SHIFT OF SHADOW -AND- SOUL

BOOK ONE OF THE SOULSHIFTER SERIES

ALSO BY HILARY THOMPSON

THE STARBRIGHT SERIES

Justice Buried
Stian's Mistake
Balance Broken
Lexan's Pledge
Destiny Risen
Atian's Revenge

SHIFT OF SHADOW AND SOUL

HILARY THOMPSON

Star Shadow Books
United States

Summary: Corentine is found to possess forbidden Shifter magic, and she must convince her people to accept the magic's return before their enemies find them.

May 2017 First Edition

Cover design by Deranged Doctor Design
Book design by Eight Little Pages
Edited by New Writers Interface

This is my dream, but you are dreaming it.
This is my wish, but you are making it.
This is my magic, but you are creating it.

What you find here, all of it, is for you.
You know who you are.

PRUSTIAN SEAN
WESTEN SANDS
MATINS HOLD
MOONSHADE CASTLE
SUNMELT LAKE
STARSHELM PALACE
CONQUEROR'S CHANNEL
WHISPERING MTS
LISTENING FOREST
SULIT
NEWMOON FALLS
RUROK
MAGI SEA
SHEDRECK RIVER
HUNGRY RIVER

N
W E
S
WHITETIDE WATCH
ESTEN SANDS
RIATA
EVENFALL FORTRESS
WESHEN CITY
WESHEN ISLE
HUSUSH
NEVERCROSS MTS
UMBREN
SHADOWSEND FOREST

I

Corentine had never been caught before, and she wouldn't be today, either. Not in the first hunt of her last summer.

There was a method to this.

The other girls bunched together on the white-sand beach, sharing whispered secrets about the boys: wondering who was the fastest, pointing out the most handsome, remembering the nicest.

But Coren cared nothing for the boys. She stepped back, as close to the dune grasses as she could get without drawing attention.

The other girls hugged their arms to their chests and waited, so close together that they would surely fall, giggling and tangling in each other's arms as they pretended to run. For them, the hunts were truly the games they were meant to be, a measure of fun in addition to the reward of food for their family.

But the hunts were not games for Coren. Before her mother had died, she had warned again and again that it was better to join the hunts than starve, but it was best to be better than the hunters.

So she waited, legs bent loosely at the knees, ready to sprint for the freedom to keep her body to herself.

The horn sounded, and she was running before the notes had spread to the waters of the MagiSea and clashed with the delighted shrieks of the other girls and the shouts of the watchers. Her bare feet didn't touch the shifting sand long enough to burn, and she sucked full lungs of salty air as she wove through the gaps in the orange-red rocks.

The cliffs of Weshen Isle had always offered her more protection than the women who lived there.

A few scant minutes of hard running and climbing put her far enough away to pause and catch her wind, but she folded her body behind a crush of bushes anyway, forever careful in case someone had managed to follow.

Coren's fingertips felt the vibrations in the ground before she heard his steps. He was closer than any boy had ever come.

She glimpsed his legs through the branches of the scrubby goshen bushes. His bare, tanned ankles were braced with thin gold rings, stacked one atop another: he was important. Perhaps the pampered son of a Weshen City nobleman, come to play at hunting in the safety of the summer games.

But the ankles before her were pacing and making no noise - Coren saw how the rings were woven through with strips of frayed leather, muffling any metallic clinks. So perhaps this boy was more than a hunter of girls, accustomed to stalking MagiCreatures in the lands beyond the women's island.

Whatever he was, he was much too close.

Coren held her breath and concentrated harder on the idea of blending into the rocks and sand. Her skin was nearly the same tan-gold as the ground, and her thick braid only a few shades darker, like the branches that twisted to conceal her. She knew she blended well. She counted on it. Even though he stood less than three feet away, she wasn't worried.

And if he didn't leave, she knew she'd fight to keep her freedom.

Sparks of adrenaline began to prick through her chest again as the ankles passed once more. She sucked in a shallow breath and gritted her teeth.

She slipped her hand down a few inches to grasp the handle of her whip, but just before she released the braid, the boy turned and left, heading back toward the beach and the men's summer camp. Coren let her breath out slowly, relieved.

Her mother had also warned her to use the whip only for hunting the island's small animals, and never to draw human blood.

She counted to eight. Then sixty-four. Then she rose, a hair's breadth at a time, her muscles screaming from the constriction. The boy was nowhere in sight, but she still raced as fast as she was able, following a convoluted route around the sharp edge of the crescent-shaped island.

The crowd of watchers on the beach had dispersed somewhat as the girls and boys began to form pairs. General Ashemon, finally satisfied that both of his sons were participating in the hunts as instructed, turned to Matron Behrenna. He noticed that she looked distinctly older than she had the previous summer, with new frown lines around her lips and a harder cast to her dark brown eyes.

"And so begins another successful hunt season. I trust your women have weathered the winter months well?" Ashemon said, watching idly as his younger son bent his head close to the curvy, brown-haired girl he'd just caught, whispering something that made her blush and smile.

Behrenna nodded in bored politeness. "We have been well. Weshen Isle provides all we need, of course, though we do look forward to your men's visits and gifts," she answered, turning to watch the General's son as well. "And has there been any change in Weshen City or Riata?"

It was the same conversation they had each summer, and Ashemon wished he had something new to tell her, though he also feared the ripples of change such news could bring.

"The city is well, and the mountain barrier holds, but Riata still spreads its greedy fingers across more and more lands to the east and west. It's a wonder there are still places left to conquer, and yet I believe the Restless King will never stop until he has added our lands to his."

"And the MagiCreatures?" she asked, turning her eyes back to the sea.

He scanned the beach for any sign of his older son, who had not yet appeared with a girl. "The men have reported slightly increased numbers and aggressiveness. I've examined dozens of suspected talismans this last month alone, but although they still fetch a high price in EvenFall, none have contained even a spark of Weshen magic." He tried to hide the disappointment in his voice, but he suspected she felt the same.

The Weshen people had been long without their ancestral magic - much longer than the elders were led to believe at the time of the Separation from Riatan society. Indeed, when the Mirror Magi had accepted the Sacrifice and transferred the people's magic to form the protection of the NeverCross Mountains, many Weshen had believed it would return in their generation.

"May our numbers increase as the days grow long," Behrenna murmured as the General gazed across the MagiSea toward the misty mountain barrier. For many Weshen, the summer hunt blessing had become as faded as the hopes of their people.

Ashemon nodded absently. On the beach, the new couples began to part again, anxious to bathe and dress for the night's celebration. The women trailed in the direction of their village, where their houses were sprinkled along the western plains and southern beaches of Weshen Isle. The men, both young and old, began to retreat to their summer camp on the northeastern side.

The Separation from Riata *would* end one day, of course. Although nearly fifty years had passed, their gods had promised the magic's return. Most believed the Magi were simply waiting for their city to recover, and so they created the games of the hunts, leaving men and women separate except for those specific activities which increased the Weshen numbers.

Even though the return of power would also mean the return of the Restless King's ever-watchful army, Ashemon hoped he would still be alive to enjoy the satisfaction of watching his people rise again to the strength and power they had once enjoyed.

"I look forward to talking more with you at tonight's feast," he said to Behrenna. She nodded, taking the cue gracefully, and General Ashemon stalked away, still scanning the beach and the surrounding rocks for his First Son.

When Coren ducked beneath the summercloth into the center room of her home, the twins were waiting, their beautiful faces pinched and mirroring an expression too serious for their seven years.

Kosh nodded at her, pleased that she had beaten the games again, but his smile was reserved and haunted. Coren lay her payment slip on the stained table and returned his smile, feeling a small guilt at how she'd poisoned him against the hunts.

Regardless of their family's views, Kosh would join the men on the mainland next summer. Like all Weshen boys in their eighth year, he would leave the island to train to become a warrior. A hunter of MagiCreatures - and someday, of girls.

Penna flung herself at her older sister, her bony fingers digging into Coren's waist. "I knew you wouldn't be caught!" She smiled, her light blue eyes shining. Coren combed the girl's pale, red-blond hair from her face.

"But what took you so long?" Kosh asked. He knew something had been different.

"A boy followed me into the rocks. I didn't see his face, but he had ankle rings."

Kosh narrowed his eyes, and she saw her thoughts reflected in his young-old face - no boy had ever come close enough for her to notice his ankles.

"The General brought both of his sons again, and there are several new sons of Weshen joining this year," Tellen called from her bed in the shade-darkened sleeping room.

"Yes. A record number of Weshen men have turned sixteen in time to join the hunts - more than any year since the Separation," Penna said, reciting a school lesson.

"Thanks to the Mirror Magi for our people's renewed growth," Kosh added, his voice quiet with the automation of expected prayers.

Coren was glad she couldn't see her cousin's face when she answered. "Perhaps I'll go and pretend to serve tonight at the celebration, to see if I can get more information. If the hunts are too dangerous this summer, we'll do without. Besides, if I go, I can bring you some treats," she said to Kosh and Penna, forcing a smile.

Penna smiled back easily, then challenged her brother to a stick-fighting contest in the common yard.

Listening to their muted shouts, Coren busied her hands and mind with preparing the midday meal. The hunting games had kept her from her real hunting today, so they would eat warmed-over meat in a vegetable broth and the rest of yesterday's bread. Tellen should bake tonight, and perhaps tomorrow Coren would hunt for rockrabbit. The remains of the island's winter stock had been pooled to create tonight's celebratory meal, and their cupboards were bare.

But in the next few days, boats heavy with meat and produce would arrive, bringing the women's island their symbolic reward for a successful first hunt.

Coren waited until well after dusk, when all the other young women had bathed and hurried, giggling, to join their hunters for the first night. Most of the older women had also gone to the feast, hoping to drink and eat well, and flirt with past lovers.

The women's village draped the hillsides and cliffs of the island, dotting the evening with pale, stuccoed houses. Most were darkened and held only sleeping children and a handful of women like Tellen - those caught in last summer's final hunts, whose bellies were now as heavy with reward as the coming boats.

As the first stars began to appear overhead, Coren bathed quickly in the clear freshwater pool centered between the women's houses. Sandjasmine vines surrounded and enclosed the pool, scenting the cool springwater. Tiny pearlescent petals clung to her wet skin as she combed her thick hair back into a straight sheen, letting it hang loose well past her shoulder blades. She wrapped herself in the simple white fabric of a serving dress, securing it at her waist with a woven cord.

A golden glow had grown on the darkening horizon, signaling the beach fires at the men's camp. Coren's stomach flipped, shrinking from the thought of joining the feast.

Although the hunt was over for the day, there was every danger in entering the men's camp alone.

A memory of her mother's last words lingered in Coren's mind as she slipped on her sandals: Sorenta had pulled her young daughter close, palms pinching the girl's cheeks and hair together as she held her eyes with the intensity only a mother can muster. Sorenta's own eyes had been bloodshot from lack of sleep and swollen from tears, marks of a grief that had taken her life soon after.

Corentine, never let them catch you. No boy must ever claim you before Weshen's magic returns, or your family will lose everything.

Coren shook her head to loosen the memory's hold and secured her whip beneath the slit skirt, spiraling the flat braid down her thigh and calf. The handle dented her skin, uncomfortable but for its familiarity, and the braid settled on her leg like a snake coiling into itself for rest.

"You look beautiful," Tellen whispered as Coren slipped into the moonlit sleeping room. Coren sat on the edge of her cousin's bed and smoothed the younger girl's sand-colored hair. Tellen's hands rested on her swollen belly. She would birth soon, and her eyes glinted between joy and worry. If it was a girl, she would stay with them on the island. If it was a boy, his father would claim him in eight short years, his mind would be spelled to forget the island, and he would return only after he was sixteen. To hunt.

Tellen reached for a sandjasmine sprig from her bed table and laced it into Coren's hair. "Be careful, cousin," she said. "Watch out for the old men, too."

Coren nodded and re-tucked the light blanket around her, then another around Kosh and Penna, then left before she could change her mind.

She had to know who had come to the hunts this summer, so she could decide if her risk was worth taking.

Her young family would struggle without the rewards of the games, but Coren had promised Sorenta. She would protect her family as told, even if she didn't fully understand why.

"Hey, boy, where's your catch?" Tagsha's slurred words brought Syashin back into the night. The older man grinned through his thick beard like he had a secret, although what he knew about the night was not the same as what Sy knew.

"Didn't see one I liked," Sy said, shrugging as if this were a reasonable excuse.

Tag laughed, his belly shaking, and Sy glared into the fire.

"Hey, girl! Bring us some more!" Tag yelled to the girl serving drinks - a job saved for girls who were too old for the hunts, or those few who refused. All of the willing and desirable girls had been caught in the sand that afternoon and were now enjoying their new games.

Sy barely glanced up as she slammed an earthenware mug on the table. Tag handed her a coin and reached to pinch her thigh, but she sidestepped him smoothly. Reshra and his girl arrived just then, a tinkling laugh and stumbling footsteps showing he had again caught one just his type.

"Oh, look at Coren! Isn't she precious with her serving tray?" Resh's catch was obviously drunk, but it was her poorly-hidden jealousy that gained Sy's interest, and he glanced up from the yellow-blue flames. The serving girl moved closer and clunked a mug before him, the wine sloshing wastefully onto the table.

A jolt rocketed through his muscles - here was the girl he didn't catch. He quickly hid his interest behind a long draught from the mug. In the shifting firelight, she had a fierce sort of beauty, her tanned skin shining like the golden claws of the poisonous Vespa bird he'd hunted only a few weeks before.

He likely could have caught her, too. He had wanted to see how fast she was, how strong. He had wanted to see where she would hide. If he were forced to hunt a girl, he would prefer to have a worthy opponent.

"Be careful with Amden," the girl said, her voice even and liquid, her eyes meeting Resh's eyes without the expected deference. "She sometimes bites, and you wouldn't want to lose something important."

Tag's guffaws echoed after the girl as she swished away before being dismissed, spilling more wine than she carried. Sy stared at her retreating form a few seconds too long, mesmerized by a dark tattoo snaking seductively up her leg.

Even Resh was uncharacteristically dumb with surprise at her daring, and his new girl was red with anger. Sy only hoped his little brother didn't get the fool idea to chase this girl at the next hunt. This could be the first girl he'd seen who was more than Resh could handle.

That alone would have made her noticeable. But this morning, Sy had thought he remembered the girl, and now he was sure. There should have been no reason for any of the girls to fear being caught, yet she always ran as though her life depended on it.

It seemed neither of them wanted to hunt like they were expected to, and Sy wanted to know why.

Resh reappeared then from behind his drained mug, eyes narrowed in calculating anger. His new girl brushed her fingers lightly across his chest, hopeful, but he merely pushed her hand away.

"What is that girl's name? I want her name!" Resh demanded.

"It's just Corentine," the girl giggled. "She's simple. Don't waste another thought on her." Her fingers finally found a place that distracted him, and Sy stood, turning away from his younger brother and his latest conquest.

He carried his mug away from the noise and smoke to the water's empty edge. The silvery moonlight spread over him, soothing his jumbled thoughts. He sat heavily in the loose sand, watching the shimmer of the sea's rippling waves.

"Tagsha tells me you are again without a girl."

Sy scrambled to rise, just as his father bent his knees to squat beside him. The General's large hand pushed his older son back to the sand, and not gently.

"Syashin…" Ashemon began, then stopped.

"I'm sorry, Father. I did hunt, but the girl escaped me among the rocks." Although he knew his failure would anger the General, Sy knew a refusal to complete the hunt would be worse.

"How could a simple young girl escape you? Your fighting skills are unparalleled among our young men. You can track a MagiCreature over any terrain and slay it with a mere longknife." The General shifted his weight and his tactics. "Perhaps you do not wish for sons?"

His question startled Sy from his glower. He rarely wasted thoughts on the purpose for the hunts, generally thinking only of the ridiculous customs his people had been reduced to since the Separation and the Sacrifice.

"Reshra is a year younger than you, and he already has one son to claim later."

"Resh isn't concerned with sons!" Sy's words were harsher than he had intended, but his father only chuckled.

"True, and that brings me to my other concern. Some of the young men hunt because they wish for the honor of sons and the improvement of our people. But many also hunt because they hunger for the girls. Yet, my eldest son does not hunt for either of these." He paused to sift a handful of the glittering sand, pearl-white under the stars.

"What do you hunger for, Syashin?"

Sy took too long in answering, and his father rose, never a patient man.

"This is your last summer, Sy. You will hunt, as I have said. And you will sire a child. Or your First Son rights and title will pass to Reshra. You owe me that much."

Ashemon was gone before the bitter words could filter through Sy's ears and stab the beat from his heart. His vision narrowed to a single grain of sand, and he felt his chest turn to stone. His father had never been a kind man, but he had also never threatened Sy in this way before.

A pounding on the sand jarred his focus back to the moonlit beach, and he looked up just as the same girl flew past, fleeing as though she still ran for her life. *Corentine.*

Without volition, Sy's muscles constricted and he was on his feet, tearing after her in the dark. If she sensed him, she ignored it as she entered the same rocks where he had nearly lost her this morning.

And he lost her tonight, the chokecherry wine and his father's words slowing his movements to the crawl of despair. She vanished into a crevice and Sy sank to his knees amongst the sandy rocks, his breathing jagged.

The next hunt would be eight days from now. He knew he must protect his First Son rights from Resh's destructive ways, even if it meant compromising what he'd always done.

Resh watched his father return from the beach, where he knew Sy had gone to drink alone. He narrowed his eyes, ignoring the girl draped across his lap.

It was no surprise to any of the men that Sy had no girl tonight. His brother hunted neither girls nor boys, only MagiCreatures and talismans.

So what could have the General looking so exceptionally fierce?

"Is it time to go back to your tent?" the girl murmured, nuzzling against his neck. Resh finished his drink and stood abruptly, nearly dumping her in the sand.

"Lead the way," he laughed, mostly forgetting his father, and fixing her in a hungry stare. "I'm sure you've been to the men's camp before."

She glared, but pulled herself tall, pushing out her lips and her breasts. "Just so you know, I always lead."

He showed his teeth and pushed ahead of her on the path, knowing she would follow and suddenly not caring if she did. The summer months were a deserved respite from hunting creatures and the creeping fear that hung over Weshen City and most of Riata, but tonight Resh felt dulled and bored with the narrowness of their lives.

His ancestors had died under the hand of the Restless King, yes, but they had also possessed things worth dying for.

This, this holding. This waiting. It simmered in his blood stronger than any liquor or lust ever had.

Coren was nearly home before she realized she hadn't brought any treats for the twins. They would understand, of course, but that knowledge only forced her frustration higher.

They were too young to have to understand. She was all they had now, but they deserved so much more. If only Sorenta had left them all with more - more explanation for her cryptic orders surrounding the hunts, more information on their tarnished family history, or more instruction for her few stolen Sulit spells.

Coren paused outside the small house a few moments, breathing deeply of the still night air, pushing each worry into the darkness where she hoped they would stay. Inside, she slid into bed and closed her eyes, pausing to count the soft breathing of three people. Tellen moaned in her sleep, likely sweaty and uncomfortable.

Thoughts swirled through Coren's head, rising and falling in a tide of images. She had learned nothing of value tonight, and nearly got caught doing it. Tellen's warning had served as a harbinger.

Right after arriving, she was cornered by a man too old to hunt, but not too old for sport. Coren had pushed away the panic and endured his greasy fingers and grating laugh long enough to hear there were two sons of the General and more than a dozen new sons of Weshen at the hunts this year, and several of them were from families important enough to merit ankle rings.

Exactly what Tellen had already known. No real gain.

As her thoughts finally slowed and drifted with fatigue, she remembered the solitary boy on the beach, chasing her drunkenly. Had he worn ankle rings?

The blurred image found its way into her dreams, keeping her from a satisfying sleep.

2

In the morning, Penna climbed into Coren's bed, her warm body adding to the sweat of the tousled sheets. Glad to be interrupted from her strange dreams, Coren slid her palm across the girl's hair, then cupped her rounded cheek. Penna smiled and moved to hold her sister's hand. Their mother had died eleven months after the twins' birth, and Coren had tried to fill her void ever since.

But it could never be the same. Not for any of them.

Shutting those thoughts away, Coren pushed out of bed and tied her long hair back. Tellen was in the main room making eggs, fresh from their midnight chickens. Kosh sat next to the firestove, whittling an arrow with his bone-handled longknife.

"Did you learn anything?" he asked. Coren ruffled his hair, and he quickly smoothed it back, huffing.

"There are several new hunters. And the General's two sons." She turned to Tellen. "But I did see Amden. She was drunk and draped all over some boy's lap."

Tellen snorted. "Typical. Always chasing the boys, instead of letting them chase her." She paused in her cooking to rub her stomach.

"Are you having any pains?" Coren asked, her eyes sharp on her cousin's face.

"Not now. But I think the baby will come soon. Perhaps even before the next hunt."

The family ate in silence until Kosh and Penna rose to leave for the children's school, and Tellen gathered her robe to visit the bathing pool. She might relax there for nearly an hour, her belly buoyant in the cool water.

Left to herself, Coren cleaned the dishes, mulling over the day's coming work. She couldn't quite shake the unexplainable feeling, left over from her dreams, that everything was about to change. She had dreamed of her little family and their village resting on the edge of a great cliff, rather than in the heart of the crescent-shaped island. The women's houses had seemed weightless, cared for by none.

In her dream, she had watched from the clouds, knowing that a single breath of unexpected wind could push them all into the MagiSea.

Restless and impatient to run, she dressed for hunting in loose pants banded at the ankle and a sleeveless wrap tunic, coiling her whip around her bare arm.

It was risky for Coren - from a family as disgraced as the Ashadens - to keep such a weapon, but it was all she had left to remind her of the warrior her mother should have become, if not for the Restless King.

Once, she had spied Sorenta chanting strange words as she wove several coarse, black hairs into the leather braid, and even now those hairs glistened when the whip was wet with blood. Although the carved handle still enclosed a defunct talisman, Coren believed it was no longer truly a Weshen weapon, but a Sulit one.

Sorenta may have lost her shifter magic in the Sacrifice, but Coren knew she'd had more than memories left from her childhood in Riata's StarsHelm Palace, where Sulit witches had once mingled with Weshen nobility and Riatan princes.

Tucked in the back of Coren's mind was a solitary spell to falsify pregnancy, which Sorenta had made her memorize at the end of the dark summer when Kosh and Penna were born, just weeks before Sorenta had taken her other spells and stories with her to the bottom of the MagiSea.

Coren's eighteen years and her family's mistakes had taught her to depend only on herself.

Before leaving the village borders, Coren paused at the bathing pool, watching Tellen doze in the morning light, her head resting on a pile of clothing, the outline of her swollen belly pale beneath the spring water. A few other girls stumbled toward the pool, eyes puffed from drink and late hours with their hunters.

Coren turned quickly without meeting their gazes. Although many were happy to trade for the meat she hunted, she kept few friends in the village.

Breaking into a brisk run, she cleared the rocks and lower cliffs easily, soon entering the wide openness of the upper plain. This was the only place she felt truly free, unshackled from her tiny, tedious life.

Here the blue-green palmpress grasses were tall, their feathery plumes nearly to her waist in places, and she could see the green-tinged MagiSea shimmering in all directions. Weshen City was barely a smudge across the water - a day's journey north by boat, she'd heard.

Beyond the city were the misty, magic-infused NeverCross Mountains, which protected Weshen City from the Restless King by cliffs more treacherous than his armies. But north of the mountains, they said, the kingdom of Riata had claimed nearly everything.

Coren often wondered what Weshen City looked like, and what waited beyond the mountains. There was no longer a reason for a Weshen woman to travel to any of those places, and none had for dozens of years. That freedom was something their mothers didn't remember, and their grandmothers never discussed.

But that freedom had existed once, so Coren idly hoped it might again.

The summer sun burned her skin with purpose as Coren wove silently through the grass. Her whip snapped the neck of a rockrabbit as it munched, barely drawing blood from the golden fur. A pair of plump groundbirds fell next, and she placed their bodies gently into her game sack, judging that she had about five pounds of meat.

She needed more. Tellen's baby would need so many things that only a trade could bring.

Coren's village duty required ten pounds of fresh meat per week; any more was hers to keep or trade. But there were very few large animals on the island, so hunting took time and patience that most of the women didn't have. Most preferred to farm or fish.

The flat leather braid of the whip grew less brown and more silver with each stroke of death, and Coren knew she needed to let it rest - needed to let the residue of blood drain away again to deactivate whatever spell rested there still. Otherwise, the blood would pull at the whip, snaking it into higher arcs and sharper cuts and faster kills.

She coiled the whip around her arm, satisfied with its familiar suctioning to her skin. The Sacrifice may protect them, but it had also made them vulnerable in a much more insidious way.

Coren breathed deeply of the salt air and rolled her eyes to the sky. Weshen women had once been the fiercest of hunters alongside their men but were now reduced to giggling girls on the beach, hoping for nothing more from life than a nice boy to honor them with a son. Their warrior lives had been taken and reduced - their focus now on survival and petty struggles.

The tall grass beckoned and she lay back, closing her eyes to the bright sunlight as the slender leaves wove together above her. For a few moments, all was bearable. The sound of distant waves on the beach. The slight movement of air upon air. The heady, green scent of the cloverhearts crushed beneath her back.

And then a scream interrupted everything. Not a human noise - a creature. Not a creature she'd ever heard, and not far away, somewhere in the wispy clouds above her.

She scanned the visible strips of blue sky, fingertips tingling on the handle of her whip as she willed her body to be still, or risk detection.

The shadow passed over her before the creature, and Coren stayed motionless, eyes wide in horror. This was a bird she had never seen - if it actually was a bird. Four wings spread lazily, spanning twice as wide as her own body length, followed by a fat, pearl-feathered belly, then scrawny legs ending in sharply-curved golden claws that trailed along the tips of the palmpress grass. A strange scent drifted down to her hiding spot - acrid and nearly metallic, like a knife blade twisting through rancid meat. Another scream floated down between the blades of grass, fading as the bird flew on.

More minutes passed than Coren's pride wished to admit as fear shook its way through her body. She knew this was no ordinary island bird. It could only be a MagiCreature.

Indisputable logic argued back: MagiCreatures never came to Weshen Isle. The creatures had always sought strong shifter magic. With the magic gone, the men were able to stay all summer on the island, on hiatus from their bloodied Riatan battles or bounty hunts for MagiCreatures and lost talismans.

But logic faded away as the image of the creature settled in her mind like a stone.

Inch by inch, Coren rose, hearing and seeing nothing more of the strange creature. Her courage built and soon she was racing back to the house, intent on one thing: her father's book.

Sy had been walking the northern beaches for nearly an hour without seeing a soul, and the quiet smoothed over his mind like a salve. Weshen Isle was beautiful, but he hadn't missed it. He hadn't been here for two summers - not since the first and only hunt he'd participated in.

Until yesterday, of course.

Now he was in his last summer, and his father was forcing him to hunt.

The men's taunts began to echo in his brain with each step. Words they used when they thought no-one was around to hear. But Sy was always around. He was better at hiding and listening, better at tracking and interpreting, better at hunting everything except girls. He always knew what the men said, though he rarely cared.

What sort of First Son would snub Weshen tradition like this?

How is he a Paladin already? If he can't catch a girl, surely he can't catch a MagiCreature.

The whole family's a waste. No wonder the Mirror Magi still keep the Sacrifice.

He stomped his feet into the sand, watching the water spike in controlled daggers around his knees, the shape dissolving as he blinked it away.

Maybe he cared a little.

But of course the Sacrifice hadn't been lifted, regardless of his father's leadership or how many babies were born each year. His teacher Damren had pointed to so many signs that the Weshen people still hadn't learned what they were meant to learn. Damren criticized how they eschewed love for lust, separating men to the city and women to the island, all in the hopes of keeping the women safe.

But Weshen women had never needed to be *safe* before the Sacrifice. They were once warriors, right alongside the men. They fought with their weapons, their fists, and their magic.

They died, but they also lived.

Unlike most Weshen, Damren didn't believe the magic was simply waiting for the population to grow. She maintained it would only return when they allowed love to return. To Sy it seemed an impossible puzzle. Which of the two must return first, if both were so tightly tied together? For him, the magic had returned first. But why hadn't it returned to anyone else?

Although his thoughts still tumbled like pebbles in the ocean, something from Sy's lifetime of training alerted him to a nearby presence. He swiveled just as Resh stepped onto the beach from a grassy path leading back to the men's camp.

"I need a sparring partner," Resh commanded, chucking a sword at Sy, and pulling another from the scabbard strapped to his back.

Sy had barely adjusted his grip before Resh came at him, as reckless with a blade as he was with everything else. For several minutes, they spoke only through slitted eyes, taunting smiles, and blow upon blow. The clang of metal echoed over the MagiSea.

"What has Father General in such knots this morning?" Resh asked, dancing backward, his dark eyes nearly black with mischief.

Sy rolled his eyes at the childish name. "Who knows." He deflected both question and blow as he thrust toward Resh's mid-section. Resh bent nearly double, holding his arms wide as though bowing, and sidestepped the gesture smoothly.

"Oh, I think *you* know. And I've come to beat it out of you."

Their blades cracked into each other. Sy grinned, enjoying the flex of his muscles. Of course, he was better than Resh. Broader and an inch taller, too. But Resh was sneaky. He did the unexpected.

Like now, as he parried, arched to one side, and threw a handful of sand into Sy's face. Sy cursed, swiping blindly at his brother even through the burn and grit. Resh only laughed, stepping back in a complex sort of dance move.

Sy hacked his sword at the empty air and called Resh a few vulgar names before blinking enough of the sand away to see his target clearly again. Then he rushed at Resh, tackling him to the ground and pinning him, his knees on his brother's chest. Their swords flopped into the sand, and they resorted to fists.

Good-natured, of course. It had been a few years since they had truly fought.

"So are you going to take Father General's offer?" Resh asked, and Sy startled badly enough that Resh got the upper hand and shoved him off.

Surely Resh hadn't heard of Ashemon's threat to remove Sy's First Son rights. He was in a headlock before he could see Resh's face to gauge exactly what he had asked.

"The training academy? Are you doing it?" Resh asked, cinching his grip on Sy's neck. Relief flooded Sy just as the blood began to recede from his brain, and he used his last bit of energy to hurl Resh forward over his shoulders. Resh landed on his back in the sand before Sy.

"Nah," Sy answered, coughing and rubbing at his neck. He stood and brushed away the sand, noting a new tear in his shirt. "I wouldn't make a good teacher. Why - do you want it?"

Resh cursed and laughed. "Are you kidding? And be stuck in Weshen City every summer for the rest of my life?" He glanced toward the women's village. "Too much fun to be had here, big brother. Not that you would know."

And he pushed to his feet and jogged away down the beach, laughing, before Sy could reach out to grab him. Sy shook his head and gathered the swords. His brother was almost too perceptive, and an excellent hunter, but he didn't want to grow up. If Resh became General, he'd never be patient enough to lead the Weshen safely out of the Sacrifice.

Sy knew this was exactly why Ashemon had given the ultimatum: Sy would trade his desires for the future of their people, while Resh was more likely to do the opposite.

Fathers were forbidden and books of magic were rarities on Weshen Isle, but Corentine Ashaden was lucky enough to have known a good one of each, even though only the book remained now.

When she reached the house, she found Tellen dozing in the shade, pretending to finish sewing a baby blanket.

"Catch anything?" she asked, eying Coren's sack.

"Not much. Rockrabbit for you tonight, though."

Tellen clapped her hands and grinned. "I think this child must be a boy, for how hungry I am!" Then she fell abruptly silent, rubbing a spot on her belly. Coren knew Tellen worried too much about the upcoming birth. Her cousin had also grown up without a mother after Nollen had died giving birth to Tellen's younger brother.

"Rest as long as you need, Tellen," was all Coren could manage to say, though, and then she pushed into the stale heat of the house. She abandoned the game sack, instead quickly retrieving the pocket field journal from its hiding spot beneath the floorboards. Tellen and the twins had no idea of its existence, and it was safer that way.

Leafing through the colorful drawings with one hand, Coren rattled dishes in mock industry. She spotted the creature easily, and a chill of truth cut through the heat of the summer-warm kitchen. *Vespa.*

A note in her father's cramped writing informed that Vespa claws were poisonous, but when drained of death, their golden hue made them valuable for jewelry. A few claws had been found since the Sacrifice, but the Weshen magi had rejected them all as talismans.

Coren's stomach rolled over at the thought of wearing those rotten-smelling claws around her neck, or pierced through her ears. People in the cities of Riata must be very different from the people of Weshen, if that was their idea of beauty.

Coren slipped the journal back where it belonged, then quickly skinned and salted the rockrabbit and set a pot to boil on the firestove, heading back outside to Tellen.

"I'm heading to Auntie Maren's. Watch the stove," she told her cousin. Maren lived in a tiny hut well outside the cluster of other homes, and she had never been anyone's aunt. But she had always watched over Coren's little family, and now Coren offered her fresh meat and small talk as often as possible.

"You're upset," Maren said as Coren opened the gate. Her thin skirt was knotted above her knobby knees and her feet were bare among the smart rows of vegetables. Three young stormcloud chickens pecked at her ankles as she pushed a few strands of gray hair back behind her ears and shaded her eyes against the sun. She nudged one away and its feathers ruffled and blackened as it squawked at her, before bustling away to another corner of the garden.

"I brought groundbirds," Coren said, shaking the sack.

"Only two?"

"My hunt was cut short."

Maren beckoned for Coren to follow her into the hut. She poured a cup of murky tea from the pot on the firestove and handed it to Coren, who accepted it. Both women knew Coren wouldn't drink it, but that never stopped the gesture.

"Tell me," Maren said, pouring herself a cup and sitting at the table.

"I saw a MagiCreature." Coren waited for Maren to scoff in disbelief, but the older woman said nothing, only sipped her tea and waited. Maren was the only woman who knew Coren's secrets, though Coren had always suspected the old woman hid plenty more of her own.

"I looked it up in Kashar's journal. I think it was a Vespa," she continued.

Maren set the mug down with a thunk, but still said nothing. A hard look had crept onto her face.

"The wingspan was two dozen feet, Maren. How is something like that on the island? And in the summer?"

"Neshra was killed by a Vespa, you know," Maren answered, staring into her tea. "It scraped its claws down his entire back, then left him to die. Nasty Umbren creatures." She took another drink, but not before Coren spotted the shake in her hand and the slight sheen in her eyes.

Coren knew Neshra had caught Maren gently each summer when she was young, then returned to her secretly each summer after she outgrew the hunts. Until one summer, he didn't come.

Coren waited several minutes more, but Maren offered nothing else. So Coren sighed and rose, turning to leave.

Maren cleared her throat. "They're drawn to magic, Corentine. Somebody on Weshen is pulling it here, knowingly or not."

"My mother's whip…" she whispered, sitting again as her heart stuttered with the thought that *she* might have called death to the island.

Maren shook her head. "Sorenta's whip holds only a dead talisman bound into a weak Sulit amplification spell. We lost the old ways in the Sacrifice, Coren."

Coren sighed. *Not all of us*, she thought, a tangle of sorrow and helplessness cinching her chest with the memory of her twin brother, Jyesh, who had been an anomaly in a race of people whose blood had forgotten its origins.

But she and Maren hadn't spoken of Jyesh in years. No-one had been able to explain why a boy who had never been off the island had known enough magic to kill a man without a single touch.

Sorenta had begged for her son's life, swearing it was the return of shifter magic and not Sulit secrets, but as no other shifter magic was found, the Ashaden family was cast into the shadows of suspicion. And as the years passed, the people stopped trying to solve the mystery, and started trying to forget what they had done to an eight-year-old child.

"One of the hunters, then?" Coren asked finally, blinking fiercely against the image of her brother being pushed from the island, alone on the MagiSea in a boat with no oar.

"Perhaps. Although I still trust Ashemon to tell us if Weshen magic begins to return. Anyone who is using magic must be channeling Sulit power, or even Umbren."

Coren shuddered at the mention of the magic that had torn her twin from her, and of the two shadowed lands that waited to the west and the south, beyond the MagiSea's protection. Even the Restless King had been unable to conquer those countries. They brought only death.

Maren drummed her fingers on Coren's arm, demanding attention again. "So you must be very careful if you go snooping about like you did at the feast."

Coren flushed - somehow Maren always seemed to know everything that happened on the island, even though she rarely left her yard.

"Send Kosh and Penna by to see me later. The pineberries are ripe, and they should pick some before the chickens get them all."

Coren felt dismissed, and she walked home slowly, her steps heavy with too many worries. If someone had found a way to channel any sort of magic, Sulit or other, she wanted to know, so she could plan to protect her family from any further accusations.

The danger in such knowledge, though…she shivered even in the summer afternoon's heat.

She'd also have to be more careful when she hunted for food, alert for the creature - even if it wasn't a Vespa, it flew like slow death. Kosh and Penna shouldn't play on the open plains alone anymore. And Tellen must be watched closely, so they would be ready when the baby came.

But above all, Coren knew she must be ready for the next hunt, as boys with ankle rings were used to getting what they wanted in life. If he wanted her, he would not give up easily.

3

Sy sat contentedly at a table between the tents, the early morning sun warming his shoulders and bare arms. Spread before him was strong black tea, fresh fruit, and soft biscuits with yogurt and honey. The flavors teased a smile out of him, although his nerves hummed like the bees in the nearby tangle of sandjasmine vines.

Resh stumbled from the brothers' tent, rubbing his eyes and ruffling his dark, close-cut hair.

"Up late again with Amden?" Sy said, knowing the answer. He regretted not demanding a separate sleeping tent. For eight nights, he had heard the girl's giggles and sighs even through the tent's thick leather divider.

"Who? Oh, you mean the girl. Of course." Resh grabbed a biscuit and grinned around a huge mouthful. "But the question is, big brother, are you ready to catch *your* first girl?"

Sy swiped at his brother, who ducked: He wasn't unmanned, he just hadn't been back to the island to catch a girl since his first summer. "At least I remember their faces and names."

"Faces are only good for kissing. Names not at all," Resh said, showing his teeth, then taking a vicious jab at his older brother's ribs.

The boys rolled to the ground, wrestling intensely. Heavy footsteps ending in large boots paused their play, and Sy looked up to see the General watching them.

"Remember what I told you, Syashin," he said, his eyes flashing a warning that skittered Sy's heart. Then he pushed into the tent, waving Tag in after him. Tag grabbed two biscuits from the table, then doubled back for the crock of yogurt, laughing at Resh and Sy tangled like pups on the warm sand.

"What was that about?" Resh asked, running his fingers lightly through his mussed hair, rearranging the dark waves to their usual perfection.

"Father is anxious for me to catch a girl."

"We're all anxious for *that*, big brother!"

Sy reached for him again, but Resh darted out of the way, smoothing his shirt and brushing sand from his pants.

"No more fighting," he said, waggling his brows. "I need to look nice for the hunts today." And of course, he already did. Sy surveyed his brother's appearance. This summer, Resh had adopted even more from EvenFall's markets, and Sy thought he must look exotic and harmlessly dangerous to the girls.

Dressed in finely-woven black pants and a dark shirt open at the chest and rolled to the elbows, Resh also wore a rich string of onyx and pearl prayer beads, and a sly smile that said he used them to ask the Magi for forgiveness, rather than protection.

"Looking for a new girl?" Sy asked derisively, suddenly feeling much *less* than his younger brother.

"Always," Resh laughed. Some of the men preferred to stay with one girl all summer, and although partnership and love had been banished along with the Weshen magic, a handful of the hunters still returned quietly to the same girls the following year.

Sy grunted and rolled his eyes. Resh certainly embraced the new Weshen life, preferring to catch a new girl at each hunt, spend each of the eight nights with her, then promptly forget her, just as he'd been taught.

Sy had always thought the whole thing false - a sorry substitute for the love his people had lost in separating women and men. But now, all his lofty opinions found him in his last summer with no heirs and his father's anger like a storm cloud in the distance.

"Seriously, Sy, is that what you're wearing? They'll probably actually run *from* you." Resh shook his head and turned back to the tent, taking his food with him.

Sy felt his face flush as he looked down at his faded hunting shirt, noticing silvery MagiCreature blood staining the front and the poorly-mended rip in his pants. His untrimmed hair fell over his eyes in shades of wet sand, and he knew his face was full of unshaven scruff. Perhaps he *should* take a cue from Resh.

The General's Second Son could have any girl he wanted, even with his careless reputation.

So an hour later, Sy stood stiffly on the beach, dressed in loose navy pants and a spotless white cotton shirt that was almost too tight across his chest. His jaw was clean-shaven, and his dark, choppy hair had been dampened and combed back. He tried to ignore the tense feeling in his gut as he watched the girls file through the rocks, clumping together in groups of friends.

Resh wasn't really helping as he waited nearby, commenting on each girl who entered the hunt.

"I caught her last summer. Boring. Oh, that one's very sweet - might be tame enough for your first time. Don't catch the brunette, or you'll never be the same again."

Sy ignored him, watching only for one girl.

Finally, he saw her: Corentine. She stood apart from the other girls, alone. She didn't watch the boys like the other girls did. She didn't search them for the familiar faces of previous lovers, or the potential smiles of new ones. She only watched the ocean and the vast blue sky. She did not appear concerned.

But she should have. Sy had spent every afternoon the previous eight days exploring every path and hidden crevice of these rocks. It was like relearning an old weapon - he didn't remember the island from his childhood, but he had practiced enough to commit the girl's possible escape routes to memory.

Syashin Havenash was Weshen City's best hunter - its youngest Paladin - and today, he was ready to prove it on new grounds. And more than anything, he was curious. He wanted to ask her why she always ran as though her life depended on it.

"Just think of it like any other hunt," Resh said, breaking into his thoughts again.

For once, the brothers agreed.

Resh grinned at a pretty blond whose blue eyes were piercing even at thirty feet, but Sy trained his eyes on Corentine, keeping the Guard with the horn in his peripheral vision.

He raised the instrument and Corentine bolted before the notes had even reached Sy's ears. He sprinted after her, his leg muscles leaping with adrenaline. Her thick braid snagged on a branch and she yanked it over her shoulder, several strands now flying loose.

Sy glimpsed the glorious, snaky tattoo on her leg and nearly twisted his ankle on a stray rock in the path.

She darted suddenly into a hidden passage, and his brain automatically searched the internal map he'd created. He cut ahead of her on a different path, anticipating where she would come out of the rocks.

Sy reached the open plain a half-second before Corentine burst from between the rock walls, and he felt a surge of excitement as her eyes widened, seeing him waiting for her. She shifted directions, barely breaking stride, and he had to scramble to follow. They cut across the plain quicker than blades flashing, and Sy thought of a Cheetana he had hunted once, sleek and confident. But ultimately his.

She slowed and he heard her curse as she veered away from another passage. The opening had been blocked by a few larger rocks, recently fallen from the cliffs above. But even though the plain was wide, it ended abruptly, emptying its grass into the ocean far below. She would be forced to double back to escape. Corentine cut past Sy, and his fingers grazed her arm, closing on air.

He poured every bit of remaining stamina into his burning legs and reached the passage ahead of her, blocking her way. She skidded on the sandy grass, sliding just close enough that he clamped his hand on her sky-blue dress. She fluttered for a moment, an insect caught in an arach's web.

Then Sy saw the hatred in Corentine's eyes, and the smile from the hunt's thrill stuttered as a strange panic rose in his throat.

But his father's glare jumped into his mind, his threat echoing with each heaving breath.

And Sy gripped Corentine's dress tighter, reaching to grasp her shoulder with his other hand.

The boy leaned closer. Coren risked another glance at his face, expecting to find the widened pupils, the swollen lips of desire and anticipation.

But it was worse than that.

He stared at her intently, gray-blue eyes narrowed and full lips slightly upturned in conquest.

Claim them with a kiss. The hunt's opening speech echoed in her mind.

He pulled her closer, and she stopped moving entirely, going limp. Playing dead. He thought this was a game, like all the others did.

Then she allowed her lips turn up in a grim smile. It certainly was a game. The boy just didn't realize that her rules were different, and he was about to lose.

Her tongue reached into the cavity of her cheek and retrieved the plump goshen berry hidden there. As his lips neared, Coren broke the berry against her teeth, bracing for the instant burn. Then, tongue searing, she shoved the pulp past his opened lips, preventing the claim.

He burst away, the shock of the acidic berry sending him stumbling backward, swiping drool from his slack jaw.

And she ran, darting around him and ignoring the pain and the blisters that were already bubbling and popping on her tongue and lips. Reaching the cliff, she hazarded a glance over her shoulder. He was tougher than expected, for he was crossing the plain too, moving quickly through the sandy grass.

"Stop!" he yelled hoarsely. Strangely, he was grinning widely, lips blackened with goshen juice and bright blood. Coren had no more ground left, but out of curiosity, she paused to watch as he approached. He walked softly now, as though she were a beast he was cornering. Perhaps he was a real hunter, after all.

Even so, the berries had stopped him, making the kiss forfeit. She could claim he hadn't actually caught her.

"So...goshen berries?" he asked, wiping away more blood with the hem of his white shirt. "I must be the first hunter ever to receive that treatment."

Coren's brain nagged at her to escape, but something in his grin made her ask. "Why the first?"

"Because surely no one has ever caught you before. And I can't imagine another girl willing to martyr her own lips just to avoid a small kiss."

He was very close now: not quite near enough to grab her, but mere steps from it. She stepped back carefully, heels nearly hanging off the edge of the cliff.

"Nothing is small when it is against your will." She watched his eyes widen as he processed the words, and then she bent her knees and pushed away from the earth, arcing back and out into the void, then straight as an arrow toward the water below. His shout was erased by the wind rushing past her ears, and then the water closed over her head with a crash.

Under the surface of the sun-warmed water, Coren somersaulted quickly and reversed directions. She surfaced only to locate the face of the cliff and gulp a breath, and she didn't dare look up to see if he had spotted her. Ducking back under the waves, she stroked hard against the current, finally feeling rock. Her lungs throbbed as her head bobbed up again, but she was safely inside the hidden sanctuary.

She took in a mouthful of seawater, swishing it back over her lips as she climbed onto the rocky ledge. The salt burned, but it would heal the goshen berry wounds faster. Looking down, she saw the blue dress was now nearly transparent. Sighing, she began to wring the water from her hair. She'd need to stay here until the dress was dry.

The sanctuary's sandy alcove was barely wide enough for two or three people, though the ceiling was high and cavernous, like an urn upturned in the sand. It was rarely used, as most of the women preferred the spacious chapel in the village center. A knee-high marble statue of the Mirror Magi waited in an alcove, delicate sandjasmine garlands enclosing the tiny conjoined necks. Several candle stubs sat nearby. Coren wondered who had been down here so recently.

She only came here once a year, to give thanks for the day the men left.

Bowing deeply now, she whispered a different prayer of thanks. She pulled a strand of prayer beads from a hook on the wall and broke a pearlescent shell in two, adding it to the small pile of offerings. Today, at least, the Mirror Magi had chosen to protect her.

She would do nearly anything to protect and provide for what was left of her family, but she had come too close to being caught today. Breaking another shell into equal halves, she sat to focus on a prayer begging the Magi to keep the boy from following through. If he decided to push the matter, his word would be stronger than hers, and she would be taken to the men's camp, regardless of the averted claim.

Though entering the men's camp was a small thing for a girl like Amden, for Coren it would be like the death of all she had promised her mother, and more recently, herself.

Sy stood on the cliff's edge for many long minutes, staring down into the churning blue of the MagiSea and trying to believe what had happened. He had seen her surface only long enough to breathe, and then she'd been gone again.

Glancing back to ensure no-one had followed, he spread his fingers and tested his strength, pulling at the sources of the salty ocean far below. A few droplets came to rest in his hands, and he smeared them into his burned lips.

All these summers, Sy had been hesitant to hunt the girls - had even gone to great lengths to be absent from the hunts. But only today had he realized the true reason for his reluctance.

Nothing is small when it is against your will.

If he hunted a girl, he wanted it to be his choice. If she was caught, he wanted it to be because she had chosen to be caught. Weshen people had long ago given up on love and magic, but Sy, alone of all the men, knew that one of these had begun to return.

He flexed his fingers once more, shifting a few more drops of seawater into his palm. The salt stung his lips a little less this time, and he turned to cross the plains and head toward the beach. He would return without a girl again, and this troubled him, but not enough to force her into the men's camp.

If his power was not just a fluke, and magic was returning to the Weshen, then perhaps love would one day return to his people as well.

The summer winds had fully dried Coren's dress by the time she entered the women's village. Her stomach growled; it was hours since she had eaten. Tellen was waiting, staring out the window with pinched lips and a creased brow. As she handed her cousin a plate of bread and cold meat, her eyes connected with Coren's, wide and fearful.

"I wasn't caught," Coren said, then pushed past Tellen into the sleeping room, setting the plate on her bed. The twins weren't home, which was a relief. Coren grimaced at her reflection in the small glass: dress wrinkled and stiff with salt, hair wildly tangled, mouth raw with blisters.

He'd come too close, but she had escaped the claim, and that was all that mattered.

She quickly swallowed a few bites of food, gathered what she needed for the bathing pool, and pushed back out of the house, ignoring Tellen's glares. No ordinary Weshen hunter could have gotten as close as he did. Only the General's sons had such training and skill, and so her information has grown.

Two questions remained, however: which son had she slighted, and how would he retaliate?

Coren rinsed the last of the soap from her skin, then stepped out of the pool, wrapping the towel tightly around her naked body. A plan was forming, and she would need to act swiftly, before the boy had time to decide.

She walked the path to her home with quick steps and chose a clean, loose dress and sturdy sandals. She would have preferred pants in case she had to run, but at least this one slit high above her knee for movement. She wove her whip around her thigh, braided her hair, and smiled softly at Tellen, who had fallen asleep again in the heat of the afternoon.

Coren knew this morning's game was far from over. But this time, she would be the hunter, and the boy would give her what she wanted.

4

Sy bent closer to the map spread on a back table in the General's sprawling tent. His fingers brushed against the raised ink of the painted cliffs that rose above Weshen Isle's beaches. Where had he lost her? Tracing the path from the beach where the hunts began, into the maze of rocks, he thought finally he knew the cliff where she had jumped.

He still couldn't believe she had jumped. A girl had jumped off a cliff to avoid kissing him. A girl had burned her lips with *goshen berries* to avoid kissing him. He should be ashamed. But instead, his fingers touched the blisters on his lips reverently. They were still a little bloody, hours later. He shook his head as a laugh bubbled up in his chest.

Corentine thought she had escaped him.

But all she had done was help him find his hunger. He would never force her into his bed, but by the Magi, he wanted to speak with her again. Perhaps he could find a solution that would please both of them.

And her words: *Nothing is small when it is against your will.* The phrase had run a loop of truth through his mind all afternoon. He'd heard it before, somewhere.

Sy tried to focus again on the map and the sound of his father's pen scratching in his journal. He remembered nothing of his childhood here; everything from before the General had taken him to the city was a shadowy blank. Even his mother's face.

The elders maintained it was better that way, and the Sulit memory charm was the only form of magic which the Magi had allowed the Weshen to practice after the Sacrifice.

Sy's roving fingertips found a rounded cove marked to the right of the plunging cliff - a place where Corentine could have easily stayed hidden. The cove opened back onto the rocky path, and eventually lead to the edges of the women's village. This was how she had escaped; he was sure of it now.

"Sir?" The flaps of the tent opened, and Tag's bulky form ducked into the semi-darkness. The General glanced up, impatient at his guard's interruption. "There is a girl, sir."

Sy stopped fingering the map to listen.

"Tell me your business, Tagsha," his father said.

"Well, she claims she was collecting berries when she came upon a creature. It…it sounds like a Vespa, sir."

"Impossible." Sy's father waved his hand, shooing Tag away. "They don't come to the island."

"That's what I thought. But her description…"

The General sighed. "Bring her."

Sy moved farther into the tent's shadows, interested but not wanting to become part of this new wrinkle. Perhaps his father had forgotten that he'd been there studying the maps all afternoon.

Tag returned with the girl, and Sy's gut twisted. Before this summer, all the girls had one face, one body, and he cared for none of them. But he remembered every freckle on Corentine's nose, every spark in her tan and gold eyes, as though he had known them forever.

Why was she here now, in his father's tent?

Her hair was damp but neatly braided, and she was wearing a clean, dry dress. She held her head proudly, meeting the General's eyes before being addressed.

"What did you see?" he asked, watching her with interest.

Sy drank in the clipped lilt of her voice as she described the bulging body and iridescent feathers of what could only be a Vespa. Yet, like his father, Sy could barely believe her. Since the Separation and Sacrifice, the MagiCreatures had never traveled to the island. Simply put, there was no magic there to attract them.

"Syashin."

"Sir?" Sy stepped forward, head bowed in deference, but his pulse quickened. Suddenly he didn't want Corentine to see him here. But he felt his face emerging from the shadows, and his stomach shrank into itself as her small feet backed up quickly, nearly to the tent's entrance.

"Allow this girl to show you the location where she believes she saw the creature. You are armed?"

Sy picked up his bow sword from the nearby bench. "Yes, Sir."

"Do not be afraid," his father said to Corentine in a rare moment of kindness. "Syashin is one of Weshen City's best Paladins, even though he is young."

Her eyes cast downward upon hearing this praise, but she did not speak. Instead, she lowered her head in thanks and slipped out of the tent. Sy turned to the General, assuming he would give him more instruction, but he was already back at work. Most likely, he didn't believe the girl, and he was just pawning her off to his conveniently-located son.

"Try not to lose her, Sy," Tag laughed as Sy pushed through the tent flap, and his father made an unpleasant noise that cut him in two.

There was no way they could have known this was the same girl who had sent him trudging back to camp in a bloodied shame today, but anger spiked in his chest at Tag's daring.

General Ashemon turned a harsh glare on his oldest friend. "Do not tease him more. It isn't effective."

"Sorry," Tagsha grinned, looking anything but. Ashemon continued to stare at him flatly, and finally he sobered. "Of course. I will stop."

"Syashin doesn't respond to shame. We've learned that much in the last few years. He believes he's being noble by refusing the hunts. Both of my sons wish to see Weshen take its rightful place in the world again, but their ideas on how to do so are like night and day. Be certain, Tagsha. Reshra is not the one we want to lead us."

Tagsha nodded solemnly. The two men had discussed as much before.

"Find out who that girl is. Who her parents are. She reminds me of someone…"

Tagsha nodded and ducked out of the tent.

The General rubbed his fingers along his jaw, clean-shaven for the summer months. He was fairly certain he knew what Tagsha would find, and if the girl could be convinced to partner with Syashin, perhaps the magic that had once surged in both their bloodlines could be coaxed awake.

It would be a delicate balance, however. Even if the Mirror Magi had begun to listen to his prayers, the return of magic would mean the return of war with the Restless King, and very few of the Weshen people were ready for such a burden.

He would not send his people to war against Riata until he was completely certain of their success.

By the time Sy's eyes had adjusted to the bright sunlight beyond the tent, he found that Corentine was already halfway to the beach path, not waiting to see if he would follow. He jogged to keep up, and she whirled to face him as he neared.

"You will not touch me," she hissed, her body lowering into a runner's crouch.

Sy held his hands palm up, a smile already crossing his face because she had recognized him. Then again, his lips *were* still blistered and raw. "I'm here to find a Vespa. No more."

"You work for the General?" She strode along the rocky path, not watching where her feet fell, yet still avoiding each hazard.

"He's my father." Sy didn't want to keep secrets from her. She may never trust him, but he felt a strange need to try.

"And yet you work for him?" she repeated, as though she had already known this.

"Of course."

"Your brother. The destructive one. The First Son doesn't work as much, does he?"

Another smile broke onto Sy's lips at her keen assessment of Resh. She was mostly right. "*I'm* the First Son," he corrected as she glanced back at him. She nodded, one corner of her lips pulling up.

"My name's Syashin," he added.

"Corentine," she mumbled, and he nodded too, as though he hadn't already known.

"How did you know what a Vespa looks like?" he asked, trying not to focus too much on the sway of her hips on the path before him.

"I didn't. Your Guard told me the name."

Sy tried to remember if that was the correct sequence. "There aren't any berry bushes here," he said instead, and she raised an eyebrow.

"Does it matter to you what I was gathering?"

"No."

One corner of her mouth lifted again, making her seem satisfied with that answer, and a small rush of pleasure opened in his chest.

The path curved and tightened so much that he had to turn sideways to avoid scraping his shoulders on the rocks. Just as he was beginning to wonder where exactly she was going, she stopped walking abruptly, and he bumped into her back.

She jumped away and focused determinedly on the sky. They had come out of the rocks onto another wide plain: one he'd only seen on his father's map. Like the women's village, their hunting plains were also forbidden to the men.

Sy scanned the area, wishing again that he could remember what it had been like to grow up on the island, running these very plains. Perhaps he had even grown up with this fierce, independent girl.

All he knew from the elders was that he had no sisters, and therefore no restrictions on who to hunt.

"There," Corentine said, interrupting his thoughts. She pointed at a speck in the distance. "That might be it. This is where I saw it, anyway, here on the upper plain."

The bird was too far away to be sure, but even from a distance, it did seem larger than any common creature. Sy moved in front of her, readying his bow sword. He expected Corentine to retreat close to the rocky path, under cover of the cliffs, but she followed him out into the tall grasses and bright meadow flowers.

He turned in a partial circle, scanning the now-empty sky. As his gaze finally rested back on her, his breathing quickened. She was bent over, her braid sliding across one shoulder. Her dress was gathered to her hip on one side, revealing a tanned, muscled thigh and that incredibly intimate tattoo - the snakka that wound from the curve of her calf to a place still beneath the fabric.

Suddenly her face snapped up and her eyes locked onto his, as searing as a goshen berry.

"Um, your tattoo," Sy managed, guilt flushing his skin.

She straightened, and he almost thought she might run. Then another satisfied smile quirked her lips. She reached down and pressed her palm to her thigh.

The tattoo slipped, slid, coiling down her leg. And Sy's jaw went slack.

She twisted the whip into a handful of loose circles and cocked her head at him. "Not a tattoo," she answered.

He felt like he was being measured, and he had the hollow fear that he might come up lacking.

"I'll send a message if I see the Vespa again," she said, then turned and jogged across the plain, toward a gap in the far cliffs. Sy knew that way lead back to the women's village, so all he could do was stare after her.

There was a distinct sensation that she'd pulled him here on purpose, as though luring an animal from its den to learn its secrets. His face stretched into a grin at the realization that she was a skilled hunter as well.

He explored the perimeter of the plain a few minutes longer, staying in the shadow of the cliff in case the creature reappeared. But there was nothing.

Just as he'd reached the path leading back to camp, though, he heard a creature's screech, and it was a sound he would always know. A sound that was imprinted in the survival part of his brain. He should run away. Far away.

But even as the flight adrenaline coursed through him, Sy's logical brain insisted there was no way a Vespa was on the island.

But he heard it again. And then something else: a human shriek.

His feet began running before he told them to, seeking the sound.

His heart nearly exploded when he rounded a corner and found a full-grown Vespa flapping at the air, and Corentine pinned against a rocky outcropping on the smaller plain, just where he had cornered her the previous day. The water could never save her now. The Vespa had begun circling her, rising higher in the air with each revolution.

Hunters called it the death spiral, and nobody survived the creature's plummet - often the impact burst their bodies open.

Sy aimed his bow sword and trained it on the Vespa, waiting for it to reach full height and begin to speed back toward the plain. He would only get one shot, and he must not pull the trigger too early, or the arrow would not fly high enough.

Why didn't she run? It wouldn't have made a difference, but he thought she would at least try to save herself.

The creature screamed in triumph and dove, a blur of swollen belly and shimmering white wings. Corentine yelled back wordlessly, cracking her whip at the air.

Instinct born from years of training pulled the trigger of the bow sword, and Sy's arrow flew true, aimed directly at the creature's heart.

Then the Vespa vanished.

A pop resonated through the air, bouncing off the cliffs, and a shimmer of dust and iridescent droplets rained down on the quiet plain. The unused arrow clattered to the ground.

The Vespa was gone. Disappeared. And Corentine was slumped back against the rock like a sacrifice.

Sy sprinted to her, a dark shroud of confusion and fear hazing across his soul.

And somewhere deep in the southern Sulit woods, far beyond where the MagiSea drained into the Hungry River, a heart began to beat again. A pale pink leaf drifted down from the trees above, followed by another, until the colors of sunrise papered the ground.

A woman - a witch - so ancient and unmoving as to have nearly melted into the ground where she waited, keeping watch over the heart, began to cackle. The sound started as a dry whisper, the air pushing cobwebs from her throat until the noise grew to reach even the starbirds perched in the branches above.

"It begins," she rasped, stroking a long, dirty fingernail across the crystal box where the heart lay, shuddering in its struggle to regain rhythm.

A snakka thicker around than a man's waist, fangs glistening in the half-light of the forest floor, wound its way around her elbow. She bent to whisper to it, and to the dust-dulled crowen that hopped onto her knee.

"*Tell the others.*"

5

Coren blinked her eyes open, groaning against the too-bright sun. All she remembered was the Vespa, diving with its golden claws aimed for her heart. How was she still alive? A face came into focus above her, and her heart plummeted.

What was that boy doing here? *Syashin*. First Son.

She would be so *mad* if she had survived a Vespa attack only to need the help of some boy - some entitled General's son.

His face disappeared and she felt fingers brush along her ankle. Panic sent her scrabbling against the rock, but she still couldn't move. Pain rocked her body as she realized the problem - her ankle was still wedged between two rocks.

He made a shushing noise, and she gritted her teeth. Coren could tell he was trying to be gentle, and she tried to hate him for it. With a final scraping of skin, her ankle wrenched free. She let go of the breath she hadn't meant to keep, along with a curse she hadn't meant to say.

He turned his face, but not before she had glimpsed a hint of a smile.

"What happened to the Vespa?" she managed, scooting a few inches away from him.

He stared down at her, his face nearly blacked out by the fierce yellow of the afternoon sun behind him. "I don't know," he said, his tone flat and careful. "It's gone."

"Then I need to go before it comes back." She pushed herself standing and tested her ankle. The skin was raw, but she should be able to walk. Yet she took two steps and dizziness washed over her, rolling her eyes into her skull.

Coren lurched forward, and the boy caught her against his broad chest, his arms warm and strong around her waist. He lowered her to the ground, leaning her against the rock as gently as though she were a small child, and this time she did hate him for it.

"Just sit here a bit, okay?" he asked. "That Vespa isn't coming back."

"Why not?" Swallowing back a lump of nausea, Coren curled into herself. She sensed him crouched next to her, and her body tensed. She was in no shape to defend herself from a hunter of women. But he didn't move to touch her again.

"Here. Drink this." He set a small water skin in the grass and settled back against the rock. It smelled faintly of lemondrine and salt. Surprisingly, the scent alone seemed to calm her whirling insides, and she took a small drink, finding it tasted mostly like fresh water. The rest of the cool liquid slid down easily, and as she removed the empty skin from her lips, she caught him watching her with a curious expression.

"Better?" Syashin asked. His eyes were darker than she remembered, like storm clouds over the ocean.

Coren nodded. "Thank you. For coming back, I mean." She felt her cheeks flush, and then she really hated him.

"What else would I do?" he asked, and his voice was so soft she could barely hear it. But of course he was right - the hunters were sworn to protect the women. Paladins supposedly welcomed the chance to battle with creatures such as Vespa.

Coren got up, more slowly this time, testing her stomach, her ankle, her head. But all was good. She stretched, feeling like she could sprint across the plains. Then a sense of what had just happened between them began to creep into her conscious, and nerves strummed across her belly.

"What will you tell the General?" she asked, working to keep her voice as flat as his.

"Nothing. There is no Vespa," he said, and his mouth closed in a firm, straight line. He reached to retrieve the water skin, then stood. "Do you want me to walk you to the village?"

Corentine blinked at him. Men were not allowed in the women's village. What was he playing at? "No. I'm fine."

She turned and hurried toward the gap in the rocks that would take her home. She knew he wasn't following, but she felt his eyes on her back until she slipped through the rocks. It was already near dinner time, and she hurried as she neared the village.

Sy didn't go straight back to the men's camp, choosing instead to roam the beaches where the hunts took place. He stared out at the sparkling MagiSea, trying to make a plan and failing. The white-gold sand was warm from the day's sun and seemed to stretch into the setting sun, golden-orange on the dark water. The cliffs here were higher, too, much of the rock slick and flat from the waves.

Creatures in general didn't vanish, but that Vespa had disappeared. Dust and droplets didn't fall from the sky unless a storm was ripping the island, yet it was as though the bird had been pulled apart, source by source. And lemondrine with salt water wasn't appealing to most people, but Corentine had drained his secret water skin and looked better for it.

He'd never seen anything like it. The lemondrine tonic was a Sulit secret…was the rest?

Sy knew SourceShifting had once been so much more than his ability to move water into a cup. Damren claimed a powerful shifter could be as destructive as separating the very matter of the world, but he'd never seen anything beyond the simple tasks she set him, as her power had weakened to nearly nothing over the years.

He knew his father still prayed for the return of magic, but he also knew Ashemon feared it, dreaded what would happen to the Weshen if the magic arrived too late, or with too little effect to shield them from the king. And so it was with this in mind that Sy had never shown his shifting to the General.

Eventually hunger drove him to the tents, and he quietly filled a plate from the common table. Nobody seemed to notice as he slipped away to sit in the tall palmpress grasses, their plumes waving gently above his head.

He had nearly finished the brown bread and grilled meat when he heard his father's voice, and Tag's, as they walked the nearby path. Sy slid down farther into the grass, not interested in giving his report on the Vespa just yet.

He still hadn't worked out what he could say to avoid creating more suspicion.

"What do you make of this creature report?" Tag asked Ashemon, confirming Sy's worry.

"I've seen nothing to indicate a creature could be on the island. The girl likely overheard someone telling stories and is seeking attention. Who could know the motivations of a young girl's heart?" General Ashemon answered, but his tone sounded strained. They had stopped just beyond Sy, and he barely breathed for fear of being discovered. "Have you seen Syashin tonight?"

"No," Tag answered. "But Resh mentioned he'd been with him at dinner."

Sy grinned. Resh would lie for him even when unasked. The brothers may not get along on everything, but when it came to the General's requests, they were united.

"Sir," Tag began after a few moments' silence, "I'd like to respectfully ask you to reconsider sending a party to rescue those Wesh. So many-"

"No, Tagsha. I've made my decision. It is regretful, and I will mourn the further destruction of our bloodlines, but it's simply too dangerous to provoke the king like that. Our duty is to protect the Weshen *here*, on our island and in our city."

Sy heard Tag sigh, disappointment audible even through the waving grasses, and he nearly leaned up and showed himself. He wanted to know more of what they were talking about.

He knew the Wesh were the half-blood and quarter-blood descendants of the Weshen who had once lived freely in Riata. Sy had met a few still living in hiding in EvenFall, and some were still locked away with the Restless King's Alchemists.

But why would a group of them need rescue, and danger or not, why would his father be so set against it? Was this decision based on a cowardly fear of the king?

The older men moved on, walking farther down the beach, and Sy rose carefully from his hiding spot, winding his way in the shadows to the General's empty tent.

"Hello, brother," a whisper in the dusk greeted him just as he lifted the tent flap.

"Resh," Sy said, straightening, but not letting go of the fabric.

"Father General is not in there," Resh said. "But you weren't looking for him, were you?"

"I'm looking for something else," Sy admitted. "Help me keep watch."

"Will you share the spoils?" Resh asked, considering.

Sy huffed and ducked inside the tent, reaching for a candle. Resh grinned and followed him inside. "I'll help you look, but I'm no watchguard."

Sy sifted through the papers on Ashemon's desk, looking for anything with the word *Wesh*. In spite of his words, Resh merely lounged in their father's chair, toying with a dagger. Finally, tucked into a journal of scribbled battle notes and hastily-drawn maps, Sy found a communication from one of the guards he knew worked undercover in EvenFall.

"This is it," he whispered. "Let's go before he comes back." He snuffed the candle and slipped out of the tent.

Once back in their tent with a new candle, he read the paper aloud to Resh.

General Ashemon, Sir,

I have come into information on a group of ten or more Wesh, traveling from Matensfold to the new auction house in EvenFall. These Wesh were gathered from the northern nobility, and though there are no reports on their abilities or health, they are indeed our people. It's an unheard-of torture to see our people reduced to the treatment of animals, and I respectfully request that you send a contingent of men to aid in their rescue and return to Weshen City.

Your servant,

Denesh Parken

"Let me guess," Resh said, stretching out on Sy's bed. "You want to skip out on the pleasures of summer hunts and go rescue these Riatan mutts."

Sy ignored his brother's careless slur as he sifted through the other papers. One was a corner of a map, showing a route traced between the two cities, with a few spots marked as appropriate for ambush. The others were a handful of sketches, showing individual people, their faces unsmiling and lean. Were these the Wesh themselves? Sy studied the drawings for so long that Resh grew bored and snatched them away.

"You'll never be allowed to go, and we both know you won't sneak away. Let our Father General take care of the mess."

"I heard him talking to Tag. They aren't going to send anyone. These people are slaves, Resh. They have Weshen blood, and they're going to be sold like animals."

Resh's eyes burned in the candle's light. "You think I don't understand? I may enjoy a girl or two and drink more than I need, but I am no traitor to our blood. But the grandmothers of these Wesh *were* traitors. They lived happily in Riata, and they bedded Riatan men. Not out of some noble love, and certainly not to protect the magic. No, they squandered our blood just like the king's army. It's *their* fault that the Sacrifice was even necessary."

"Many of them had no choice," Sy insisted. "The king seduced many of our people to his land, only to turn on them in an instant."

Resh only stood straighter. "Still, you forget your duty, Sy. If the General says no, I say no. *That* is how

Weshen work, Sy. If you don't obey him, the men will never obey you."

Sy noticed an anger in his brother's tone that made him wonder if Resh were only speaking of these papers. A tickle of pride snaked up his spine and his eyes slitted at Resh's insinuation.

"Our father may be more cautious than we are," Resh continued, "but he's kept our people safe all this time, and his father before, and his before that. One day it will be your job, and you'd do well to learn which battles can be won and which will only be suicide."

And with that, Resh gathered the papers and stomped out of the tent. Seething, Sy barely resisted running after his brother to retrieve the papers. If the General found them snooping, they would be put under watch like children until the summer was over, and he needed freedom to move about the island, especially after what he'd seen today with Corentine.

Returning, Resh said, "I've put everything back. You're welcome."

"Do you never question our father?" Sy asked, blood still coursing too quickly in his veins.

"Of course, but it does no good." Resh bent and drew two cups from his trunk, along with a bottle of brown liquid.

"If things were different, it would," Sy said, turning to pace the narrow tent.

"But things are the same, Sy. Always the same. Here," he said, handing Sy the mug. "Drink to our fallen brothers, and pray no more may die."

Sy glared over the rim of the mug, but he did drink. Prayer was needed, of course, and obedience to a strong leader. But sometimes so was action, and suddenly it was as though his role and Resh's were reversed. Seeing the Vespa today made him feel reckless, and the sloth of these summer days seeded a restlessness he hadn't felt in years.

He knew better than most how the Magi had begun to answer prayers for renewed protection. He knew better than most that things were not the same, and he wondered if his father and brother would accept the magic once they learned his secret, or continue to fear it.

Downing the rest of the liquor, Sy counseled himself to be patient. For now, the secret should stay kept.

Maren sat alone at her table, peering into the bits of tea leaf in the bottom of her empty cup. A tawny catten purred on the stool next to hers, and Maren petted its silky back absently.

There had been a death today. She could see it with the borrowed Sulit spell and swirl of the lemondrine leaves.

A retribution, of sorts. Maren smiled, an image of Neshra appearing clearer in her mind than in many years. Even if it wasn't the same Vespa, she felt he was finally avenged.

Then another thought entered. In her haste to celebrate, she had nearly forgotten. Maren swirled the leaves again, counterclockwise with the drops of liquid in the cup, and her expression darkened. The cycle was not complete, not even close. Instead, the circle in her cup was more of a ripple, with ever-expanding consequences.

In spite of all Sorenta's secrecy and Maren's cloaking spell, Corentine's shifter magic had awoken today, and now she must be told the last of her mother's secrets.

Soon other magic would begin to awaken, and then the General would have a decision to make. Maren wasn't certain he would be strong enough to choose wisely, and so she knew she must ready herself.

The Weshen magic was born to bring light into the shadows and darkness. But it had always been both a curse and a blessing in the cycle of power, for the strongest light creates the darkest shadows.

Maren rose and set about preparations, including packing clothes for tomorrow, making pineberry cookies, and preparing more tea. Her help would be needed, and soon.

Left alone, the catten stretched and yawned, then knocked Maren's mug onto the floor with a single swish of its bushy tail. Growling, it licked a single paw in satisfaction.

"Coren!" a voice screamed as she entered the common yard near her home. Penna rushed at her, her small face wide with fear and panic. The little girl barely hugged her before sprinting away again, toward their house, and Coren broke into a run.

A wail burst through the summercloth as they stumbled inside.

There were too many bodies in the sleeping room, and it took Coren more than a few seconds to realize that Tellen was birthing.

She shoved through the older women who had come to help and knelt by the narrow bed. Tellen's face was red and sweaty, and her eyes were full of pain and terror. Penna darted in and laid a cold cloth over Tellen's forehead just as she opened her mouth to scream again. Her body rocked in the bed as the labor pains coursed through her.

When she quieted again, Coren could hear the women behind her whisper and breathe. She burned to tell them to leave, to get themselves away from her house. But they knew more of this than she did.

For the second time in one day, Coren needed someone else to help her and her family survive. And oh, she hated it.

Kosh came in and left again, shooed away by the midwives. After some time, Penna was also asked to leave. Coren told her to find her brother and go see Maren and pick some pineberries for Tellen. The house was silent for several moments, and Coren turned to see the women watching her doubtfully as well, as though wondering if *she* should go too.

It was this look which finally fixed her fear into something that clutched and squeezed at her throat. She stumbled to her knees next to Tellen's bed.

It had been too many hours. Too many moans. Too much blood.

She pushed away these thoughts and buried her face in the sheets next to Tellen's slick neck. She prayed, whispering fierce bargains to the Mirror Magi into the fabric. Eventually, Tellen woke from her drowse and turned her face, feverish lips resting on her cousin's cheek.

"It's okay, Coren. You'll all be fine," she whispered.

And Coren was undone. Shattered.

She sobbed and clutched at Tellen's arms, hugging her cousin's limp body as the older Weshen women hovered over them, finally unsure what to do to relieve the girl's suffering, or that of her family. Coren had never wished more for the power of magic - any magic.

But Sorenta had left her nothing but warnings of her whip and a single spell, to falsify a child. Not to save one.

Finally the baby was pushed and pulled from the womb, but no cry greeted the waiting women. The cord of life had wrapped tightly around its tiny neck, and Tellen stared vacantly at the bundle of still blankets that the midwife held out to her. The woman bent to place the baby in her arms, but Tellen didn't even lift a finger to grasp her dead child.

The sun had sunk below the horizon, the sky faded into a sweeping darkness before Tellen gave up her tenuous hold on life. Coren swore she could feel her cousin's soul brush past as it tore free from her broken body, caressing her hair and cheek in a breeze that shouldn't exist.

As a clump, the women left quietly. The house had been dark and silent for a long time when Coren heard Penna and Kosh pad into the room. Penna set a basket of berries on the nightstand. None of them spoke a word.

Instead, the twins knelt on either side of Coren, their small bodies pressed close to hers, and together they recited prayers for Tellen's soul, then for the baby's, to find eternal rest.

What should have been a life was now a double death, and Coren feared that sort of heavy omen. It spoke of an imbalance in the world - too much dark where there should have been light.

When they finished the litany, she woodenly instructed the twins to fetch Auntie Maren and their few other friends.

And numb to her exhaustion and loss, Coren set about preparing her cousin's body for the pyre of water and fire.

6

Sy's mind rejected sleep.

Instead he sprawled on his bed, which was aggravatingly lush with crisp cotton blankets and feather-down pillows. A cooling ocean breeze drifted through the tent's open window flap, moonlight slanted across his bare stomach, and a small insect plodded along the canvas ceiling. A girl was murmuring behind the divider wall, and he could hear Resh laugh, low and sultry and full of leisure.

So much had happened in just a single day, and Sy had no more patience for his brother's casual ways or their pampered summer lives.

If the magic were returning, Weshen was hurtling once more to a future of war, an arrow flying at the heart of the king. Sy worried the king would disappear and deflect the arrow again, but he wouldn't dissipate like the Vespa.

King Zorander Graeme had a singular way of reassembling his sources, coming back generation after generation to hunt the Weshen hunters into an early extinction.

The possibilities and then the impossibilities rose in waves, beating against him. Suddenly growing too restless even to pretend sleep, he pushed out of his bed so quickly that it nearly tipped, the blankets sliding in a heap to the woven floorcloth.

He went over each of his lessons, from childhood on, as he paced the square room of his tent. During the Sacrifice two generations before, the Mirror Magi had sucked all the magic from Weshen people and blanketed the NeverCross Mountains with it, creating impervious protection from Riata. Stories were told of those Weshen left defenseless beyond the mountains, and how the Restless King had found them all and scraped the magic from their bones.

Since then, everyone inside Riata and out believed that no Weshen would be born with magic until the Sacrifice was no longer needed to protect them.

And yet…there had been banishments in Sy's lifetime due to the use of magic. Once even a young boy, rumored to have shifted a *man* back into mere dust and droplets. Some maintained he had used Sulit or Umbren spells instead, and after seeing what Corentine had done to the Vespa, he guessed it must be the same magic. But which…Sulit, Weshen, or Umbren?

If only he could question Damren now, or search her salvaged books.

As Ashemon's First Son and a respected Paladin, he was permitted to travel as he liked. He had sought out the most vicious of MagiCreatures in hopes of finding their talismans' power. It had all come to nothing until three years ago, just before his first summer hunts. Deep in the caves of the NeverCross Mountains, he had found an even larger source of power: a library of lost magical lore, and Damren, the woman who had become his teacher.

No girl from Weshen Isle was likely to have access to any sort of magic.

And yet.

She had known a Vespa. And Vespas were drawn to shifter magic. Lemondrine tonic was a Sulit concoction, but it restored shifter magi when they had depleted their power, and she had drained his waterskin without flinching at the taste.

Excitement filtered into his limbs, quickening his pace. He peered around himself in the dark, realizing he had paced his way out of the tent completely, and down to the ocean. His toes were sunk deep into the damp sand.

A flicker of light farther down the beach caught his restless attention, and he walked to a small rise in the encampment. Slightly below him, near an isolated portion of the women's beach, a great bonfire raged, surrounded by a small group of dark figures. He didn't remember ever seeing the women celebrate on their own before.

He moved carefully down the slope and toward the gathering, careful to stay out of sight.

Abruptly, Sy realized he was watching a funeral.

The melody of wailing grew louder, then shifted into a haunting song. The bonfire began to move, pushed slowly into the water, toward the faraway mouth of the Hungry River. It had burned down enough that Sy could see a flat platform holding a wrapped body, and a smaller bundle set atop, now fused together in ash. Mother and child.

His heart fell in grief for this tragedy.

As the raft floated farther out to sea, the singing quieted, and the figures on land began to move away, a few at a time. Some were hunched over with old age, and two were small - other children. There were not many.

As the fire floated along its ocean path, the beach emptied, except for one lone, dark shape kneeling in the sand. Sy had crept close enough to see the profile of her face, ghosted in the silver moonlight.

Of course it was Corentine.

His heart twisted in sympathy for this girl. He barely knew her, and yet he felt a certain responsibility for her now. He wanted her life to be simple and happy, her days to be carefree like the other girls'.

Even as he thought this, though, Sy realized such a change would make her a different person - perhaps a lesser person.

When life hit hard enough to crack, people either came apart or they healed stronger than before. Corentine was strong for a reason, he was certain.

The tide had shifted and water had begun to lap at her dress, swirling the fabric around her, but still she didn't move. Sy remained, watching in solidarity, wishing he could comfort her, but knowing he wouldn't be welcome.

He had just turned to go, feeling he should leave her to the solitary prayers, when a shriek of grief and despair

- maybe even anger - erupted from Corentine. The air seemed to course with invisible lightning up and down the beach, and Sy felt the hairs on his neck lift.

He choked out a curse, then clapped a hand over his mouth against the sound, watching in shock as the shape before him on the sand shrunk in on itself, becoming smaller. Younger. A girl of maybe ten now crouched in the surf, her face raised to the moon as a sob wracked her body.

And Sy's walls of logic and careful observation collided, crumbling with the force of an unavoidable truth. He knew, and his soul swelled with the knowledge and the hope of change.

There was no question in his mind any longer. He knew *this* magic - could even perform it himself. Corentine was no traitor: she was a Weshen shifter.

And she had somehow learned Double magic.

Sulit witches had begun to gather in the Listening Forest. They whispered their true names to the pink-leaved trees, which passed the knowledge on the air to the renewed heart.

"I am GrandScream."

"SmokeFist."

"You will call me ShadowStrike."

"BloodChaser has come."

And the coven was formed, and the covenant was signed.

The heart sighed in satisfaction of its second life, stretching wide enough to reach the cold walls of the crystal box. The box itself sparkled with dew in the shadows, and the witches watched it with covetous eyes. One day, if they survived the coming trials, one of them might earn the heart's favor.

"Which of you will go to StarsHelm Palace?" the trees asked the witches.

The witches laughed, the sound like a splattering of summer rain on the leaves of the Listening Forest.

"Be still, my heart," ShadowStrike answered. "For one of us has been waiting in the palace all these years."

7

It was late afternoon when Coren woke, and the sun was heavy and hot as it slanted in the window. She blinked into the thick silence of the house for a few seconds before the events of the previous day and its long night poured back into her like a tidal wave.

Thank the Mirror Magi for Auntie Maren, who had taken the twins home with her last night as Coren waited alone in the sand, performing the final parts of the vigil. She had stayed much longer than tradition expected, watching the pyre and questioning the gods' plans until the fire was too small to see, drifted into oblivion on the southern MagiSea.

The waves of grief shoved at her again and again, her breath coming in short gasps and heaves until she could focus enough to remember the methods that had saved her when her mother died. Systematically, she wiped her tears and closed her heart. She shut away memories of Tellen and hopes for a new baby. She stomped down any idle thoughts of traveling beyond the island or Vespas or magic or odd General's sons.

More than ever, she must be strong. For Kosh and Penna. No matter what the gods gave her to bear, her reason for living was still to protect her family.

Coren rose shakily from the too-hot bed in the too-empty room and staggered to the pitcher of water. She gripped it with both hands and gulped straight from its rim. Her body felt as though it hadn't had food or water in days. And although she knew it wasn't true, she also knew their cabinets were too bare for comfort.

Perhaps the supplies from the men would be enough this year. Perhaps - and Coren hated herself for thinking it - but perhaps having fewer mouths to feed would help it to be enough. And yet, she knew that somehow her family's history would shadow them forever, keeping their house lonelier and more frugal than most.

So Coren began to dress for hunting.

As she wrapped the whip around her arm, another unwelcome thought flickered into existence in her tired brain. She could let the General's First Son catch her. She could offer him a son. Girls who provided a male heir to such a boy were honored and cared for, even beyond the child's eighth birthday.

But her throat closed, her heart nearly ripping open again at these thoughts. No. She would simply hunt more often, and Penna would practice her sewing instead of her fighting. And Kosh would be gone in a year.

Fighting tears harder than she could remember since her mother's death, Coren raced toward the plains.

Her sack filled rapidly with groundbirds, rockrabbits, and even an oversized snakka, which she coiled tightly and knotted with twine. Its unmoving silver form looked a little like her whip, which was shimmering between brown and silver-streaked bronze, and nearly burning to the touch.

Coren was suddenly fiercely glad something else had seen as much death as she had.

The sack was heavy over her shoulder as she trudged toward Maren's. The wild energy that had sent her to the plains was gone. Penna ran to her as soon as Coren opened the gate, the small girl's embrace nearly buckling her knees. Coren managed a smile for the sweet child. She and Penna would have each other, at least.

Kosh appeared then and relieved her of the blood-stained sack, holding it high to keep it from Maren's catten. He began to spread the animals on a bald patch of Maren's garden, examining their joints and wounds. He would skin and dissect them too, if allowed.

Coren had often watched him take apart each beast to see how it worked, then rebuild the tendons and bone in much the way the King's Alchemists were said to do with their magical machinery. In another world, she thought, one without need for the Separation, Kosh could have trained for such an honorable job, instead of the inescapable and violent deaths that awaited Weshen hunters.

"You and the twins are welcome here any time," Maren said in a low voice, as they watched the twins argue over what to do with the snakka's luminescent fangs.

"Thank you. For keeping them last night. But I will manage, like I always have. Tellen isn't the first to leave me." This last part was more an admittance of self-pity than Coren normally indulged in, but Maren just sighed.

"Have some tea," she said instead, taking a sun-warm mug from the garden wall.

Coren took the mug obediently and stared into its cloudy liquid as though it might give her a vision. She glared at her wobbly reflection - Maren certainly had persistence. Never failed to offer the nasty stuff.

A sigh escaped her, but when she inhaled again, the tea filled her nostrils with lemondrine and salt. And suddenly that scent had a context - it smelled just like Syashin's water yesterday. Coren raised her mug and took a small, exploratory sip. The flavors, which shouldn't even have been drinkable, flooded her cottony mouth with relief.

She turned up the mug and drained it in one long drought, feeling energy sear through her limbs like lightning across the sky.

Maren grinned and squeezed Coren's arm with a bony hand. "I thought you might eventually learn to like my brew."

Coren looked at her sharply, but the old woman only cackled. Her muscles tingled like they needed to be stretched with movement, although she'd been running the plains for hours that morning.

"Where did you get this recipe anyway?" Coren asked.

Maren grinned and glanced back to the children. "Depends on who is asking."

Coren rolled her eyes. "*I'm* asking, Maren. Just me."

"Then I got it from a Sulit witch."

Coren nearly dropped the mug. "What did you say?"

Maren smiled around a sip of tea. "The Sulit used to be our friends, you know. Allies, even. Before we shut out the entire world trying to lock the door behind the Restless King. He's taken so much more than you know," she added, her expression darkening like the feathers of one of her prized stormcloud chickens.

"I've had that drink before, you know," Coren said, ready to drop her own information on Maren's unsuspecting mind.

"In my kitchen."

"On the plains. After that Vespa disappeared. Ashemon's First Son gave it to me."

Maren watched her closely, one eyebrow raised in interest. Waiting. Coren sighed. Why did she even try to shock the woman? "How would we know if the magic were returning?" she asked instead, finally putting words to thoughts she'd pushed away for years.

Maren shrugged and leaned forward conspiratorially. "How can something return when it never really left?"

"Maren, what do you really know?" Coren leaned heavily against the garden wall. She needed answers, not riddles.

"Yes, I've kept many secrets from you, and I'm sorry. But your mother…"

"Was insane. I know. But none of the Weshen have had magic in two generations!"

Maren said nothing, but simply upturned her mug. Instead of spilling on the ground, though, the liquid churned in the air, a tornado of tea. A smaller spiral of white salt separated itself, followed by a few drops of murky yellow juice. The rest, water clear as the air, formed itself into a crystalline sphere. Coren steadied herself against the wall and bit back a curse as she watched Maren run a finger through it, spinning the sphere in mid-air but never breaking its edge.

"How long?" she whispered. She knew little of Weshen magic, but control over matter - sources - this was more than Maren's Sulit spells.

"All my life, dear."

"But why…" The magic wasn't *returning*. For Maren, it had never left. Were there others then?

"There is no-one else now, at least not among the women," Maren answered, her odd skill of hearing the unspoken barely registering this time. The water, lemondrine, and salt surged together again and poured itself back into the mug.

Maren set it down on the garden wall and fixed Coren in her blue eyes, storm-dark and piercingly honest.

"It's time for me to give you my story. When I was a young woman, I went to school in Riata for a time. I knew many Sulit witches. When we were forced into the Sacrifice, I feared what would happen if all the magic were taken, and no-one was left to teach a new generation. So I asked my closest Sulit friend for a cloaking spell, and I hid my shifter magic from the elders."

Coren felt her mind spinning, feeling like her world was about to tip off the edge of the cliff from her dreams. "Why-"

"When Sorenta came crawling through the passage, orphaned and rage-filled and already so, so powerful, I decided to cloak her budding magic, too. I did it out of selfishness, and fear of loneliness, and perhaps love for her mother, who was also once a good friend. So we alone kept our magic. But the Sulit spells are insidious. They have a way of taking over, crusting like barnacles over rocks. Our magic was cloaked, but over time it dulled, like a muscle that has atrophied."

"So Jyesh…what he did…" Coren managed, gulping back a half-sob.

Maren nodded. "Was shifter magic. I think when you and Jyesh were born, the magic did indeed transfer to both of you. But instead of Sorenta's magic increasing to share with you like it should have, the Sulit spell sliced it in half. That was the beginning of her madness, as though half her soul was stripped away. Then when Kosh and Penna were born, there was nothing left inside of her."

Coren slid down the garden wall, her legs folding beneath her in the dirt. "Then why did my father leave her, in her weakest moment?" she asked, because she couldn't stop herself from asking. "Why did he desert us?"

Maren knelt beside Coren, a soft hand resting on her shoulder. "To find a remedy, dear. He loved Sorenta so, so much."

"More than his own children. We needed him!" Coren bit out, blinking tears of hurt and anger from the corners of her eyes. But she knew nothing would have changed if he had stayed. Kashar couldn't have stayed on the island to raise them.

Then something else occurred to her, knifing through the self-pity. "That's why I must never be claimed, isn't it. Because my magic will be cut in two, like hers." She glanced up in time to see Maren frown and nod. Her mother's words began their well-worn steps through her mind: *your family will lose everything.*

"She prayed you would find and keep your magic until the Sacrifice was reversed. And now here you are," Maren said, something like a proud smile tugging at the corners of her mouth.

"But the Sacrifice hasn't been reversed," Coren said, her nerves strumming. "If I'm found out, I'll be banished just like Jyesh."

Maren sighed and turned her eyes to the sky. "I won't let that happen."

"It happened to him," Coren whispered, shutting her eyes and locking away the memories.

"But we didn't know - we didn't even realize the magic had passed into his blood until that very day," Maren said, a raspy catch in her throat. "I won't let it happen to you," she repeated.

Just then Penna burst through the nearby rows of plants, Kosh following close behind. The air around them seemed to swirl and shimmer as they wove through Maren's vegetables and chickens.

Maren made a noise that was open to interpretation, just as Coren sighed and pushed to her feet. She'd gained the sort of knowledge today that could change her world forever, but instead of powerful, she only felt heavier and more tired, The burden of this new secret weighted her like the stones Sorenta had filled her pockets with, just before diving from the cliffs of Weshen Isle.

Nothing was ever enough, and everything was always too much.

"Are we going home tonight?" Kosh asked, leaning in to squeeze her waist. Coren nodded absently, and they scampered away to gather their things.

"Do you remember the cloaking spell?" Coren asked when the twins were out of sight.

Maren nodded. "But I need a few days to prepare it. Go home. Rest. You need to be in control of your emotions - calm - for the spell to work properly. That was always a problem in your family," Maren added, a shadow of sorrow passing over her lined face.

Coren hesitated, wanting more information, but she sensed Maren was not ready to give it.

Perhaps the old woman was right, and things would be taken care of with a little rest and a spell.

Or perhaps Coren was right, and they had already begun the slow slide from the cliffs of Weshen Isle.

The shifter magic was simply a new puzzle for her to worry into submission. In the meantime, she had the hunts to plan for.

She despised feeling weak instead of strong. Standing tall was her only defense against the unfair blows life seemed determined to throw her way. So, because she had learned that even pretend strength helped defeat real weakness, she left Maren and strode after the twins, out of Maren's garden and down the rocky path toward the village.

Resh stalked behind his father, silent as a shadow. It was several minutes before the old man noticed him in the dusk.

"Reshra, did you need something?" he asked, turning to examine his Second Son.

"I've heard a rumor, and I want it confirmed."

The General's brows drew together and his shoulders squared. Resh knew he hated being questioned directly, and that was precisely what he had set out to do tonight. If Resh played the game well enough, his father would spill his secrets before his son's blood.

"The boats of food for the women come tomorrow, correct?" Resh began.

Ashemon nodded, crossing his arms before him. "That is hardly a rumor."

"That is hardly my main request. Once the boats are here, send me back to Weshen City with a few men. Let me find the Wesh slaves and bring them home." Despite what he'd said to Sy about the Wesh, rescuing them would increase their numbers in much more useful ways than the children toddling the island.

"How do you know about that?" the General asked, his voice low and dangerous.

Resh kept his eyes steady, merely shrugging. "I listen when people speak, even if they aren't speaking to me. So you confirm there are Wesh slaves traveling to EvenFall?"

"The mission is suicide, Reshra," he answered, his posture finally slumping. Resh narrowed his eyes at his father's weakness. "The route is filled with places to die, and though I wish we could collect all the Weshen blood here and protect it, I must be true to those who have served me their whole life."

"And so the Restless King wins again," Resh taunted, baiting the cowardice into the weak moonlight. He noticed Ashemon's fists clench, and he prepared to sidestep a blow.

But Ashemon only turned away. "Say nothing of this to anyone, Reshra. Especially your brother. Let nothing distract him from the hunts this summer, and when we return to the city, I promise I will send someone to investigate further."

"By then they will be sold and scattered. Why do we hunt for infant heirs when we could be rescuing an army from Riata?" Resh asked before he thought better of it. Ashemon whirled on him, gripping his son's finely-made collar.

"It is all I am willing to offer. I will not sacrifice full-blooded Weshen."

Resh held, never blinking, never flinching, and soon Ashemon let him go. "I'll watch over Sy," he said, smoothing his shirt again. He had heard the implication in his father's voice. Shifter magic had always traveled in Weshen blood. The more blood, the more magic, or so the elders claimed.

All Resh understood was that his father was choosing to save the potential for magic over the real increase in numbers. Choosing to wait and pray for more instead of acting with what he'd been given already.

The General turned his face to the rising moon. "He needs an heir, Reshra. The men…they talk."

Resh eyed the General, hating the weakness in his father's admission."I know what they say. Remember, my General. I listen when people speak."

"Then listen to me. Forget about the Wesh. The Magi will help us survive, and until our power returns, my job is to keep the blood flowing in our veins, not spilling on the ground."

Resh nodded, though he felt like spitting at his father's feet. The man cared too much for the promise of magic. Resh was prayerful, but he drew the line at superstition.

The old men of the city grew fat waiting for a fairy tale to come true, while more of their people died in a war the Restless King still fought. And Resh feared his brother would be no better as General, as Sy clung to the hope that the magic would return, along with the love.

Resh shook his head. When examining history instead of fireside tales, the stories showed time and again that the one who acted first had advantage over the one who waited for the action to come.

Coren allowed the twins to run ahead of her on their path back to the women's village, giving her time to think on what she should do next about the magic she potentially possessed, the summer's continuing hunts, and the persistent First Son.

Unlike Sorenta, Coren was not interested in dying. Did she have the power to do what Jyesh had done? She shuddered, thinking about how she may have already done it to the Vespa.

Until the cloaking spell was ready, she must be ready to protect herself from the one person who had seen her shift.

The house was quiet when she entered. Penna and Kosh had already tumbled into bed, groggy with sleep. Coren pushed Penna's limp hair from her forehead and dropped a kiss there. Kosh's arm dangled from the side of the bed, and she lifted it back to rest on his small round belly.

Her attention snagged on the snakka fangs, glinting on the table. She needed information about Sy, and they would be a good bribe for someone who was poised to share such secrets. This, at least, was a task she could accomplish tonight. Gritting her teeth against the decision, she started out the door, walking toward Amden's house.

As luck would have it, Amden was outside her home, scattering feed for her chickens. A chair with sewing on it rested near the door, and when Coren glanced at the fabric, she realized it was a baby blanket. Amden was also wearing a ridiculous skirt, banded high on her ribs and full enough to hide her figure, fashioned of delicate lace and a netted fabric that floated around her ankles and shone like spiderwebs.

A gift from Weshen City, expensive enough to be from a General's son.

"Are you with child?" Coren asked, then realized it sounded too blunt. She didn't say anything to soften the question, though.

Amden only laughed and glared up at Coren. "I certainly hope so. I have lain with the General's son enough times to make him an army of heirs."

"Syashin," Coren said. This was not the sort of secret she had hoped for.

Amden snorted. "No, the other. Reshra. Syashin is the First Son, but he prefers boys." She giggled, although spreading rumors like this could mean punishment. Weshen were not expressly forbidden from choosing their own kind once they had provided heirs, but it cut too close to the reasons behind the Separation. Love integrated with their shifter magic in unexplainable ways.

Coren glared at Amden, who showed her top row of teeth.

"Has he not caught girls?" Coren asked finally.

"Oh, I'm sure he has," Amden shrugged. "Why are you so curious, anyways?"

"I haven't meant to be. Actually, I've brought you a present. For your baby blanket." Coren held out the fangs and Amden smiled possessively.

"Those will be the perfect fastener for the blanket of a General's heir," she said. "Now that I think of it, he did catch that one girl a few summers ago. The quiet one. Lorenya? Yes, she's the only one I can remember."

"That's nice. Congratulations on your news, Amden."

"Well, I believe I'll go to bed now, and rest my body." She turned her back and went inside, shutting the door of her house firmly. Amden and Coren did not like each other, but they were each good at understanding what the other wanted.

Coren crossed the village square and walked down a small lane to reach Lorenya's house. There were several small children still playing tag in the yard, and a battalion of different-colored chickens hunting for insects in the grass. Lorenya sat in the grass, stitching together gaps in torn clothing by the bright light of the moon.

"Hello," Coren said. Lorenya looked up suspiciously, and for good reason. Although the women of Weshen Isle all knew each other, Coren rarely approached any of them.

"Do you have a minute? I have a strange question. I'd appreciate it if you didn't tell anyone, either." Of course, Coren knew she had no way to hold Lorenya to such a request, but it couldn't hurt to ask.

"Okay," Lorenya nodded simply. She rose and walked into the house, waving at Coren to follow.

They sat at her table and Lorenya lit a single candle. Coren pursed her lips, unsure how to begin.

"Amden told me you were caught before by the General's son? Syashin?" she asked, deciding to just jump in the middle.

Lorenya startled, then flushed. But she nodded. "Two summers ago. No. Three. It must have been his first hunt too. He was my age, but he seemed so much younger. Why do you want to know this?"

"He's tried to catch me. I'm…I'm afraid of him," Coren lied. Although she wasn't so sure it was a lie anymore.

"Syashin would never hurt you." Her face flushed again, and Coren saw a hardness come into her eyes. "But if he catches you, be sure Reshra will follow. He wants everything his brother has."

Coren grew wary of the anger in her voice. She needed to be careful. "Amden said…well, she said he prefers boys."

Lorenya raised her eyebrows and smiled, the shadows clearing from her eyes. "Perhaps she says that because he has never tried to catch her."

Coren grinned. She wondered why she had never talked to Lorenya before.

"Anyways, I don't believe that. He *was* very shy. He's noble, actually. He has ideas. He believes in love…that it could exist for Weshen again." She added this last bit softly, casting her eyes to the table.

The two girls sat in silence for a minute, then a crying child burst through the door. She was tiny, with tousled hair and a scrape on her knee. Coren found herself examining the child's eyes to see if they matched Syashin's. They did not. Lorenya gathered the baby into her arms, murmuring reassurance against her plump cheeks.

Coren turned away, thinking of her own mother, and how she did not remember her like that. She rose and moved toward the door. "Thank you for talking with me."

"Come again," Lorenya invited, smiling. "And Coren? Be careful. Syashin is gentle, but he is nearly grown. I don't think he's caught a girl since me, and he never returned to me either, although I hoped he might. This is his last year, and if he has decided to hunt again, there is a reason."

Coren nodded and left the house, her stomach churning. This much she had deduced. If he had no heirs, and this was his last summer, she knew exactly what he would want.

Her protection wouldn't come in the form of a mouthful of goshen berries, but in the ability to trade something worth his silence.

8

All night again, Sy had been forced to listen to Resh and his girl. The General's Second Son seemed bent on making enough heirs for a battalion by the end of the summer.

Perhaps I could simply claim one of them as mine, Sy thought with a snort.

Sy watched the light begin to filter into the tent, his eyes dry and his head pounding as though he'd drunk too much wine. And all he could think about was how to see Corentine again before the next hunt. They needed to talk about the Vespa. And about the hunts themselves.

Sy knew he couldn't risk her escaping again, not if he wanted to salvage his First Son title from Resh's destruction.

Perhaps he should just forget about hunting her and bed some foolish island girl to appease the General.

Rising and dressing quickly, he pushed irritably through the tent flaps and began to walk, not thinking of any certain destination. He passed the General's darkened tent, the path to the women's village, and the sentries who watched the water before reaching the ocean itself.

Sy waded into the water, its cold waking his skin and asking his heart to pump faster. A current pulled at his calf muscles, teasing him to follow it into deeper water.

Here on the island, surrounded by the waters of the MagiSea, he could feel the sources in the water much more strongly. He imagined shifting them apart - removing the salt and the air bubbles to leave fresh drinking water. Would he ever be powerful enough to do what he believed Corentine had done to the Vespa?

He longed to practice his shifting as he did with Damren, but it certainly wasn't safe here, even for him.

A shout rang out behind him and he turned quickly. The sentries were scattering, one running toward the General's tent. Sy gazed into the horizon, shading his eyes against the morning sun.

A ship was just barely visible, coming toward them from the direction of Weshen City. A grin broke across Sy's lips - this was how he would see Corentine today. She would come with her family to claim their supplies from the mainland. He splashed out of the water and headed to his father's tent to ensure his part in the ceremony.

A few hours later, the sun was beating down on his back. He paused often to wipe sweat from his brow. An interminable line of women and children leaned patiently against their three-pronged barrows, waiting for their parcels of supplies - dried meat, preserved vegetables and fruits, sacks of wheat and oats and sugar.

Sy hadn't seen Corentine yet, but the General had been pleased with his offer to officiate. For now though, he handed the scroll of family names to Tag and ducked into the tent for a mug of cool water. Standing in the shade, he scanned the line again, finally spotting her.

She stood quietly, not talking to anyone around her. Two small children hovered nearby, playing games as they waited.

For a second Sy's heart stilled, thinking perhaps she *had* been caught before. Then he peered more carefully at the children, and he realized they were far too old to be hers. He was a little ashamed at the relief that washed over him. A growing part of him had begun to hope that if Corentine were caught, it would be by himself alone.

Finally she approached.

"Name?" Tag said, glancing at her, then back to the General's tent.

"Corentine Ashaden, daughter of Sorenta," she answered. "And Kashar," she added, as though reluctant to name her father.

Sy's head snapped up at her answer, and his eyes studied the proud line of her shoulders. "Kashar the Deserter?" he asked, receiving a glare from Tag. His stomach rolled, thinking of what taunts and injustices she must have endured with such a disreputable father.

But Corentine kept her eyes down, nodding as she pointed to the children. "And Penna and Kosh, also children of Sorenta and Kashar." Her voice was resigned, and Sy pondered a man who was steadfast enough to father children with the same woman, so many summers apart, yet would abandon his people for Riata.

He swallowed his water the wrong way as he glanced again at the children and realized they were twins. An extremely rare occurrence in Weshen - a sign of blessings from the Mirror Magi.

"Don't forget sister of Jyesh the Banished," a girl's voice rang out nearby, clear even over Sy's coughing. Corentine swung around, and for a moment Sy feared she might punch the girl. Nerves strumming, he struggled to remember stories of Jyesh, but the name was only a shadow in his mind.

Still, if her brother had been banished, then it was more than just Corentine. Her bloodline must have powerful magic. Sy struggled to hide his growing excitement, afraid she would see the grin tugging at his lips.

"Here is your portion, then," Tag said, his voice low and weary. His glance lingered on the small girl and boy as he dumped parcels in the barrow, barely filling it. With a quick elbow, Tag slyly knocked an extra sack into the barrow, and Sy turned away to hide another smile.

Tag made a mark on his list. "Wait," he said as she turned to go. "You are missing Tellen, daughter of Nollen and Bagesh?"

Corentine gasped a little, the sound ragged as she inhaled deeply. "I will always miss her. She died in childbirth two days ago."

Then she swung the barrow so forcefully it nearly tipped and stalked away from the crowds of watching women. Tag glanced at Sy in distress, his embarrassment at having caused her pain evident on his open face. He made another mark on the list, then handed it toward Sy.

But Sy no longer felt excited about Corentine's magic, and he regretted ever being eager to help with this charade.

He simply turned on his heel and pushed away into the crowds. Other than the hunts themselves, he'd never taken the time to notice before how truly unfair Weshen practices had grown since the Separation. Once fierce hunters as well, the women were now trapped here. They had little game to hunt. Barely enough land to farm.

They had grown soft and submissive, all in the name of protection from the Restless King.

And then the men came each summer on the pretense of rebuilding the Weshen race with the humiliation of the hunts. The men presumed to offer the women a year's worth of food, but those with shamed families were denied their equal portions. Kashar had deserted his General. Jyesh had been sent to die on the MagiSea.

Yet the ones left behind suffered the most.

Sy picked his way along the rocks, glaring into the brightness of the MagiSea. Magic surrounded them, and it had even touched his blood and her family's. But it remained just a whisper of what they would need.

For too many years now, the Mirror Magi had only taunted Weshen with a promise of bounty.

General Ashemon had watched the exchange from the darkened shadows of a nearby tent. The girl was indeed who he had suspected, her family was exactly as Tagsha had reported, and he was extremely interested in Syashin's reaction to her misfortunes.

The boy had grown to care for her, and that could be made useful.

He gathered a string of prayer beads from his altar and fastened the tent flap securely. Refusing his best friend and his son as they pleaded for the lives of slaves weighed heavily on his heart. If only the magic were to return in full, like the tide overturning the pebbles on the beach, his hands would not be so tied, or his choices so absolute.

His people may not be quite ready to face the Restless King again, but Ashemon knew they simply wouldn't remain the same race for another generation. Too many of the old ways had been lost already. Weshen was growing soft, and one day, their safety would be breached.

The answer could lie in the combined bloodlines of Syashin and Corentine. Her family may have been troubled in recent generations, but the Ashadens had once been some of the most powerful of the Weshen shifters. It was time to pray more insistently to the Mirror Magi for relief from this Sacrifice.

The Restless King would never rest. The crown of Riata was nearly complete, and Weshen was the jewel he had sought his entire life.

Coren knelt in the water-cooled sand, thankfully alone, her knees dipped into a tide pool, her shoulders shaking with rage and sorrow. How could Amden have been so cruel as to bring up Jyesh? As if her fragmented family weren't already getting a reduced portion for her father's desertion.

Then the guard who had asked if she missed Tellen. It had been innocent, but it had nearly broken her on the spot.

Of course, Coren had broken and healed so many times. She would heal again, and she would be stronger for it. She had made it to the house in a state of numbness, left Penna and Kosh to sort the supplies and run without thinking, ending up in the shallow waters just beyond the cove of the Mirror Magi.

Nothing was ever enough, she thought again, *and everything is always too much*.

She fisted her fingers in her eyes, pressing back the hot tears. The wind brought relief in cooler air from the green and blue MagiSea, and she felt the sand seem to twist and writhe beside her as her chest heaved and the water lapped at her skin. Finally the heat lifted from her face and she pulled her hands away, calmer and emptier.

It was easier that way, to be empty.

Coren bent closer to the pool, reaching to cup the water and wash the tears from her face.

But instead of her own reflection, Penna stared back at her from the water. She gasped and fell backward, the rocks digging into her palms as she caught herself. A few seconds passed before she bent to look again, her heart pounding in her ears.

Not Penna - Corentine. Younger. As a girl of ten or so. The year her life had shattered into pieces so small they had never quite fit back together.

She scrubbed her eyes with the seawater, ignoring the burn of the salt. She looked again and saw the same thing. Her body began to shake for a new reason. Why couldn't she see herself in the water, as she should be?

Was this shifter magic, too? It was nothing like pulling salt from water, as she'd seen Maren do. Nothing like what Jyesh had done, pulling a man apart, bit by bit.

Then the air around her seemed to shimmer and undulate, as though its actual movements had become visible. Coren watched the water, mouth gaping open, as the reflected girl shifted back to her usual appearance. Had she imagined it all, then?

Coren felt her stomach flip, and the nausea began to rise.

Several handfuls of sand sifted to the earth around her, forming miniature dunes in the tide pool, as though the breeze had been holding them aloft while it waited for her to notice.

Then a rock fell and clattered somewhere behind her and she jerked upright, scanning the coast and tree-lined path to the village, half expecting to see the Vespa back to hunt her.

Instead, Syashin stepped from the tall brush, coming slowly onto the crystalline sand as if afraid to startle her. Again, Coren was struck with how he moved like a true hunter, sleek and silent. Stalking. She backed up instinctively, but her feet sunk into the wet sand of a tide pool, the cave walls at her back.

She had nowhere left to go. Perhaps she should just surrender and have it done and become like all the other girls on the island.

"I'm not going to touch you," he said, his face drawn in anger. Or maybe disappointment - it was difficult to understand his lowered brows and sea-dark eyes. He stood several feet away though, waiting, demonstrating the truth of his claim. "I just want to talk to you."

"You shouldn't be here," she blurted. Despite her despairing thoughts of a few seconds before, she didn't even want to talk to him.

He shrugged and kicked at the sand few feet away, evidently not going anywhere. "I'm sorry about the rations. Tagsha was just following the rules."

Coren narrowed her eyes. "I'm used to it. And he didn't know about Tellen." She was relieved that her voice didn't shake when she spoke, not even Tellen's name.

"Still. I'd like to help. Somehow." He seemed very uncertain, like he had no idea why he was here or what to say. That made two of them. He wasn't supposed to seek her outside of the hunts, and Coren wished he would just leave.

"Look, I'm fine. I've been taking care of my family for years. Jyesh was banished when I was eight, Kashar deserted when I was nine, and my mother died when I was ten. I can handle it. Thank you, though," she added when she saw the stricken look he wore at her list of small tragedies.

She stepped out of the tide pool, bending to brush sand from her bare legs.

When she straightened, he was mere inches from her. His hands clasped her shoulders, lightning fast, and she struggled to twist free of him, adrenaline spiking through her.

She would fight him if he tried to force her, but she knew he was much stronger.

"I know what you are," he whispered then, his breath hot on her cheeks. Coren stopped moving, not even gathering air. Her heart pounded and her vision tunneled to his face.

Had he seen her younger form, too? What did he think she was? Sulit witch or Weshen shifter?

His eyes were storm-dark and so, so close. He was beauty and terror and confusion all in one. "I know what you are, because I'm one too," he continued.

She startled at the unexpected admission, her body jerking against his.

"One what?" she whispered, unwilling to give up a single, damning word.

He released her shoulders, one finger at a time, as though testing her decision to stand or run. But he didn't step back. Instead he filled the small space between them with his cupped fingers. His thumbs brushed her stomach and he lifted his eyes to hers, then nodded down at his hands.

She followed his glance, and it was as though her entire world tilted and began the agonizing slide off the cliff of her dreams.

If this were real, then all of it was…Maren, Jyesh, Sorenta, *herself.*

The air held invisible and stagnant in his palms began to shimmer and glow, then a small pile of sand began to appear, a few grains at a time, flowing into his fingers from the wind. Soon his hands were overfilled with the pale granules. She gasped as he slipped his fingers from beneath the pile, and the grains hovered weightlessly in the small basin between their bodies before slipping toward the earth again. She felt their small patter on her bare toes.

"I can SourceShift," he said, his blue eyes lifting again to hold hers like the sand in his palm, and she felt a similar sense of weightlessness, just before anger began to slide in like the hot summer sun breaking from behind a bank of clouds.

Maren may claim to trust the General, but his own son had shifter magic, and none of the women had been told.

"You cannot deny me what I saw," he continued when she remained silent, his voice low and dangerous. "You have shifter magic too, Corentine."

"Show me again," she managed, biting at each word as it left her lips. If he was using shifter magic…then probably *he* was the one who had called the Vespa to the island. The General's First Son was putting her whole world in danger.

He held his hands before him and the water behind her began to lap gently at the rocks, as though the tide were coming in. Then she saw a narrow stream of water hovering by her left elbow, and another at her right. They joined and circled her body for an instant - a thin but solid ring of water at her waist.

She raised one hand and trailed a finger in its reality, her anger distracted by how this power held every beauty she'd imagined magic to be, and more. Her brain thrilled at the possibility that shifter magic might return to the Weshen people in her lifetime. The Restless King could be beaten. The women could leave the island. The hunts would never bind her brother and sister.

Then he called the water to him, forming it into a palm-sized sphere, which rested in one hand. The other hand spread across the sphere, pulling white crystals to its surface.

"Salt," he said, not looking up at her.

Coren nodded tightly as she watched a pile of white salt grains appear in his other palm. Just as with Maren's tea, the water grew a tiny bit clearer. He dusted the salt into a nearby shell and cupped his hands around the sphere. Some of the water broke free and trickled through his fingers.

Then he stood and reached his cupped hands cautiously toward her lips. Growing more excited as she imagined how her life could change if the magic had returned, Coren bent her mouth to his fingers and tasted the water.

Fresh.

She looked up at him, fixing her wide gaze on his sea-dark eyes, and his hands jerked away from her mouth, the remaining water spilling to the sand at their feet.

"That's kind of like what you did to the Vespa, isn't it?" he prompted, staring at the droplets left on his fingers. "You took it apart, separating its organs and skin and feathers into separate sources. It vanished because you dissolved it into air and bone dust and droplets of blood."

"I had no idea what I was doing," she warned. "I know nothing of shifter magic. Or any other kind," she added, in case he might try to accuse her of using Sulit spells.

But even as she spoke, a gruesome memory Coren had worked hard to repress shoved back into her mind and her knees faltered. Syashin moved like lightning, catching her shoulders and helping her sink to the cave floor next to him. She slumped against the wall, breathing thinly. As much as she knew she needed him to keep her secrets and keep her safe from banishment, he should know what and who he was really sharing his ideas with.

"My brother…Jyesh. Everyone thought it was Sulit magic, but what you just described is exactly like what he did. But he did it to a man." That sort of power seemed so different from the pretty spheres of water and neat piles of salt, and she wanted none of its destructive power. Not here on the island, where there were too many precious, fragile things she cared for.

Syashin sucked in a strangled breath and ducked down to look directly into her eyes. "*That* was your brother? I…I always thought that was more of a legend."

Coren shook her head firmly, trying to numb herself again to that horrific memory of watching a screaming man dissolve into air and bone dust and droplets of blood. She had often wished it were only a nightmare or myth.

Jyesh had been just a few days past eight when he had done that. Eight years old, when the men came to take him to the mainland. Instead he had been banished.

The youngest ever. And the only since.

"He was my twin," she whispered.

"Twin?" Sy managed. A curse of disbelief hung in the air between them as he stared at her, eyes flickering back to the statue of the Mirror Magi. "And your siblings are also twins? Your family is blessed by the Magi."

"My family is *cursed*!" she cried, her voice echoing off the walls of the cave. The water behind them churned and frothed with the incoming tide. "Magic has brought nothing but pain to my family!"

She clamped her lips shut around the rage that threatened to escape her. A few beats of silence granted her the space she needed to calm her emotion, although she could still sense his shock from her revelation.

"Tell me what else you know," she said, softening her tone as much as possible.

He sighed and leaned back against the smooth cave wall. "Shifting uses mirrored abilities. I can shift the salt from the water, which is a weak version of what you did to the Vespa - disintegration. I can also join the sources again, which is called fusion."

She nodded, although the words were not familiar. The opposites made sense in their mirrored religion. The magic could take sources apart or put them back together. If only life were so easy.

"Some can also shift their appearance into another version of themselves," he continued carefully, watching her. A shiver danced over her shoulders despite the warmth of the sun. Surely he had seen her younger form, then. "And there were once Weshen who could take other forms. But nearly all the practical knowledge has been lost. Weshen believe the magic is gone, but that's true only in Weshen City and Weshen Isle. In Riata, there are still those who practice, although being caught with shifter magic is a sentence of slavery or death."

His voice had grown bitter toward the end of the brief lesson, and she wondered what he had seen on his travels. But there was a different, much more important question on her mind.

"So the magic is returning. What does the General have to say?" she asked, and his face paled. He was silent a beat too long, and her heart sank in her chest, beating instead in the pit of her belly, telling her to run and run and run, far away from this First Son.

"I'm the only shifter in Weshen City, and I've told my father nothing." Sy's gaze was distant.

"Nothing," she repeated, her fantasies of the women taking their warrior places next to the men shifting away like the sand through his fingers.

If the General did not know of the magic, perhaps he would not believe in it. And if he did not believe...

"Will you help me hide my magic, then? Or will you unwittingly destroy everything I hold dear?" she blurted, unable to hide any longer that her life had suddenly grown infinitely more dangerous. "I can't be found out. You cannot tell anyone! Please!"

She knew she was begging, and she would hate him forever for making her do it, but all she could think of was Jyesh, sitting small and proud and accusing as the Weshen sent him to sail the MagiSea alone. That could not become her fate. Penna and Kosh couldn't lose her - she was all they had left. They were all *she* had left.

"Please," she repeated. "What will it take?"

9

Sy's stomach bottomed out at her desperate question. His heart felt like a battlefield the morning after, strewn with good intentions and the reality that had cut them down. He didn't want to ask this of her. He hadn't meant this to be a bargain.

But perhaps this way, they could solve both of their problems.

"Tomorrow is the hunt. My father said I must…" He stopped, keeping his eyes to the sand, but the silence finished his request.

Her hand fluttered to her chest, pressing just above her heart. "You wish an exchange," she whispered, her fingers scratching lines in the sand between them.

His head snapped up, but she wasn't looking at him. A curious sort of fear flashed through him.

It was not a small thing to ask, but it was against both of their wills. Perhaps that made them equal.

"I'm sorry. I don't wish for anything that you wouldn't wish for. But the General…he will pass my rights to Reshra."

Her shoulders wavered with a shiver. "Keep what you've seen a secret, and you may catch me tomorrow," she said, the strength in her voice surprising him. Finally she raised her eyes to meet his, and the gold in them burned in the candlelight. "For show. But I will bear you no heirs. I would sooner sail the MagiSea alone."

He flinched at her harsh words, and a glimmer of regret shadowed over her face. But she said nothing to back down. And really, Sy didn't want her to. He realized with a start that he had begun to care for her enough that he would fight to keep her from being hurt. Somehow, it had grown to more than sympathy for the vicious blows life had given her.

"There is a way to falsify a child, at least in the beginning," she said, watching him carefully. "This is one of my family's secrets. But if your father insists…"

Sy felt his shoulders sag, and he moved to stand, knowing it had grown late. "He will insist."

He extended a hand to her to help her stand, but instead she stood and shook it, as though sealing a transaction. He tried not to let that hurt, but he wished, now more than ever, that the Weshen ways were different. "I need to go now," he continued, keeping his eyes hidden from her. "I will see you tomorrow, at the hunts." He turned and stepped toward the cave's entrance. "And Corentine," he added, guilt banding tightly across his chest, "don't let Reshra catch you."

"Why would he catch me?" she asked, her eyes narrowed.

"He wants anything I have. And he thinks I have you."

It was a simple answer, all too reminiscent of Lorenya's description of Reshra. Coren wished the girl hadn't been quite so accurate. But even through the skin of fear, her pride bristled at the arrogant assumptions of both boys.

General's sons, she thought in disgust.

"Neither of you *has* me, nor will you ever. I've never been caught, and I've avoided it with great skill, and I will not be caught in my last year." This time, her voice could have frozen the entire cove.

Sy ducked his head, unwilling to meet her eyes. He believed this, of course, but Resh…

"I have never been caught before," she said again, a challenge in her eyes. She knew he could dispute the truth of such a statement, yet she made it, and he let her.

"I promise not to hurt you," he said instead.

"And you will break that promise," she answered, turning away and darting from the cove before he could find the words to reassure her otherwise.

Coren ran the path to her home, repeating instructions to herself like a mantra. She would not feel fear of Reshra. She would not feel fear of her bargain.

She *would* hide her magic until the General announced its return himself.

Syashin's expression as she had left had not been victorious. Instead, his eyes had flashed with a curious sort of fear at their agreement. That alone gave Coren hope that perhaps he did not truly want to ask this of her.

It didn't make a difference, not really, but then again, it did. If they made this deal against both of their wills, then perhaps that equality would allow her to survive this summer.

Maren's cloaking spell would soon be ready, and if the magic truly was returning to the Weshen people, perhaps Coren might still become the warrior she'd idly dreamed of and hunt the Restless King herself.

She paused outside the entrance to her yard, gazing at the stars above as she entreated the Mirror Magi for their protection, thinking of Sy's statement that her family had been blessed. Certainly, twins were once considered a blessing. But that was when the Weshen had magic, and twins symbolized embodiments of the Magi - the two sides of shifter magic, split between two minds.

Now they were just a reminder of the power her people had once enjoyed. Her thoughts filled with long-buried memories of Jyesh, Coren slipped inside and beneath her covers without a sound.

Resh was sitting on his brother's bed when Sy stumbled into the tent. A mug of liquor rested in his hands.

"No girl tonight?" Sy asked, stalling for time as he tried to gather his thoughts. He knew why Resh was here.

"Never the night before a hunt, brother. You know that. So. Why Corentine Ashaden?"

Sy startled at the sound of her name and Resh laughed, the low crackle of a boat breaking on the sharp rocks. He took a deep draught, then offered the mug to his brother. Sy shook his head, and Resh shrugged.

"Yes, Sy. I know who she is. I know her desolate family and her lack of friends in the village. I know her brother was accused of Sulit witchery and her father was a traitor and her mother lost her mind before drowning herself in the sea. I even know that her grandmother was cozy friends with the Sulit in StarsHelm once upon a time. What I don't know is why my brother, who must be *desperate* for an heir, has chosen so poorly. Such a girl will never be suitable for a General's son."

"She runs in every hunt, yet has never been caught. She is worthy of my skill," Sy tried.

Resh narrowed his eyes and lay back on the bed. Sy was left standing in his own space, shifting from foot to foot like a nervous child.

"Father has commanded you to hunt this summer, hasn't he?"

Anything Sy might say would answer the question, so he stayed silent.

"But surely there are better ways to produce an heir. This girl may even be barren, and you will have wasted your last summer." His tone was soothing, as though there were nothing more he wanted than to solve Sy's problems. He finished his drink. "I can show you a few girls who are more than ready for your heir."

"And why would you help me, little brother?" Sy finally sunk onto the edge of the bed, shoving Resh's legs over and fixing him with a serious look.

Resh glared and sat back up. Sy knew he hated reminders of his status as Second Son. But he wanted him angry enough to slip up and tell the truth. Surely he had guessed their father's gamble. Did Resh hate his status enough to hurt his brother, or love him enough to help him?

Resh stood and kicked at the pillow that flopped onto the floor. "You shame our family, Sy! A General's First Son who does not hunt? Do you know the rumors the men laugh about when you are not around the fire? What I hear when they think I am not near?"

Sy shrugged and lay back on the now-empty bed. Rumors meant nothing to him.

"They say you prefer boys."

Sy only watched his brother pace. He'd never been with a boy, but he'd never accepted that as a slur, either. Before the Separation, love had just been love for the Weshen.

"They say you are afraid of the girls."

Sy sneered. He was never afraid of what he was hunting.

"They say you are probably not a great hunter at all, and perhaps Tag has killed your MagiCreatures all along."

"Lies! And you know it!" Sy had finally had enough of his brother's taunting. He lunged for Resh and tackled him to the floor. Surely the men were not so stupid as to believe any of this ridiculous gossip.

But Resh only laughed as he struggled to push Sy's hands from his throat. Rolling to the side, he leaned against the bed to gain his breath and patted the ground next to him. "Sit with me. Of course I know these rumors are not true. But you must have a real reason for avoiding the hunts. Tell me. I can help."

Sy eyed his brother as he sat, but offered no answer or explanation.

Resh shook his head, gazing at his brother in a sad sort of wonder. "You are a contradiction. A ruthless killer of creatures who is afraid to take a girl, or a peerless Paladin who fails to track a single female along a rocky beach. And what did I find out when I set out to catch the only girl you had ever caught? *Lorenya.* Yes, you think I don't know their names. But that one I remember."

Sy suppressed a groan and shook his head, as though this could erase what he knew Resh would say. Surely Resh hadn't only caught her because of competition. He had to reach Coren first tomorrow.

Resh leaned in and gripped Sy's arm. "She told me strange stories, brother. She nearly cried when I asked her about you. She told me you weren't like the rest of us - that you were meant for something larger. She told me you believed in *love.*"

He let the last word soak into the silence around them. Sy mentally smacked himself - why had he ever spoken such things to a girl? "I was a stupid young boy then, Resh. I would never try to undermine the Sacrifice. If our elders claim the magic of love was a casualty of losing our shifter magic, who am I to contradict?"

Sy hoped the words sounded better to Resh, because they echoed falsely in his mind. Of course he wanted to contradict the elders. He did it regularly on his long hunts, when proximity to the NeverCross Mountains allowed him to visit his hidden teacher.

If shifter magic could survive the generations, love could as well.

"So how exactly do you plan to help me?" Sy asked, hoping the change in topic would help Resh to just forget about the rest.

Resh eyed him but answered the question. "I want you to catch a girl. I'll point one out to you tomorrow. Catch her. Take her. Lie with her every night. Then catch another one. Prove them all wrong. Take back our father's name, Sy. Don't you realize that your actions reflect on him? On me? His men must respect him to follow him. You're corroding that with every hunt."

"And what of Corentine?" Sy whispered, unable to help himself.

"Forget her. It does you no good to focus on one girl. This is the purpose of the hunts. It's why the elders created them. If you spend too much time with one girl, you might start to believe in something as crazy as love…or magic. Those are things Weshen are no longer permitted to rely on."

Sy groaned and leaned his head backward onto the edge of the bed. His hands scrubbed at his eyes. He ached to show his magic with Resh, to share Corentine's power. But even in his excitement, he knew it wasn't enough to save them from the king, and in sharing he'd only be giving Resh another reason to dislike Corentine.

"Besides," Resh said, shoving at Sy's shoulder, "the adrenaline from the chase makes things better. The thrill is like an aphrodisiac. Even when the first-summer girls hesitate at first, it is a small thing - a part of the game."

Reshra's words - *a small thing* - rattled in his head, reminding him of Corentine.

Nothing was small when it was against your will.

"Games are for children," Sy retorted, feeling like sand clogged his veins. How could he understand this strange girl more than he understood his brother?

"Then consider it part of the hunt!" Resh's anger flickered back to life, his muscles tensing. "Why should we not hunt women in the summer, when we hunt MagiCreatures every other season of the year! Our purpose in the winter is to harvest the creatures' bounties and hunt talismans and protect our people from the Restless King. Our purpose in the summer is to produce heirs, so our race does not dwindle into nothingness! When we are strong in numbers again, we will be able to take back our place in Riata!"

"But our *place* was to use magic to protect people from the creatures," Sy argued. "Without magic, we are worth nothing more than any other race of people."

"We do not need magic to overthrow a king who does not have magic," Resh said.

Sy didn't answer or look up. Just as he knew magic still existed, he was sure the king would know that as well. The world was not as simple as it appeared from the beaches of Weshen Isle.

"But brother, you're better off forgetting that girl," Resh warned. He looked into the still-empty mug and glared. "We can't always have what we want, no matter how powerful our desires."

"She said I can catch her tomorrow," Sy answered finally, a little ashamed at the hope that swirled in his gut.

"Fine," Resh said, aggravation pushing him to his feet. "Catch her if you must. But Sy. Please take her. Even if she is unsure. Remember - it is her Magi-inspired duty to provide a Weshen child to replace herself, if not to grow our numbers. Remind her of that."

He pushed aside the flap to his section of the tent, looking back darkly at his brother.

"Remind her, Sy. Or someone else will."

Resh left his brother with a stricken look on his face and strolled down the beach, out to the water's edge.

He hated roughing up Sy's mind like that, but he just couldn't remain silent when his brother insisted on believing in such fairy tales as love or magic.

Something in that girl had grasped his brother's mind, and Resh didn't like it. He hated it, in fact. Even the youngest boys in the training academy knew that to show sympathy for the creature you hunted was to open yourself to attack.

He hurled the mug into the sea, watching the ripples as they widened and dissolved into the soft waves. He needed a plan. Resh knew he would never grow as tall or strong as his brother. He would never be the fiercest fighter.

But he had something Sy didn't: Resh thought in layers.

Opening Sy's eyes to what the hunts really meant - that was one layer. Embarrassing his brother, so he felt the need to resurrect the General's respect. Another layer. But he needed more. The girl obviously couldn't be trusted. She was playing the oldest game the women knew - building Sy's anticipation by refusing him what the Magi instructed her to offer freely.

And her family…before the Separation, they'd practically been a coven of Weshen witches. He didn't believe for a minute the girl was innocent in his brother's fascination.

Resh walked the length of the beach, his eyes alternating between the stars and the camp behind him.

Magic and love had been taken from them before they were born, and Resh didn't waste time missing what he'd never known. Weshen knew only war and death, and it would be that way until they had the numbers to defeat the Restless King.

If it came to war and numbers, Resh took comfort in knowing he had a small army at his disposal. Picking up a handful of pebbles, he skipped them one by one across the water, watching how each ripple he created layered on top of the others, forming a complex pattern that shifted the water's surface completely.

IO

The morning was already hot.

Sy pushed back the curtain that separated him from his brother. Resh blinked at the intrusion of sunlight. He scrubbed at his face and cursed at Sy.

"The hunts begin shortly," Sy said.

Resh flopped an arm over his eyes, his mouth twisted in an ugly grimace. "I'm taking the day off. The girls will cry, but it can't be helped."

Sy studied his brother. An empty bottle of wine was toppled next to Resh's empty mug. Resh rarely missed a hunt, but it wasn't unheard of. He *had* been drinking a good deal the night before.

"Go," Resh muttered. "Catch that girl and get her out of your mind. Make me proud, big brother," he laughed, turning into his pillow.

Sy snorted but left his brother to sleep. He arrived at the beach just as the girls were lining up along the water's edge. Corentine was in her usual spot, closest to the paths back home. She didn't even glance in his direction, and it made him smile.

For a brief second, Sy considered taking Resh's advice to just find a girl who wasn't such a challenge. But somehow he knew Corentine would not be false with him, so he would complete his promise as well. He would keep her secrets.

The horn sounded and she was gone before he could blink. He shook his head at her stubbornness and started after her, but halfway onto the beach, a curvy brunette with mischief in her eyes collided with him, nearly toppling them both. He clutched her slim arms to steady her, and her full lips stretched into a grin.

"Hello, First Son," she said, bending her head low.

Sy blinked, his brain slow to process what she had said. "Sorry, I didn't mean to…" he began, but she drew closer to him, tilting her face up at his. Her lashes swept her cheeks demurely, but Sy had the distinct feeling she was anything but.

"I'm sorry," he repeated. "I'm after a different girl."

Her eyes flew open, the hurt in them obvious, and he felt slim fingers grip his arms.

It's okay," he whispered. She glared.

"You caught *me*," she said, her voice low with anger.

Sy could feel eyes on his back, and he knew the General was likely watching this unfold. There was an outcropping of rocks nearby, and he pulled the girl behind them, sheltering them both from the watchers on the beach.

"Look, I don't mean any harm. I wasn't watching where I was going. Please excuse my mistake."

"Oh, you've made a mistake all right," the girl hissed, her eyes narrow now with fury. "But you can still make everything right. Claim me with a kiss and all will be forgiven," she said, pressing close to him in yet another twist of emotions.

Something rolled in Sy's belly, but he wasn't quite certain what to name it. He tucked a finger beneath her chin and studied her face. "Go home. There is no shame. You were caught, and I let you go, that's all."

"The only shame is on you, First Son," she spat, stepping backward. "Your brother will not like what you've done here."

"Reshra?" he said, a darkness spreading in his chest. Had Resh somehow set this up to distract him from catching Corentine? Sy inhaled deeply to calm himself. "Go home," he repeated, turning to go.

"If you have no intention of continuing the Weshen blood, then perhaps you don't deserve to be First Son after all," she called after him.

Rage simmered hot beneath his skin, but Sy forced himself to turn away. He sprinted up the rocky path, hoping Corentine was still waiting for him.

Coren paced in the shade of the single tree on this plain. Where was Syashin? Surely he should have found her by now, or he was not the hunter everyone seemed to think. Probably she should have let him catch her on the beach, like the other girls, but her pride had bucked at such a show of weakness.

Just as she was about to give up on his coming, faint footsteps sounded on the rock path just beyond. She turned, surprised at the smile that tugged at the corner of her mouth. Biting it back, she ducked deeper into the shadows, her heart beating hard with adrenaline at what she had agreed to.

"I know you're here," a voice called, even before the figure came from behind the rocks.

Coren frowned and peeked around the trunk. The voice was Syashin's, but not.

And then he was upon her, darting behind the tree and pinning her against its rough bark. Panic seized her heart as she saw not Syashin before her, but his brother. The destructive one.

"You're not so hard to catch," he grinned, his near-black eyes flashing. Reshra clutched her forearms, pressing them crossways to her chest. His smile sliced through her thin armor and spilled everything she had ever held dear onto the grass before them.

How could she have been so stupid? Her lips trembled, trying to form words, but there was no time for anything as he bent his mouth to hers, as gentle on her lips as his fingers were fierce on her skin.

"I claim you with a kiss," he whispered against her lips. His knees pressed hard against her thighs, keeping her from kicking out.

Coren moaned and struggled against him, frantic to escape. But there had been no goshen berry ready in her cheek today, and the cliff's edge was too far away for jumping. She couldn't even free an arm to grasp her whip.

She had been caught.

In her last summer, despite all her skill, she had been caught.

Reshra laughed softly at her struggles. He was simply stronger than her. He nuzzled his face into her neck, his breath hot on her skin. "Relax, simple girl. Today I claim you for Syashin. Be sure to keep your word and offer him an heir, or I will catch you again and again and *again* until you give me one."

To her horror, Coren heard a whimper escape from her lips. She had known fear, but it was nothing like the paralysis found in this loss of power and pride. His teeth scraped lightly along her jaw as he returned for a second kiss, but Coren suddenly found her eyes staring levelly at his belt. Her arms slipped easily through his fingers and he stumbled back.

"What is this?" he hissed, staring down at her shrunken form in shock and agitation. Coren frantically looked at her hands - child's hands. Child's feet, now tiny in her sandals. Child's body, swimming in the blue dress she was wearing.

Vomit crept up her throat as she realized she had shifted into her younger self.

Would Reshra understand what she'd done?

Glancing up, she saw him start to lunge down for her, but she ducked and ran, kicking off her sandals, tripping over her dress, straight into the grass that was now tall enough to hide her eight-year-old form. Heaving, she wound a random spiral through the grass, desperate to lose him.

The plain grew silent as she stopped running and crouched in the dirt, lungs straining. She listened intently, ear close to the ground, but heard nothing. Either he had left or was waiting for the chance to ambush. If Syashin was Weshen's best Paladin, Reshra must be second best.

Panic beat against her lungs as she realized Reshra's discovery had destroyed her bargain with Syashin. He could have her banished this very day.

If Reshra understood she'd used magic, he would certainly assume it was dark, just like people had assumed with Jyesh. Syashin's promise of secrecy and Maren's cloaking spell were her only hopes for surviving the summer, but she worried neither would be enough if she failed to produce an heir for the First Son.

Coren grasped that if *he* came to claim her, the magic would surface again like a shield, and she would end up sailing the MagiSea alone. This truth knocked the wind out of her and froze her fingertips to the dirt.

"Corentine?" a voice called, and she had to force herself not to bolt from the cliff's edge like a rockrabbit.

Adrenaline shot through her veins, but she focused on the voice as it called again. Her pulse steadied as she realized it was Syashin. Constricting her muscles around her lungs until her breathing slowed, she stood an inch at a time. Her head rose above the grass again, and she saw her body had stretched back to its normal length. Staying low, she scanned the plain but saw no-one other than Syashin waiting for her by the tree. She swiped at her cheeks, swiftly erasing a few hot tears.

"Corentine!" he called again, waving as he saw her. Keeping her eyes moving, she walked carefully toward him, composing herself more with each step. Somehow, she didn't believe Reshra had completely gone. Syashin smiled, holding her sandals out to her.

Should she tell him what Reshra had done? What she had accidentally revealed?

But if he knew Reshra had seen her magic, he may not be willing to lie to his brother. He might take back his promise of protection. Her instincts whispered she should wait.

"Sorry I was delayed," Syashin began, but she just shook her head.

"I must learn control," she blurted, working to keep her voice steady. "I cannot be found out. My family depends on my hunting and care."

"The twins - you're their only caretaker?" he asked, watching her carefully. She nodded, feeling her face darken with desperation. How long until Reshra figured out what he had seen?

She must make it home today, and every day after.

"Control is about emotion," Syashin said, lowering himself to the ground and settling his back against the chokecherry tree. "If your emotions have control, you won't." He patted the grass next to him, and she sat, keeping more than an arm's length from him. He frowned a bit, but Coren just glared.

"You know that you'll need to enter the men's village with me tonight, right? My father will want to see you." His voice was full of uncertainty. Coren closed her eyes and lifted her chin to the sky, her skin sensitive to both the dappled shade and the patches of sunlight filtering down to them.

"I will stay in your tent tonight," she whispered. "On the floor." Her eyes opened to meet his and seared them in place just as the acidic juice of the goshen berry had burned his lips.

"So…emotion," he said after a beat of silence, glancing down at his fingers in the grass. "When you're afraid, your magic might manifest as a defensive reflex."

Coren felt her stomach flip. This she had already learned. "And why have my powers only begun now? I've never done anything like this before this summer."

She bit down on a rant about how Sorenta should have told her before, how Maren should have helped her earlier.

Syashin shrugged. "I've prayed to the Mirror Magi for years, questioning my magic. And in answer, I found you. I don't know why the magic is returning in us alone, but surely the gods have a plan."

Perhaps, but why did the gods' plan need to involve her family so heavily? "How did you learn to control it?"

He gazed into the leaves above them, as though trying to decide his answer.

"Why do you hesitate to tell me anything? Surely you know that nothing I repeat would be trusted. My word means nothing to Matron Behrenna or the General." She could hear the frustration in her voice, and she hated how helpless she felt.

Maybe she should learn to *use* this power, instead of relying on others to help her hide it.

He studied her for a minute more. "When I travel for hunting, sometimes I…hear rumors. Sometimes I pursue them, and sometimes they are true." He glanced behind himself, then back to her. "I've found a teacher."

"A teacher," she repeated.

"Not every Weshen entered the Isle or the City during the Sacrifice, right? Well, Damren stayed behind and hid herself and her magic."

"In EvenFall?" Coren raised an eyebrow. He'd just told her how dangerous it was to have shifter magic in Riata.

"Hidden in the mountains, actually. I see her when I can, on my hunts and when I go to EvenFall to sell talismans."

"Talismans," she repeated, wishing he would get to the point.

Syashin gestured to the whip peeking through the slit in her dress. She tugged the fabric over it and he grinned. "Talismans are weapons or protective jewelry made from the MagiCreatures."

"I know what a talisman is," she said, aggravated that he thought her so ignorant. And what did talismans have to do with teaching her control? She pressed her lips together, praying for patience. "This is just a whip. Talismans carry magic."

"They did, once. But when the Weshen sacrificed their magic, the talismans lost their purpose as well. Mostly." He gestured toward the hidden whip again. "Does it still warm to your touch?"

Coren glared, thinking of how many times Sorenta had reassured her it was only a weapon. Nothing more.

"It glows silver with the blood of a kill," she hissed without thinking.

He leaned forward to grasp her arm, his eyes inches from her face. "It's a true talisman, then! They're extremely rare, and even the few we find no longer work. How did you get it?"

She blinked at his proximity, shrinking into the tree trunk and yanking her arm away. "It was my mother's," she whispered, lowering her eyes from his.

"Did she have magic?" he asked. "Did she use Sulit magic? What you're describing sounds like dark magic layered on a true talisman. Activating it, maybe."

But Coren didn't answer his burst of questions. She wasn't about to admit a single other fact that could be used against her. "The only thing my mother ever told me of magic was that it ruined lives," she answered instead. A truth of its own.

"I should go," she said, growing fidgety. She hadn't learned anything, and he was taking too long in his explanations. She must return home soon, or she'd need to explain her absence to the twins. Keeping this secret from Kosh and Penna - Kosh especially - was going to be tricky.

"I have so much to teach you, if our bargain is to be useful," he said, staring down at his fingers, now empty in his lap.

She paused. Unfortunately, she *did* need him to help her hide her magic for a few more days.

"Perhaps we can meet in the cove again? I need to see to the twins' dinner. Then I can put them to bed and meet you before…" she trailed away. She knew she'd have to enter the men's camp with him, meet his father to keep up the pretense.

For years she'd avoided being caught with skill and determination. She should hate Sy for his part in her broken promise to Sorenta, but something in his open, honest eyes prevented that seed from taking root. None of this was his fault, and he had promised to help her.

Though she'd been raised to trust no-one, Coren realized she believed Sy would be honorable with her.

She glanced to him, finding him staring at his hands, where blades of grass were slowly growing from the specks of green he held. They formed into a loose flower shape, which he handed to her. She took it, wondering at its ability to be both grass and flower.

Familiar and yet wholly unexpected.

He stood and offered her his hand. Although her mind was still automatically suspicious of the gesture, this time she allowed it.

"Thank you," she whispered. "For being different. I owe you more than I can give." She was suddenly intensely grateful that although it was the Second Son who had truly caught her, it was the First Son who stood before her now, gentle and noble and everything his brother did not appear to be.

He tugged her fingers to his lips and brushed them with a kiss.

"You're worth more than what you can give me," he answered.

She closed her eyes as he let go of her fingers, denying herself any reaction to the tender gesture, and when she opened them again, he had gone.

The sun already rode high in the sky as she ran the beach back to the women's village.

II

Corentine did not meet Sy in the cove after the sun had set.

He waited and waited, pacing the narrow space and glancing at the statues of the Mirror Magi with each lap. When he saw them from the corner of his eye, they seemed to shimmer and nod at him, but each time he passed, they were nothing but carved white stone.

As darkness claimed the cove, Sy gave up and headed back to the men's camp, shoulders slumped in defeat. He chafed against the men's laughter around the newly-built bonfire, each clink of mug upon mug like a blow to his chest.

Corentine had changed her mind, and he would have to accept his fate and his father. He shouldn't expect her to solve his problems.

As he neared his tent though, she stepped from the shadows and slipped close to his side without a word. Her fingers closed around his forearm, tugging him toward the edge of the celebration, where Ashemon and Tag sat drinking. Though he felt the tremble of her body as she shrunk against him, her steps did not falter.

Despite the guilt that swam in his gut, he allowed himself a single grin in the darkness.

"Good night, Father," Sy said, hoping to avoid conversation. Tag smiled proudly up at him, his eyes crinkled as he took in Corentine's silent form and bowed head. Sy had hidden his grin from the men and the firelight, and as Ashemon nodded to him, he felt sick at gaining this approval. He swiveled and led Corentine into the shadows beyond the firelight, hurrying them to his tent.

When he held aside the door flap, she darted inside, scanning the space like an animal searching for escape.

"I'll go get us a drink," he offered, and she nodded too quickly, pacing the length of the tent in only a few strides. "I'll be right back. Just have a seat," he added, a little worried her nerves would send her skittering out to the ocean as soon as he'd left. But she had come, and he should trust her to stay, just as she was trusting him to keep her secrets.

Getting the drinks took longer than he wanted, as several men stopped him to discuss some small matter. None of them said a word about Corentine, but Sy guessed their change must be due to her presence. He hated that Resh had been right about how to earn and keep the men's respect.

Sy realized as he said good night to yet another man that he hadn't seen Resh all evening, and he hurried his steps back to the tent, not liking the possibility of Resh being there alone with Corentine.

But he found her undisturbed, curled on a corner of the bed, head propped on several pillows and eyes closed. Her dress had slipped from her shoulder, and her skin looked warm and soft in the flickering candlelight.

Sy's chest grew tight with relief and gratitude and, he hated to admit, a nervous anticipation of things that would never happen tonight. Watching her, he felt something like the warm spread of magic, growing from his center and tingling through each of his fingers. It was not the same as when he called the salt from the sea, however, or the green from the grass.

Instinctively, he knew it was because he had grown to care for her in some small way - he was invested in what happened to her, even beyond his part in her life.

Just then, Corentine moved and opened her eyes, and he saw her whip coiled around her leg, her fingertips hovering near the handle. His hope for friendship stalled as he realized that as peaceful as she looked, there was a tautness to her muscles, like an animal playing dead until a predator left.

"Stop staring," she said, her voice light and gentle. "Reshra has already been here once to ask where you are, and I don't like being watched by two brothers in one night."

Although it sounded like a joke, he turned on his heel and pushed through the thick curtains to Resh's room.

"What have you said to her?" he growled at Resh, who was lounging in bed with another mug of liquor and an untouched plate of food.

But Resh only laughed, a soft chuckle that strummed Sy's agitation. "I bow to your skills, First Son. She appears to be here of her own free will."

"You will do nothing to that girl!" Sy continued, advancing on Resh. He burned to question his brother about the other girl from this morning's hunts, but Corentine might flee if he left her alone longer.

Resh drew his body gracefully from the mussed blankets, standing firm and toe-to-toe with Sy. "You're right, brother. I will do nothing to that girl." He paused to take a drink, showing his teeth in a grin as he lowered the mug. "As long as *you* do something."

He held Sy's glare for a long moment, then slipped out of the tent without a glance backward.

Coren heard none of the words spoken between the brothers, but she heard the tent slap open and steps move away. She knelt up on the bed, readying herself to sprint if the wrong brother returned.

She had no desire to meet Reshra again. Although he hadn't even come near enough to touch her, he had whispered, "Do not harm my brother, or I will tell everyone exactly what you are."

The threat still echoed in the air like a swinging blade, and Coren fought the urge to duck and run from whatever evil thing he might have decided she was. Perhaps she was self-centered in her reasoning, but she believed the power to harm lay solely with these two handsome, privileged brothers - one light like the morning sun, and one dark like the crescent moon.

She felt like the sand, with no power at all, or the shadows, which were only a consequence of the games between light and dark.

Coren pushed aside these thoughts and tried to relax when she saw Sy press aside the divider wall.

"He's gone. I'm sorry," he said, glancing at her, then quickly away. Indeed, his eyes landed on everything in the room except her. He was clearly uncertain what to do with her in his space, and Coren was surprised to find she did have a strange sort of power here, in his bed.

It wasn't the sort of power a girl like her had ever wielded, and it made her just as nervous as he seemed to be.

She tucked her legs beneath her, making room for him. Still, he hesitated, and she used the seconds to examine the dagger strung at his belt, the strong shoulders under a summer-thin shirt. His hair hid his eyes with choppy, sun-glinted waves, and his jaw was sharply drawn with the shadow of scruff.

Finally he sat at the opposite end of the bed, still avoiding her gaze.

"I'm sorry I didn't come to the cove earlier," she said. "It was too hard to lie to the twins. I'm still not sure Kosh believed me. But my friend Maren will watch them tonight. You smell of the sea," she added.

"Sorry," Sy said quickly, jumping up and shrugging his shirt over his head. He turned his back to her and grabbed a cloth. Wetting it with water from a jug, he scrubbed at his skin.

Coren watched him, biting back a grin. "It's not a bad smell," she said, careful to make her voice gentle.

He turned toward her, and their eyes locked. She immediately wished she'd kept her mouth shut.

The ridges and planes of his chest held a beauty all their own, and against her will, her fingers slid across the blankets toward him. Would his skin be as smooth as it looked?

Flushing, she corralled her hand beneath her leg. "Sorry. I just meant…I mean. You can sit," she finished awkwardly. No wonder Sorenta had warned her away from the hunts. This was horrible.

She'd much rather be running on the open plains, her whip flashing into the tall grass.

"No, I'm just…sorry." Syashin pulled a clean shirt from a bag, but sagged down next to her without putting it on. "I'd rather face a whole flock of Vespas than feel like I'm forcing you into anything," he said, his eyes finally meeting hers again.

Coren sighed. At least they had that much in common. "It's not your fault. It's these stupid hunts. Our traditions and rules. All of it is stupid. I mean, haven't you ever wanted more?"

"More?" he repeated.

She sighed again, leaning her head against the tent behind her. "No, you wouldn't, I guess. You can travel as you like, do what you want. You're First Son. You can do anything." She closed her eyes against the injustice of the truth.

"And you think you can do nothing?" Sy asked, realizing the accusation lacing her words. He wanted to contradict her, but he knew she couldn't possibly understand how trapped he was as First Son.

She flopped back onto the pillow, sliding her legs under the blanket. Her legs were inches from his now, separated only by the thin fabric. "I'm trapped here, Sy."

Those words, repeated on her lips, and something about the way she shortened his name, made him full to bursting. He wanted to fix every problem she'd ever had, but even as the emotion swept through him, he knew it was ridiculous.

She was just as capable as he was. They were just separated and trapped by the Weshen ways.

"We can change it," he whispered. "Together. If we both have magic, then maybe the Magi are reversing the Sacrifice…maybe it's time for Weshen to reclaim its place." He didn't agree with Resh on many things, but there wasn't a man in Weshen City who hadn't wished it were time to fight the Restless King for their rights again.

And just maybe, if he could find the perfect time to speak to his father, he could show him that magic *had* returned to the Weshen.

Then they would be free to fight the king and rescue their people languishing in Riata, like the Wesh slaves the General was leaving to die.

"We're on the edge of a cliff," Corentine answered, her soft voice interrupting his thoughts as she stared into the candle's yellow flame as it flickered shapeless shadows onto the walls. "We'll all go into the sea if we shift the wrong rock."

He was about to ask what she meant when he heard steps from the next room. Resh had returned, and Sy doubted he would leave them alone. He slid down and parallel to Corentine, blocking her from whatever was coming. Her palm landed on his bare chest, as though to shove him away, but she didn't.

"Well, big brother." Resh's presence filled the room, almost seeming to snuff out the spare light. "I see you have an idea of what comes after the hunt. Don't worry, Coren. I'm sure you two can muddle through what goes where. Even creatures do it, you know."

Sy half-twisted in the bed and threw a vulgar curse over his shoulder, and Resh laughed, but he left.

Turning back, he realized Corentine was shaking, her fingernails curled into his skin like tiny half-moon blades. He cursed again, but softer, his hand hovering over her, unsure what to do. "What is it? I'm sorry - he's gone."

She raised her head from the pillow then, and her smile lit the room. Shaking with silent laughter, she flipped onto her back, her head much closer to the crook of his arm. Something had shifted in these few seconds, and his head was spinning with confusion.

"This is so ridiculous," she managed, pressing at her eyes, her smile fading. "What our people have been reduced to. Look, Sy. My mother taught me from birth to avoid the hunts. There are many reasons why I can't go back on my promise to her. I won't even be trying to give you an heir. But I promise to pretend here with you for as many nights as are needed, and I can even pretend to be with child for your father, too. I owe you that much, and more."

"But then next summer, when there is no child…" He didn't want to say what they both knew.

"Of course I'll be shamed. But that's nothing new. I'll be too old to run in the hunts then, but I have other ways to take care of myself and my own." There was a resolution in her eyes and the set of her lips that spoke of a will so great it could change the world, and Sy marveled again at her strength.

"Your family is lucky to have you," he whispered. His hand landed between them, the backs of his fingers brushing against her side. The fabric of her dress was warm with her body's heat.

"You *are* noble," she said then, glancing sidelong at him. "Lorenya told me that. Yes, I sought her out," she smiled when he startled at the name. "Sy, if anyone can change Weshen for the better, I think it would be you. You've had every opportunity to treat me how they expect you to, yet you haven't. That should be enough for me to help you win your father's approval."

He noticed she used *should*, rather than *is*, showing her continuing hesitance. "I'd be nobler if I didn't have to ask you to lie for me."

"But you're not asking me to lie *with* you. That's a key difference, and I promise I'll remember it." She closed her eyes, and he marveled as her face relaxed into a different sort of beauty. Carefree, in a way her open eyes never were. He marveled at how she allowed his presence, as though she had begun to trust him.

She certainly hadn't let down the fierce guard she kept around her life, but at least she had ceased the offensive.

Several minutes passed with only the sounds of the ocean at night, and Sy found his eyes growing heavy. He reached over to pinch out the candle, then rested his head back on the pillow, Corentine's slim body still a few careful inches from his, and he slept.

When he woke later, it was still dark and quiet, but the space beside him was empty and cold.

12

Coren wandered the beaches of Weshen Isle alone for several hours after slipping away from Sy's tent.

She tried over and over to pull the water into ribbons or to move even one grain of sand. She tried to imagine taking a creature apart, not with a knife as Kosh did, but with her mind. She tried to figure out how to shrink her bones and make her reflection in the black water resemble her memory.

But she might sooner figure out how to fly up and touch the stars above.

Whatever magic had swirled awake in her blood was unresponsive and useless, except when she was in danger. But after watching Sy and Maren use their power, it was obvious she should be able to control her shifting, instead of it controlling her. She wanted answers, and she didn't want to wait a minute more.

She couldn't very well ask Sy tonight, with Resh keeping such careful watch. Which left Maren.

Determined not to let the old woman sidestep her questions any more, Coren turned and hurried home.

Maren was there, having spent the night to watch over the twins, and she was awake, sitting at the kitchen table as though waiting. Coren nodded at her, then padded to the beds where Kosh and Penna slept peacefully, kissed them both gently, and returned to the kitchen. Two warm mugs rested on the table, the scent of lemondrine and salt wafting through the early morning air.

"I need to know everything," Coren began.

Maren only smiled and sipped her tea, each movement agonizingly slow. "The cloaking spell will be ready tomorrow evening, at moonrise," she answered, finally resting the mug on the worn wooden table.

"What if I don't want the magic to be cloaked?" Coren asked, the edge of a dare entering her mind. What if there were others like her, confused and also thinking they were alone? She could show the General, and he could contact the elders in Weshen City. He could tell the people, and their world could change with just a few words.

"It must be cloaked," Maren said, breaking into her wild thoughts. "Ashemon will not believe in the return of shifter magic to your family. He believes your family is cursed, and he's waiting for his own."

"His own what?" Coren asked, running a finger over the rim of her mug, trying to conjure a separation of salt from the water inside. What would the power feel like, if she could control it?

"Ashemon has always assumed his family will see the return of shifter magic first. Once, an elder told him the

Magi would honor his family, so he's waiting for his First Son to receive the shifter magic."

Coren opened her mouth to inform Maren that Sy had indeed received his magic first, but then she thought again of Jyesh. Her brows drew together in confusion.

"Ashemon even planned it this way," Maren continued.

"Planned?" Coren realized Maren was trying to tell her something, and she focused her gaze on the old woman.

"His First Son was not conceived in a random hunt. He hails from two very powerful bloodlines."

She fixed a heavy gaze on Coren, who blinked several times as she ran through the short list of once-powerful shifter families. Many had been wiped out in the battles with the king. Sy couldn't be related to her family, or they would never have been allowed to run in the hunts together. That left…

"Ashemon took our son to the mainland several years early to better monitor any magic that may develop."

"Your son…" Coren whispered. "Syashin Havenash is your *son*?"

Maren looked away, her silence the answer Coren needed. But the trace of a smile drew her cheeks back. Weshen women had once been proud of their abilities to both hunt and produce hunters, to wield magic and produce magis.

"With the *General*?" Coren sputtered, shoving her chair from the table and pacing to the window above the sink. The moon still hung in the sky like a lopsided grin, but the night was fading into pale blue-gray. "But…but Neshra!"

"Neshra was before, and Neshra was after as well. There are layers upon layers of secrecy and plotting here, Corentine." Maren's voice held a sharp warning. "The General's family knew the Sacrifice was necessary. But they never stopped working to be ready for the reversal. Ashemon knew nothing of my cloaking spell, but he knew the magic had once swirled in my blood, just as in his family's. Sorenta would have had nothing to do with him, and so he approached me. Together, we made an agreement. A trade."

"Does *he* have magic still?" Coren nearly growled, thinking of how his father, the previous General, had banished her brother.

"No, it was sacrificed, along with everyone else's. His family is powerful in other ways. But Syashin does have magic, doesn't he?" Maren smiled in satisfaction.

Coren stared at her. "Have you known all this time?"

"Of all the things I have done, Syashin is my highest accomplishment," she said, slanting her eyes toward Coren. "And I *am* sorry I didn't tell you sooner, but I would never want to influence your feelings for him."

Coren had no idea how to respond. To think she had once been a child with Sy…that he might have played in the same yard as Kosh and Penna often did. The ripples of this revelation were more than her brain could understand. "What was your agreement with the General?" she asked instead.

"I would provide him an heir, and he would never banish one of my family."

"Including your heir, who was likely to have magic," Coren guessed.

"Precisely."

"But that courtesy didn't extend to my family. Wouldn't extend to me now," she added, coming back to sit across from Maren. "Why doesn't he remember? Why don't I remember him? He would have been at your house when Mother took me there!" Her brain was stuck on the missing memories.

"The memory spell is perfect, my dear. You two don't even remember what you don't remember. But yes, he spent his first few years chasing stormcloud chickens in my yard, just as Kosh and Penna do now."

Again, Coren felt as if the earth beneath her was cracking. One of them had indeed moved the wrong rock, and entire pieces were breaking off and splashing into the sea.

"Why wouldn't Sorenta have given Ashemon a child?" she asked, needing more specific answers to help her comprehend this twisting truth.

"She and Kashar always felt more strongly about the role of love in the existence of magic. Sorenta didn't believe such a plan would work." Maren's smile was smug, and Coren shook her head a little at the memory of her iron-willed mother. If kept secrets were a sort of magic, Sorenta had left her a powerful inheritance, indeed.

"I wish I knew the rest of her story," Coren said. Regardless what shifter magic rested in her veins, learning these stories had certainly begun to invoke a taste for that power in her, enough that she wanted more.

"Sorenta rarely spoke of her family or her time in Riata. She was much like you. Strong and silent."

And wrong about so many things, Coren thought. "What of this can I tell Sy?" she asked, itching with the need to discuss these revelations with someone who might understand the sliding feeling of learning so many secrets at once.

"These are your stories now, too. Tell them to whomever you wish, but know that stories can have as much power as magic."

Coren nodded, a promise to be careful. Maren had protected her for years, and she knew the woman always would. Knowing she was Sy's mother...certain things about the First Son made so much more sense now. "Thank you, Maren. I owe you so much."

"You owe me nothing. One day, I think, we'll all owe *you* our lives. You and Syashin...you were made for great things."

Coren smiled even as she shook her head. "I'll be happy enough here, watching Kosh and Penna grow. Being an old chicken lady with you."

Maren's eyes grew distant, and sadness pulled at her brow. "My dear. Your blood was not created to be *enough*. It was created to be *everything*. Although it's true that the magic never left Weshen completely, it's also true that the world believes it did. And when the foundation of people's beliefs shakes, so does the foundation of the world."

"What do you mean?" Coren asked.

"I mean things will change soon. The signs are here. The General sees them. The Matron does too, even if she does not tell us. Surely the Sulit witches see everything. And somewhere in the bowels of his cold

stone castle, the Restless King also has the power to
see."

Several minutes of silence passed between the two
women. Sunlight had begun to slant in through the
window, across the swept floor in a prism of light.

"I need to find Sy," Coren said, realizing that these
secrets were just as important as her learning to hide or
control her magic. Maren nodded, her eyes carrying an
old sadness that Coren could see had been made plain
and fresh once more.

Sy sat at the table outside his tent, trying to enjoy the
morning sun and the simple pleasure of another good
meal.

But things had changed, and the biscuits, honey, and
yogurt did little to curb the hunger Corentine's presence
had awoken. It wasn't just that he imagined holding her
close, his hands on her smooth skin.

After last night, he did want more. More from the
world, more from his people, and more from himself.

"Sy!" The whispered call was right and wrong all at
once. Corentine had left his tent in the night, but
sneaked back this morning. It wasn't normal, and
anything out of the usual pattern could be dangerous if
people saw. Still, he rose quickly enough to knock over
his stool and greeted her with a smile as open as the
horizon.

"I have things to tell you," she said in a low voice as she neared. She glanced around, skittish and careful, and his smile faltered.

There were only a few tents here: his and Reshra's, the General's, and those of a few other boys from noble families. A thick stand of goshen bushes and clumps of palmpress grass separated them from the other tents and the main feasting areas. It was still quiet, and no-one had stirred from bed since he'd sat to eat. But soon people would be coaxed awake by hunger and the need to stretch and piss away the wine they'd drunk at the feast the previous night.

Soon the girls would begin to trickle out of the tents to pad home to the women's village, dresses wrinkled and hair mussed, but chins held high with the pride of a successful hunt.

He motioned to the tent, but she shook her head slightly.

"Alone," she whispered, and darted away in the direction of the beach used for the hunt ceremonies. It wasn't as hidden as the plains or the cove, but at least it would be empty this early in the morning.

Sy took a few extra minutes to clean up his breakfast, watching to be sure no-one who may have seen her stepped outside their tents. A last peek into his shared tent, though, showed Resh was no longer in bed, and the blankets were cold. Sy hurried to find Corentine.

She was a speck on the far end of the beach already, nearly where the sand wrapped around to face the Sulit lands.

"I know why you have magic," she said as he approached, still keeping her voice low.

He blinked at her and his steps paused, mouth open to ask but uncertain if he truly wanted to know.

"Your mother. And her mother. And hers. My mother, and her mother, and hers. We are both born of it. The magic never left, Sy."

"Who is my mother?" The question slipped out without his permission. He snapped his mouth shut and shook his head, his hand held up as though to stop the words. "No. It's still better if I don't know."

"My friend claims the signs of change are here, and that the Matron knows. She claims the Sulit witches will know."

Sy glanced across the water, where the Sulit lands were too far to be visible on the horizon, misty and unknown. None of the Weshen had gone west to Sulit since the Separation. And to his knowledge, none had *ever* gone south to Umbren.

"Sy," Corentine whispered. "Your father knows, too. He knew your mother's magic when he found her. He knew when they had a child that this boy - you - was likely to inherit that magic. Sy, have you been honest with me? Has the General never *once* said *anything* to you about your magic?"

Sy's face had been growing more flushed with anger at each of her words, and all he wanted to do was let out a roar of anger. How dare she accuse him of lying, when all he'd done was be honest with her? If all she said were true, his father had been very deceitful indeed. He didn't know whether to thank Corentine or curse her.

Instead he broke away into a run, jogging at first, then sprinting along the water's edge, in the direction of the men's camp.

"Sy! Stop!" Corentine yelled to him, but the rush of wind in his ears and fury in his heart made her seem like an echo, far away and unimportant. He sensed her footsteps pounding behind him, but he was farther along and faster in his rage. She would not catch him until he had found his father.

But as she tackled him from behind, he couldn't help but grin through his haze of anger. This girl was truly his match in every way, as if they had been made to either complement or destroy each other.

He preferred the first, and so he didn't struggle.

"You will not do this!" Corentine said fiercely, scratching at his back as she worked to pin him to the ground, arms behind his back and face in the sand. "You swore to keep my secrets, and by spilling these, all will come known!"

He relented completely, letting his limbs go limp. "I'm sorry," he managed, spitting sand from his mouth. "Please get up and I swear not to be so rash again."

She slid off his back into the sand next to him, and he flopped over. "I should not have told these stories to you," she said, almost to herself.

"No!" he countered, brushing his hand against hers. She moved her hand from his reach. "Corentine, thank you for telling me. I won't break your trust again. I swear I won't hurt you."

"And you will break that promise," she whispered, watching the ocean waves and repeating what she had said before, when their bargain had first been made. "Men have always hurt women. The Restless King hunted Weshen women, enslaving them for their magic. Killing them when they tried to save themselves."

Sy remained silent, although he had heard stories that both supported and contradicted her words. Many of the Weshen women had wanted the attention of the king. *Sought* it, much the same way some of the girls sought his brother on the beach. For honor, and for pride.

"And the Separation took half of the women's utility. We were once strong hunters, just like you and your men."

"I know," Sy answered. "But it was done for protection. The magic was in your blood - in the women's blood. The men couldn't have that blood spilled recklessly by MagiCreatures."

"It was still a strength, and it was taken. We're still captive here on Weshen Isle, and it's all because of the magic and the men. The Sacrifice took everything." She pushed up and began to walk the line where the water lapped onto the sand, quickly sucking away her footprints. Sy scanned the beach carefully, but there was no movement at the men's camp in the distance.

"What does it feel like?" she asked quietly, staring at the water frothing around her bare feet. "When you choose to do magic?"

Sy rose and stood beside her. "It feels like power, rushing from the core of your being and filling every arm, leg, finger, toe."

"Mine doesn't feel like that. When I tore apart that Vespa, or when I shifted younger, I was nauseous. Unbalanced. As though I were doing something foreign to my body."

"That's because your power is untrained. Uncontrolled. Imagine the storms that come to the island. Some are gentle rain, coaxing life from plants and feeding the water back to the ocean. Shifting one source to another. But some are tempests, powerful and destructive. The shift becomes violent, like a break."

Corentine looked up at him, understanding in her wide amber eyes. "I must become like the rain, then." She closed her eyes and held her hands over the water, cupping them the way Sy had done in the cave. "Teach me," she whispered, and his chest tightened at her vulnerability, standing on the empty beach with closed eyes and outstretched palms.

"Think of your center, where your strength comes from. It's not the same for everyone, my teacher says. Open the channel of your endurance, the way you do when faced with a difficult task. The very strength you use to survive is the strength you use to shift," Sy said, watching her hands fill with water even as he spoke.

He grinned in complete amazement at how fast she learned. It had taken him months to learn to find such strength.

"My strength comes from my family, and what I must do to protect them," Corentine said. Her eyes still closed, she moved her hands around the water, letting it form a sphere that she was no longer touching. The sphere rose between them and spun, the salt gathering in clumps at its edges like tiny continents on a miniature world.

"I can feel them. The sources," she whispered.

Then the salt separated from the water a bit at a time, the grains floating away on the breeze. Sy bent his lips to taste the water, and it was fresh.

"Congratulations. You've mastered something which took me many months."

"Because I'm a woman, and we have always been the keepers of magic," she teased, rewarding him with a smile that stirred his center. In that moment, he felt powerful enough to shift mountains.

She pulled his hand from his side and turned it palm up, resting the sphere of water there. Then she pulled more water into her hands, moving them in circles to coax the water into a ring, its width as much as her arm. She spun and rotated it between them, playing like a child with a hoop. Laughing, Sy waited until the angle was right, and he tossed the sphere through the middle of the hoop.

But Corentine controlled both, merging them into a flat disc of water that she then hurled across the sea. It skipped across the water's surface, and Sy marveled as the disc refused to merge with its source. For several seconds they both watched it, mesmerized by the crystalline light reflecting from her creation.

"What is the meaning of this?" a rough voice yelled, breaking into their bubble of wonder. The disc crashed into the sea, and Corentine bolted without even a glance at Sy.

He pushed down the sick that crept up his throat as he turned, searching for the right words that would defend instead of condemn.

Tag was there, his face dark with confusion and accusation and betrayal. He would never understand. Sy hoped he might be able to convince the burly man to stay quiet for now, but explanation would be required, and his father would soon know that magic had again come to the island.

And from Corentine's family. Again. But if the General knew already…

"Tag, please," he started, but they were both interrupted by a scream. Sy felt the blood drain from his face, and he swayed on his feet as he turned to see what had happened.

Farther down the beach, Corentine lay crumpled in the sand, her face bloodied as she tried to scoot away from Resh.

"Sorceress!" Resh screamed, his long fingers pointing like bony daggers hurtling toward Coren's chest. She felt herself flinch as if the word itself had pierced her, as if it alone could take her very life.

"Sulit witch! Traitor!" The shouts seemed capable of echoing to every corner of the island. She tried to get up, to run, to vanish into her younger self, but her body and its magic were both frozen in the face of this fierce boy. He yanked her to her feet, wrenching her arms behind her and cinching her wrists together with his leather belt.

"Tagsha, get the General!" he yelled. Coren moaned, stumbling against his pressure to pull her up the beach. "Quiet, girl. My brother is too trusting, but I know your family's true story. You will not ruin him." He bent closer to her ear, his breath hot against her already flushed skin. "Your witch grandmother Lorental single-handedly forced the necessity of the Sacrifice. Your *family* is responsible for the downfall of our people, but *you* will never hold that power on these shores!"

Coren's head spun with his accusations and the repercussions of what had just taken place. Surely he must be false. One family alone couldn't have caused so much. Maren had said…but Maren might have been wrong, if she only knew part of the story.

But none of it mattered now, because the only thing left for her future was banishment.

13

"Tag. Please wait," Sy pleaded, turning to the man who had always been more than his father's guard. Tag looked between the two brothers, torn between duty and love, responsibility and trust. "Tag. It's not what Resh thinks."

"Was she not using magic?" Tag asked, his voice cracking. "I saw…I don't really know what I saw."

Sy opened his mouth to deny it, then hung his head. There was no use. Tag had seen something, and Resh knew something of what it had been. The General would need no other convincing.

"Tagsha!" Resh yelled, half-dragging Coren as they neared. "I command you to find the General!"

Tag glared at Resh. "You should not have tricked me into this!" he called.

"You are under oath, Tagsha. Now that you know, you cannot keep it." The look on Resh's face was triumphant, even from so far away. In that moment, Sy learned what it was to truly hate a brother.

In Weshen, under General Ashemon, the law was the law. Sy's brain raced to find another way, a loophole, even as he ran to catch his brother.

"Resh, please wait. There's an explanation."

"Of course there is, brother. This girl is the newest in a coven of Weshen witches, bent only and forever on their own aggrandizement, no matter how it might hurt our people. She may seem down on luck now, but her dreams are that of victory. Are they not?" he sneered at Coren, who glared and spat blood onto the ground before them.

"How dare you hit a woman!" Sy yelled, raising a fist as if to pay the blow back to his brother.

But Coren said, "Stop. That part was an accident. There is nothing more you can do. I have disobeyed my mother, and this is my penance." Her voice was bitter and resigned, as though she were actually beginning to believe Resh.

"But is any of this true? Your family?" Sy whispered, hating that he needed to ask the question to settle his doubts.

She looked to the sky, avoiding his eyes. "It may be. It may not be. I know little of my family. Certainly we have been cursed by many kinds of magic for too long."

Sy felt his heart cracking for the sorrow she had known, and the hardships she would surely find today.

They were nearing the center of the beach, where several men had run from their tents, and even a few of the girls. Resh's shouted words must have drawn them from their breakfasts and lingering kisses.

The small crowd of women and men stuttered and murmured, uncertain of how to react to such a display.

More people continued to hurry from the tents onto the beach. Resh screeched the damning words again and again, stopping only when the General tore through the door of his tent, striding onto the beach.

Ashemon stalked toward his youngest son and the girl he had caught on the wrong beach, murder on his face.

For a second, Coren thought the look was directed toward Reshra.

If only Maren were right about the General's bargain.

If only that bargain included her.

The people had begun to clump together, closing in on them, then backing away, like the tide sucking at the sand. She saw many familiar faces, now made grotesque by fear and the lust for spectacle.

The General came to a stop several yards from Coren, looking between both of his sons and his guard.

"Reshra. Hush your cries," he barked. Resh glared but clamped his mouth shut. Coren pushed her back straighter, twisting her wrists in their bindings, although she couldn't quite rid her shoulder of Reshra's grip. Ashemon turned to her then, pinning her in his hard gaze.

"Tell me, girl. Do you deny my Second Son's accusation?" He was not yelling, but the crowd and the morning were so quiet that his voice echoed off the cliffs.

Coren did not answer, nor did she flinch at his words. There was no going back to before, even if she were the only one who had realized it yet.

Perhaps there had never been another option. Not for her family. Between the Restless King and the Mirror Magi's elders, her family members had all been dead the second they had been born. The unfair truth of it swept her suddenly, and the currents of anger pulled her under.

There was an odd look in Ashemon's eye though, as if despite the fury rolling from every movement, he was reluctant to broach this subject. Thanks to Maren, she knew some of the General's old secrets, but she also knew people change. Since Sy seemed to mistrust him now, she would do the same.

"Do you wish a trial?" he asked then, and the whispers began. Trials were reserved for violent acts, never magical ones. Whatever game he was playing, she would have no part in it.

"You pretend to offer me a trial?" Coren sneered, finally finding the strength to wrench her arm from Reshra's grasp. She stood as tall as her slim form could stretch. "My *brother* had no such trial. *Your father* sent an eight-year-old boy to die alone on the MagiSea! And now you will surely threaten me with the same, although I am the only caretaker to two young children. What *worthy* Generals!"

Reshra yanked hard on her bound arms, causing her to stumble to her knees. Several of the watching women gasped, though Coren thought she heard one laugh.

"I deny nothing," she called, her voice reaching toward the crowd like a slap of its own. "Your Second

Son may be a lusty shame to our people, but he is not false."

This time she managed to twist completely away from Reshra, springing up several feet away from him. She glanced back at him with a look of challenge as Sy stepped slightly between them.

"I know nothing of Sulit magic, only the power the Mirror Magi have cursed my family with!" she continued, twisting to watch every judgmental face before her. "Perhaps before you banish me, you should send someone to the temple in Weshen City to ask the sages why one family has been so chosen for the magic's return!" Coren's voice rose and rose, spiraling through the gaping crowd. "Ask them why, if shifter magic is supposedly gone, and the women are trapped on this island, why have the banishments remained necessary!"

She finally managed to twist her hands free from their leather binding and swept them around her. The crowd shuffled away and pushed each other back, as though ducking her very movements. "You have all played a part in driving my mother insane, my father to desert, and my brother to die! Give me a boat and my siblings, and we will leave you forever. I will have no part of your future!"

Coren realized she was nearly wild with grief, near to doing something she could never be forgiven for. What would these actions mean for Penna and Kosh? But she seemed powerless to stop the rage from pouring forth, and Ashemon was staring at her with something like curiosity, almost inviting her to continue.

"Our ancestors made a cruel bargain to protect all Weshen people, denying our nature to protect our existence, but you have not protected my family! You have *not!*" She ended on a wail, the anger dissipating as the heaviness of what would surely happen next weighed on her soul. She began to slump to the ground.

Suddenly, Coren felt a gentle pair of arms wrap around her, the familiar smell of Sy envelop her, overwhelm her, and she allowed herself to sag back into his chest.

There were several beats of silence as the General stared between Coren and his two sons. Neither Reshra nor Syashin moved a muscle, both staring defiantly at their father. The crowd too was silent, waiting for their General, and the cry of a dawngull was the only noise on the beach.

Then Ashemon's eyes hardened, and Coren knew in that moment that she had lost. She hadn't realized she was still grasping any hope until the General's eyes sucked it from her soul. Her chest heaved against Sy's arms in a helpless sob.

Ashemon spoke, his voice louder this time. "Then you admit to practicing magic prohibited by the Mirror Magi and the elders of Weshen. We will harbor no such traitors. You are hereby banished from Weshen Isle and Weshen City from this day forward, until your last. As per our custom, you have one hour to pack your things and say goodbye to your family, who will stay here. Those children have done nothing wrong, and you will not destroy their lives as you have your own with these slanderous words. The Weshen people will gather here, on this beach, to offer you the Last Meal."

Sy let a wordless roar from his lips and charged at his father, hatred in every unbalanced step.

"This is not right, and you all know it!" he yelled, sweeping his arms across the motionless crowd. "Father," he said, turning to the General, "it's my fault she's been discovered. I asked her to show me what I suspected. She denied any knowledge, and I forced it from her."

"How could a son of Weshen force knowledge of magic when he has no such knowledge?" the General roared back. Coren slumped to the sand, her muscles giving up. Sy needed to be silent, but she had given him a reason to shout. Now this would be on her, as well.

Sy did not flinch at Ashemon's question. Instead he turned to his brother. "You have always wanted what I have. Now you may have it all!" Turning in a full circle, he stared down anyone who would meet his eyes.

"People of Weshen, if you continue to listen to the history our elders cling to, instead of what future the Magi have given us today…if you choose to banish this innocent girl, whom you have persecuted for her family's perceived failures, then you must also banish me, the First Son of your revered General!"

And with that, he lifted his hands wide, calling the ocean water to him. Wide, thin waves soared above the crowd, and their silence broke into gasps and shrieks and even delighted laughter, from a few. As one, they ducked and cowered beneath the suspended droplets. Then Sy gathered the water into a swirling ball of pure white-blue, taller than the people, a world unto itself.

Coren watched with a split sense of awe and despair as the sphere floated down to rest in the sand, a blurry barrier further separating them from their people. She heard a strangled noise and turned to see Reshra, ragged shock and possibly a painful knife of regret slicing across his finely-cut features.

She wondered what the General could say to this display of power? Would he accept it? Sy looked back just then, his wide, desperate eyes catching the question on her face.

Abruptly his power seemed to flicker, and he let go of whatever control he had over the sphere. The water splashed in a great wave at his feet, soaking himself, Reshra, and Coren.

Something had changed in the General's expression during this demonstration, but Sy no longer cared. If his people rejected him, he would welcome the freedom that would come from banishment.

He alone, of all the Weshen, had the skills to ensure it did not result in death. He could survive the journey, and he and Coren could start a new life in EvenFall, far away from the judgments of their people.

The General's anger swept silence through the crowd, however, smothering even Sy's reckless thoughts. The words came out as bites of bitterness. "You, Corentine Ashaden, daughter of Sorenta, and Syashin Havenash, son of Ashemon, are both hereby banished from all territories of Weshen for the use of prohibited magic, by order of the Mirror Magi and all of Weshen."

Sy nodded numbly and began to move away, unable to process the thoughts and emotions beating at him like tidal waves in a summer storm. The General reached to grab his shirt, holding him close and whispering, "Foolish boy. Why have you hidden this for so long, only to reveal it before everyone? The people are not ready, and there is nothing I can do to save you now! Go. Pack your bag."

It was more of a goodbye than Sy had hoped for, and he stared after the General as the broad man stalked away. It seemed his father did indeed know about the trickle of magic returning to his people.

But if he had known this all along, why hadn't he asked Sy, or tested him to find the magic? Why would he continue to stopper its reveal, when the return of Weshen magic could represent freedom from the Restless King's grasp?

And as he drowned in this new wave of questions, Sy realized he could never truly abandon his people.

Instead, he needed to get Corentine to the mountains, to Damren. Then together they could work to save Weshen before it sank into the ocean, too stubborn to fight the destruction that was coming.

If he could master his magic and kill the Restless King, Sy would earn back his people's acceptance, and he could return to claim his place as First Son, and later, as General.

Resh watched as the crowds parted wide for Sy and Corentine, as though the people feared the magic might rub onto them. He blinked after them, still calculating where his plans to help his brother regain the hunts had gone so, so wrong.

Resh had made mistakes today, but none so crippling as the mistake his father had made, every day of the brothers' lives, in failing to tell them the truth. He'd seen the very first, fleeting look on the General's face. It had not been fear, or anger, or even mistrust. It had been pride, and worship, and hope. Even if Ashemon hadn't known of Sy's magic, he had to have known its return was imminent, and not in the mythical future.

Betrayal coursed through Resh's mind as he remembered all the time spent on his knees in the temples, praying for a way for Weshen to rise once more.

What possibilities for their people's revenge had been squandered by Sy keeping this glorious secret? What could possibly have been gained by such a thing?

He knew Corentine's family had once dallied with Sulit witches. The girl had somehow inverted the hunts, claiming his brother's mind and body, and Resh still vowed to never trust her motives or her magic.

But if Sy had magic too, it would certainly be Weshen. Never dark.

If their shifter magic was indeed returning, then Weshen's future was within reach. The Restless King could be killed.

Resh jolted to life and rushed after his father and brother.

Sy stormed into their shared tent, Resh only steps behind. Sy didn't even glance at him, instead grabbing a worn leather rucksack from his travel trunk and shoving in clothing haphazardly. Resh watched him, uncertain what to say or do, then pushed aside the room divider. He yanked a box from beneath his mattress and took out an offering.

It wouldn't be enough.

"You can take mine," Resh said, hating how his voice cracked with regret. But it was enough to jolt Sy out of his movements. He glanced over his shoulder, his eyes taking in the favorite knife Resh was holding.

But Sy only turned back to his bag. "Too late to be sorry for what you started," he muttered.

"Brother…I never knew." Resh's voice was tight with the effort of apologizing.

"You never asked," Sy tossed back belligerently.

Resh cursed and chucked the knife into Sy's bag. It fell with a soft thud against a pair of boots. Sy didn't touch it.

"We're not children any more, Resh," he said, keeping his back turned. "This is a real war, and my family just surrendered me to the enemy."

Resh wanted nothing more than to pummel Syashin out of his anger and stubbornness. But he clenched his jaw against the sensation.

Sy was the strength. Resh was the sly. He must be smarter about this.

Just then Sy turned and pinned his eyes on Resh. "I'll survive this, little brother. Be watching for my return."

Determination flared in Sy's expression. Resh knew if anyone could live through such a punishment, it would be Sy.

"And Resh, if you care for me at all - if you ever have - be sure the people are ready for the return of the magic. Because when I come back here, I'll be bringing the future with me. The Restless King *will* fall to our hands. He will not last another generation, and his sons will never see the throne!"

Resh felt himself nodding, but even then, as he imagined an empty throne in StarsHelm Palace, the regret began to twist and grow into jealousy. Syashin, the First Son, had always been taller. Stronger. Better with every weapon, including the one that was his own muscled body.

Now he was conveniently the first to receive the shifter magic as well? Resh narrowed his eyes. He needed answers, and he wouldn't find them on Weshen Isle.

14

Ashemon entered the tent just in time to hear his First Son's claim, and to see the look of jealousy twist into his Second Son's face.

"Syashin, I never wanted this for you." Ashemon knew his voice betrayed his fatigue. This was nothing like what he had planned. He wondered how strong his son's magic was, even as he reminded himself one magi would never be enough.

"You *planned* this for me," Syashin hissed, as if somehow throwing Ashemon's thought back at him. "Corentine learned of your plan to awaken the magic. And guess what? It worked. But the women have more of it than you know."

The girl's name reminded Ashemon of something else he had planned, much more recently. Perhaps, the two of them alone on the MagiSea…perhaps his son's magic could be put to use after all.

"I'm aware that some of the women have a weak sort of magic still," Ashemon admitted. "Some of the Wesh in Riata retain the gifts as well, though none so strong as what our people once possessed."

Reshra made a noise then as if to protest the very idea, but Ashemon held up a silencing hand. Both of his sons quieted, their years of training evident. Ashemon nearly smiled at the display of obedience.

"The Mirror Magi know all. Surely they have tolerated the determination of certain families to retain their magic in secret. Our elders also know the importance that the old ways remain alive. But Syashin, know this: Weshen people are not ready for the magic to fully return, and *none* of the people who have the magic in their blood are ready to fight the Restless King."

Syashin's face flushed with this implication, but Ashemon stared him down. "You may think you are ready to fight. But Zorander Graeme has conquered fourteen nations in his lifetime. What is one half-magical boy to him?"

Ashemon watched as Syashin's shoulders slumped in agreement, and his chest warmed in satisfaction that his son would do nothing rash. "But you are right on one matter," he continued. "The Restless King will never survive your generation. Though we believe dark magic prolongs his life force, still he grows old and weak with wanting."

Syashin's eyes widened in surprise, but he asked no questions, whether from residual anger or good training, Ashemon wasn't sure.

"Father, what are you talking about?" Reshra asked, his voice rising in disrespect. Ashemon resisted the urge to backhand his Second Son, but only just.

"I will tell you what you need to know, when you need to know it. Just like the other men and women of Weshen," Ashemon said evenly. He stared at Reshra, glad he was still several inches taller than the boy. Reshra would need much harder discipline now if he were to take Syashin's place for the summer months. It may be Ashemon's fault, but the boy had grown too soft with women and drink.

"Now, go help Tagsha drive the people to the beach. Ready the *Alimente* for your brother. And Reshra..." Ashemon waited a few seconds until Reshra had given up his full, grudging attention. "Fill it well if you want to see your brother again."

Reshra nodded, though a scowl darkened his face as he left to prepare the unique vessel. Ashemon turned in time to see Syashin hide a grim smile. He watched the young man before him for a long moment, taking in the shoulders and chest broadened with muscle, the too-long hair and faded clothing that spoke of a warrior rather than a pampered prince. Glancing in the bag behind Syashin, he could see more weapons than shirts.

He allowed himself a single, brief smile.

"My son, I did not wish this for you," he repeated, struggling to clear the sorrow from his voice. "It is true that I sought a strong Weshen woman to be your mother, and that I hoped the magic would lie dormant in your blood until the right time. But I don't believe today was the right time. Shifter magic alone will never be enough to fight the Restless King - it never was. He has more strength than you could imagine, and only a meticulous plan will topple his reign. You and Corentine must use your banishment well. Gather information. Train. Learn. Hide in the mountains, but do not venture past them. I will come for you when the summer is done, and we will conceive a plan together."

He clapped a hand to his son's shoulder, hesitated, then drew Syashin in for a full embrace. The boy allowed it, but Ashemon felt the mistrust still stiffening Syashin's shoulders, and he closed his eyes in appreciation.

General Ashemon knew he had made many mistakes, but his First Son was not one of them.

Coren stumbled to her house through a blur of tears. How had this happened so swiftly? How could she possibly explain what had happened to Penna and Kosh?

Why was *her* family the one who tumbled from the cliff to the MagiSea first? Was it true, what Reshra had said - that her grandmother was somehow responsible for the Sacrifice? He could be lying, but what would he have to gain in a whisper?

What secrets had Sorenta taken with her into the dark water?

The questions blurred into a whirlwind as she stepped inside the summercloth, but the sight that met her arrested all movement. The blur of tears and panic broke like glass shattering, and her home snapped into focus sharply. Every cupboard had been opened and emptied. Every trunk overturned.

She darted into the sleeping room, and it was the same. Clothing was scattered. The beds leaned against the wall.

And Penna and Kosh were nowhere. Pricks of dread needled through her dazed confusion.

Coren's breath came in shallow gulps as her eyes darted from one empty space to the next. Sinking to the floor amid the chaos, she used several precious minutes forcing herself to focus. She chanted a simple prayer to the Magi until the repeated words calmed her breathing, and she opened her eyes again.

Looking around the house carefully, analytically, she realized it was their essential items which were gone - even her things.

Someone had done this with intention...but who? And for what purpose?

Nothing of value was left for her to take on the boat. Not only had she been banished, but robbed. Leaning against the wall, Coren closed her eyes and rubbed at her face, smoothing away the tears and massaging her furrowed brow. She let the anger seep into her bones. She would not be beaten this way. She had survived a Vespa attack. She had *torn apart* a Vespa with shifter magic.

That was something no-one could steal from her. She would be banished, yes, but she would honor Jyesh's memory by surviving. Perhaps she was so strangely strong because his spirit remained with her. Perhaps his magic had blended with hers when he died, their sources shifting back together in a reversal of their separation in the womb.

Yes. Family was the answer.

It occurred to her that maybe there *was* one valuable possession left. She knelt and pulled at the loose board in the floor, breathing a deep sigh of relief when she found her father's journal still there. As she lifted it, though, she noticed a scrap of paper below it.

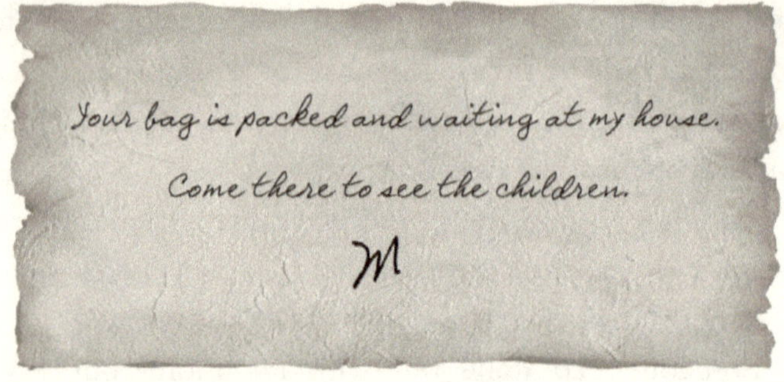

Coren crushed the paper between the pages of the journal and cursed in frustration and relief. What was the old woman doing now? She sprinted out of the house, dodging quickly into the brush to avoid any inquiring eyes. Several minutes later, she arrived, breathless, at Maren's yard.

Penna and Kosh waited there for her, their young faces streaked with tears.

"It's okay," Penna whispered, hugging Coren tightly. "You will survive. We will see you soon, at Rurok! Maren says."

"Rurok?" Coren said, jerking her head up to look at Maren, who had bustled into the yard with a large rucksack. She handed it to Coren, who shouldered it dumbly.

"Yes. We're leaving as well. You certainly can't take them with you, and I won't have these two banished as well. First Jyesh, then you. It's only a matter of time until their magic manifests. The General is an idiot who goes back on his word, and he can't be trusted." The woman's words were matter-of-fact, but Coren sensed the deadly fury in her every movement.

Of course. Syashin should never have been banished. The General had promised to protect him. But what could he have done, with all the people watching and hearing Sy's challenge?

"Ashemon has never been a fearless leader," Maren answered. "The people are not ready, true. But his influence could have brought us together today to *become* ready. Instead he chose to bow to their ignorance and prejudice."

Kosh wrapped his slim arms protectively around Coren and Penna, squashing his sisters together. "Now I won't have to go to the men's city and be trained to forget you both. Now I'll be a refugee in Sulit, and the witches will help us find our power. Surely we will have magic, too," he said, his child's face stretched into an excited grin.

Coren clutched their thin bodies close to her, her body shaking as the tears began again. The twins had simply accepted the complete reversal of their world. Burying her face in their hair, she murmured thanks to the Mirror Magi for their resilience, and for Maren, who would defend them with her life.

"But *Sulit*, Maren? How can you get there? How can you even know the witches will still welcome you?" Coren asked, the reality of Maren's plan sinking in, now that her soul had quieted somewhat around her siblings' safety.

"I can't. Witches are fickle sometimes. But we were friends once, and I will not stay on this island a day longer, Corentine," Maren said, embracing her fiercely. "I've stayed all these years, hoping to be of help when we Weshen banded together to reclaim our magic and our love, but I am *through*." Her hand sliced the air, leaving a shimmering trail as it moved. Coren wondered just what sorts of magic Maren still hid.

"The Sulit witches can be dangerous, but perhaps not so much as our own people. We'll leave from the northern beaches while the crowds are distracted with the banishment ceremony, and we'll meet again one day, in Rurok. Syashin will know where the Sulit capital is, even if he's never been there. He should be willing enough to take you there, after all the trouble his father has caused. Stupid men," Maren practically spat, her eyes sparking.

"But Maren, the Hungry River…" Coren trailed away, imagining the treacherous journey Maren was describing. One pull of the wrong current and the remainder of her family would be swallowed whole. Just like Jyesh had been, and all the dead they had sent to the mouth of that river.

Maren made a dismissive noise. "I can navigate those waters. There is still magic in me yet, and the water sources were always mine to control. Perhaps they will listen better, the farther we get from the island. And

Neshra drew me a map, once. We will aim our boat directly west, into the mouth of Shedreck River. It's not nearly so hungry. From there we can travel north through the Listening Forest. Rurok is at the top of New Moon Falls."

Maren paused, seeming to realize then that Coren had been staring wide-eyed at her ranting. She put her hands on Coren's shoulders and looked straight into her eyes. "We *will* see each other again. Trust in yourself and your magic. Trust in the love of your family. That love is *power*, girl. Do not forget it."

Coren nodded, wishing so much to believe in Maren, just as she always had. Yet it was growing harder and harder with each passing second, like grains of sand slipping from beneath them. They were all tumbling from the edge of the cliff.

The ripples of the ocean as they hit would surely reverberate across the whole world.

Maren reached her arms across the twins to Coren, and the four of them clung together for a few brief seconds. Then the sound of a horn on the western beach broke them to pieces again.

Coren swiped at the fresh tears on her cheek and joined hands with Penna and Kosh. "I know it will delay you, but please see me off," she whispered. She knew she could be strong if they were watching.

She must not break before the General and his cruel collection of followers.

Together, the four of them walked slowly to the beach, where every person on the island had gathered. Banishment was a rare event, but still, everyone knew the ceremony. Tradition provided one hour to pack what could fit in one sack, one longboat, and one Last Meal. No sail, and no oar. The banished were truly set adrift for their actions.

When they inevitably died on the MagiSea, their dangerous magic was dissolved back into its source, and swallowed by the Hungry River.

Each Weshen household helped provide the Last Meal. Coren had always thought it a mockery of the sense of community Weshen boasted. What good is community when you are being banished?

But the families stood before her now, each holding one piece of food. She was allowed one bite from each piece, symbolizing how the community was always willing to help the banished survive, but also how the banished knowingly refused their help by committing acts of treason in their use of magic.

Jyesh had not eaten a single bite of the offered food, snubbing the false ceremony of help from the people who had deserted him. Jyesh had sailed into the MagiSea without a crumb in his belly, and the look on her twin's face had filled Coren's stomach with knots and her dreams with screaming for months afterward.

She could only hope that the expression on her face would be as powerful a reminder for the Weshen people, but her experience had shown it was unlikely. They would forget her, as they had largely forgotten her brother, her mother, her father.

And yet, Coren managed to shove her pride far away. This was not the time for a show of dignity. She meant to survive. And so she ate enormous bites of every piece of food offered, filling her cheeks and nearly gagging as the food filled her mouth.

Glancing to her side, she noticed Syashin began copying her actions, and a strange sense of relief flooded her, pushing her spine even straighter. She was not alone, and at least he, too, seemed interested in living.

She burned to ask him why he had thrown away his future by showing his magic, why he had cast his lot in with such a family as hers, but they would have the rest of their lives to discuss these things.

15

The Last Meal was complete. Sy's stomach ached from the amount of food he had consumed, and his very jaw was sore from chewing. But he had to admit it was better to begin their journey well-fed.

The line of women and men parted before Corentine and him, and everyone pivoted to face the ocean, where a small boat was waiting, the name *Alimente* painted on its side, and Sy caught Resh's eye. The brothers nodded at each other in a strained sort of understanding.

Sy watched the twins press their bodies against Corentine. Their faces were streaked with dried tears, but they were each strong-faced and silent now. As Corentine straightened from the embraces, the twins moved back to stand with an older woman. She glared ferociously at the General, as if she might tear him apart with her bare fingers, and Syashin was surprised to see his father duck his head as though in shame. He blinked between the two adults until Tag gathered him in a bone-crushing hug.

"I swear I'll see you again," he whispered to Sy before letting him go and shoving him a bit toward the boat. Sy climbed in, careful to stay straight and proud.

Corentine stumbled, splashing water all over her dress. She had likely never been in a boat, Sy realized, and he held a hand out to help her. She took it without looking at him, then sat stiffly in the stern, arranging her damp dress over her legs and holding her chin high with pride.

Tag leaned in, grasping the boat. Corentine slid her eyes to him, leaning away from his bulk. Just before heaving the boat from the sand, Tag fixed both of them in a heavy glare. "*Survive*," he commanded. "Weshen may depend on it."

Sy nodded, noticing a sheen had covered Tag's eyes. He didn't share the man's sentimentality, but there was no question that they would survive.

The boat drifted without purpose for several yards before catching a small southern-bound current. There was no song of lamentation for the launching of their boat, only silence. Sy kicked his sack to the bottom of the boat. Corentine stared blankly at the sparkling water stretched before them, her face as smooth as the sea on a still morning.

It reminded him a bit of how she always began the hunts - never worried about who was watching her, only what she had made up her mind to do. It wasn't long until the faces on the shore were indistinguishable from one another. And not much longer until the shoreline had blended into a smudgy horizon.

Sy settled into the bow of the boat and positioned himself to watch for the appearance of the Umbren shore. That would be his cue to start turning the boat northwest, away from the dark southern shores. Then he would need to navigate past the Hungry River, which joined the magical continents of Sulit and Umbren. But that would be many hours from now, perhaps even after the sun had set.

"We have time to rest," he said, and his voice sounded much too loud in the quiet of the open water. Corentine didn't even look at him. Guessing now was not the best moment to form a plan of survival, he lay back against the bow of the longboat. "We can drift several hours before needing to direct the boat. I will keep us safe," he added. Still, she stared into the distance, as blank and unmoving as an icy rock cliff, as though she didn't even care that he was in the boat.

Sy shoved his hand through his hair and sighed, filled with shame for how her family had been treated by his. How could they possibly learn to trust each other now, even in such a situation where that trust was needed to save their lives?

Suddenly unbearably weary, he leaned against the smooth wood of the *Alimente* and closed his eyes against what his father had done, and his own part in pushing her to acknowledge her magic.

They were adrift in the MagiSea with a boat, each other, and what they had packed in one hour. Coren had no idea how long their journey would be, but she knew they were meant to die on the water and be baked into white bone by the sun, then sunk into the MagiSea, which would absorb their forbidden magic.

And the people of Weshen believed they would be safer for it.

As the afternoon wore on, interminable, neither of them spoke a word. All her previous questions disappeared before the empty expanse of the water, and all her tears dried to salt in the breeze. Although Coren knew it had all been out of Sy's hands, she had nothing left to say to the boy who, despite all his promises, had indeed hurt her in the worst way possible.

Feeling as empty and flat as the horizon before them, she pulled a loosely-woven shawl across her face for shade and let the hot sun and her full belly finally lull her to a fitful, dozing sleep. Her body needed the rest, so she didn't fight it. Long minutes or maybe hours passed as she began to relax into a deeper sleep, only to be ripped upright by a sudden, fierce shriek.

A Vespa. She would never forget that sound.

Panic shot through every limb, but before Coren could even move, Sy was on top of her. Gripping her waist, he yanked her into the bottom of the boat, her body pressed beneath his. His heart hammered against her chest so hard that her own seemed to match it through their clothing, two wild drum beats of fear. He pulled a coarse blanket over them just as a giant shadow seemed to block the very sun.

And they waited, still as mice beneath a wheeling hawk.

The creature circled once, twice. Surely it could see them, Coren thought, her throat constricting, or smell them, or whatever sense Vespas had in plenty. And then the boat was jarred nearly to the water as the monster landed on its edge, a thick golden claw plucking at the weave of the blanket. Sy's hand moved, quicker than thought, covering her mouth and preventing the scream she barely knew was poised on her open lips.

Coren had imagined dying on the MagiSea a thousand times, but never once at the mercy of a Vespa. She tried desperately to focus the same magic that had dissipated the previous creature, but it was like a candle sputtering in too much melted wax. She had nothing.

The bird shifted on its perch and Sy ducked his head even closer, burying his face against the curve of her neck as the claw shifted downward, slowly ripping the blanket open an inch at a time. Corentine froze, her mind searching for a way to protect him. She didn't want to acknowledge it, but the thought unfurled deep in her belly: she *needed* Sy to survive.

If that claw scratched his skin, if he bled, the Vespa's poison would kill him before the banishment could. Time seemed to stand still as they both struggled not to breathe, and Coren begged the Mirror Magi for a reprieve.

And then the Vespa simply left, the boat rocking gently from its departure as its call faded in the breeze, seemingly pushed away by nothing but prayer. They were free to move, yet neither of them did.

Coren only realized she was shaking when Sy finally took his palm from her mouth and circled her shoulder gently against his chest. His mouth closed against her neck in a not-quite kiss, and she tensed for new reasons, her stomach tightening against his movements.

She may need him to survive, but she was determined never to need him like that.

She was suddenly overly aware of the sweaty heat of their bodies pressed together: her shoulders tucked between his, her ribcage rattling against his pectoral muscles, her hip bones cutting into his abdominals.

Sy pushed up onto his elbows, his eyes dark and liquid like the ocean just before a storm. The blanket still covered them, casting the minutia of their world into deep shadow. His eyelashes blinked down slowly, and his lips began to curve upward.

"Get off of me," Coren whispered.

His mouth straightened and set in a hard line and his brows lowered nearly to a glare, but he rose, shaking off the blanket. Coren sat and scooted swiftly back until her shoulders bumped the stern of the small boat. He knelt, surveying the bright, empty sky. There was no more sign of the Vespa except their lingering unease.

"Why didn't you fight? I thought you were a great warrior. A Paladin," Coren said, her sneer doing a poor job of covering her discomfort.

"There could have been more than the one, and my weapons are packed away. I wouldn't risk your life."

The answer surprised her, but she only glared. "I've killed one before, remember?"

"A happy accident. You're untrained in your magic and your fighting." His words were simple and flat, but they skinned her pride like a fillet knife. She hated the raw feeling of needing his help.

The wind began to blow again, as if it too had paused to watch the Vespa. The breeze gently pushed her hair from her sticky neck. She gathered it to one side, weaving it into a thick braid of earthy browns.

"Perhaps you should train me, then. Begin by showing me how to create a sail." It was a taunt, something she knew was likely impossible, but Sy answered with a wry smile.

"It's not so easy as you think. But it can be done."

Coren shrugged, daring him with a raised eyebrow. His smile hardened and widened, and he held his hand toward her as though offering it. Before she could refuse it, though, she noticed a blue fabric begin to form in his palm, the threads weaving through his fingers.

It was several long seconds before Coren realized he was stealing the thread of her dress, and she gasped in shock and anger as the cloth swiftly disappeared well above her knees, the threads dissolving from her browned legs and winding into his hand.

"Stop!" she cried, embarrassed by the note of panic in her voice.

He obeyed, but it was too late for her modesty. Coren saw his eyes fixed on her upper thigh, where the handle of her whip rested against her skin, beginning the flat, thin braid that spiraled down to her ankle.

"Your mother's whip." He pointed, wrapping the last bit of blue thread around his palm like the women who wove clothing on the island. "What sort of creature made its talisman? What dark magic keeps it alive?" he insisted

But Coren had no idea. And she wouldn't have told him now if she did. Instead, she lunged forward, grasping at the strings he held, but he snatched them away, holding them to his chest.

"This is fusion, the mirror magic to disintegration." He looked down his hands, running the thread through his fingers as he wove the thread into fabric. "Many generations before the Restless King was even born, people called the Weshen creators, but no human can truly create. We're shifters. We move sources from one place to another. A sail is made from cloth, and so these threads must come from somewhere." Syashin locked his eyes on hers and grinned without real humor. "Your dress is more useful now."

Coren huffed, but she didn't reach for the scraps again. She wanted to see him work. She knew she needed to learn from him if they were to survive.

Sy finished the sail and began to form a tough rope from the leather of his belt, then shifted the top board of the boat up into a short, bare mast. Although they sat much shallower in the water this way, he was then able to string the slim blue sail. Coren felt the gentlest push of the wind as the sail filled.

"Now we will move faster toward our end." Bitterness and exhaustion laced his voice. He leaned back heavily, closing his eyes against the sun and throwing a muscular arm over his face. Coren wondered how much energy he had just used, and how long it would take him to recover.

"I don't know anything about the whip's origins or its magic, other than what I've told you," Coren said finally, her words meaningless except as an offer of peace. He slit open his eyes and watched her, waiting for more.

Keeping secrets wouldn't help them survive now. Hiding their abilities out of pride or fear was a senseless act.

So she pressed the handle of the whip against her thigh, triggering it, and the flat braid stacked in loops around her ankle. She leaned over the water, waiting, conscious of Sy's eyes on the curve of her back. Soon a bright yellow fish swam too near the surface and she lashed out, the braid cracking the water. The fish's body bounced into the boat, its neatly-severed head still floating next to the boat.

"But I do know how to use it for that," Coren murmured, keeping her eyes on the fish.

To her surprise, Sy grinned, laughter shaking his shoulders. "If Resh had managed to catch you, things would have turned out so very differently. You would have torn him to shreds, leaving me with the unsavory task of revenge. Maybe this end was inevitable."

Coren hesitated for only a second. "Reshra *did* catch me."

Sy sat up straight, his body an angry question. "What do you mean? When?"

"Yesterday, just before you came. He was waiting on the plain before you got there. He claimed me with a kiss but said it was for you. It means nothing now," she added. And she meant it.

Although nothing against her will was small, their current situation was so largely wrong that those past insults had shrunk to insignificance.

He leaned forward, searching her eyes. "Corentine, I'm truly sorry for the grief my family has brought yours," he said, his voice barely a whisper. "I promised not to hurt you, and I've broken that more completely than I ever imagined possible."

She couldn't even glance at him, fearing the past weeks would be too much to bear and she would collapse into sobs.

"Surely the Mirror Magi have plans for us, and we will not die on this water," she whispered instead, hearing the question in her voice and despising its weakness. Staring into the depths of the water, she trailed her fingers through its sparkling surface, wondering what magic still swirled below.

As Corentine's fingers twisted in the deep waters of the MagiSea, those reverberations rippled across the miles of ocean, like a displaced source seeking something new to bond with.

Miles and miles to the south, but closer to a Weshen woman than many generations had seen, those same waters began to lap at the shores of Umbren, seeping into the roots of the thick trees in ShadowsEnd Forest. Rivulets of enchanted water worked inland, loosening the dirt and feeding the thing that had slept in the earth of Umbren for decades, shattered into pieces and bound long ago.

The darkness of the forest sparked with a light unseen since the Separation, and Shadow began to stir.

A Vespa's cry echoed on the breeze, and the trees began to whisper their green-black leaves with an ancient enchantment.

> *The Shadow is good, the Shadow is bad.*
> *The Shadow will take all that you had.*
> *The Shadow is near, the Shadow is far.*
> *The Shadow knows all that you are.*

16

"**W**hich direction is the Hungry River?" Corentine asked, breaking the silence. Sy was wary of the flatness in her voice and the rounded slump of her shoulders.

The wind had pulled the little boat gradually west until Weshen Isle disappeared into the horizon. Now, there was nothing to see in any direction. Nothing except sea and sky and each other. Not a bad view, in his opinion.

Sy lifted his eyes to the blue above them, considering the position of the sun. "That way," he pointed. They were drifting west and slightly south, but he wasn't worried. He'd been watching the timing carefully.

Too soon and they would be sucked north into the treacherous rocks surrounding NewMoon Falls. Too late and they would be pulled down into the black mouth of the Hungry River, or worse, to the shores of Umbren, a place of darkness and death.

"The current will pull us to the river eventually if we don't begin to row," he added.

"How can we row with no oars?" Corentine glared at him. "If you shift more wood from the boat, we'll sink, and besides, you'll likely pass out from exhaustion."

Heat rose in his already sun-warmed cheeks. So she had noticed how much shifting the sail had drained him. Sy knew he had little practice in sustaining his magic; he'd always been able to replenish his energy with the tonic his teacher had shown him how to make. But there had been no time to make more before leaving. Once they were safe on the shores of Weshen City, he would fill a sack with enough lemondrines for the journey.

But for now, all he could do was wait until his body had rested sufficiently.

"There is wood to use," he answered. "This boat has a false bottom. Resh was supposed to pack it with weapons and food."

"And you trusted him?" Her laughter was more cutting than the winds of the NeverCross Mountains, but he supposed his family deserved it.

"I did, and I do. Reshra may be a lot of things, but my brother would never see me die."

With that, Sy bent and fumbled for the hidden latch. Finding it, he raised an uneven rectangle of the boat's bottom. Beneath it was an assortment of knives, a wrapped portion of dried meat, a sack of dried beans in a shallow cooking pot, and a disassembled bow sword. Sy noticed a sheaf of papers and smiled as he lifted a corner: Resh had even stolen and packed the map to find the Wesh.

His heart sang with the knowledge of what he could now do, once they survived the MagiSea. Surely such a deed could turn this curse of banishment into a blessing for his people.

Not ready to ask Corentine to share this new burden, though, he shoved the papers beneath the crude medical kit and a thick blanket, pushing everything back into the compartment.

Sy began to break apart the false covering, finding it to be more than enough source material for an oar. Corentine watched him without comment, but her gaze had grown shrewd again, and she sat straighter. Not for the first time, he wondered if she would actually follow him once they were on the mainland.

"We can visit Weshen City for heavy winter clothing before entering the mountains," he said, sorting through the knives.

"My family is going to Rurok, Maren and the twins. She said I must meet them there," Corentine answered, and Sy clenched his jaw. That was the worst plan he'd ever heard. He noted the square of her shoulders. She would think nothing of trying to follow them.

"Rurok is suicide!" Sy tried to keep his voice steady, but his stomach rebelled at the thought of the young twins adrift on the Hungry River, food for the sharp-toothed mouths of Sulit witches, or worse.

Corentine fixed him in a stare that sucked him dry. "Your *mother* is taking my brother and sister to Rurok. I am to meet them there," she said again, emphasizing each word carefully.

His mouth opened, then snapped shut. "My mother," he whispered. Forbidden words, for a son of Weshen. How did she know this? Why would she tell him now?

Corentine's laugh was bitter. "Yes, the woman who raised *me* after my mother threw her life away is the same woman who raised *you* until your life was stolen. Her name is Maren."

Sy blinked out at the broken-mirror surface of the MagiSea, everything else forgotten. He turned the name over in his mind, but he had no memory, no emotion tied to its soft syllables. The elders had done their only allowed spell with the perfection of practice.

"Why is she leaving the island?" he finally managed.

"Because of your father. Ashemon came to her years ago to make a child of magical blood. She loved a man named Neshra, and still your father asked this of her. He *knew*, Sy. He wanted to continue the bloodlines. He even promised her you would never be banished." A derisive snort told what she thought of his father's promises.

Sy glanced up, grateful to find she was no longer watching him with that piercing stare. His world was crumbling, and for the first time since the banishment had begun, he felt truly abandoned by his people. His father's words, and Tag's, as he left.

All for nothing. For show.

The General could have stopped the banishment. Had *promised* to. Why would he make such a child - such a promise - if he didn't intend to keep either one?

Sy gripped his temples and stared into the boat's false bottom. He was being punished, he knew now. Not cast aside, but punished for not showing his magic to Ashemon, for not hiding it from Resh. For not producing a Weshen son.

And then he realized the piece he had missed. Shame broke into shards of fury. Their double banishment in a single boat was unheard of. What his father obviously hoped might happen between them, alone in this narrow boat…Sy glanced up quickly at Corentine, certain that guilt lined his face. Certain she would see it and assume he had held a role in placing their fates here, adrift together on the MagiSea.

Corentine's eyes rested on the water, though, and several minutes passed in silence. Sy wondered what he should say, but words were scarcer than land. Finally, Corentine began rummaging in her sack. She pulled out a rolled paper, spreading it on her knees.

"So will you help me navigate to Rurok, or should I swim for it?" she asked, and he let out a deep breath he hadn't even realized he'd been holding. She didn't suspect, and he'd give her no reason to. She lifted her eyes to meet his and pointed at the map, silently repeating the question.

He adjusted his cramped position, stretching his legs carefully. The boat dipped too close to the water, and he watched a few drops slide down the wood. "I can't go to Rurok, Corentine. Weshen men are forbidden there. We have been for generations - even before the Sacrifice."

Corentine studied him as though she didn't believe it. And he didn't blame her - it wasn't a thing people even spoke of anymore. Few of the Weshen even traveled far outside of their own land now. The ones who did were only allowed to hunt MagiCreatures in the open southern plains of Riata, then trade in EvenFall and dart back across the mountains before the king's men scented them.

"But the women? Children?" she asked.

Sy shrugged. "As far as I know, they aren't forbidden. But I'd be killed on sight if the rumors are true."

"What's *your* plan, then?" she asked, bending to study the paper in her lap. Her emphasis gave Sy the distinct feeling she still intended to head to Rurok once they hit land. He leaned forward enough to see that what she held was a crudely-drawn map. She didn't hide it from him, but she didn't offer him a better look, either.

He pretended to study it for a moment. What would entice her to give up her fool plan of Rurok? Even if this Maren woman were able to reach the city without drowning, the witches were just as likely to drain their blood for spells as anything else. Of course, he wouldn't be telling Corentine this bit. She'd be in the water and swimming in a second.

"I'm going to rescue a group of Weshen slaves," he said, the specifics of a plan crystallizing in his brain. It wasn't what Ashemon had instructed, but Sy was growing less concerned with his father's wants. Even betrayed and banished, Sy would work for the return of his people's magic and love and land. But he would do it his way, and not his father's.

"They're being transported from MatinsHold to EvenFall, and I think I could free them and send them through the passage to Weshen City. Then I could go to StarsHelm Palace, kill the Restless King, and take back everything we used to have."

He imagined returning to the city and increasing their numbers not with a single infant, but with a dozen Wesh. Even Corentine should be interested in a plan like this.

"You will die doing it," she said. But she was studying him wide-eyed now, the map forgotten.

He nodded, holding her eyes, marveling at their mix of shimmering brown and bronze. "But I will also die not doing it. Better to die fighting for what should be ours."

Corentine considered him for a long moment, then rolled the map tightly and shoved it in her sack. "I thought all the Weshen captives would be dead by now."

Sy shook his head. "There are many of our people still stranded in Riata. They couldn't return to Weshen City for the Sacrifice, or refused to. These slaves are their descendants. Half-bloods. Now they're mixed with non-magical Riatan families in a foolish attempt to draw the Weshen magic into their bloodlines."

"They're forced to breed?" she asked, her eyes flashing.

"And more, I'm sure." He could plainly see the horror and bitter realization spilling onto her face.

Setting her mouth in a firm line, she seemed to make a decision. She bent and drew out a water skin, tossing it to him without a word. He unscrewed the lid, and the heady smell of lemondrine made his muscles tremble in anticipation. His eyes rolled back as he drank deeply, though not nearly as much as he wanted.

"Where did you get this?" he asked, handing the skin back to her reluctantly. Someone on the island knew how to make the tonic. Maren, perhaps?

She ignored his question and gazed into the horizon for a long moment, lost in thought or a memory.

"I've dreamed idly of becoming a Weshen warrior for so many years," she whispered to the wind. "Now it seems the impossible is suddenly here, and I want a chance." She turned her head and fixed her eyes on him.

"I want my life and my family's name to mean something again."

He struggled to find the words that would embrace her, keep her from thinking she was worth so little.

"I will travel with you to StarsHelm, Syashin, First Son of Weshen," she continued, and he winced at the formal way she addressed him. "Together we can rescue these slaves and slay the man who destroyed my family and reduced our people to game-players and bounty hunters."

"And your brother and sister?" he asked, although his chest was swelling with how quickly she had chosen *him*, chosen *his* quest and made it hers as well.

"They'll wait for me to find them, and Maren will keep them safe. I trust her with everything."

Coren wished she were as certain as her words sounded on the open air. Yes, the Restless King should die for what he'd done to the Weshen and all of Riata, and certainly no-one should ever be forced into slavery.

But if the twins died because she neglected to find and save them, then Zorander Graeme would have still won.

She closed her eyes against the hot sun, pulling the shawl back over her face. All her life she'd wished to travel beyond the island. But for a brief moment, her mind filled with regret and desire for a quiet, safe life of hunting groundbirds and growing old with Maren. But safety was no longer an option for her, if it ever had been.

Why had her family suffered so much more than any other? Was it punishment for their ambition, as Reshra had insinuated? Tendrils of unease began to wind around her heart. She knew Sorenta had lived in fear of the magic - her mother had grown up knowing its power to destroy, as it had consumed every good thing in her life.

Coren knew she might slip down the same road of shadow, not quite dark, but not quite light either.

"The shifter magic is part of you, Corentine, even if you know nothing of it," Sy said, and she shoved the shawl away, snapping her eyes to his. He read her thoughts too closely. "You might as well start to learn how to control it, so you can help us."

And not hurt us further, she added to herself, guessing the unspoken end of his sentence.

Regardless, Coren knew he was right. If she had known how to control her magic, perhaps they would never have been found out. So she pushed away the dark thoughts of her mother and watched intently as Sy finished using the slim slats of wood to form an oar. Then she took it from him, exchanging it for the water skin again. She examined the oar from each angle while he drained the last of the tonic.

"It looks carved this way. From a whole piece of wood," she marveled, angling it against the sunlight. Shifter power, even in its weakened form, was impressive. "No wonder the king wanted Weshen people on his side."

"That's only the beginning of our powers," Sy murmured, his eyes drifting closed as he leaned back into the *Alimente*'s prow. "One day, we'll have it all again, and then we'll take back our land. We'll be a free people again."

She handed the shawl to him so he could cover himself, and she began to row, testing the oar against the gentle current that marked the direction of the Hungry River.

As the water parted around the oar, she watched how she could control its motion and the resulting ripples. Sitting taller in the boat, she began to fortify the decision in her mind, forming her foundation of strength with promises to herself.

She would meet Sy's teacher, and she would learn power and control over her magic.

She would travel to Riata, help rescue the slaves, then find the Restless King, who had ripped her family apart.

She would be the wind and the storm. She would be the shadow that snuffed the light from his patchwork kingdom.

If Zorander Graeme were restless, Corentine Ashaden would be ruthless.

The sun grew hot in the sky, and she knew they were both burning. She also felt the beginnings of real thirst, and she fantasized about the streams of the upper Weshen plains, where the water was somehow always cold. Sy stretched and sat up, reaching for the oar. She relinquished it gratefully, rubbing at her shoulder.

"I haven't seen land in hours," she complained as she draped the shawl over her face again. His cheeks were red, and his forehead gleamed with sweat. They both needed a bath.

"Not seeing land is a good thing," Sy reassured her. "If we get close enough to *see* Umbren, it'll be too late. We'll be caught in the current and lost to the Hungry River."

"And NewMoon Falls? How will we avoid those?" she pressed, suddenly needing more information. The heat and open water were making her itchy, and her nerves felt stretched like a hide on a rack.

But Sy shrugged, apparently not sharing her anxiety. "It's not the falls we need to worry about. It's the rocks. But we should be able to stay far enough from them to be safe."

As he rowed, he directed her while she started to make more of the lemondrine tonic. It wasn't much of a recipe, although here on the water it would take time they may not have. Lemondrines Maren had packed from the island trees. Heat from the sun to draw the oil from the peel. Water and salt from the MagiSea to mix.

As she carved the peel into slender sections, Coren wondered how they would continue to make the tonic, once they were too far from the island trees and the sea. But too many other questions swirled in her brain, which pulsed with heat. She put her effort into surviving the despair of the endless water instead.

The afternoon slid into evening, and although this brought relief from the sun, Coren recognized the change in the water. From the south it came at them like a crawling, living thing, sucking at the bottom of the boat and pulling them relentlessly toward the Hungry River.

Sy grunted through the effort, paddling hard to correct the current. Too often, he was forced to flip the oar to Coren and rub the cramps from his muscles. The sun sunk to the edge of the Sulit forest before them, its orange-red rays concentrated in a fierce line above the treetops.

"That old woman is a fool to leave the island," Sy grunted as he heaved the oar to her. "How could she make it past this?"

Coren said nothing. In her mind, no future existed except one where she would see her family again. Maren wouldn't risk their lives without good reason. She dug in harder against the current, setting her teeth against the burn of her muscles and the sting of sweat on her raw palms.

Suddenly her grip on the oar faltered, and she felt the slick wood slip from her fingers as though the water had tugged back.

"Sy!" she gasped out. He lunged forward, grabbing at the oar, nearly tipping the boat, but they were both too late. The narrow tool slipped into the water, bobbing just out of reach. Coren cursed violently and wiped at the sweat on her face.

"I'm sorry-" she started, but just then a wrinkle in the water made her pause. She squinted into the depths but could make out nothing clearly. The shadows were knitting too quickly into the blanket of night.

"It's okay, I'll just jump in and get it," Sy answered, eying the dark water. He didn't want to get in, though. It wouldn't be a simple swim. The bow of the boat had begun to twist and drift, exactly in the direction he knew they didn't want to go. He heard Corentine begin to protest, but he was already sliding into the water.

They needed that oar to make it to safety, and with her inexperience, she'd likely tip the boat. Then they'd both be lost.

A few short strokes brought him to the oar, and he threw it back to Corentine. She clutched it to her chest, and he grinned even though it brought a scowl to her face. He kicked out hard toward the boat, but the current sucked at his legs like thick mud. Shaking the spray from his face, he noticed that the *Alimente* seemed farther than it should be, farther even than when he had started back. He stroked out again, but each time, any progress was eaten by the sideways movement of the boat, as though an invisible wall kept them apart.

"Turn the boat north," he called, glancing over his shoulder. The woods of Umbren loomed in the distance, an indistinct black mass. "It's getting too close to the river's mouth."

"But you're not close enough!" She reached the oar out over the water like a lifeline. It was nowhere near long enough. He swore in his head, knowing she was right.

"Just row north!" He pushed as hard as he could against the current and gained a few inches, but his energy was nearly spent.

This was magic, he knew. Whether it was Sulit or Umbren didn't matter. Something wanted him in that water.

Forcing away the first tendril of panic, Sy kicked again solidly. Only his brutal training as a son of Weshen allowed him to fight through the sensation of the current wrapping around his legs.

Even so, unwelcome images flashed through his mind: fingers reaching up from the deep dark to pull him under. The great mouth of the river, opening wide to swallow him whole.

Whispers of a breeze began to swirl around him, and he thought he heard the cackles of witches on the air. Salt began to burn in his eyes from the fruitless splashing.

"Back to your forest graves, witches. You will not have me tonight," he whispered fiercely, his muscles trembling as he shut his eyes against the taunting distance between him and the boat. "Corentine, direct me with your voice!"

"Straight forward," she called back, and he kicked. "A little left!" And he kicked, filling his mind with her voice and memories of her smiling at him in the sun. Of her sleeping peacefully in his bed.

"Almost there!"

His fingers brushed the bark, and he lunged upward, gripping the sides of the boat and breathing much too heavily for the brief distance he'd just swum.

But even his gasps weren't enough to erase the laughter dancing on the sweet breeze now.

"Do you hear that?" he managed to gasp as he hauled himself into the boat, collapsing in a soaked heap at her feet.

Corentine cocked her head, listening to the night air. She shrugged.

"Just row," he whispered hoarsely. "We're way too close to the Hungry River."

The heart was beating too fast. The dark waters of the MagiSea had felt the boy, and frothed the mouth of the Hungry River, sucking at his flesh.

The heart wanted that boy. His body was strong. Smooth and young. His Weshen fingers held the beautiful magic the heart had dreamed of for so long. It beat frantically against the crystal box, the squish of soft flesh waking the witch who had been sleeping nearby. She pushed the tangle of mud-brown hair and green-black vines from her face. An insect squirmed at being exposed, rooting back toward her scalp.

"Patience, my love," the witch cooed, murmuring an ancient incantation that gradually calmed the beating heart. "We will have all that you want, and very soon." She bent her head closer to the box then, listening, interpreting the beats.

She nodded, a tendril of vine tapping the ground as she moved. "Yes, the boy is strong and handsome. I have seen him in my dreams. But my heart, other choices are coming to us. Other young, fresh bodies."

The heart had slowed again to the steady beat it had maintained for so many, many years. The beat spoke of patience, endurance, and knowing.

The witch stroked a dirt-blackened nail across the top of the box, smiling. "Yes, there are many boats on the water tonight."

17

Coren slumped back in the hull of the boat, her salt-sore eyes closing in relief. The night had been a dark, shadowy blur of aching muscles and whispered curses as they pushed with everything they had to outrun the greedy currents of the Hungry River.

But now, the first slivers of a pale morning sun slit open the darkness above them, and their boat drifted easily north again, away from Umbren and toward the Sulit coast and NewMoon Falls. The falls would be another type of trial, but after a full night on the water, she was more confident now, and a spark of hope had begun to grow where before there had been only despair.

They were going to make it. Actually make it. She smiled softly to herself.

A scuffing noise caught her attention, and when she peeled open an eye, she caught Sy watching her.

The smile faded, but she held his gaze for a spare second, nodded that she was okay, then blinked away.

His expression was too intense, as though he wanted to ask her questions far deeper than the water around them. That, she couldn't do. Not today, and not for many days after today.

Sorrow still rippled beneath the surface of her exhaustion, pulling like the currents below the *Alimente*, threatening to suck her under to drown in the depths of loss.

Deliberately, she turned her gaze to the last few stars and the ghost of a moon that lingered in the sky. *We made it*, she repeated stubbornly to the darkness lapping at her mind. So would Maren and the twins.

"I've spent my whole life staring at the stars, dreaming of the world beyond the island," she murmured a few minutes later, when she could trust her voice to be steady. "But I never really believed I'd see them from a different place."

Sy nodded, his face turned to the lightening horizon. He dipped the oar in the water, alternating sides as he worked to keep them parallel to the rising sun. "They will always be the same stars, but now they will always seem different," he answered. She heard the wistfulness in his voice.

What would he miss, in his banishment?

Did he hope to see his family again too? Would Reshra's mistakes be forgiven, and his father's stubbornness overlooked? She guessed he would be loyal to them, but she hesitated to make him choose, and to hear his choice.

"We should eat now," Sy said, beginning to shift the salt from a skin of sea water. Coren nodded and unwrapped the dried meat Reshra had packed in the boat's secret compartment. Listening to the dawngulls overhead, they renewed their strength as the sun rose.

Despite rowing north, they had also continued to drift west, and suddenly the Sulit coast seemed to swing out into the MagiSea to meet them, its shoreline like the curve of a scythe against their progress. Sy pushed them harder toward the center of the MagiSea, his muscles flexing and stretching beneath his thin shirt.

"That's where I hope your friend makes it with your brother and sister," he said, jerking his chin to the northern side of the peninsula they were passing, where black-barked trees arced over a tapering river, trailing corkscrew branches of whisper-pink leaves.

Coren noticed he hadn't claimed Maren as his mother, but the motion of the trees seemed to draw her into herself, and she simply forgot what she'd noticed.

"There?" she whispered, her gaze intent on how the slender, ebony branches seemed to reach toward them, beckoning them gently with a flutter of sheer rose.

"That should be the Shedreck River," he answered, the same sense of wonder evident in his voice also. The oar slid to the bottom of the boat as they both stared, mesmerized, into the hazy maw of the smaller Sulit river. "It leads to the heart of Sulit."

"The heart," Coren repeated, leaning over the edge of the boat to see it better. Something gray-blue and smoky danced and swirled at the edge of the shore, and a charming laugh floated on the breeze. The ends of Coren's hair trailed in the unstirring water as she bent even lower and the unguided boat drifted west, closer and closer to the river.

"The heart," she whispered once more.

"Yes, that's it," SmokeFist cooed from her perch in the highest tree, just above the opening to Shedreck River. Her laughter was a light caress on the wind, her breath stirring the sand on the beach below her into a swirl of golden beckoning. "Come into our home, daughter of Weshen. You are welcome here."

The girl was bent nearly to the water now, her brown and bronze hair loosened from its braid, floating on the surface of the MagiSea. Her amber eyes fixed on the mouth of the Shedreck, and SmokeFist reveled in the glorious sensation of the magic in the water meeting the magic in the girl.

"Yes," she repeated, excitement leading to impatience. As soon as the girl's body hit the water, the magic would do the rest.

Growing greedy, the witch twined her power like a twisted black branch across the breeze, hoping to reel her target in just a few more inches.

Just a few more…

Sy registered the thickening purpose in the air, and it activated his trained instincts, snapping him back into his own mind just in time. He spat a curse, reaching to yank at Corentine's arms just as she began to tip head first into the glistening water. He heaved her back in the boat, and the craft rocked wildly as they tumbled together to the bottom of the boat, droplets of the sea shimmering like oil as they squirmed down the wood.

Corentine was limp in his arms, though her eyes were bright. Glassy and almost feverish, they flitted from side to side without seeing him, as though she were watching a dream with eyes open.

"Come on!" he yelled, his face too close to hers. She flopped against him, awake but lost. Her lips parted, whispering nonsense. And he knew, he knew. The Sulit witches were out there, waiting for them. Waiting for her.

"Coren," he begged, shaking her harder. "Don't go with them."

A roar began to register in his ears, and he realized they were even closer to NewMoon Falls than he had thought. Maybe if he could get them farther from Sulit…

He pushed Coren down into the hull of the boat, making certain none of her body was touching the water, and began to row furiously.

Coren opened her eyes, seeing nothing but blue sky. Her mouth was dry, so dry. She coughed and tried to shake her head free of the webby feeling left from a summer's afternoon nap.

Her body rocked left and right as her bed tumbled strangely beneath her. A face appeared above. "Kosh?" she murmured. No, not Kosh. Too old.

"Corentine?" a voice said. She knew that voice…how did she know that voice?

"Drink this," the voice said, and Coren found a skin placed to her lips. *Yes.* She was so thirsty. She scrunched her eyes against the sour, salty flavor, but her head was tilted back and the liquid poured down her throat anyways. Coughing again, she tried to spit it out, but a hand clamped over her mouth. "Swallow it!"

Gulping and spluttering, she swallowed what she could without choking, struggling to free herself from the rough hand over her face. Some of the haze retreated from her mind, and she began to remember.

Of course that voice didn't belong to Kosh.

Syashin.

Fingers forced her lips apart, and more of the salt and sour poured into her mouth. She gagged and bit down on one of the fingers, but the liquid slid down her throat anyways, burning all the way to her gut.

"Drink it!" he repeated, his arms holding her close to him. She felt the liquid settle in her stomach, sloshing and scraping at her insides. But it burned away the confusion too, and as she blinked again and again, the world came back to her. She relaxed against Sy's grip, and he removed his hand, his fingers ending in a sort of caress along her jaw.

"I thought you were lost to the witches," he breathed.

She sat up slowly and scooted around to face him. The boat bounced over a wave, and her stomach churned, forcing her over the edge. Sy lunged for her, his arms closing around her waist as she retched into the sea. She allowed him to pull her back, slumping against the side of the boat.

She was so spent she couldn't even care that his arms still rested at her hips.

"Better?" he said, his voice wary.

She nodded. "I'm sorry," she said, her voice rasping against the rawness of her throat.

They both sat up, and he retreated to the bow of the *Alimente*, eying her. "For a second there, I thought you were going to start swimming for shore."

Coren tried to smile, but she was starting to remember just how close she'd been to doing exactly that. "*That* was Sulit magic?"

Sy nodded. "I've been trained to resist it. Or at least recognize it."

"How?"

He gazed out over the water several seconds before glancing back to her. "There are captives…witches. In Weshen City. Once hunters have reached Paladin status, they can train with the Sulit."

"Prisoners?" Coren repeated, the nausea threatening to return.

"Sulit magic isn't like Weshen magic," he answered. "The Weshen have always had to protect themselves. Now more than ever."

She didn't answer, knowing he was right. And just now, she was intensely glad he had been trained to recognize and resist the witches. But what price had the Weshen paid for such training? What unforgivable things had been done?

"We're very close to the falls," Sy said a few moments later, and Coren realized she'd been hearing the roar of water on rocks for a while now. "We need to go northeast, and now that the sun is up, we'll be looking directly into its glare. It'll be hard to see the rocks around the falls," he continued. "But we have to row back around the top of Weshen Isle to get to the city."

He handed her the oar and Coren nodded grimly, steering the boat while he stretched his arms and drank deeply once more. "There," he said, pointing ahead as he reached for the oar again.

First, all she could see was white mist. Then it separated into the spray and foam of water crashing down from unseen heights. The rocks loomed next, black and slimed with the remains of the sea.

Coren quickly learned that the larger, vertical shafts of stone, although terrifying, were less treacherous than those half-hidden beneath the churning water. These appeared from almost nowhere, smacking and scraping the fibers from the bottom of their boat.

"Watch me, not the water!" Sy called back to her, and she fought to obey, though her eyes itched to search instead for the rocks waiting to break them open.

Several times, Sy chucked the oar at her without warning as he bent double to shift the wood back into place, plugging a crack in the bark. When that happened, she struggled to push them from the path of each rock, sometimes the width of the oar blade being the only thing between the *Alimente* and its destruction.

The look on Sy's face alternated between desperation and determination, and Coren's gut twisted with worry and helplessness. But what could she do besides follow his direction? This was so far removed from anything she knew. A few times she tried to shift away water that splashed into the boat, but it returned almost immediately. The spray and the sun glinting off the water nearly blinded them.

Finally the boat swung free of the falls' grasp, and as they entered the calmer water near the Weshen shoreline, Coren felt a smile of relief break across her salt-cracked lips, and a laugh bubbled up from her throat. She could see the NeverCross Mountains clearly for the first time in her life, jagged and emerald and onyx, and impossibly high before them.

They drifted easily now, parallel to the shore, and Coren closed her eyes, whispering a prayer of thanks to the Mirror Magi.

Somehow, for reasons yet to be disclosed, their gods had saved them from banishment. She knew there would be payment due for such a favor, but for now, she was simply grateful to be alive.

18

Sy watched her as she mumbled what sounded like a prayer, her face turned up to the brilliant sky. He knew he shouldn't be caught staring, but she was so beautiful, even disheveled and exhausted from their journey. Perhaps because of that.

Corentine twisted back to watch the falls retreating into mist again. He could barely glimpse a glint of metal at the top of the falls, on the Riatan side, so he pointed to it when she glanced back to him. "The Restless King has been trying to build a bridge across the ridge of the falls for nearly a year. Rumors are that he means to conquer Sulit next."

"Conquer Sulit!" Corentine said, her eyes widening in shock. She lowered her voice. "No-one could conquer Sulit. Right?"

Sy shrugged and adjusted their course slightly. Anyone could conquer anyone, he guessed. Some just took longer.

"Rurok is there, at the western edge of the falls." He gestured toward a black mass of what could be towers, rising above the splash and steam of the falls and the fog of the forest. "If he makes it across the falls, he could attack the capital city."

"Maybe that would be for the better," she mused. "Maybe the witches would be the ones to finally beat him, and we could all be free."

Sy snorted, pushing the boat around a slight curve that blocked Rurok from their view. "Witches don't deal in freedom."

"I've never met one," Corentine said, and he heard the slight disbelief in her voice.

He guessed she was thinking of her family, apparently headed to Sulit right now. Swiveling back to look directly at her, he said, "I truly hope Maren knows what she's doing taking your family there. But all I've seen of witches is destruction."

"Maybe because all you've seen are prisoners," she said, turning her attention to the cliffs above them. He sighed and focused on watching the shore. Eventually the sound of the falls grew too distant to distinguish from any other sound on the water, and Sy knew they were approaching the beaches that surrounded Weshen City.

Corentine stretched her legs. "Most of the men will be on Weshen Isle, right? What can we expect when we land?"

"I have a spot in mind," Sy said, handing her the oar and rolling his shoulders to ease their cramped fatigue. "It's close enough that we won't need to walk far, but we can still hide the boat."

"Won't the men see us and stop us?" Corentine asked again.

"They'll never see us with me leading," Sy said as he grinned at her. She didn't smile back, and he resisted the urge to sigh again. He glanced back to the shore, where the beach was gradually widening from a strip of sharp pebbles to a walkable swathe of sand and scrubby grasses. "The only men in Weshen City right now are a few guards who lost on out on summer duty, the old teachers, and the boys too young for the games."

"Surely they all know the difference between a man and a woman, though," Corentine said, gesturing to herself. His grin widened, but he bit it back as her face flushed and she glared at him. Gods, but she was prickly about her looks. "I just mean that even if they don't know we're banished, seeing a woman in their city would be a problem." Her voice was not hiding her annoyance, although she had pushed back the glare to a mere grim stare.

"Which is why we'll be careful to stay out of sight." Sy shrugged. He knew every door and secret passage in Weshen. "But we do have to stop in the city to gather what we'll need for the mountains. It's always cold that high up."

He pushed up and leaned forward, reaching for the oar. His fingers brushed hers in the exchange, his eyes snagging on her gaze. Was there something new in the curve of her lips just then? His chest tightened, but she blinked away quickly, fixing her amber eyes on the shore instead.

To the south, Weshen Isle was a narrow line on the horizon, nearly a day's journey. In order to avoid the

Hungry River and NewMoon Falls, they had traveled a wide half-circle against the tides and currents, effectively almost circling the island.

"There!" he said a few minutes later, pointing at a tight inlet where the rocks had created something more like a harbor. Navigating the constricted opening would be easier with a bit of magic, though. "Pull at the water to help me," he called back to her as he knelt up in the boat to get a better angle to steer. "Move it in a channel!"

"What?" she asked, her voice laced with irritation.

"Imagine the water under the boat and shift it away like you're digging a channel!" he said. He knew she must be trying, because the tiny craft swayed and bucked as the water dipped and rose beneath it. Sy's balance faltered, and he fell hard against the side of the boat, but he was laughing as he righted himself.

"You need practice!" he teased as he knelt again.

"Well, I'm getting it now!" she retorted, squinting her eyes nearly shut against the light. The boat jerked down as though falling into a crevice, and Sy shouted, "Easy!"

Coren's face heated at his command, but she pushed aside her embarrassment and focused instead on the shore, which was approaching too quickly for her taste. Feeling self-conscious, she tried moving her arms in wide, gentle sweeping motions, as if she were swimming. She imagined pushing the water from her path. And to her surprise, the boat straightened, righted, and its course smoothed. A wide grin pushed onto her face.

She was using *magic*. And she was *helping*.

The crunch of sand on the bottom of the boat broke her concentration, and as the boat beached itself neatly, the water rushed back at them from both sides, its spray reaching several feet above their heads before it crashed down, drenching them.

She spluttered and scrubbed the salt from her eyes, but she could hear Sy laughing. He reached for her hand and she let him. Together they stumbled onto the beach, collapsing onto their knees in relief and exhaustion.

"You're incredible," he whispered, rolling to his back.

Coren slid her eyes to him, but he wasn't watching her. His arm was thrown over his face to block the sun, and his chest was heaving with fatigue.

He was so different from what she had expected. A First Son, a noble of Weshen. A lethal, highly-trained Paladin. All of this should have created someone as arrogant and entitled as Reshra seemed to be, yet Sy was nothing like his brother.

In a different Weshen, in a different time, Coren thought fleetingly, she might have allowed herself interest in such a boy.

Then again, Sorenta's threat that a boy would cause her to lose everything seemed a bit like old news. Sy and his brother had both already earned their parts in that prediction.

Sy was aware that she studied him, but he resisted meeting her eyes. That comment had slipped out against his better judgment. It was true - she *was* incredible, and so much more than a girl he had been commanded to hunt. But because she was more, she must also be less.

They both rested in the sand a spare few minutes, then Corentine pushed upright, her movements stiff. Her dress was ruined, ripped where he had stolen the fabric for the sail, and crusted with salt and sea.

"We need food," she said, kneeling beside the boat. He saw her begin to concentrate on shifting the water from the bottom of the boat. Their bags were soaked through: they'd be lucky if the food was even edible.

"You're doing well. It's faster to just make a hole in the wood, though," Sy said, coming up close beside her. She flushed and sat back, looking embarrassed. "No, Coren, it's okay. It takes a while for the magic to make sense - to be useful," Sy added. She really had done a fantastic job with their landing. Pure instinct and power.

Damren would be thrilled to gain her as a student.

He motioned to the bottom of the boat, where he shifted the wood, forming a narrow slit in the boat's structure which allowed the water to drain. Together they hauled the boat completely onto the sand.

"Still, I should have thought of that," she muttered as she brushed the sand from her hands.

"Can you *close* the hole?" he asked, wondering if her instincts would also lead her to the mirrored abilities.

Corentine stared intently at the hole in the wood, her brow wrinkling in concentration. Sy saw her fingers moving too, as though to knit the sources back together.

But nothing happened. She scowled at the hole, and Sy held back a smile.

"It's just your lack of training," he reassured her. "The easiest skill to learn is disintegration. Fusion is more complex, like the difference between sorting beach pebbles and weaving fabric. It won't take you long to learn what little I know," he added, wishing he could give her more.

"How long did it take you?" she asked, wringing water from the blanket and dumping the contents of her sack on the beach.

"I've been sneaking away to study with Damren once a season for two years now. But only for a day or two at a time. More and I'd be missed. Someone would have tracked me."

"Do you think Reshra ever tracked you?"

He considered. "I don't think so, or he would have said something."

Coren turned her attention back to the waterlogged supplies, wary of Sy's glances, which she seemed to find each time she looked in his direction. Although she'd grown more comfortable with him, she didn't want to encourage any interest.

He may be handsome, but she wouldn't disregard Sorenta's fears surrounding the hunts, and Maren's warnings concerning children. Coren had lost home and family, but gained power, and she wasn't about to jeopardize any advantage she had for survival in this new world.

They worked to spread their soaked belongings along the strip of beach grass. The matches had remained intact in their wax-sealed box, at least, allowing a hot meal of boiled beans and jerky. "What next?" she asked.

"We need to sneak into Weshen City for supplies. Then we climb," he answered, pointing at the cliffs which towered above them, just beyond the narrow strip of beach. She stared up at them, unable to even see the tops of the black cliffs.

"How many men will be in the city?"

"A few dozen. But it's much different without my father to keep them in order. Usually they're drunk by nightfall."

"Drunken men are more dangerous."

"Possibly. But they're slower," he grinned.

"And Rurok? Is it truly impossible?" she asked, a swell of emotion choking her words. She missed Penna and Kosh s much.

Sy's grin faltered. "Coren," he began, his voice sinking into regret.

"I know…I know I promised to stay with you, but my family…" She was grateful to him for keeping her safe, but how could she just abandon Maren and the twins?

He glanced up at the cliffs, then across the water toward Rurok, as though measuring. His shoulders slumped. "I don't know. I've never been there. Just…please come with me to meet Damren. Let her teach you how to control your magic. Then perhaps…we can…"

Coren found herself nodding, but she felt like a coward. If only she could know they were safe. She rose and strode toward the sea to rinse her bowl, blinking back the tears that had begun to pool in her eyes. She plucked some mostly-dry clothing from the sand and scanned for a concealed place to change.

Hidden behind a grove of young lemondrine trees, she stripped the ruined blue dress from her tired body. The comfort of loose hunting pants and a tunic with good movement in the arms soothed her, and she coiled her whip around her middle, just beneath the tunic.

Armed and covered, she felt better, more herself. Just as she bent to gather her ruined dress, a breeze began to swirl the fallen leaves at her feet. Bits of crumpled leaf caught at her ankles as they hovered, then settled back on the ground. Coren folded the dress and turned, but a wide, green leaf drifted up to cover her eyes, and when she plucked it away, the flesh of it withered and turned to dust in her hand, leaving only the lacy structure of its veins.

Coren noticed the same hypnotic pull of magic she had felt near the shores of Sulit as she stared at the leaf's exposed innards. There was something there, but her brain couldn't quite make sense of it.

"Sy?" she called, walking toward him. The leaf warmed in her hand, though, and she dropped it on the ground. It fell to the sand, too heavy in its quick descent. Coren stared at the leaf, her eyes widening as some of the veins began to glow like iron in a forge.

Then she slumped to her knees in the sand, realizing what the leaf was: a message from Maren. The words were plain now, written in tiny, looping letters formed from the red veins of the disintegrated leaf.

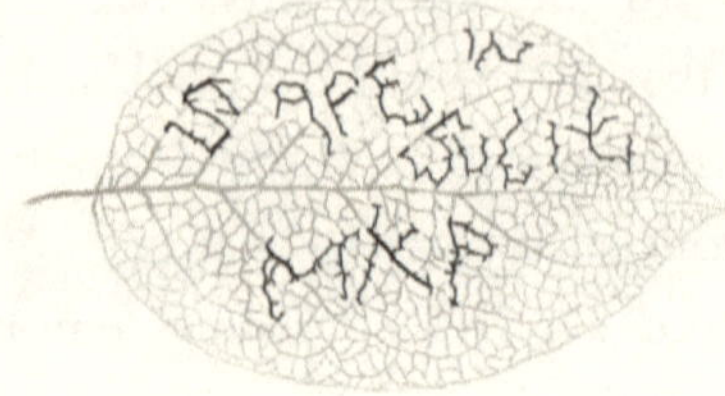

"Sy!" she called again, her voice more urgent. But when she bent to pick up the leaf, it crumbled into the sand, leaving nothing at all as evidence of what she'd seen.

"I'm by the boat!" Sy called. She saw his arm waving as he tugged a shirt over his head.

How would she explain this to him? Would he even believe it? Coren remembered how the Sulit magic had wrapped itself around her, nearly pulling her into the depths of the MagiSea. No, she decided. Sy wouldn't trust this message. He didn't know Maren like she did. He would think it was a trick, pulling her to Rurok instead of the mountains.

Coren gazed into the distance where she knew Rurok lay, too far to see. For a moment, the air felt like fingers on her face and an embrace around her shoulders, and somehow she knew her family truly was safe. As Maren had said, the Sulit witches had been their friends once.

She would trust her family to wait for her. She would trust in their safety, or she would learn enough magic to bury the witches alive.

"I will come for you," she whispered to the breeze. "But I have things to do first."

Swiping at her cheeks one last time, she tied her hair back in a loose pile at the nape of her neck and hurried back to the beach. Sy had left their bags empty, packing their belongings instead into the bottom of the boat. She helped him haul it beneath the lemondrine trees, angled to blend into the trunks.

"It's fine if you stay here," Sy said as she rubbed at a knot between her shoulders. "You could rest. I won't be gone long."

"No, I want to see the city." She picked up her pack. Looking inside, she frowned. It was *too* empty. She bent to rummage in the boat, choosing a light wrap and a few knives.

"I know I can get in and out quickly, but it isn't that safe," he said, fidgeting with the zipper on his bag. "If the men see you…"

"They won't see me. You're confident in your abilities to keep hidden, and I'm confident in mine. I want to see the city," she repeated. No longer trapped on Weshen Isle, she meant to see and learn everything she'd spent a lifetime missing.

He didn't argue further, and that pleased her. She shaded her eyes against the sun, hiding her smile.

They walked in the wake of the tide, letting the water erase their footprints. The sun had begun to slant behind them, disappearing into the western horizon.

"Entering the city at night will be best," he said as they picked their way through a group of tall rocks. She began to smell smoke and something dirtier. Soon a stark, densely-wrought iron gate loomed before them, bolted to a rough stone wall taller than two men together. At the top of it waited thousands of tarnished spikes, ancient but still sharp enough to slit the feet of anyone trying to scale the wall. A salt-bleached skull was impaled through the eye socket on one of the stakes.

Coren knew the mountains hadn't always been Weshen's main defense from Riata, but seeing such a cold welcome made her miss the openness of the women's island with a sudden, aching ferocity.

She hadn't realized she'd stopped frozen, staring at the wall, until a light touch on her arm broke into her thoughts.

19

Sy watched Corentine study the city wall before them, thinking how young and vulnerable she appeared.

Weshen Isle had been hard on her, but he knew the world beyond the island could be much harsher.

"Are you okay?" he asked, wincing at the words.

"Of course," she snapped, stepping forward and to the side, just beyond him.

She tugged a thin brown wrap from her pack and looped it up around her shoulders and head, hooding her face and camouflaging the curves of her body well enough. She was taller than many women, and slim. She might pass for a young boy in the semi-dark.

"Keep your hands down," Sy said, continuing his evaluation out loud. "They would give you away. But I'm sure we won't be seen," he added. He'd sneaked in and out of Weshen City dozens of time; he knew its every trick.

Corentine narrowed her eyes and arranged the fabric to cover her hands.

Sy slid up to the gate, watching for the pair of guards to pass each other. No-one came or went through this gate in the summer, so it wasn't heavily monitored. The guards arrived, paused to grumble a few words, then continued their rounds, each heading in different directions.

Once they had gone, Sy led her to a small door, inset in the stone wall just beyond the gate. He knew it would be locked, and he hoped Resh had remembered this. Sy set his pack on the ground and knelt beside it, feeling along the seams. He felt Corentine's eyes on him as he searched for what he hoped his brother had provided.

He grinned as his fingers brushed slim metal sewn into the side of the bag. Ripping the loose stitches, he held it up for her to see.

"See, Resh is on our side," he said, reminding himself as much as her, but her expression remained skeptical.

The key slipped into the door's lock and turned with a precise click he appreciated, and the two of them darted into the opening. Corentine crouched in the shadows of the nearby guard building as Sy locked the door behind him, then brushed their tracks from the mix of sand and dirt that made up the bare outer ring of Weshen City.

Several yards in, the dirt turned to grass, dotted with scrubby lemondrine trees and grazing animals. They navigated to the next circle of the city in quick bursts of running and hiding. Although they saw only a few men, and each was as drunk as Sy had predicted, he was still careful. It would only take one to recognize him or to rouse an alarm.

"This is the market circle," he whispered to Corentine as they ducked behind a long-empty fruit stall. Weshen City had a slightly abandoned air to it, with far too few people left to fill its many buildings, and here in the summer nights it was even more pronounced.

"It's lonely here in the summer," he whispered to Corentine as they waited, watching another guard walk through the market. "I stayed here two years ago when the others were on the island."

"Your father didn't force you to hunt the girls that year?"

Her voice was bitter, and he clenched his jaw. "I was injured from a real hunt. The boat journey would have disturbed my recovery. And it was Reshra's first summer," he added, reluctant to agree with her. "Father was less strict then."

"And who did you catch the following summer?" she asked.

"Last summer I was on a mission to EvenFall and didn't make it back in time for the boats." This was most of the truth.

She turned her head to regard him in the pale moonlight, the hood shadowing her face. "So you truly have only caught Lorenya?"

He startled, nearly giving away their position. How did she know that name? The women must gossip as much as the men. His mouth straightened to a grim line.

"I have often disappointed my father," he answered, answering her indirectly. The guard left the area, and it was safe to move. He beckoned, and they sneaked across the open space, keeping to the edge.

The market stalls were decrepit, falling to pieces where they lay. Sy bit back the disappointment that always accompanied his thoughts of what his people had once been. Now, their numbers were so few because of the Restless King and the Shift following his crowning.

Sy pushed open a wooden gate, and they passed into another layer of the city. "This is the commoner circle, where most of the men live, and next is the government circle."

"Where you live," she guessed. He nodded, uncomfortable with the distance she kept placing between them. Man, woman. Commoner, First Son. He hoped he could prove to her one day that they weren't as different from each other as she believed now.

There were more people outside in the commoner circle, though still fewer than a dozen, enjoying the summer night with fires in the common areas. The smell of an animal roasting on a spit made his mouth water.

"Ay, who's there?" someone called out just as they slipped behind a square stone home. Corentine bent double next to Sy, her body close enough for him to hear the thump of her heart.

"Only me, you old girl-dodger," another voice bellowed. Sy felt Coren relax behind him. The two men bantered for several minutes, then stepped inside the house. Light flooded the alley where they were hidden, and Sy glanced back to see Corentine's eyes widen in alarm.

He held up a finger for her to wait, and sure enough, the shadows of the men flashed over the lighted alley, then away. He knew they were likely sitting and drinking or playing cards at a table, and wouldn't notice anything outside the window. Sy pressed his body to the wall of the house and ducked past the window.

He turned and beckoned to Corentine, and they sprinted across the street and into another alley, weaving between the narrow homes and across abbreviated lawns. All of the homes had once been well-kept and filled with Weshen woman and children as well, according to his father's stories, but they were decidedly run-down and somber now.

They slipped easily past the wall into the government circle. It was silent here, and Corentine turned to him questioningly.

"Only the students will be here, with a few of the teachers. Very few guards this far in."

"Where are the students?" she whispered.

He shrugged. It had been many years, and he'd never stayed in the student quarters, only in his father's spacious home. "Hopefully in bed by now. This way." He navigated them around the dormitories and training hall, into the very heart of the city. With each circle, they had been slowly climbing in altitude, and he smiled at the thought of showing her Weshen City spread before them, dotted with small fires and smoking chimneys.

His father's home was also the main government building, and although it needed repairs like everything else, it was still the grandest of all the Weshen structures. Its bulk and towers were on the highest ground of the city, and spoke of a time when their people were wealthy, respected, and most importantly, a time when they had never needed to hide who they were.

"Our people's history," he murmured, gesturing around himself at the grounds, where grids of ancient, twisted lemondrine trees marked paths of now-overgrown paths of rosewhip vines, their spicy-sweet fragrance heavy in the night air. Corentine reached to grasp a blossom in her fingers, its width as much as her palm. A tendril of the vine stretched and curled around her wrist like a child's finger.

"I never imagined any of this," Corentine said. Her voice echoed in the night, and she shook her hand free of the vine and ducked behind him as the words echoed off the stone façade. As he scanned the area for signs they'd been heard, Sy tried to look at the building from her eyes, and shame crept across his shoulders. Of course, the men's way of life was greatly reduced from how it was before the Separation, but to Corentine, such a building must look as foreign as the NeverCross Mountains and the city of EvenFall would.

The Weshen women had the sea and the plains to run, and he had always envied them that. Life on the island had seemed simple and pleasant until he'd begun to pay attention. And now, watching her survey the vast city spread below them with a frown, he felt anything but proud.

Ashemon hadn't slept since he had sent Syashin on the *Alimente*. The entire night had been a blur of prayers to the Mirror Magi, and the lonely day had passed with more of the same. His heart ached with the heaviness of what he'd been forced to do. But as the second night approached, with the creeping dark came Tagsha.

"Ashemon, you know I'm with you in everything," the burly guard said, barging into Ashemon's tent. He set a tray of food and strong tea on the table and waited, shuffling his feet.

Ashemon barely looked at his friend, but he did rise from the floor where his personal altar was still open. He sat heavily on the bench, reaching for a mug.

"It had to be done, Tagsha. The people aren't ready to fight. Syashin's magic isn't enough for all of us." He knew most wouldn't question his actions, but Tagsha was different.

"But banishing your *own*?" Tagsha continued, his fist hitting the table harder than necessary.

"Syashin will survive."

"But will he ever trust you again?"

Ashemon glared at the guard. "That is not my first concern in this matter." He began to eat, stacking the meat and rich cheese between thick slices of bread. He had not eaten since watching his son's Last Meal, but he knew his strength would wane if he did not break his fast.

"Perhaps you should send Reshra to the city to wait for them. That will be the hardest part of the journey."

The General looked flatly at his oldest friend. "Each part of their journey will be hard. Reshra is not ready to understand the magic. He resists."

"He resists because you never told him of its existence! You never told any of us!" Tagsha exclaimed, the hurt evident in his voice. He turned his head away when Ashemon tried to look squarely at him.

"Weshen is not yet ready," Ashemon repeated. "I made Syashin on purpose - I prayed he would have magic. But he is one son among hundreds of Weshen sons. It is not enough for a revolution of our fates. The girl's family has strong magic, though. Their children, perhaps..." His voice faltered as he realized he'd never told this plan to Tagsha either.

"My General, you do not know your son at all if you think this banishment will force him to claim the girl. He will discover your plan and distance himself from her out of spite."

"I appreciate your ability to speak freely with me," Ashemon said, the growl in his voice speaking the opposite. "But again, you do not know everything. I have told Syashin that if he does not provide an heir this summer, his First Son rights will pass to Reshra." He pinned Tagsha in his gaze finally.

Tagsha glared. "That was not wise-"

Ashemon held up a hand. "So yes, I believe this banishment is the perfect solution. Syashin has come to care for the girl. He sacrificed his position for her. But he must learn to put his people before himself, and providing an heir is a good first step."

"And so we are to wait for the next generation? Our people must continue to suffer this self-inflicted banishment until the magic is born again into Sy's child? Why not now, Ashemon? Why not us?" They had held this debate before, but never had Tagsha been so adamant.

"Weshen is not *strong* enough," Ashemon insisted, shame slumping his shoulders. He wanted nothing more than to fight the Restless King. To regain their ancestral lands. But he would not risk the end of their race to do it. "I will not lead my people to slaughter, Tagsha."

Tagsha pushed up from the bench. "But you will send your First Son."

He left his dinner on the table and pushed open the tent flap. Turning one last time, Tagsha glanced at Ashemon, the sorrow evident in the slump of his shoulders. "Make no mistake. When we return to the city after the summer, Syashin will not be waiting for us."

He closed the flap, leaving the tent silent behind him. One of the candles on the altar sputtered and died, and Ashemon sighed deeply. Tagsha may be right on this one.

Perhaps he should send Reshra after Syashin, to convince his brother to wait in the mountains.

The second candle stuttered out then, leaving Ashemon in complete darkness. "I should have told him of his heritage," he whispered, beginning another prayer to the Magi as he rose and left the tent. He crossed the clearing to his sons' tent and pulled open the flap, calling his younger son's name. Hopefully, there was no girl with him tonight.

But no noise greeted him, no movement within.

Ashemon entered the tent and looked in both small rooms. Both beds were empty, and both sides of the tent looked abandoned, cleaned of personal items as though the summer had ended. His heart began to beat faster, a heavy knowledge growing there.

Rushing to the dock, he noted the expected absence of the *Alimente*.

And then he counted two other spots, emptied of their vessels. He knew - his heart knew - that his younger son had already left the island. But with what purpose in mind?

And who could have taken the other boat?

"Tagsha!" Ashemon roared. He needed a count of the men, and soon. Then a new thought exploded into his brain. He remembered Maren, her eyes slicing him to ribbons at the Last Meal.

Her eyes had been murder. Treachery. *Treason.*

"Tagsha, we need a count of all the people on the island. Immediately!" he yelled at the guard lumbering toward him.

Coren pushed her eyes up again at the enormous building before her. How much bigger could the king's palace possibly be? The main door itself was as tall as the city walls, bolted through with bars of iron wider than her body. Syashin unlatched a narrow side door, and they slipped inside.

"This is an old servants' entrance," he whispered, locking the door behind them. "Of course, no-one has servants anymore." His voice sounded guilty, as though he recognized how out of place she felt.

Inside, there were rooms upon rooms, connected by hallways with ceilings so high they faded into shadows above her, lit only by the soft moonlight streaming in the multi-paned windows. Syashin led them into the main entry vestibule, which was large enough to hold dozens of people and hung with dusty tapestries she could barely see in the dim light. Gripping the curved wooden banister, she followed him up a sweeping staircase that parted halfway up, offering a choice.

Syashin pointed. "That half is the government side. This half is quarters for the General's family."

"You have *half* of this building as your home?" Coren couldn't help the comment, although she regretted it when she saw how his cheeks flushed. Yes, their lives had been very different, but he had never tried to make her feel small.

He had never treated her as a General's son might be expected to treat a common girl.

They entered a hall of closed doors. "These are bedrooms. Mine and Resh's, and my father's. And guest rooms."

"Why didn't your father ever have more children?" Coren asked idly, running her fingers over a locked door.

Syashin shrugged. "He had at least one other that died young. I always thought he was just too busy training to become General."

"Perhaps he needs to keep your brother more busy," she said, her voice flat.

"This is mine," Syashin said, opening a door and moving past her. He stepped to the window and drew the heavy curtains shut the last few inches, removing all moonlight from the room. She stood completely still, afraid to move in the thick dark. Then there was a squeak of metal, and a soft glow emanated from lamps on either side of a large bed.

"Gas lighting," he said, his voice low and apologetic. Coren bit into a sigh. Yet another thing the women had always done without, except for the Matron, and a handful of women who had been favored by certain wealthy sons. Certainly her own family was more used to moonlight and candles.

He moved deeper into the spacious room, disappearing behind yet another door, but Coren felt odd following him. It was such a private space. Something in her still needed solid distance between them, so she continued down the hall.

One door stood carelessly ajar, as though its occupant would be home any moment. Curious, Coren pushed it open a few more inches and crept inside. The room was as large as Syashin's but cold and surprisingly bare. The curtains were drawn completely back, and moonlight streamed in, silvering the white bed and pale wooden furniture. Something of it all smelled familiar. She rifled through the papers on the desk, noting how a pen had broken and splattered its black ink over the pages.

On one, she noticed a signature that explained the note of familiarity: she was in Reshra's room.

Narrowing her eyes, she advanced to the closed doors on the opposite side of the room. What secrets might a Second Son keep? What could she take of his that would be equal to what he had taken from her?

Nothing. Even if she set fire to the building itself, it still wouldn't be enough.

But it wouldn't hurt to look for a prize anyway.

Opening one door revealed shelving for an impressive array of weapons. She palmed a stiletto with a bone handle, inlaid with colored crystals that reminded her of the MagiSea. Many of the other weapons were far too heavy for her to manage on the trip up the mountains, and she preferred the simplicity of her whip. But this knife was pretty, so she wrapped it back in its leather and slipped it in her pocket.

The second door opened to reveal stacks and hanging bars full of winter clothing - hunting gear and furs and leathers. She turned a small knob on the wall, and a gas lamp above her glowed to life. Coren pulled a coat from a hanger, but it was too long for her arms, too large across her body. The other clothing was the same. Cut for a tall, strong General's son. Finely tailored to suit the arrogance that he wore as well.

Near the back, she found a cloak that could likely be cut to length, hooded and lined with silver and black fur. But as she pulled it from between the others, a flash of bright satin caught her eye. Shoving the menswear aside, she found a second rack, a rainbow hidden behind the dark clothes.

There was nothing practical on this rack, but the beauty…Coren sighed into the soft sheen of the dresses. Her calloused fingers stuttered across the expensive fabrics, tracing the beading and intricate embroidery. What were dresses doing in Reshra's closet?

She remembered Amden's skirt then. A fluff of impractical lace and cloud-like tulle. Since Coren had never been caught in a hunt, she had never received a gift like this from a Weshen boy. She would never admit to jealousy of those girls, but here in the soft light and silence, she *might* admit to coveting the specific right to *be* impractical.

The right to own something not for its usefulness, but simply for its magnificence.

And of course she'd heard of the legendary presents given by Reshra, Second Son of the General. It was one of the reasons so many Weshen girls were willing to set aside their pride and be caught by the conceited young man. But here in the semi-darkness in the private room of a very dangerous Weshen son, Coren's fingers clutched possessively at the water-blue dress in her hand.

She'd never had anything like it, and by the Magi, she wanted it.

Pulling it from the rack, she held it to her body. The length was perfect. The skirt was full and heavy with crystal embroidery. It must have cost a fortune. Enough to feed her family for a year. Still, she ached to slip it on, to feel the satin next to her skin.

"No," she whispered to herself, pushing aside the coats again to replace it. These dresses were not for girls like her.

"You should take one," Syashin said, his voice carrying from the door of Reshra's bedroom. Coren nearly dropped the dress, her face flaming at being caught in such a place, with such a symbol of all that she hated grasped in her greedy fingers.

"You'll need dresses in EvenFall and StarsHelm. We can buy some, but coming to a dressmaker dressed like a man would alert the wrong sorts of people. Take one," he repeated, walking toward her.

Coren started to shake her head, then stopped. Her fingers curled into the dress, and she knew she would take them all if she could carry them.

"I guess I have a right to choose a dress," she said, gazing at the heady mix of satin and velvet. "Your brother did catch me, after all."

"And so did I," Sy said, his voice rough with an anger she didn't quite understand. "These are mine." He stepped into the closet with her. She felt the heat of his body in the narrow space between the racks of clothing. He held out a strand of pearls, long enough to loop her neck three or four times. Each pearl shimmered like the depths of the MagiSea: colors of the sand, the dark green kelsh plants, and the white-blue of the upper waters.

"Take them," he said.

She allowed him to drop them into her palm, where they pooled and cascaded through her fingers like droplets of home.

"Thank you," she said, her eyes fixed on the riches in her grasp, wishing they were not so close or so alone. Wishing her skin were not so warm from his nearness.

A few seconds passed, and still she kept her eyes on the clothing. Finally, she felt Syashin move away, back into the bedroom.

"Take the dress, Coren, and a plainer one, too. It should be nearing daybreak soon, when the younger boys will be off to training. Their rooms should be empty, and we might find other clothing to fit you there." His voice sounded far away and tired, and as Coren dropped the pearls into her bag, she regretted how she must treat him. But regardless of how her body might respond to his, she knew her mother's advice held truth.

She needed every shred of her magic, and losing any of it to anyone could mean death when she met the Restless King.

Coren chose a second dress too, midnight-blue and cut with a more practical high-necked velvet bodice and slim wool skirt. She folded the dresses and the hooded cloak into her satchel, frowning at its new heaviness, then turned off the light and followed Syashin out of the building.

They had been inside longer than she'd thought, and the sky was streaked with pink and orange.

They wove silently through a series of gates and narrow alleys until they reached a two-story dormitory. Banging doors and the shouts and laughter of young boys reached her then, and her heart ached uncontrollably for Kosh.

She was fiercely glad he would never know this life, but she was crazy with fear that he might not survive what life he had left, traveling to Sulit with Maren. And if he did survive, at what cost?

"They should all be gone now," Syashin whispered, tugging her out of her miserable thoughts and leading them to the laundry room. "The younger boys do the washing, but they're all at breakfast and prayers now. Take what will fit."

20

Sy watched as Corentine quickly plucked fitted pants and tunics from the drying lines, holding them up briefly. Most would be heavier, sturdier material than what she'd brought from the island. He handed her several pairs of thick knitted socks and a pair of boots he'd guessed might fit. She slid a foot in and nodded.

"I'll never be able to carry all of this up a cliff," she protested as they stuffed her bag nearly to bursting.

"The NeverCross Mountains are always frozen," he said. "And EvenFall is expensive. I don't have a lot of Riatan coin."

He knew they'd both struggle with the packs, but it was the best way. The climb to Damren's hidden home was only a day's length for him, but she may be much slower. And once they crossed the mountains, there would be many days of hard travel in Riata.

"I want to go to the armory next. I have a few weapons, but I need backups and things to sell.

And you'll need more than that whip." He still wasn't sure he trusted that weapon.

"I'm fine with my whip," she replied curtly. "Really, Syashin, I can't see how we'll carry all of this."

He heard the frustration in her voice and noticed she'd reverted to his full name. "I'll help you, but please trust me when I say you'll be glad to have these things later. Corentine, remember, we're never coming back."

She glared at him, and he hated himself for reminding her. How could either of them forget something like that? Obviously, she hoped to see her family again, and although he knew it was unlikely, he too still harbored hope that Resh or even his father might find them later, with a ready army of Weshen. But these were idle hopes. Preparation was wiser.

He led the way through the few streets to the community armory, their progress painstakingly slow in the early morning light. This task would be more dangerous, as there was never a time when the weapons were left unguarded.

But Sy knew all the rooms by heart, and he hoped to find one of his father's left unlocked or unwatched. He didn't dare venture the NeverCross Mountains and into EvenFall with only a single bow sword and a handful of throwing knives.

"Here," he whispered, peering in a window. The room within, as well as the nearby windows, was dark and still. Perfection. He pushed a knife through the soft wood and pried the lock away with a popping sound. He grinned. It was a fact he had viewed with shame before, but today he was glad the buildings were in disrepair. The window slid open with a screech that made him cringe, but after waiting several moments, it seemed evident that no-one was coming.

Tucking their bags out of sight in an empty doorway, Sy hopped onto the ledge and hefted his weight through the opening, then held his hand down for Corentine. She struggled more, being several inches too short for the jump, and he hauled her body across the sill. They landed together in a heap on the floor, and Corentine scrambled to stand and distance herself from him.

He sighed to himself, wondering if she would ever trust his honor. He turned away to search the weapons for a few particular favorites, while she idly opened cabinets and drawers.

"Almost done," he whispered, handing her a set of finely-fletched arrows for his bow sword. She wrapped them in a cloth with the other weapons he had chosen, fitting everything into yet another bag taken from a peg on the wall.

But just as she closed the buckle, heavy footsteps sounded in the hallway just beyond the room. There was no time to escape back through the window; the first lock on the door was already beginning to rattle. Sy kicked the newly-filled bag to a corner, pushed Corentine down behind a massive trunk of old blades, and flattened himself against the wall behind where the door would open. If they were lucky, the guard would just open the door, glance around, and leave without seeing anything.

"The noise was from in here, I think," a gruff voice said as the first lock clicked open. Realizing there was more than a single guard, Sy cursed under his breath. If they were caught, they could be sent out to sea again, or the men might decide to keep them prisoner until the

General returned. Sy's stomach flopped at the idea of Corentine in the Weshen City prisons.

Too soon, the man started on the second lock.

"Arash said all the young pups were accounted for at breakfast," another voice answered.

"Eh, he's been drunk the whole summer." The door swung wide, forcing Sy to soften its landing with quick fingertips so that it wouldn't smack his nose. He couldn't see anything of Corentine. Hopefully the men wouldn't, either.

He thought he recognized the voices, but it had been too long since he'd spent more than a few weeks in Weshen, preferring the travel and trials of the MagicCreature hunts.

"Who'd be man enough to sneak into the General's armory, anyway?" the first one wondered, his dull voice reflecting awe at the guts of such a task. "Course I'd like to look around in here myself." The men laughed, and Sy's hopes for an easy escape disintegrated. These men were simply too curious, and now they had a legitimate excuse to snoop.

"Eh, the General's gone soft these last years, waiting for that rogue son of his to man up and make some heirs," the first voice said, and Sy's memory slotted together the pieces he'd been searching for: this was Melshen. Irritation prickled over his shoulders, his muscles tensing. He had heard Tagsha warn his father about this man, recommending his removal from armory duty. "Lots know it. Ashemon's losing respect."

Sy narrowed his eyes at Melshen's disrespectful words, feeling his face flush at the realization of the gossip his own actions had caused. Reshra had been right. Sy's refusal to sire a child truly was reflecting badly on the General. How much worse would the news of his banishment be received?

He gritted his teeth, pushing away the hot feeling of shame to focus on how they might escape.

Then Melshen grunted, striding forward. "Hey, window's open!"

Sy cursed himself again for this new mistake. The men certainly wouldn't leave quickly now. Might as well make his presence known, and hopefully protect Corentine from discovery. Both men had gathered at the window, peering out with their backs to Sy, but it was possible they might see her if they turned in the right direction. Quickly, Sy stepped around the door, blocking their exit, as though he had entered from the hall.

"Melshen! You will ask my forgiveness for such a slander to my father and myself," he growled, standing tall and straight. The shock in their eyes was plain, but Melshen still recovered quickly, jangling his keys as his lips curled upward. His other hand drifted toward the knife pushed into his belt.

"Well. Our young First Son. Certainly didn't expect you to be here." He glanced around the room, his beady eyes glinting in suspicion. "Get tired of the girls on the island? Or did you find a way to skip out on the hunts again?"

The other guard laughed at Melshen's joke, his fat belly shaking, and Sy snapped. Melshen was broad, but Sy was faster, and he was on the man in a second, holding Melshen's own knife held to his throat.

"My business here is none of yours. But you will *not* slander my family. I'm doing you a favor by repeating myself. Now, beg my forgiveness, and I might spare your life."

He heard the slightest gasp from behind him, and both guards' eyes swiveled toward the trunk. Sy let out another curse just as the fat guard strode past him and yanked Corentine from her hiding spot.

"What's this? A girl? Perhaps you're wrong, Melshen, and young Syashin isn't a beach runner after all!" The broadest man Coren had ever seen held her tightly by the arm, snatching her shawl and pulling it halfway back. She stumbled toward him, twisting to remove the fabric.

His face leered as she spun, the covering unraveling and her panic rising as they stepped closer and closer, locked in a dance of desire and destruction.

"Or perhaps our future general pitied our lonely summer and brought this pretty doll for us to play with!" he cackled. A meaty hand brushed and grappled at her breast, and Coren felt a great rage well up in her, black and fiery red.

She would *not* be touched against her will.

The whip slid from her middle and snaked across the floor, flicking at the man's feet. The handle was instantly warm in her palm, and its dark magic seemed to call to her boiling blood, making the whip in her fingers seem to move on its own.

Coren's vision crowded with shadows until all she could see was the man before her. Like a flash of light in the dark sky, the whip snapped across the man's massive chest, and a bright line of blood appeared. Shouting a curse, he let go of her arm, and she darted away toward the opposite wall.

Struggling to suck air through her closing throat, she shook her head and tried to blink away the odd bits of darkness in her eyes. She bent to retrieve her shawl and was knocked off balance as the man grabbed at it, yanking it from her fingers.

"You're not getting away from me after that," he roared, swiping at the droplets of blood on his chest. His eyes glittered as he moved to corner her. Coren risked a glance at Syashin, whose face was a mask of rage. The guard he was struggling to hold back made a noise as if to speak, but Syashin pressed harder against his throat, his leg stretching to pin the man's arm before he could retrieve his weapon. The man was thick with muscle, but Syashin appeared to be better trained.

Coren knew they should flee now. Forget the bag of weapons, jump out the window, and run. But something in the whip sang a song of blood in her mind, its handle seeming to stick to her fingers. The fat guard watched her like a hunter, trying to measure her movements, but Coren had no intention of being touched again.

"You're just a girl," he sneered. "Now put away that whip and come do what you were made to do."

A mask of calm slid over her, hiding the boil of rage behind a sheet of unforgiving black ice.

"Nothing," she whispered, watching as her hand struck the man again, higher this time.

"Nothing is small." Another line of red appeared, like a ladder up his bulging chest, and another.

"Corentine!" she heard Syashin yell, but his voice sounded so far away. Farther than home, and farther than the Restless King, and farther than happiness.

The handle was hot in her hand and the whip was slick and nearly black with blood, pulsing gloriously with magic as the life of each droplet seeped into the weapon's strengthening braid.

"Nothing is small when it is against your will!" she hissed, striking one last time. This fresh cut finished her task, opening the artery in his neck, and he staggered back, clutching at the red liquid that flowed in an entirely wrong direction. He stumbled heavily against the wall and slid down as she advanced in measured steps. A wet trail of crimson marked his descent.

"*That's* what I was made to do," she whispered, her voice echoing in the shadowy corners of her mind. She felt as though something had taken her hostage, and everything else had fled. She knew, on some dark level of her soul, that what she'd done was horrific.

But she no longer remembered how to find the part of her that cared for men like this.

So with her slippered foot, she pushed the man over, watching intently until the last bit of life faded from his eyes.

Gradually, she became aware of the silence around her. Her body swiveled slowly, her eyes dragging over the room as though it were the first time she'd seen it. Syashin was watching her with an unavoidable, grim expression of horror on his face. The other man had been bound and gagged while she had worked, but fury crowded his brows into his eyes, and she knew he was cursing her.

Glancing back to the dead man, she realized a curse was exactly what she deserved. Light splintered into her shadowy vision, the pain squeezing her eyes shut, and Coren sprinted to the window, slumping over the sill just in time to retch into the street below.

What had she just done? And *why*?

Sy had no idea what to think.

Corentine hung over the windowsill, and he heard her still gagging. What had she just done?

The man lay slumped against the wall, tracks of blood still bright on his chest. Sy *knew* what she'd done, and yet, he didn't know. Corentine had completely come apart - her mind cracking open to reveal something darkly different inside. Sy had seen the presence hovering in her eyes, darkening them from tan and gold to black and amber, like the molten insides of a forge.

He'd seen the reddish glow of the whip's handle, as though she had gripped hot iron without flinching.

It had been slightly terrifying, but Sy couldn't help but notice he was also unavoidably intrigued.

Such power. And in a Weshen *woman*. It sounded like the stories of old. He'd stolen a restricted book from Weshen City's sparse library once and reveled in reading the adventures of the times before the Separation and the Sacrifice. When the women hunted alongside the men, fearless and fierce.

Watching the young girls giggle on the beach each summer, he'd never quite believed the stories could be real. Watching Corentine, he'd begun to believe.

But was that even Weshen magic? Sy feared something entirely different was lurking in the braid of that whip.

He looked down at Melshen, whom he had wrestled to the ground as soon as the other man had pulled Corentine from her hiding spot. Tightly bound, Melshen was slumped over, looking very similar to his partner, except for one small, yet very significant difference: Melshen was still alive.

Sy crouched, busying himself with tightening the man's bindings and checking the gag. Melshen tried to yell something beyond the cloth in his mouth, and Sy pressed the knife point to his throat again. He quieted, and Sy rewarded him with a blow to his temple. His eyes fluttered closed.

What was he going to do with these men? Both presented serious problems.

"I'm sorry," Corentine whispered from behind him. He glanced up and saw her face was ashen. She glanced at the body against the wall, then quickly away. "What will we do now?"

"I don't know," Sy admitted, looking around the room. Melshen would obviously tell everyone, and he and Corentine could be imprisoned if caught. But as much as he hated the man, there was no reason to kill him too.

Even if they just left the guards locked in the room, the others would notice their friends' absences before the next meal.

"We'll leave them here," Corentine said, her voice gaining surety with each word. "Your father knows we planned to survive. So let everyone know we did. You can leave him a note if you wish. Tell him I killed the man. The people of Weshen *should* know that we're alive!"

Her eyes were blazing with fury and determination. Sy rose and nodded, swept into her ferocity like a boat caught in a current. He regretted what had happened, but it was true they were already outcasts. Outcasts created by his father.

"Okay," he agreed. A hint of a smile crept onto her lips, and his chest tightened. "Let's go, then." He stooped to pick up the bag.

"Don't you want to leave a note?" she asked, eying him.

He actually didn't want to leave such an admission, but he shrugged, trying to be nonchalant. "Melshen will tell them what happened."

"But he'll lie, won't he. He wouldn't want to admit his friend was bested by a woman." She scrutinized Sy, then each guard, and he could tell her mind was working out the path he hadn't wanted her to find. "He'll tell the General you did it. *You'll* be the murderer."

"It doesn't matter," he sighed, wishing she weren't so perceptive.

"It does! You shouldn't be taking blame for things I've done! I want you to write a note! I want you to tell Ashemon the truth. I want..." She bit at her lips, and he watched her intently. She shook her head, refusing to continue.

"You want them to know it was you, don't you?" he asked, realization washing over him. She was proud of what she'd done. Perhaps only a little, as her cheeks were now flushed in embarrassment or shame. But she owned her actions.

Corentine turned away, resting her hands on the windowsill. "I want them to fear me," she whispered. "So please just write the note."

So he did what he'd become quite good at - following her direction. He rummaged in the cabinets of the room, finally finding spare paper and a pen, and he wrote his father a quick note. He half expected her to read it over his shoulder, but Corentine remained by the window, staring into the street below.

Sy lifted the dead man's shoulders with a grunt and placed the paper beneath him, where Melshen wouldn't see it until it was too late.

Sy tossed the bags out the window, and they dropped down into the empty street.

"We need to make it back to the boat as quickly as possible. And we can *not* be seen, not after this."

She nodded, her expression grim, but not exactly sorrowful.

Sy tilted his head at her. Especially now, he figured she could handle what he had planned next. "How do you feel about tunnels?"

Shadow could feel the blood that had been spilled with its weapon.

The iron tang floated on the air, crossing miles and miles of city and ocean and forest. Now that the ancient blood in the whip was awake, the magic would strengthen. And as did the magic, so too would Shadow strengthen.

It flexed its limbs, breaking free of the cassocks of dirt, the crevices of ancient tree bark, and the hidden undersides of green-black leaves. Breaking free of the binding spell that man had used so many years ago.

The Shadow was good, and the Shadow was bad.

The Shadow remembered, and it vowed to take all the man had.

For the first time in so many years, Shadow stood. It was not whole, and still so weak, but the scent of blood in the summer air would be enough to sustain its journey.

Shadow slunk east and north along the coast of Umbren, slipping silently between the trees of ShadowsEnd Forest and toward the NeverCross Mountains.

21

"Tunnels?" Coren repeated, staring at him blankly. Animals used tunnels. She'd never been inside one.

Syashin nodded, beckoning her down the narrow street, his body flush with the stone wall of the armory as he crouched beneath the windows. Turning the corner, she could see the building butted up against a wall, creating a dead end. Syashin motioned her to a hidden door, flush with the stone, its wood bleached with age to the same mottled gray of the blocks surrounding it. Glancing behind them, he pushed open the door and slipped inside the darkness.

Coren hesitated just a moment. There was something about such underground darkness that pulsed a warning in her brain. He reached out a hand, though, and she took it, joining him as he latched the door behind them.

"No-one comes down here anymore, and most of the men have probably forgotten it exists," he said.

They were standing in complete black, but she heard him rummaging in his bag. A scritch echoed, and a flame sprung to life. He touched the match to a candle, and the light grew enough that Coren could see the stair landing. Only a waist-high railing separated them from darkness.

"These stairs lead down into the sewer system and the old mines, but what we want is the escape tunnel built for the royalty when the city was first laid out."

"Where does it go?" she asked, her voice muted by the dense black.

"The edge of the city, near the base of the mountains. From there we'll double back to the boat, grab whatever else we need, and head west."

"West?" she repeated. "I thought the mountain passage was just outside the city."

"It is, but we aren't going through that passage. If we're going to see Damren, it's easier to reach it from just west of where we docked the boat."

"And what about the Wesh slaves? Shouldn't we go to EvenFall now?" she asked.

"According to the papers, the auction isn't for nearly two weeks. We need to let Damren train you."

He started down the steep stairs, his bag brushing both railing and wall. She hurried to follow close behind, not anxious to lose the few feet's worth of light the candle threw out.

Coren had never been afraid of the dark. Hunting or walking outside at night or being enclosed by the sea and rock of the Mirror Magi's cove were one level of darkness, though. This was an entirely different sensation, and her nerves tightened with each step down.

It took mere seconds for the door to fade into the shadows around them. All she could see were the few steps before her, and Syashin's form. All she could hear was the light echo of their boots on the stone staircase.

"Eighty-eight," he said.

"What?" she asked, startled.

"I heard you counting. There are eighty-eight steps."

Coren hadn't realized she'd been counting out loud. "And then what?" she asked, her voice sharp with embarrassment.

"You pray I remember the right tunnel."

She thought she heard humor in his voice, but she wanted none of it. "If we get lost down here…"

"We won't, Coren." He slowed without warning, and she bumped into his back. He twisted around and held up the candle so she could see his face. "I know these tunnels, I promise."

"Then we have nothing to worry about," she said, stepping up one level to distance herself again.

"I didn't say that," he answered, lowering the candle. "There are plenty of creatures that live in the tunnels."

Coren glared at his back and hurried to follow. If it were any other boy, she would assume he was just trying to scare her. But Syashin had a way with honesty that was more frightening because it was unexpected.

"What sort of creatures?" she asked.

"Ratten, and snakka, and of course lots of arachs, but never the giant ones. I haven't been this way in at least a year, so there may be more. It's a different world underground."

Gradually, she grew used to the dark and had found a bit of confidence by the time they reached the bottom of the stairs. Syashin held the candle up and around, showing brief glimpses of their surroundings. There was a bricked channel of water and sludge that explained the fetid smell of rot and waste. Several round pipes along the wall continually filled the channel, and the dank water flowed past them into the farther darkness.

"Sewer," he said, unnecessarily.

The patter of tiny feet sounded beneath them, stopping when Syashin held his candle down toward the noise. Coren saw a palm-sized, furred animal with large beads for eyes staring back at them. Its tail curled up and over its body, ending in a flicker of whitish light.

"TunnelRatten," Syashin said. "They can't see in the dark, but they do carry a torch wherever they go."

Coren almost smiled until the creature leaped at them, its mouth snarling open to reveal finger-length fangs. She gasped, but Sy smacked the creature in mid-air, sending it flying back into the darkness. She heard it plop into the water beyond.

"They also bite. Not poisonous, but painful," he added.

Coren let out her breath. "Good to know," she said, uncoiling her whip.

"Any MagiCreatures down here?" Corentine asked. Sy held the candle toward the dirt, showing her where to step and avoid the sewage channel.

"I've never seen one." And he hoped he never would. The escape tunnel was too narrow for fighting. He held up the candle, searching for the right place along the back wall until his fingers brushed the ridged doorway carved in the rock.

"The secret passage is right here. It's a tight squeeze for a few minutes. Push your bag in front of you and turn sideways." He ran the candle flame up the slit in the wall to show her, then took a deep breath and ducked inside.

It was a mental exercise, this tunnel.

Only a few steps in, the passage narrowed to a level of discomfort. "Designed to keep people out," he huffed, struggling to crouch and manage the candle and his bag all at once.

"Including us," Corentine said, her voice muffled.

The ceiling lowered again, forcing Sy to his knees. "This is the worst part," he said, and Corentine snorted. "On your belly."

He leaned the candle against the rock wall and pushed his bag ahead of him into what looked like barely more than a snakka hole.

"Sy, I don't think I can go in there," she whispered.

He glanced back at her, seeing her eyes huge and glassed with panic in the candlelight. "It's the only way. I'll be right in front of you."

"Surely this isn't where the nobles of Weshen would have come to escape," she insisted.

"The nobles of Weshen have always been warriors," he said, hoping to challenge her pride.

She shook her head, still staring blankly at the hole. Sy reached over to grasp her hand, and she blinked down at their fingers.

"Coren, it's the only way," he repeated. "The whole city will be searching for us."

Slowly, she began to nod, and he breathed a sigh of relief. He hurried to crawl into the hole, pushing the bag before him and keeping the candle close in case snakkas or arachs decided to investigate the intruders.

"Talk to me," Corentine whispered, a note of panic still lacing her voice.

"When I was a boy, Resh and I would come down here to escape training sometimes. He was fearless. Always leading. We explored most of the mine shafts and the sewers, and we followed this tunnel all the way to its end a few times. Once we even found a bone-handled stiletto. It had these crystals cut into it that were like the sea, all shades of blue and green. Resh was so sure it was a talisman, left over from before the Sacrifice. But it never tested well. I think he kept it anyway."

"He did," Corentine interrupted, surprising him. "I think it's the one I took from his room."

Sy chuckled. "Well, it's probably in better hands, now. But he'll ask for it back if he finds out. And here we are," he said, hauling his body through the last bit of tunnel and into a space big enough to be a bedroom. He helped Corentine to her feet. A pool of water rested in the center of the rock room, and very high above them was a portal to the afternoon sky.

"Resh and I never did figure out where that opens to, but I think it's somewhere in the animal pastures. From here, it's less than a mile of easy walking. No more crawling under the city."

"Thank you," she said, keeping her eyes down as she brushed dirt from her clothes.

Sy opened his mouth to answer, but a low growl sounded instead, echoing around the cave. He pressed Corentine against the wall where they'd just exited, his fingers reaching reflexively to his back.

But of course, the bow sword wasn't strapped there. It was zipped snugly in his pack. All he had was a candle stub and the short dagger at his belt.

The growl intensified as the beast stepped from the shadows, and he heard Corentine gasp.

"Cheetana," she whispered, and Sy had just enough presence of mind to wonder how she knew the name before the MagiCreature leaped at them.

Coren barely thought before shoving in front of Syashin, brandishing her whip. The braid lashed out at the MagiCreature, wrapping around the paw that swiped toward her and leaving a bright line of blood.

The beast growled again but retreated around the edge of the room. It licked its paw and paced the water's edge. As the light from above caught its fur, Coren marveled at its beauty. The sleek, velvety fur shone in rainbow shades of hot oil; black swirled with midnight and teal blue. Jade green ringed its eyes, and its claws shone silver even in the shadows.

"Get back," Syashin whispered, his fingers grasping at her shawl.

But she ignored him, stepping forward so he was left holding only fabric. Even she knew a dagger was no match for a MagiCreature. Paladin or not, he would be dead before he got his bag unzipped.

Something in the beast's eyes held her, though, and a sense of rightness and recognition settled over her, like the way she felt when running the plains or swimming the sea.

"You will let us pass, and I will let you live," she offered to the Cheetana, even as part of her balked at the idea of speaking to a creature.

Her whip flicked at the water that separated them. Ripples formed and grew, reaching the opposite side.

"Let us pass," she repeated, her voice low.

"Coren-" Syashin's plea was cut short by the Cheetana leaping across the water, pinning Coren. She cried out as her head cracked against the rock floor. Syashin shouted and darted toward them, his dagger flashing, but the creature snarled and swiped at him. He fell back hard, head smashing against the rock wall. His eyes fluttered closed, and Coren wrenched her arm from beneath the Cheetana's claws.

Her whip cracked the air and wrapped itself tightly around the creature's chest, squeezing.

"I am no threat to you, Cheetana," Coren whispered, staring into its black eyes. She wasn't afraid, and something told her the Cheetana wasn't either. She could feel its power: magic and muscle tightly wound into each movement.

"Our magic is not so different. Let us pass." She didn't want to kill such a glorious creature. It was nothing like the Vespa.

The Cheetana dipped its muzzle closer to her face, and Coren shrank beneath the muggy heat of its breath. A black tongue darted out and tasted her temple then, and Coren yanked on the whip, hearing the intake of breath from the creature.

But then she stopped. Where the Cheetana had licked, Coren could feel her skin tingling, and in her mind, a thought was forming.

A thought that was not hers.

You have taken enough of my magic. Release me, and I will release you, daughter of Weshen. Release me and go, but beware. The Shadow follows you.

Coren gaped as the Cheetana stepped back, pinning her with only a stare, its paws flat on the ground on either side of her. Syashin moaned where he lay, and Coren glanced at him, then back to the creature before her.

"Go," she whispered, pulling her whip away gently, so it wouldn't cut the Cheetana's flesh any more. "Go, before he wakes."

With another leap and a scattering of pebbles, the MagiCreature was gone, vanishing into the shadows of the tunnel beyond them.

Coren staggered to her feet. "Sy?" she asked, bending over him. A gash on the back of his head had begun to bleed, but he opened his eyes.

"It's safe," she said before he could try to speak. "She ran."

He grimaced and rolled onto his hands and knees, then stood slowly, bracing himself against the wall. Coren hovered, unsure how to help.

"We need to move," he whispered, bending to pick up his pack. His body began to sway, however, and Coren had to dart beneath his arm to help him regain balance.

"I'll get the packs," she said. "You just tell me where to go."

"One way out," he managed, sliding his hands along the wall as he walked. "Need to go. Before it comes back."

His words were a little slurred, and Coren worried he'd hit his head too hard. But they couldn't stop yet. She didn't think the Cheetana would come back, but then again, she hadn't thought MagiCreatures could speak, either.

And what had it meant? How could she take its magic?

Her thoughts were a jumbled mess as she helped Sy through the rest of the tunnel. Thankfully he had been right about the distance, and she saw daylight ahead not long after the attack. Coren immediately dropped the bags when they reached the exit, rubbing at her sore shoulders.

"You stay here," she said. "I'll check for guards."

He moved to protest, but only a simple shove from her was needed for him to slump down against the bags.

Coren readied her whip, but several minutes spent prowling the tunnel's exit turned up nothing dangerous. She recognized a straight line of lemondrine trees and knew they were indeed very close to the boat.

Turning back, she helped Syashin to his feet. She shouldered the bags again, and together they trudged the final distance to where the *Alimente* waited for them, untouched.

"We should rest," she said, dampening a rag and blotting the dried blood gently from Syashin's hair. His eyes slipped closed again, and Coren sighed. This would be a long evening.

Resh reached the city just before sunset.

"Open!" he shouted at the outer gate, rattling the iron. "Open under the command of General Ashemon Havenash!" He knew it was suspicious. No-one ever came back from the island early, and anyone whom the General had sent should have a gate key.

But Resh had given their key to Sy, and he sincerely hoped his brother had been here to use it.

He wasn't surprised when the guards approached in a trio, bow swords pointed directly at his head and heart. He held his hands up to show he wielded no weapon.

"Second Son!" one of them called back to the others. "Step aside," he said to Resh. He pressed his face to the gate and peered around Resh in the gathering darkness, looking for any traps or tricks.

"It's only me. I've come from the island with news. Bring me the Summer Commander."

The guard nodded and began the complex process of unlocking the gate. Once Resh slipped inside, the man quickly latched and locked it back, as though afraid of the very shadows beyond the wall.

Resh cut a straight path through the circles of Weshen City, followed by one of the gate guards. When he had made the decision to leave Weshen Isle in the starlit night, he had dressed to command, and now his summer-weight cloak rippled behind him in the breeze, and his tall leather boots echoed nicely as they struck the cobblestones. His hand rested on the hilt of his best sword at his waist, but he ignored the stares and questioning whispers that swirled at his back as he stalked the streets toward his father's home.

"Bring the Commander to me," he repeated as he reached the General's mansion, shutting the door in the guard's face.

As he waited, Resh called a servant to bring him food and drink, and he threw open the doors to his father's meeting room. He had a glass of fine liquor in hand, and his boots were kicked up on his father's writing desk when the same guard knocked tentatively on the door.

"Sir? I apologize for the delay, but there's been a problem. The Summer Commander, well…"

"Tell me," Resh said, keeping his voice low and dangerous.

"He's just been found unconscious. And his partner is dead!" The man rushed out the last part, and Resh set his glass on the desk with a thunk. He hoped it was evidence that his brother had made it to the city alive, but why would Sy need to kill one of their men? It wasn't like his brother. Resh lowered each boot slowly, then rose, moving to stand over the man's bowed head.

It must have been the witch's doing. Perhaps she had even spelled Sy to help her escape. It wouldn't be unexpected from a family such as hers.

"Show me," he said, and the man's breathing shallowed as he bobbed his head in deference.

Resh smiled as he followed the man, his fingers drifting again to the sword at his belt. Oh, how he enjoyed this feeling of being in charge. He glanced back at the mansion once more as the guard motioned down the rosewhip-lined path.

One day, all of this would be his.

He'd dreamed of being General before, but his loyalty to Sy and the Weshen traditions had always clipped his desire. Now that his brother had been banished, Resh had no plans to let him return and assume the General's position.

He followed the man through the city streets and into the armory.

"Here, sir. In your father's vault."

This also spoke of his brother's survival. If Sy had made it this far, he would certainly have come to gather weapons. Resh pushed through the other guards at the door and surveyed the scene.

"Nothing has been moved?"

The men shook their heads. "We just found them, sir, right before you called for Melshen."

Resh approached where Melshen lay, bound and gagged. There was a welt on his temple from being struck, but his chest rose and fell in sleep. He lived. The other man was not so lucky.

Blood had dried in a brownish circle around him. Resh bent and examined the man's wounds without touching him. What sort of weapon had done this? It was no sword or dagger. Perhaps a stiletto. But the slices were so long that surely the man would have been able to dodge better than he obviously did.

Then he noticed a smear of fingerprints on the man's shoulder and the wall behind. "Move him," he commanded. One of the guards tugged at the man's huge body until it slumped forward and to the side, revealing a paper stuck to the wall with dried blood.

Resh peeled it away delicately, moving to the window to read.

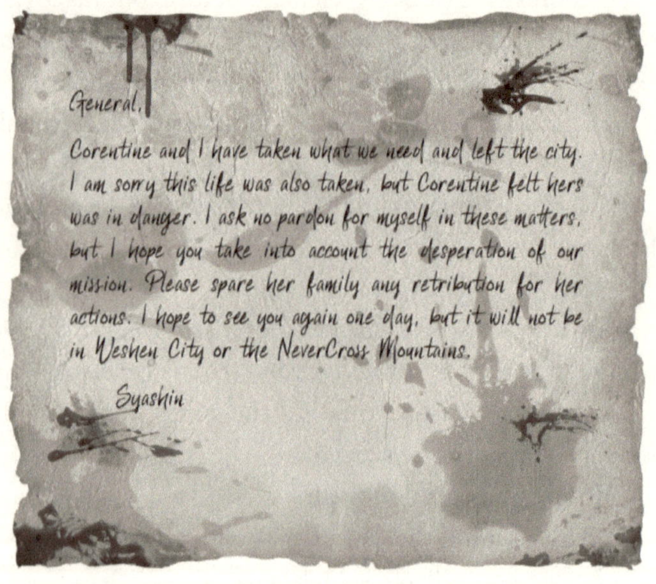

Resh crumpled the paper into his pocket. Had Corentine killed this man, or had Sy killed him for her? The language seemed purposefully vague. Either way, though, he knew he had been right. Sy would never kill one of his own unless it were a fight to the death, and there was no other smear of blood in the room.

The girl was at fault. Sy was blinded by her power.

"Appoint a new Commander," he ordered the guards watching in silence. He drew the sword from his belt, the song of it leaving its scabbard sweet in his ears. This would be a perfect chance to cement his authority and rid himself of a guard he'd never trusted to begin with.

He gestured to the dead man. "This poor soul was bested by a witch who has enchanted my brother's heart, and I fear Melshen's heart is also compromised."

Melshen moaned just then, and his eyes fluttered open just in time to widen as the sword of the Second Son plunged into his heart.

"Search the city for the witch," Resh said, calmly drawing a black cloth from his scabbard and wiping the blood from his sword. He ignored the shocked gazes of the men and strode from the room. Making certain none of the guards had followed him, he ducked into a nearby room and locked the door.

Slumping against the wall, he yanked his string of black beads from beneath his shirt and began to pray, his fingers shaking. "Magi, protect our people from the Sulit witches, who have come again to ruin us. Help me see through the mist they weave against reality, and guide my sword to the heart of their power."

His eyes closed, and he continued to repeat the prayer, even as his mind wandered to his brother and Corentine.

He regretted killing a Weshen. But if the guard had seen either of their powers and could gossip to the others, then his life was a necessary sacrifice in the game of witch against Weshen. The Sulit witches had compromised his people's freedom in Riata so many years ago; he had learned this much from the ancients in EvenFall two winters ago.

Later, the General had confirmed Resh's inquiries, although he insisted the witches had no ability or reason left to attack from beyond the barriers of the MagiSea.

Resh, however, believed they might still attack from within, their magic passed along in whispers through families just like Corentine's.

22

Sy awoke with a pounding headache. He yawned and looked around him in the pale dawn light. Corentine slept nearby, curled in the hull of the boat, a light shawl covering most of her face and upper body. He gingerly felt his head, where he remembered striking it against the rock wall. Though tender, it didn't appear to be bleeding.

Again he glanced to Coren. She had saved both of them somehow - he didn't even remember what had happened after he struck the wall. Cheetanas were one of the strongest MagiCreatures, and clever as well. He'd never known one to abandon a fight. He shook his head, thinking again of how powerful Coren was. The thought was clouded, though, by the memory of his father's maddening decisions.

If the General had told the right stories or even paused long enough to ask the right questions, Sy and Coren might be heroes instead of outcasts, helping their people search for magic in their blood.

Instead, they were unlikely to see anyone they knew again.

Sy pushed to his feet, brushing away the sand and cave dirt that had collected in his clothes. He rummaged in a bag and found an empty water skin, then walked slowly to the shore to fill it, stretching his stiff muscles. He shifted away the salt and drank the skin dry, then repeated the process before his headache began to recede.

Coren stretched in her sleep, then she settled again, her form quiet.

He decided to let her sleep as long as she needed. They could reach Damren's home with a good day's climb, but she would need her strength. Turning back to the water, Sy wandered along its edge for several minutes before he noticed the prints.

They were almost washed from the sand, but they were there. Human.

Sy scanned the beach. All was clear and quiet. What was left of the prints seemed to lead toward an outcropping of tall rocks, though, and he wondered if perhaps someone had hidden there. Sy moved closer to the water, careful to allow the tide to erase his own prints.

Just as he reached the rocks, a figure dressed all in black stepped into view, separating slowly from the lingering darkness of early morning. Sy felt his face harden into a blank stare.

"Hello, brother," Resh said. "I see you found the prints I left for you. How were the tunnels?" He half-turned in the direction of the tunnel's exit, and the wind caught his cloak, billowing it behind him. "Just as when we were children?"

"Resh," Sy said, nodding a cold greeting. "You left the island."

"Indeed. Our father would have sent me anyways, so I thought to do it on my terms. The girl still lives."

"Corentine is fine," Sy answered, although he could tell Resh hadn't asked a question. How long had Resh been tracking them? Had he been to the city?

"So she is," Resh agreed, studying him. "But are you, Sy? Are you fine? Or has the witch woven her spells so tightly that you no longer even know?"

"Corentine is no more witch than I am. You and Father would both know that if you'd stopped to listen."

"I think she's woven her magic around you so delicately that you can't even tell what is your thought and what is hers. I found your note," Resh sneered, and he held up a crumpled paper like evidence. Sy narrowed his eyes.

"So you think I'm lying for her? Yes, she killed a man, but in self-defense."

"She should be dead for all she's done."

"And yet she lives. The Mirror Magi have allowed her to live." Sy saw the falter in Resh's expression, so he pushed the point. "Don't you think the Magi would have wiped away her magic if they didn't want it? Drowned her and dissolved her blood back into the MagiSea? We *survived*, Resh. We passed the shadows of Umbren, escaped the mouth of the Hungry River, and the pull of the Sulit shores, and the NewMoon Falls, and we *lived*. How many can say that?"

Resh considered his brother for a few scant seconds, then shrugged. "And where will you go now, since you are alive but homeless? Without family or friends?"

Sy bit back the disappointment he felt from Resh's response. How he wished his brother believed in the magic and what it could do for them. "We're going into the mountains. Perhaps on to EvenFall, maybe even StarsHelm." He was deliberately vague, not certain if Resh would try to follow them, but knowing his brother would complicate things, as always.

Resh raised his brows but kept his voice neutral. "The General told you to wait in the mountains for his return."

"The General banished me. I care nothing for his return." Sy picked a pebble from the crevice of a larger rock and skipped it across the water. "Besides, you put the map to the Wesh in the boat."

Reshra raised an eyebrow in answer. "And what of Corentine? How will you protect her on such a mission? You and I both know the mountains themselves are dangerous. EvenFall would be purgatory for a Weshen woman, and StarsHelm certain suicide. You claim to care for her, but all I see is a plan to get her killed."

"Corentine can take care of herself," Sy said, feeling a smile creep onto his face.

"She's a witch, Sy."

"No. She's a Weshen."

The brothers considered each other as the waves lapped at their feet and crashed against the rocks. Overhead a bird screamed, and Sy only broke the stare to ensure it wasn't a Vespa.

"Report back to the General if you must. Tell him we survived. But be sure he knows that I won't be waiting for him when he comes home from the summer hunts." Sy held Resh's eyes a second more before stalking back to the boat.

Coren watched Sy approach from far down the beach. He looked recovered, at least, but as he neared she saw his face taut with irritation.

"What is it?" she asked, shaking her shawl free of sand.

"Are you rested? We should go," he answered. Coren eyed him for a few seconds, but he said nothing more. Shrugging, she bent to begin the process of sorting and packing their supplies into a manageable bundle.

"Take the winter clothing, and the dresses for EvenFall. And the weapons," Sy added.

"What about the food?"

"Only enough for a few meals. Damren's home isn't far. And we can melt snow to drink."

"What about the lemondrines?" she asked, gesturing to the nearby trees.

"Yes, bring a few," he answered, impatience lacing his words.

Coren flicked her eyes to him as they packed in silence, but he kept his head down. Coren's mind kept returning to what she'd heard in the cave.

When a MagiCreature had *spoken* to her. Then again, perhaps she'd imagined it all. After all, she'd hit her head as well.

As soon as they had packed and hidden the leftover supplies with the boat, Sy led her up the beach, to where the mountain face dipped in on itself, creating a sunless cove.

Coren shivered as the mountain suddenly seemed to surround her. Every corner and ledge were dark with shadows, and the Cheetana's warning danced through her mind.

That warning alone insinuated that she hadn't imagined the creature. Shadows had never been anything more than a lack of light to her, but the Cheetana had spoken as though the shadow were an entity in itself - a monster dangerous enough for a MagiCreature to fear.

She wanted to ask Sy, but something in the stillness of the cooler air stopped her, as though the whole world was holding its breath to see what would happen next. If something called Shadow had indeed followed them here, she didn't want to invite it further by speaking its name.

The mountain stretched its spiny crest into the sky, losing sharpness to the blurring mist of the clouds. The temperature had dropped noticeably in the sunless shelter of this cove, and Sy knew the wind would strengthen and grow full of ice as they neared Damren's hidden home.

"Let's climb," he said, turning to Coren, who had been staring into the shadows of the rock around them. She had experience with the cliffs of Weshen Isle, but he wondered if they could truly make it. How long would their luck last? As she met his eyes, though, she only lifted an eyebrow in challenge and set her jaw.

They began the ascent, their heavy bags dangling by ropes clipped to their waists.

"I miss the island summer," Coren grumbled as she moved steadily below him, placing her hooks and toes in the vacancies left by his climbing. She was already breathing harder, and he smiled to himself as she cursed the dresses and furs that were weighing her down.

"I'd rather be back there too," he returned. "I've already spent much of the winter doing this. But I'm grateful to be free of the hunts," he added. How would the summer have ended if her magic hadn't manifested?

Would he have really obeyed the General and fathered a child, either with her or another girl? The thought seemed too bizarre, and he rejected it, focusing instead on the gray and black-streaked rock before his eyes.

They climbed in silence for over an hour before Sy found his first resting place. There were four, each a quarter of the way. Over the many times he had visited Damren, he had grown smart enough to leave supplies at each stop, and this practice served him well now, as Coren ducked into the shelter of the tiny cave. There was barely enough room for both of them.

Sy brushed the snow from a narrow bench he'd once carved from the ice and drew the fire box from an alcove at the back. The box had an outer shell waxed against moisture, and when Sy removed it, he found the matches and several corn cobs still dry from his previous visit. He'd need to remember to bring more to fill it when they rested here again on their journey into EvenFall.

The fire was soon burning hot, and Coren smiled to herself as she held her fingers to the warmth. They ate a little bit of dried meat warmed over the fire, and melted snow in a skin to drink.

The day continued slowly, broken into quarters by their climbing and stopping until finally, they had reached a ledge which seemed to be a dead end. The rock above them was slick and impossible to climb, and before them on the ledge was only more of the solid mountain.

"Now what?" Coren asked, surveying the mountains around them. Her voice was soft with exhaustion, but she hadn't complained again. She was even stronger than he'd hoped. "We don't have to sleep out here, do we?" she asked, a shiver coursing through her shoulders. It had grown nearly dark, and day was ending.

"Nope. We're actually here. The entrance is hidden." Sy grinned. This was the best part. He brushed snow from the rock to find the secret markings. "Accessible only to shifters. Damren has plenty of space inside though, and once, she had a handful of shifter students to help her build and maintain it."

"Was it a school?" Coren asked, leaning against the rock face. Sy shook his head. He glanced behind them, noticing how quickly the shadows had gathered for the night. An uneasy feeling hurried his searching as he turned his attention back to the rock wall.

"Damren told me once that she wanted to form one, but luckily for us, she never got that far. The Separation and the Sacrifice made schools a target. The others were all ransacked and destroyed by the Restless King. Since hers hadn't really been official yet, Graeme's soldiers knew nothing of this place."

He found what he'd been looking for and began to shift aside the stone of the mountain. A sliver of light from within began to show, and he glanced back to see Coren's eyes widen as she watched. It was almost too dark to see now. He wondered if a storm was coming, and said a quick prayer thanking the Magi that they had arrived before true night. "To my knowledge, Damren is the only source of magical lore that survived the Sacrifice, at least on this side of the mountains."

Soon there was a gap large enough for them to squeeze through, and Sy pushed the bags inside, the wind pushing puffs of snow in as well. "Come on," he said. "We need to shift the rock back once we're inside."

Shadow had watched them climb the mountain all day. It, too, had been climbing, but the light of day made its progress slow and tedious. It took strength to shatter itself into the tiny pieces that fit between the rocks, and even more strength to gather those pieces back together. There was precious little food on the mountain, too.

But once the magical cycle was more complete, Shadow would once more be able to move as it pleased.

Patience was needed, and Shadow had waited a long, long time already. What was a few weeks of human time to such a creature?

It caught the scent of the girl again and slithered faster up the rock face. They had stopped moving. The time could be perfect, if only…A hissed growl echoed off the icy rocks as the boy sealed the mountain shut behind them.

Shadow could not pass *through* rock.

But surely they would come out again, and then Shadow would be ready. Waiting. Patient.

The darkness grew thicker as night settled into the cliffs, and Shadow scraped its finger idly across the rock, leaving no mark. Soon, though. Soon it would be able to leave marks, and not just on rocky mountains.

It turned its hollow eyes to the night, watching for any movement that might become a source of sustenance.

23

"**S**yashin?" a thin voice called out as they stepped inside the mountain.

"Yes, Damren, it's me! I've brought a guest!" he called back as he finished sealing the strange mountain-door again. Coren rubbed at her tingling cheeks, relieved to feel that even with no fire visible, the inside of the mountain was free of wind, and therefore much warmer.

She'd kept her complaints to herself, but she never wanted to climb that mountain again.

"This way," Sy said, excitement lacing his voice. He shouldered their bags, and Coren hurried to follow him through a low-ceilinged tunnel. She sighed - if she never saw another tunnel after today either, that would be quite fine. But seeing as they hadn't even *crossed* the NeverCross Mountains yet, she seriously doubted either of her wishes would be granted.

Sy led her into a more open room, with a book-filled table in the center and several empty hooks on the wall.

An eight-candle sconce rested dangerously close to a stack of books, and Coren tried to resist moving it. Sy dropped the bags and hung his fur cloak on one of the hooks, then reached for hers. Coren let him have it reluctantly, still shivering. The ice that had formed along its edges was now melting and dripping all over the stone floor.

She had just reached over to move the candles away from the books when a stunted, wrinkle-faced woman bustled into the entryway. The woman glared at her hand on the candle, and Coren tucked it behind her, embarrassed. Books were important, though, she reasoned. The titles were too faded to read, but the spines looked promisingly broken.

"Damren, this is Corentine," Sy said.

Damren looked her over carefully, appearing to take measurements. "Welcome to my home. You'll do."

"Do what?" Coren asked, startled at the old woman's abrupt manner.

"You'll do as a student of shifter magic, of course. There's no other reason to seek such a place at the snowy top of the NeverCross Mountains. Besides, Weshen women don't travel anymore. If you're here, it's because you need a teacher. Now, get on in here, and I'll get you some hot soup."

Coren watched Damren turn and hurry down the hall she'd come from. "And take off those wet boots!" she called back over her shoulder.

Sy obediently shed his boots, lining them under his cloak like a boy at school, and Coren couldn't help but smile. She quickly did the same and followed Sy into the next room, where a fire burned brightly in its grate, heating the close-quartered kitchen gloriously. Damren sat in a rocker so close to the fire that Coren marveled the woman wasn't up in flames. She reached a ladle into a hanging pot and stirred vigorously. A few drops splashed out and sizzled on the wood below.

"It's early yet for your visit, Syashin."

"Something's happened, Damren. We've both been banished." His voice trailed down at the end, and Coren wondered again whether she would truly be welcome here. Would Damren blame her for Sy's troubles?

Damren stirred her pot one last time before turning to them. "Sit," she said. Coren nodded in thanks, but so far she didn't feel particularly welcome. In fact, she felt very much lacking as Damren's bright eyes looked her carefully over once more, her face a wrinkle of reserved judgment.

Damren gestured to the rough wooden table. Two benches gathered beneath it, and Sy scooted onto one, leaving room for Coren beside him. She glanced at the woman, who was still watching.

Coren sat across from him instead, and a hint of a smirk crossed Damren's face before she stood and reached into a cupboard to fetch bowls.

Damren's hands shook as she carried the bowls, but Coren felt she didn't want any help. Several drips spilled onto the table as Sy received his bowl and thanked her, the grease shining in the firelight.

"Who is your mother?" Damren asked, reaching toward her with a steaming bowl. Coren blinked at the suddenness of such a question, but she'd known enough old women to realize her answer would likely make a difference. That was, if Damren knew much of Weshen families. Even so far from Weshen gossips, Coren found herself reluctant to share.

"Well?" Damren prompted, withdrawing the soup.

Coren narrowed her eyes. Evidently, the woman's question wasn't idle. "Her name was Sorenta Shonen. She died when I was ten."

Damren nodded perfunctorily, her mouth grim as though she'd already known this, or suspected it. Finally, she set the bowl before Coren. "I know of her. We all did. Quite the strong, haughty family. Her mother was Lorental Shonen?"

Coren shrugged in agreement, gulping a steaming mouthful and reveling in the warmth as it coursed down her gullet. Regardless of what other Weshen thought, her family was hardly proud of itself. She'd barely heard a word about her grandmother her entire life.

"All I know is my grandmother didn't make it through the mountains during the Separation. Sorenta was an orphan by the time she made it to Weshen City, and my father Kashar was a young half-Weshen knight who deserted the king to help her home, then deserted her later to go back to StarsHelm. The Restless King took everything from my family. That's why I want to learn whatever magic I have, and quickly enough to kill Zorander Graeme before he finds out the magic is back," she added, setting her bowl down so abruptly that she added to the spills on the table.

She wiped at them with her sleeve, suddenly embarrassed by her outburst. What did this secluded old woman care about her family's struggles? Why should anyone believe her naive claims of vengeance?

Should she ever be face-to-face with the Restless King, he could cut her down in a second.

"Yes, you do have much to learn," Damren murmured, staring intently into the fire.

Coren guessed she wasn't just talking about learning magic, and she flushed.

"Damren, do you think the magic is returning to all the Weshen?" Sy asked.

"How many more?" she asked.

"Just us," Sy said, his voice defensive.

"And my brother, who was banished for it," Coren added. And her mother and Maren, she thought, who had never actually lost their magic.

Damren nodded, watching her so closely that she seemed to be listening in on Coren's thoughts. "Two in one family. Same father?"

"Twins," Sy answered for her. "And there are two younger. Also twins."

Damren looked sharply at Sy. "Two sets?"

"They're too young," Coren protested. She wasn't ready to discuss Kosh and Penna's potential for magic, not with this crusty woman.

"Not much younger than your brother when he was banished," Sy countered. "Your *twin* brother," he repeated, emphasizing the so-called blessings of her family.

Coren glared at him, and he pressed his lips together, moving his gaze to his empty bowl.

"Two sets of twins in one family," Damren muttered, rising to refill Sy's bowl. Coren sighed. It had always seemed to her like a slap from the Magi to be blessed with a twin, only to have that twin ripped from her because of his magic.

"So if the magic is returning to Weshen now, why us, and what is its purpose? Do you know?" Coren demanded, growing tired of the woman's continued scrutiny. She still hadn't decided if Damren and she would get along.

"Of course I know why. Do you?" Damren asked, turning to Sy.

Sy shrugged. "Because it's needed?"

"Magic does not appear simply because it's needed, or because we wish for it. Magic plays by rules, not by desire."

"The Weshen have recovered their numbers?" Coren guessed, although she knew that couldn't be true, or the General would have reacted very differently to her discovery. Damren only snorted and slurped from her bowl.

"Love," Sy whispered then, and Damren cackled.

"My favorite student," she said, pinching his cheek affectionately.

"Your only student," he laughed.

"Not anymore," Damren replied, sliding her eyes toward Coren. "But yes, shifter magic responds to the love between partners. And the children born of that love. Not only magic was lost during the Sacrifice. And not only magic has returned to the Weshen people."

Damren gazed intently at Sy, but he turned his head away, his face flushed.

"I know my parents loved each other," Coren offered. "Maren told me that's why I have magic. But then

Kashar abandoned her. So it seems love is as fickle as magic."

"There could be many reasons for his leaving," Damren said, her voice low. "Magic is born of love, and love is born of magic. It's circular and eternal unless one is removed. Then the circle is broken, and both are lost. Who is to say which should return first?"

"Well, how do you explain Sy, then?" Coren challenged. She knew it was rude, but the logic wasn't sound.

Damren shrugged. "Perhaps the General loved Sy's mother."

Coren made a disgusted noise. "I know his mother. Maren made a bargain with Ashemon, nothing else. A bargain he broke when he banished his own blood. That man is incapable of love, as are all the Weshen men."

Sy set down his bowl and turned his face from her, and she realized he was hurt. Maybe even insulted. But it was true - Weshen men hunted, and they killed, and they deserted.

But in her experience, they did not love.

"So then Neshra didn't love Maren?" he asked, provoking her. Coren glared, contemplating tipping his soup into his lap.

"Neshra?" Damren repeated, watching the fire. "The name is not familiar."

"Neshra Shennar," Coren supplied, but Damren still didn't answer.

"You've been gone too long, Damren," Sy said gently. "You can't be expected to know everyone."

"Shennar," she whispered, nodding as though the name had finally reached her. "Another strong family."

"But the Magi banned love between partners until the magic returned. The hunts ensure that no-one even has time to learn it," Coren said, still stuck on this piece of the puzzle. "None of the other Weshen will have magic until they give up the hunts. My mother told me as much, but I was too young to understand."

She thought again of Sorenta's warnings, which she now knew were cautions to wait for children until she was in love.

"Why do you think my father set us adrift in one boat instead of two?" Sy burst out, his voice still hurt. "His methods may be terrible, but he understands love must return too."

"But we aren't in love!" she protested, her face hot. "We care nothing for each other!"

"Nothing," Sy repeated, pushing up from the table and dumping his bowl in the sink. He stayed there, his back as solid and still as the rock walls around them.

Coren gulped. He cared for her, and if she were honest with herself, she cared something for him. It couldn't be love, though. They'd only know each other a few weeks. But he cared enough that his fool father had seen it, then gambled on it with the life of his First Son.

"The greater the love, the greater the magic," Damren said, her voice soothing the tense line of Sy's shoulders. "Love between partners strengthens each person's magic, and the children they produce are stronger for it. Your family, Corentine, was once the most powerful family Weshen knew. Their shifter magic was unparalleled in the community. You may not see it now, but your family was once made of love."

"There is nothing left of that now. My family is gone. Scattered. Dead." The words caught in her throat, choking her.

"Yet here you are," Damren said. "Learning magic." She didn't say the rest, but Coren heard it. Felt it. The old woman expected her to learn love as well.

"No matter what I am here to learn, what matters is that we help our people, both enslaved and in hiding. The Restless King's days are fewer than they were before this summer," she muttered. She must remember her true purpose here - otherwise her banishment would mean nothing. Her life would mean nothing.

"Where will I sleep?" she asked, turning back to the table. Sy's face was still turned from her, and he stared unmoving at the fire as Damren rose to show Coren to her narrow, cold bed.

"That girl is our people's greatest hope for salvation from Zorander Graeme, you know," Damren said to Sy when she returned to the kitchen.

"I've wondered as much," he whispered.

"And you're learning to care for her, aren't you?" Damren asked. She didn't expect an answer, but she smiled warmly when Sy met her eyes. But even though he agreed with Damren, something in him resisted calling it love. What bond he felt developing was still more like family or friendship, though he hoped to someday feel the strength of emotion Damren spoke about.

She rose and rested a hand on his shoulder. "Life has been hard for you. Both of you. And it's just the beginning. But if you have each other…"

"Don't say it, Damren. There's so much to do. We could both die in EvenFall."

"You could," Damren agreed, clearing the other bowls. "But think on this, Sy. Her family was once rumored to possess Triple magic."

He turned to her sharply. "Triple? What is triple?"

Damren snorted. "I've taught you so much, and yet I've taught you nothing. Single magic is?" she prompted

"SourceShifting. Controlling the matter," he answered, the diligent student.

"And Double magic?"

"SelfShifting. Controlling how you look."

"And Triple is SoulShifting. Controlling where the soul resides."

Sy stared at her, unable to absorb such an idea. "So someone could shift a soul from its body?"

Damren nodded. "And into another body. Make no mistake, Syashin. Triple magic is not always good. Weshen magic works best in pairs, and Triple has no pair. It's unbalanced. And of course, Triple magic is rumored to be the *true* reason the Restless King coveted Weshen women."

"If a soul could be shifted into another body, that person could live forever," he whispered.

"Yes. Triple magic hasn't been seen in many, many generations. Even before the Separation and Sacrifice.

But that girl…there's something powerful in her. Sleeping, yes. But powerful."

She fixed Sy in her gaze and continued. "Even in these few hours since your arrival, I've felt my magic strengthening. Powers I haven't felt since the Sacrifice are whispering through my veins. This girl, Syashin, is like a hurricane. A storm on the water. If her power cannot be controlled, if her path veers…" Damren broke off, watching the effect of her words on Sy.

He shook his head, brushing away the idea. "Coren is better than that. She wants what is best for our people, I think, even though she's been treated poorly."

"But would the Weshen people trust *her*? Enough to lead them? Where there is no trust - where there is doubt - there will be a need to prove, and the possibility of a great bitterness rising in her heart."

"I'll watch over her, Damren," Sy answered. He didn't think Coren was bitter enough to turn black inside, but he also remembered the stories of her father, her mother, her brother. Desertion, suicide, and murder. None of it boded well for Coren. He thought uneasily of the guard they'd left behind in the city.

If her family's magic swirled in her blood, perhaps their darkness did as well.

"The Shadow sees everything," Damren whispered, almost to herself. "The Shadow hides the messes that the light and dark make, and it is a master at making the unequal seem equal. Wouldn't your young beauty prefer to be seen as an equal?"

Sy nodded, the fear bubbling into his chest.

"Then you must watch her for signs of the Shadow."

Sy's brain was racing. It had been a long time since he'd been afraid of the Shadow. By now it was a bedtime story he and Resh used to scare each other with. But what Damren spoke of was ancient and different.

"May I go to the practice room?" he asked, his limbs suddenly restless. He needed to pause his whirling mind, and the best way to do that was to beat it into submission with the fatigue of training.

"Of course. But don't be up too late. We begin at sunrise, as always," she grinned, bowing to him. He returned the gesture, then took the stairs up to the vast inner room carved with the power of many shifters and designed specifically for combat practice.

Sleep was impossible, despite Coren's intense fatigue. The bed was too comfortable, or too narrow, or too far from home. Something.

Finally, she gave up and lit a candle, then padded down the silent hall to the bathroom Damren had shown her. Splashing icy water on her face, she held up the flickering light and studied herself in the sliver of mirror. The early-summer sparseness and then the journey had taken the plumpness from her cheeks, and the sun glinting off the MagiSea had darkened her skin and lightened strands of her hair.

She looked older. Harsher. More like Sorenta. Her mother had been beautiful, once, and Coren remembered her vanity. Once, when her mind was nearly lost to delirium, Sorenta had described a StarsHelm ball she'd attended as a very young girl. A ball at the palace, given by the Restless King himself. Her eyes had sparkled as she listed the foods, the colors, the names of well-known and well-to-do guests.

Coren shook the memory from her mind. Such beauty had never counted for much in her world. Sorenta mourned the loss of her wealth as much as the loss of her mother, and the two were twisted together in Coren's mind as well. Love and money and magic and power. All things the Restless King had stolen.

Once, all things that had been forbidden or out of reach for her.

Now, all things she could regain for herself. For her people. Perhaps even for all of Riata.

Coren showed her teeth in the mirror. *Foolish girl*, she admonished herself, turning to head back to her room. She'd be lucky to make it to StarsHelm alive, and the Weshen people had never cared much about saving her.

A rhythmic thumping reached her from somewhere in the mountain. What were Sy and the old woman doing now? She shouldn't have left them alone after dinner.

The door next to hers was ajar. She peeked inside: another closet-sized bedroom, empty except for Sy's bags. A third bedroom was completely empty, but a fourth door was shut tightly, warmth and a dim light seeping from beneath the door.

The thumping continued, so she followed it, the vibrations in her bare feet helping her trace it to a staircase cut from stone, leading up to a wooden door.

The door was open an inch, and she pressed her eye to the slit, finding a room that seemed to be scooped right from the stone. Torches flared in alcoves every eight feet or so around the walls, glimmering like fiery crystals behind their glass screens.

Sy was in the center, his feet and chest bare, using a long wooden rod to hit a human-sized bag suspended from the ceiling. He moved around the bag in a fluid circle. As the bag swung with each hit, he ducked and leaned, each time knocking it away before it connected with his skin.

And once Coren noticed his bare skin, it seemed that was all her eyes cared for. The torchlight cut his arms even more sharply, and beads of sweat trailed between his broad shoulder blades and across the rippled muscle of his stomach.

As quietly as possible, she pushed the door open a few more inches, forcing herself to study the other walls. Each wall had a variety of weaponry, plus bars, bags, and pulleys obviously designed for physical training. There was no sign of Damren.

Sy stepped away from the bag, grabbing a cloth from a nearby chair. He wiped his face, then turned directly toward the door.

"Join me, Coren," he said, his voice now the only noise in the night.

Coren's breath jumped at the surprise of being found, then come twice as fast as he strode toward the door, pulling it open and grasping her hand to pull her into the room.

"I always train when I can't sleep," he said, releasing her hand to latch the door. She wondered if he'd left it open before in hopes she would come find him.

She tried to keep her eyes everywhere but on him. "I don't even know what most of this is." She gestured around at the implements hanging from hooks on the wall.

"Each day we'll try a new one until you learn."

"And when will we go rescue the Wesh and find the Restless King? I care nothing for mastering weapons."

He smiled, handing her the rod. "But you must master them if you hope to be any use in fighting the king. We have time to train before the auction. Damren tells me that when you are master of your body, you are a better master to your magic, and it will be more powerful."

"And are you? Master of your body?" she asked, twisting the rod and finding its balance point. It was heavy, but not unwieldy. She flushed as she realized the implications of what she had asked, but Sy wasn't watching her.

"I am as my father says. Weshen's best Paladin," he replied, facing the weapons rack. Coren thought there was a note of bitterness in the words, but all thoughts were swept away as he turned around and swung at her with a new rod.

He moved slowly enough for her to block, but she felt the thump reverberate in her arms and shoulders. She was already sore from the day's climbing, and it would grow worse if they continued.

But her mouth set in a grim line. If he could train after such a day, so could she. Readying herself better for the next blow, she held up the rod and blocked him again. He twisted and turned it as he wove around her on the mat, still in slow motion, but she managed to block each blow.

"You have quick reflexes," he said, grinning.

"A lifetime of hunting with a whip," she countered. She noticed he increased the speed of his movements slightly then, but still she matched him. The night was quiet except for their controlled blows, and she found her questions bubbling to the surface of the silence. "Tell me more of the magic. Single magic has fusion and disintegration. What about Double? All I've done is make myself look younger. Can I look older?"

"Yes, but that's not the opposing magic." He leaned his rod against the wall and sat, beckoning for her to do the same. "Double magic is tricky. SelfShifting can go within or without. Within, you can shift your appearance younger, older, or even alter it to look like someone else. Though I've never been able to do that," he admitted.

"And without?" she prompted.

He stood and retrieved his water. He offered it to her first, but she shook her head. Coren watched him drink, her stare letting him know he wouldn't be able to avoid her questions.

"Without means shifting to something not human," he said finally, his eyes meeting hers.

"Not human," she repeated.

He nodded. "No-one alive can do it anymore. But once, the strongest of the Weshen hunters were able to claim a certain MagiCreature - only ever one per hunter - and shift into a mix of creature and Weshen."

Coren stood, her muscles restless, as though they could learn to shift into a creature that very moment.

"This is how we can beat him!" she whispered. "This is the magic that will be the Restless King's undoing!"

"This magic was the Weshen's undoing," he answered softly, and her shoulders sagged. Of course. This was exactly the type of power a king would conquer a nation to get.

"But if he doesn't know the magic has returned…if he doesn't suspect," she tried.

Sy nodded. "That's our only hope. To train here, where our secrets will stay safe, and travel to StarsHelm undetected."

Coren smiled. Yes, this could work. They had a willing and capable teacher and a safe place to practice. Even her family was protected and waiting for her return. "This has to work," she said.

Sy held his hand out to her. "Come with me. I want to show you the library."

"Library!" Coren repeated, her spark of excitement flaring again.

Sy laughed as she hurried from the room. He barely had time to grab his shirt from the floor, and by the time he blew out the torches, she was waiting at the bottom of the stairs.

His chest grew tight watching the gleam in her eyes as he led her down a different hall and into the vast circular cave that was Damren's library. The center of the room was open except for one wide table, and a path spiraled around the room and up, lined with shelves of dusty volumes.

"This was Damren's real passion," he said, watching as Coren splayed her fingers over several spines. "Before she was a teacher, she was a student, and before she dreamed of training Weshen to use magic, she dreamed of studying magic. The training and teaching only became necessary with the war. These are mostly rescued books from Weshen City's libraries." He pointed to a prominent shelf, less dust-filled than the others.

"This is incredible," Coren said, her face shining as she turned to him. "I thought all of this knowledge was lost." He let her roam while he searched for the book he'd brought her here to see.

"These are the Weshen shifters," he said, spreading the book flat to show her the pages of gloriously-colored drawings that had entranced him since childhood. This was the very book he had once stolen from his school library, lost long ago but found in duplicate here in Damren's library.

Coren slid the book she'd been leafing through back on the shelf and hurried to join him. He heard her quick intake of breath as she ran her fingers lightly over the illustrated pages.

There were men with the brawn and ruff of a Grizzlin, taller and twice as muscled as a normal man. Women with the wings of a Vespa, spread twenty feet on either side of their shoulders, and golden claws extending from their fingers. Young men and women both with the pointed, curious ears and silken tails of Sun Kitsuun, their hair blended with coppery fur, and some with the ebony-blue and silver hues of the sly Moon Kitsuun.

One had eight shiny, jointed legs springing from his spine, holding his body aloft like the Giant Arachs, and another's skin had been replaced with the glistening jade and teal blue hide of a Cheetana.

"They're beautiful," Coren breathed, flipping through page after page of the fantastic creations.

"Unfortunately, there's no way to know if any of this is possible," Sy said, sitting with a yawn. The need to sleep had finally caught up with him.

"If it was possible once, it is possible still," Coren answered. She looked up at him and closed the book, tucking it close to her chest.

"Damren begins training early," Sy said. "And if we truly mean to rescue those Wesh slaves, we have limited time. Perhaps two weeks."

"Why are they called Wesh?" she asked, standing.

He lowered his eyes. "It's a slur. The *en* was removed, showing that they no longer have enough of the women's blood to be considered truly Weshen. I shouldn't use it."

She watched him intently. "Thank you for showing me this," she said, her eyes locked on his instead of the books.

Sy smiled, finally feeling as though he'd finally given her a gift to enjoy instead of another trouble to overcome.

24

Damren's bell did indeed ring before Coren was ready to get up. She pulled the blanket over her head and groaned at waking before the sun breached the slit of skylight above her.

But soon Sy was knocking on her door. "She won't stop, Coren!" he called. "Just get up and deal with it!"

Coren huffed and shoved the covers away. The chill of the rock room woke her stiff muscles slowly, but soon enough she dressed and headed to the kitchen, yawning.

Sy greeted her with a warm mug of strong black tea, and she smiled gratefully at him, inhaling its steam and sweet, fortifying scent. Damren sat at the table spooning oats and sugar into bowls. Coren idly wondered where the old woman got her food, but that wasn't what she planned to ask first.

Instead, she set the mug down and placed the book of shifters open on the table.

"Can you teach me to do this?" she asked, pointing to one of the Weshen-Cheetana shifters.

Damren took an enormous bite and watched placidly as Coren began to fidget, growing impatient. Then she smiled. "No."

"No?" Coren echoed. "Why not?"

Damren only continued eating.

"You'll have to master Single magic first," Sy cautioned, sliding a bowl over to Coren. "And physical training."

Coren nodded, her eyes distracted by how his sleeveless tunic exposed the muscle of his arms. Why did this boy care for her? What did that mean, after everything else was stripped away?

"What will I learn today, then?" she asked, blinking back to the Cheetana in the book.

"Today we see what you can do," the old woman announced. "Eat fast. I'll be in the training room." She dumped her bowl in the sink and padded away.

Coren bent her head and kept her eyes on the pages before her as she ate, letting Sy finish and leave as well. Only then did she sigh and slump against the tabletop.

She could not afford to get distracted by thoughts of love, or anything even close. Things had been so much simpler before, when she lived on an island and kept her heart an island.

Unreachable by no-one except her little family.

Damren's bell jarred her up again, and she glared at the empty kitchen. She knew it wouldn't stop, though, until she had learned every scrap of magic Damren had to offer. So she left her bowl in the sink and sprinted up the stairs to the training room.

When she pushed open the door, a similar sight greeted her. The torches were lit, and Sy was again shirtless. Coren huffed, and she could have sworn Damren grinned before chucking a rock at her head.

She barely ducked in time and whirled on the woman. "What the Magi was that for?"

Damren answered by throwing one at Sy. Coren's eyebrows shot up as he raised his hand and the rock disintegrated in mid-air. A pile of dust drifted to the mat. Coren turned to Damren just in time to see a second rock heading her way.

She tried to focus her magic, but it was too late, and the rock smacked into her hand. Pain shot through her palm and into her wrist, but she said nothing.

Damren grinned and threw another rock.

It went like that all morning, and although Coren quickly learned not to keep her hand in the rock's path, the most she managed was to break the stone into chunks that clattered to the floor.

"What's wrong with my magic? Shouldn't I be learning faster?" she complained, massaging her wrist after yet another rock had connected, her power a split second too late.

"Most of your magic before today has stemmed from emotion, yes?" Damren asked when they paused to rest and restore their strength with lemondrine tonic.

Coren nodded, draining her glass.

"But you've had a brush with Sulit magic?" Damren continued. "Is it still in her system, perhaps?" she asked Sy.

"I gave her the tonic immediately after. It should all be cleansed from her body."

"Wait, isn't the tonic *from* Sulit?" Coren interrupted, remembering Maren's story.

Damren watched her, as though calculating. "The Sulit created it, but they have no need for such restoratives. Their magic comes from the power of nature, which restores itself naturally. Weshen magic restores naturally as well, but the tonic speeds the process, and has helped a few of us maintain our strength since the Sacrifice."

"Maren used it for that," Coren acknowledged. "I got a message from her," she blurted then. "On the beach. I think she sent it with Sulit power." She explained the leaf to them. Sy's eyes widened and Damren's narrowed.

"It was a rare Weshen who was able to befriend the witches," Damren said, "but the message sounds genuine from both witch and Weshen."

Coren nodded. "If they wanted me to come to Rurok, all they had to do was threaten the twins. But if they're safe, I know they'll wait for me there. I just wish I could send them a message back. That I'm coming, but I have things to do." She lowered her eyes to her empty glass, trying to push the wave of sadness away, but like all waves, it rolled over her resolve, leaving her adrift.

"Hey," Damren said. When Coren looked up, Damren hurled a rock right at her face.

And this time, it exploded in a puff of dust and sparkling minerals, the sources suspended in the air as Coren tried to slow her breathing, realizing she'd done it. She marveled at the cloud floating between them.

Damren cackled, her form hazy through the sources. "And you didn't even need the hand motions."

Sy stepped around the wide sphere of dust and grinned at Coren. "The hands help, like a crutch. But this was like the Vespa all over again."

"Except now I know what I'm doing," Coren answered. She concentrated on the sources, their differences now as obvious as the temperatures of the sea's surface and its deeper currents. She willed them to separate, like with like, and soon several piles rested on the floor of the room. "I don't even know what to call these sources. How can I feel their differences so easily?"

"The same way you know light is different from dark," Sy answered. "Now that the magic is awake, it's a natural part of your senses."

"For many students of magic, the need to know conflicts with the ability to do," Damren said. "You're limited by your imagination because you've seen very little." She stood and walked around the sources, and as she moved, the different colored dust at her feet began to move.

"A Weshen magi can be a laborer," she said, and tiny bricks formed, laying themselves atop one another in a wall barely two inches high. "Or she can be an artist." The bricks melted away, and the sources swirled together to create a figurine of a bird in flight, sparkling feathers covering its mottled body.

Damren sat back in her chair and took another drink. "Or, a Weshen magi can be a warrior." The bird's wings stretched wider, its body slimmed and lengthened, and its beak grew more pointed, until a stone dagger rested before them on the floor.

Coren bent to pick it up, and its new form held true, as though it had been carved from the rock wall with tools rather than assembled with an old woman's mind. She turned and hurled the dagger at a wooden target, where it embedded itself near the edge.

"Sy, practice with her. I believe I need to lie down," Damren said then, and rose stiffly, hobbling toward the door. She brushed away Sy's attempts to help, turning back to them before she opened the door. "There is nothing wrong with your magic, Coren. You're stronger than Syashin was initially. But your mind is cluttered and your heart overfull with confusion. The magic must have room to grow." She didn't wait for an answer, only slipped away.

"Shifting drains her quickly," Coren observed when they were alone again, avoiding Damren's comment. These were things she'd already sensed in herself, and the boy in front of her was a source she needed to either separate or fuse into her heart.

But she feared the idea of caring for someone. Of depending on them. Love might shift him into the perfect weapon, ready for someone to aim at her heart.

Sy turned and walked back to the training floor, selecting the same two rods they had used the previous night. "Part of it is her age, she tells me. Just like the body and mind weaken over the years, so does the magic."

"And if you shift to a younger version of yourself?"

"It doesn't stay. You can only hold that form as long as your magic is strong. A few minutes, maybe more for some people."

"Can you do it? SelfShift?" Coren asked

Sy nodded and leaned the rods against the wall. His form flickered, and a slight haze grew around him, as though Coren were seeing him through the shimmery heat of summer. And in an instant, he stood before her, a boy no taller than Kosh. His hair was cropped close to his head, and his chest was the unformed plane of youth, but his eyes were the same.

Coren stared into his eyes too long, trying to remember the little boy she had once known in Maren's yard before the elders had charmed them both to forget.

"I wish I could remember," she said, as his form shifted back, the limbs stretching and muscling before her eyes, the hair seeming to grow inches in seconds. But the eyes were the same, and they didn't break contact until Sy reached for the wooden rods and chucked one at her.

"We can make new memories," he said, shrugging as he began to circle her.

She smiled and struck at him, and the training began again. Sy was harder on her this morning, hitting with more speed and force. Finally, her belly growling with hunger for the noon meal, she managed to strike in such a way to knock his rod to the floor. It clattered away as she pressed the end of hers to his throat.

He grinned. "Good. But don't forget about your other weapons."

"Magic?" she asked. But he shook his head, and faster than she could react, he had knocked her weapon away and swept her to the floor, his forearm in position to crush her throat. Panic swelled in her chest as she clawed at his arm.

"Weapons are useless and magic is dangerous if you can't control your body," he said, his voice low and gravelly. His weight bore down on her, his body coming close to full contact. She stilled under him, no longer trying to struggle away.

Coren's mind stuttered through several responses, but just as she opened her mouth, the kitchen bell rang, and Sy removed his arm, standing and holding out a hand to help her up.

By the door was a stack of towels. Sy threw her one, then took one himself, scrubbing at his face. As Coren wiped her neck and just lower than her shirt's collar, her eyes wandered again to his bare chest, wondering why those ridges and smooth, sun-darkened skin were so pleasing.

"Do all boys look like this?" she wondered.

"Look like what?" Sy asked, lowering the towel.

Coren felt her cheeks flame. She truly hadn't meant to ask that aloud. "Like you," she mumbled.

Sy grinned, his face flushing too. "In EvenFall you'll see much less muscle. More fat. People who have too much to eat and never train. Or people who have had too little to eat all their lives and are wasted to nothing. But soldiers and Weshen boys look like this because we train every day. Resh has better abs," he pointed to the squares of his stomach, "but his arms aren't as strong as mine."

"He's strong enough," Coren muttered to herself, remembering how easily he had pinned her against the tree. Her stomach churned, but then she reminded herself how much had changed. "But I'll be stronger next time."

"I saw him on the beach," Sy said, guilt flashing across his face as he met her eyes. "Before we came here.

He left the island and went to Weshen City, following us."

"He hates me, doesn't he," Coren asked, thinking of the look that had swirled in his dark eyes. She somehow wasn't surprised that Reshra had followed them. She didn't think he would stop, either.

"Resh doesn't understand you. He'd never seen anything except Sulit spells until he saw ours. I think once he gets over the shock, and I can convince him it's shifter magic, he'll be intrigued. Interested in how useful your power can be. He was so curious why I chose you at the hunts."

Coren frowned. She didn't like the idea of drawing *more* of Reshra's interest.

"Why *did* you keep trying to catch me? Why not just go after one of the easy girls?" she asked, lifting her sticky shirt enough to wipe the sweat from her stomach and lower back. "Surely many would offer you an heir." Her eyes slid down his skin once more, daring to notice how his trim waist tapered into sharp indentations at his hips, and how those lines dipped lower, beneath the band of his training pants.

Sy set down his towel and stepped toward her. "I didn't want one of the easy girls. Maybe I'm like Resh that way. I wanted to understand you - to know why you ran from the boys instead of playing the game."

"And do you know now?" she asked, holding her ground as he took another step. They were close enough for her to touch if she raised her hand. She tucked it behind her, her fingers brushing the rock wall.

Sy nodded. "But I'm curious. The more I learn about you, the more I want to."

"To what?" she whispered.

Sy was silent for a beat. "To learn," he answered, taking a final step.

"If I tried to kiss you, would you let me?" he breathed, his eyes flicking down to her lips.

Her stomach flopped, twisting tight. Would she? He hadn't hurt her in all this time. He was safe. He was certainly handsome. And a kiss wasn't an heir.

Before her nerves could win, she nodded, hating how vulnerable this admission made her. A faint smile crossed his lips, and he leaned in slowly, brushing his mouth carefully against hers. The slightest of touches, then he pulled back. She had barely felt the heat of him until she rested a hand against his chest. She could feel the pulse of his heart beneath the warm skin. He glanced down at her hand between them.

"Stop?" he asked.

Coren smiled shyly and slid her hand down his front, removing the barrier as she rested her fingers at his waist. She arched her neck, offering her lips again, and he bent to her, more urgent this time. He slanted his mouth over hers, and she parted her lips, suddenly interested in the way he might taste. Her hand slid around to his back and tugged him closer.

Sy slid his hand into her hair, cradling her head from the rock wall and tilting her chin back to find the base of her neck. Her breathing quickened as the scruff of his unshaven chin scraped her jaw. And then their lips were joined again, and her breath was his breath, and they both learned something more.

It was Sy who broke away first, his eyes strangely shuttered. He smiled at her, though. "Thank you," he whispered. "For not pushing me away."

Then he picked up their empty glasses and damp towels and turned toward the door. "We should go. Damren doesn't like to wait for meals."

Coren nodded. "I'll be right there," she said and watched him go, her fingers brushing against her lips as she puzzled over his odd expression. Although her skin hummed with a sense of satisfaction, she still didn't feel the way she had expected.

For years, she'd rolled her eyes at the other girls' giggles and flushed faces around the boys.

Instead of light as air, she felt even heavier. Somehow, she'd expected a kiss to be *more*. She'd assumed it would make her *want* more. And she couldn't be certain, but the uncertain expression in Sy's eyes made her wonder if maybe he felt the same way.

Perhaps, although life and magic had thrown them together, love wasn't in agreement.

Or perhaps love just wasn't made for people like her, she thought wryly, walking over and tugging the stone dagger from the target. That was the more likely possibility.

Sy ignored Damren's glare as he took his plate down the hall into his room.

He was confused, and he just didn't want to talk to either of the women.

He'd been thinking of kissing Corentine for days now: imagining it, dreaming of it. And now that he had done it, he was more uncertain than ever. The whole time he had felt a strange sense of detachment, as though his lips hadn't connected to the rest of his body.

He hadn't felt the kiss anywhere but his lips - and he'd expected to. He'd expected to feel more, to want more. To want to push her hard against the wall and slide his hands down her side to her slim waist and lower.

But as much as he'd expected the desire - even *wanted* the desire - it simply wasn't there.

Leaning back on his bed, he sighed. He'd wanted to learn more about her, and he'd accomplished that. He just hadn't expected to learn more about himself in the process. Perhaps their experience in the hunts had tainted their touches forever.

Perhaps when they reached EvenFall, or StarsHelm, or even later when the Weshen were free to love and partner again - perhaps then he would find a girl that made him feel everywhere.

Love existed, Sy was certain of it. He'd just have to wait a little longer to find it.

Damren's bell rang again to begin the afternoon session, and he breathed a curse, knowing she would only train him harder if he were late. When he reached the training room, Coren was already busy trying to learn fusion with a glass of tonic. She had separated the sources, but they refused to rejoin.

"How am I supposed to put it back together if I don't know how it goes?" she said, the frustration evident in her voice.

"Stop thinking so much," Damren retorted. "Just feel the sources. Listen to them. They'll *tell* you where to put them."

Coren huffed and closed her eyes, tilting her head toward the glass before her. Sy suppressed a laugh. He remembered this part of his training all too well, and it had taken him many days to learn. Days they didn't have, though, if they were going to have a chance to rescue the Wesh.

"Here," he said, walking to her. He dipped his finger in the water, then the salt, and then the sticky lemondrine. Then he pressed the mixture against her temple. "This is where you hear the sources. In your mind, not your ear."

Coren looked up at him, her mouth parted and brows drawn in confusion. "They speak in your mind?"

Damren snorted and Coren flushed.

"Not in words. Sources aren't sentient," Sy explained, ignoring the old woman. "But if you quiet your mind, you'll feel it, like a magnetic pull. You'll understand where they need to go."

Coren's eyes closed and her face relaxed. He touched her other temple with the mixture and waited.

The minutes passed in silence with no result, and he was trying to figure out another way to explain it to her when she figured it out. The salt began to roll, grain by grain, up the side of the glass and dissolve into the water, and then the murky lemondrine droplets did the same. Sy felt the side of the glass, and the heat needed to complete the tonic was there too, just as it should be.

Coren's eyes opened, a smile spreading across her face. "I did it, didn't I?"

"Great. Now do it with the rock," Damren said, earning a glare from Coren.

"I heard the sources," she said, turning her face up to Sy's. "I felt them in my mind, just like you said."

"Well, then I guess you don't need me anymore," Damren cackled, but she didn't move to leave.

Coren stood, an odd nervousness to her movements. "That's not the first time I've felt the magic with my mind, though," she said. "The Cheetana. When you were unconscious in the cave…she spoke to me. She licked my temple, here," Coren said, touching the place where the salt and lemon had dried on her skin.

"A MagiCreature spoke to you?" Sy said, trying hard to keep the disbelief from his voice. He'd never heard of that. Of course, she'd hit her head in the cave, too. Maybe she'd dreamed it.

"What did it say?" Damren asked, her voice sharp, and Sy snapped his attention to her. Was it possible, then?

Coren blinked at the woman. "She said I'd taken some of her magic, and I should go. That the shadows were following me."

Damren rose so quickly her chair toppled over. "*The* Shadow," she emphasized.

Coren nodded, taking a step back. Sy nearly pulled a muscle trying to get to Damren before she crumpled to her knees.

"I…I need to sit in prayer," Damren said, her voice weak. Sy glanced back at Coren apologetically but didn't stop to explain before helping Damren to the door, then down the stairs and to her room. Damren sat heavily in her rocking chair and shooed him away.

"Don't leave her alone, Sy. We're safe from Shadow here, but if she were to go outside…"

"But Damren, we'll *have* to go outside. We have maybe a week before those Wesh should be transported."

She shook her head. "She won't be ready in time. I'm sorry, Sy. I know you want to help save those people. And they deserve to be helped. But something your father *does* realize, and that you'll need to understand as well, is that sometimes you can only save one. Syashin - make no mistake. If it comes to that, you must save Corentine. Her power…"

"Rest, Damren. Pray. I'll work with Coren and bring dinner in later. We need you, too," he smiled, forcing a soothing tone to his voice, even though all he wanted was to argue with the stubborn old woman.

By the Magi, he intended to rescue those Wesh. It may seem like a choice to Ashemon and Damren, but not to Sy. If it came to a choice, he would leave Coren here with Damren while he traveled alone.

His mind spinning with this new plan, he shut Damren's door and returned to the training room. When he got there, though, it was empty.

Coren wandered the spiral of the library, wishing she had known these books her whole life. Wishing she had known her magic longer, so she could control it.

And more than anything, wishing she could understand the darkness that had settled in her heart. She couldn't quite pinpoint when it had begun, when it had shifted from frustration to rage.

But she raged.

She pulled out a book at random, but the words refused to form before her eyes, and she shoved it back unread. There was no organization here. She kicked at a shelf, wondering which of these books held the secrets to MagiCreatures who spoke in your mind, or SelfShifting with the abilities of a Cheetana.

She imagined the power she would hold over the Restless King if she could merge her body with that of the beautiful Cheetana. Then again, the animal had been easily captured by her whip. Perhaps a stronger creature would be better.

"What are you searching for?" Sy asked from below. She leaned over the railing to look at him. He sat backward on a bench, resting against the study table as he gazed up at her.

"How to SelfShift with a Cheetana," she admitted, hating the petulance in her voice.

"Damren will never teach you that. It was one of the first things I asked for, as well."

"Then I'll teach myself," she said, toying with the sources of the railing. She separated a handful of the metal easily and fused it into a spike, thin and deadly. It pleased her how simple the magic seemed after the day's practice.

Soon maybe she wouldn't even need a teacher. She contemplated throwing the spike at the spines lined before her in the attempt to spear the right book. That seemed as good a method as any.

"What do you know of Shadow?" Sy asked. He wasn't watching her, only staring down at his legs stretched before him.

"I've never heard of it," she said, although this wasn't entirely true. Sorenta had occasionally muttered in delirium about shadows in the singular form, and although she'd asked about the dreams, she'd never gotten a comprehensible answer.

"Shadow is Umbren, and ancient," Sy answered. "We know little of it, but it has always been, and it always will be. Some say the Shadow can be good or bad, but it's always been a tale of nightmares for the Weshen."

"Umbren is blood magic," Coren recalled, and he nodded. "Is my whip *from* Umbren?" she asked abruptly, remembering how each time she took an animal's lifeblood, the whip seemed to grow stronger. And now animals weren't the only thing she had killed with that whip. "Is that why this Shadow thing follows me, because I killed a man with blood magic somehow bound in that braid?"

Sy's brows were drawn in confusion. She knew her logic must sound ridiculous and incoherent, but she had no patience to explain. Something in the darkness of her heart nodded at this reasoning.

"I have no way of knowing," he said, but his voice was low and troubled. "Have you ever felt a soul?" he asked then, changing the subject so abruptly that it was her turn to frown at him. She walked down the stairs slowly, circling him as she headed toward the ground.

Souls didn't have substance to feel, did they? They weren't sources. But sick swirled in her belly as she remembered Tellen's passing, and how it had felt as if her cousin's very soul had brushed against hers. "No," she said, swallowing against the sensation.

Sy watched her, tapping the pads of his fingers soundlessly on the table behind him.

"Yes," she whispered, stopping at the top of the last step and using her magic to shave the iron spike into flakes like black snow. She blew gently on them, and they drifted in the air, like feathers shorn from an invisible bird.

"Damren told me yesterday of Triple magic. I think it's what the king covets, and if we can find it, we can change *everything*," he answered.

"What is it?" she asked, still intent on the flakes floating in the air, like broken pieces of shadow.

"SoulShifting."

The word yanked her out of her reverie. "SoulShifting," she repeated in a whisper. Even the word was the stuff of ancient magic. "And who has done it?"

"Damren says no-one for generations. But once, long ago, it was *your* family, Coren. Damren said that long ago someone in your family was able to pull the soul from one body and push it, still living, into another body."

"Life and death. A shifter who could control the very source of life," she nodded.

This.

This was something a king would grow restless to find, willing to tear apart countries and families in the search.

This was something she could pour her heart into learning.

25

Sy rose early the next morning, even before Damren. He listened at her door but heard nothing, so he began to prepare the strong tea and oats that had prefaced each day of his training.

"Is Damren okay?" Coren asked, coming into the kitchen and rubbing her eyes.

"I haven't seen her yet, but I think she will be." He set a mug before her and smiled at how she bent her face to inhale the steam.

"How many days do we have before the Wesh are moved?" she asked after a sip.

"Six, if the papers are correct. But we need two of those to get down the mountain and through the passage. I think we'd have a better chance taking them from the auction house in EvenFall than on the road."

She tilted her head at him, her brows drawn. "I would have picked the opposite."

He grinned. "But I'm a Paladin and the General's First Son. This is something I've trained for my whole life." He shrugged when she glared. "It's time all my lessons work for something other than hunting creatures and talismans."

"So what do you plan, exactly?" she muttered, turning her attention to a bowl of oats.

"I know the auction house, and where they keep the slaves. I've been there with Father before. And I have contacts in EvenFall that can be persuaded to help, I think. They can certainly help me hide the slaves much easier than I could on the road. Plus they'll be closer to the passage to Weshen."

"Four more days," she said, setting down her spoon and shaking her head. "I'm afraid I won't be ready."

"You won't be," Damren said from the door. "Which is why you will stay here with me, while Syashin goes alone to EvenFall."

Sy glanced down at his breakfast, not wanting Coren to see his agreement.

"No!" Coren said, startling Sy with her forcefulness. She pushed away from the table, seething at both of them. "I have lost everything. My family, my home, my simple existence. In one day I began to live an entirely different life. But I gained so much, too," she continued, controlling her voice better. "I have the power to help these people - *my* people - and I would be no better than the dark kingdoms if I refused to help them. Killing the king is a dream, certainly. But this. This is something I *know* I can do."

Sy could tell how much it pained her to admit all of this. Even though Damren had said nothing, he knew she would never agree to Coren going. Not with the threat of Shadow so heavy on the old woman's heart.

He didn't truly understand the threat, but he trusted Damren, and so in that moment he made a decision. He would train like normal for four days, then leave in the secret of the night, without telling either of the women. Neither would be able to follow him - Damren was too old to travel the mountains, and Coren would have no map.

Nodding at the decision, he took the last bite of his breakfast and stood.

"Ready to train?" he asked Coren, catching Damren's eye and winking to let her know he would smooth the situation.

Coren scraped what was left of her oats in the trash and followed him from the kitchen, shoulders slumped. As Sy left, he saw Damren sit heavily at the table and bury her face in a mug of tea. These women were too similar, he thought.

The morning went quickly, and so did the days that followed. Each day, Coren grew in leaps of magical power, impressing even Damren herself, although the old woman never complimented her. Coren pushed away fatigue and injury and the despair Sy had seen those first nights and focused like the noon sun on the task of learning to control her power.

And each night, he knew she sat in bed for hours, reading by candlelight. He expected her to tire, or get frustrated, or her enthusiasm to wane, but using her magic seemed to energize her. She learned weapons far beyond her whip, which Sy was grateful for. If that whip did indeed have anything to do with Umbren blood magic, it was probably better that she didn't use it.

He wondered if the whip itself could have sparked her to kill that guard in Weshen City, and if that were true, what else could it whisper to her?

The morning of the fourth day, Coren stood in the training room, demonstrating for Damren as though it were the final test in school.

"SourceShifting," she announced, pulling water from a bucket and separating it into droplets. Then she fused the drops into a spiral that wound around her body and up to the ceiling, like the spiral stairs of the library. She moved the stream of water much like a whip, striking out at a punching bag. The bag swayed gently with the force, but Damren only grunted.

Coren dumped the snakka of water back in the bucket and glared.

Turning to the wall of weapons, she chose a club of wood and iron. Disintegrating it into piles of sources, she swirled the dust together on the floor, using the training mat as a canvas and the dust as paint.

"That's beautiful," Sy said, and Coren smiled. But Damren only sighed and tapped her foot.

Coren squared her shoulders, and Sy knew she was near the end of her patience. She began to fuse the sources back together, forming the weapon again in seconds and hurling it at a wooden target. The target cracked in half, its pieces falling to the floor with the club. Damren nodded slightly.

Sy pressed back a smile as he saw Coren's jaw clench. Damren had always been the same to him, but he was used to it.

"SelfShifting," Coren bit out and closed her eyes. Sy watched, wide-eyed, as she shrank again to a girl of no more than ten, clutching her too-large clothes around her tightly.

She held the form for nearly two minutes before her body began to shimmer and stretch back to its normal size. Sy could see the weariness around her eyes - using this much magic at once was exhausting. He tossed her a skin of lemondrine water, and she nodded in thanks.

"Is that all?" Damren asked, yawning as Coren lowered the skin.

"It wouldn't be all if you'd teach me more!" Coren finally exploded. "I have spent every hour working for your approval."

"And I will never give it," Damren answered, grinning. "It's pointless to work for the approval of others. Work only for the approval of yourself. *That* is power. *That* is true magic."

Coren clenched her fingers into fists and opened her mouth, then closed it. Instead, she stalked from the room, slamming the door behind her.

"You shouldn't tease her like that, Damren," Sy said, smiling but shaking his head.

"It's not teasing. It's the truth. She wants to impress me, but I've seen too many arrogant magi in my time. Trying to impress others only brings the darkness of jealousy."

"She's already as capable with her magic as me, and in only four days," Sy pointed out. Her progress was almost unbelievable.

"True. But she still has much to learn - much of her shifting is that of an artist rather than a warrior. And her stamina is weak. She must learn to ration her power and not be so dependent on the tonic. It will be difficult to find lemondrines in Riata."

"So she can come with me tomorrow?" Sy asked, surprised.

"Of course not. I'm talking about when you return from your mission. By then, I hope to have trained her enough to resist Shadow."

"So it's possible to resist?"

Damren shrugged. "Anything is possible. But Shadow has just awakened from long decades of sleep. It will be hungry."

"Which means it will be weak," Sy reasoned.

"Which means it will be desperate," Damren returned. "Shadow is an ancient, used to waiting. But anything magical that has been denied its magic for so long will be desperate to gain what power it can."

Sy crossed his arms, feeling she wasn't only speaking of Shadow, but also of Corentine and himself.

Coren stalked down the hallway, wishing with all her heart that she was back on Weshen Isle, running the sunlit upper plains.

In that moment, she hated Damren more than the Restless King, and she felt she might do anything to be free of the old woman. What was the purpose in rationing out her training and only teaching her a useless bit at a time?

Coren had heard Damren's comments to Sy, and they made her blood nearly boil because she knew the woman was withholding knowledge. Of course her skills weren't that of a warrior - she'd never been in a battle, had never trained like Sy at the boys' school, and was certainly not learning any of that here, except what Sy was teaching her.

The old woman had no idea what life was like outside of her hole in the mountain.

Her room seemed too hot, as though the air itself were angry, and the entire hallway stunk of stagnant air. The kitchen was no better, and even the library held no interest for her, with its jumbled shelves. She needed to be alone, and she needed to see the sky and the sun. Not from a sliver of skylight.

She needed the sky vast and ever-reaching above her.

So with Sy and Damren holed up in the training room, likely discussing how else they could hold her back, Coren strode to the entryway and the solid wall she now knew could be shifted to make into a doorway. Patting the rock the way she'd seen Sy do, she felt the sources inside its solidity. She could feel where the thinnest part was, and she began to shift the sources aside to make an exit.

Soon a glimpse of white snow and a gust of icy air brought a smile to her face, and she shifted faster, ignoring her fatigue.

A slim opening formed, just enough for her to squeeze through, and she was free. The cold ripped tears from her eyes, and she briefly thought of going back for her cloak.

But she didn't need to be out here long. She just needed to see the sky.

Stepping farther out onto the ledge, Coren spread her arms wide, breathing in the biting air. The sky was immense and white-blue above her, and the forests below were nothing more than a greenish-black smear. Snow swirled around her feet, whipping at her thin training clothes.

"Corentine!"

She yelled a curse, refusing to look at Sy.

"Coren, this is insanity! You know what could be out here!" he called again.

She sighed, pushing out a puff of white air. "Yes, Sy. The Shadow. Are you afraid to speak its name?" she taunted, turning to look back at him. He was waiting just inside the slit she had created, his shoulders too broad to follow.

"There are shadows in all of life!" she called, gesturing to the crevices beyond the ledge, the hollow of Damren's cave home behind him, the dark trees below, and the ocean far in the distance.

But even as she spoke the words, she felt a creeping sensation behind her own back.

Turning, she saw nothing but rock and snow and the normal play of sunlight and shadows. The wind seemed to ripple the white and gray and black together, though, almost as though it were capable of shifting the sources too, fusing them to create a new being.

Coren shivered.

"Please come back inside," Sy called again, already moving to shift the rock away enough to join her.

Her spine slumped as she admitted she couldn't stay out here. The cold was too much. Her hot anger and pride had frozen, leaving her with regret for how she'd acted. She turned and edged back into the mountain, and the two of them together shifted the rock, shutting out the rest of the wind and snow.

Inside was darker by comparison to the white world outside, and Coren found herself examining each corner's worth of shadows to see if there was something innately evil about the fusion of light and dark.

"I just don't understand why she keeps so much from me," she said as she followed Sy into the kitchen.

"Damren has always held her knowledge close," he answered, beginning to warm water for tea. "She comes from a generation of superstition, and rightly so." He turned and pinned her in a serious gaze. "Remember, Damren is old enough to have seen our secrets betray us, and our magic turn from a blessing to a curse."

Coren nodded, her regret swiftly congealing into guilt. "I'm sorry. I just...I really need to go with you to EvenFall. I need a purpose beyond learning. I need to help someone besides myself. I can't have lost everything I love for nothing!" She paced the small kitchen, still too restless.

"Come on," Sy said. "Let's go use some of that energy to train. You need to work on your hand-to-hand, in case your magic and weapons fail."

She rolled her shoulders, wishing he weren't so single-minded. Then again, it would feel nice to throw a punch right now. She nodded. "As long as Damren isn't there judging me."

Sy laughed. "She went to lie down. We'll be alone."

Coren's stomach flipped at that. They hadn't been alone since the night they'd kissed. Her imagination spiraled into thoughts of training in hand-to-hand with Sy, all alone in the torchlight. She followed him up the stairs, building little walls around her emotions with each step.

She couldn't allow herself to be distracted by curiosity; she needed control.

When they finished, hours later, Coren felt satisfied. She had kept her eyes from Sy's muscles, mostly, and had even connected a few punches and kicks. They would both be bruised tomorrow, and that pleased her.

"I'm going to take a bath," she announced, and Sy nodded, heading to check on Damren.

Coren watched him go, granting herself a moment to examine the tangle of thoughts surrounding Sy. She cared for his happiness, wanted him to stay safe, and she was distracted by his body. But something in her still resisted the idea of love or lust growing between them.

Like a wall of clear ice, something was keeping them from falling where others wished them to fall.

Her muscles burned from the day's training, and Coren built the fire high to warm her bath. She relaxed deeply into the water, letting it ease her aches. Rinsing soap from her hair, she evaluated how much more defined her arms were becoming, and looking down, she appreciated the new firmness of her thighs and stomach.

Coren had always been slimmer than many of the island girls, but here in the mountain she was growing sleek. She smiled, remembering the Cheetana from the tunnel, and how every part of her body was learning a purpose now.

A purpose that was so much more than attracting a boy in a hunt. Each day, Coren was forming and refining her body into a weapon she could use to save her people.

The soap was gone and the water cooling around her when she heard a noise, like the door creaking open a few more inches.

"Sy? Damren?" she called, but the steam was thick in the room, and she could see nothing when she pulled open the curtain. "Sy?" she called again. Surely he wouldn't come in when he knew she was bathing. She began to shift the water in the air, gathering the steam into spheres and rings of water.

As the air began to clear, a shadow seemed to slink out the door, as though someone had been standing in the hall, watching.

Uneasy, Coren drained the bath and dried herself quickly. She hurried into her steam-dampened clothes, thinking how something about the dark and the silence of the mountain had her feeling very, very exposed.

She pushed the spheres of water droplets still hanging in the air back into the tub, where they broke apart and drained, chilling the room. Coren wrapped her hair in the towel and nearly ran down the hall to her room. She saw nothing and no-one in the hall, and her room was silent and empty. She hung the towel to dry, and quickly braided her hair and tugged on her slippers. Palming a knife, she wrapped her whip around her middle, under the tunic's cover.

Although training had finished for the day, an ominous sensation hung in the quiet air. A whisper lingered at her ear, telling her the fight was far from over.

Sy leaned against the wall of the kitchen, his bare feet propped up by the fire. He had been helping Damren harvest the lemondrine peel from her many hothouse trees, and the kitchen smelled heavenly sour-sweet.

A pile of peel waited on the table for him to slice and boil, but the water wasn't quite ready, and for now Sy was content watching Damren's precise movements as she pulled apart the sections of fruit and squeezed their juice into a shallow silver bowl.

"It's lucky the lemondrines were ready to pick," she said, not lifting her eyes from her task. "Having you two here has depleted nearly everything I'd saved from the last harvest."

"I'm sorry," Sy said, smiling because he knew she loved having them there.

"Corentine is progressing well with her control, yes?" Damren asked, casting him a sideways glance.

"Much faster than I ever was able to," he agreed.

"Soon we can see about finding you two a MagiCreature to bond with."

The words straightened Sy from his lazy pose. "Am I really ready for that?" He'd spent so many boyhood nights poring over the glorious drawings of Weshen men and women with wings, tusks, clawed hands, tails like barbed whips, wanting that power so much his young body had trembled with anticipation.

Naturally, Damren had told him it would be impossible to complete that stage of magic without the Magi's reversal of the Sacrifice.

"What's changed, Damren? Do you think the reversal has begun?"

She shrugged. "You've changed. And she's changed. I know nothing of the Magi, for they don't deign to visit an old woman locked in the mountains. There is indeed magic in the air, but not all of it is Weshen. If the magic of the two dark kingdoms is growing, it can only be in response to the Weshen magic growing. Balance in everything, remember."

Sy nodded distractedly, his head filled with the old images he'd once lulled himself to sleep with.

Damren held a handful of peels out to him. "The water is ready," she prompted. He obediently began slicing the peel in tiny sections and dropping them in the boiling pot before him. The sharp scent of lemondrine oil permeated the room, spread by the tendrils of white steam.

"There is a book in my room that I've been saving. I think it's time I shared it with you," she said, smiling when he caught her eye over the steam. Damren finished the last of the juicing and rinsed her hands in the rock basin that served as her kitchen sink.

"I'll fetch it now. You keep working on those peels."

"Yes, Damren," Sy said, grinning in excitement as she bustled out of the room. She'd always been as much of a taskmaster as the General and his teachers in Weshen City, but he'd never minded taking her orders. He hungered for the magic she knew, and he was willing to do anything she asked to get more of that precious knowledge.

The steam thickened from the boiling pot, and he cranked the chain, raising the pot a few inches. It wouldn't do for all the water to boil out before the peel cooked through.

Sy shifted some of the steam away from the fireplace so he could better see his work, and he noticed a dark place in the corner of the kitchen. A shadow where none should be.

A chill raced up his back, despite the heat at his face.

"Damren?" he called, standing. She'd been gone a while. He placed his handful of peels on the table, keeping the small knife out. There was another dagger strapped to his belt, and he palmed it as well. Something sinister hung in the very air.

Silence. Sy shifted more of the steam, and the shadow seemed to dissipate with it, slinking away, out the open door. He left the kitchen and shoved the paring knife in his belt, exchanging it for the eight-candle sconce from the entryway.

He had just started down the blackened hall when he heard a hoarse cry.

"Damren!" he yelled, breaking into a sprint. He burst into Damren's room.

"You will not have her!" the old woman shrieked, staring wildly into the darkness. Her arms were up, and Sy felt the magic swirling from her fingers. She was shifting the particles in the air. "Sy! It's here! Help me find it!"

Sy felt for something to shift, but all he felt was the chill air of the rock room. He tried shifting the heat of the candle flame, but fire had never been his to control. It was too ethereal - his magic depended on the substance of a source, not the movement of its particles.

"There's nothing here," he said, but even then he began to feel it. The shadows in the corners were growing, fusing together.

Darkness snuffed out one of the flames, and then another, leaving a single light against the black room.

Damren shrieked again, waving her arms in a complex shift, but despite her efforts, the last light shrunk into itself, dying a slow, slow death.

"Sy?" a voice called from the hall. Coren.

"Stay aw-!" Damren yelled, but her voice ended abruptly in a terrible gurgle, and Sy charged toward where he knew she had been.

The darkness was thick around him. Palpable. He felt its form as solidly as Damren's in his arms. She slumped to the ground, heavier than he had prepared for.

Yelling wordlessly, he charged into the center of the dark, and somehow it burst backward against the wall, exploding into shards of harmless shadow.

A single candle flame sprung back to life, reviving as the air in the room stilled and returned to normal. Sy chased the bits of shadow around the room, searching for whatever he had just disintegrated, but there was nothing.

"Corentine!" he yelled, desperate that whatever it was had not found her.

"I'm here." Her voice came from the hall, just beyond the door. "I felt it too. Like fingers of ice and despair on my skin." She entered the room and took the sconce gently from his shaking hand. She lit the other candles one by one, and as each light grew to envelop the room, Sy fell to his knees.

Damren lay crumpled before them, her throat slashed open. The floor was lurid and sticky with her fresh blood.

Coren gasped. "What did this?"

Sy could barely answer through his grief. Damren - who had helped him when no-one else could. Dead.

He had failed her completely, utterly, in the only way that mattered.

"Shadow," he whispered, finally. "The Umbren Shadow is no myth or children's nightmare. It's awake, and it was following us."

Coren knew better than to keep asking him questions, though she burned with them.

Whatever had done this to Damren seemed to be gone, though she and Sy checked every corner and nook in the bedrooms and hall. He grew more listless with each step. Coren knew he needed to grieve, so while he continued to look, she cleaned and prepared Damren's broken body, arranging her on the bed as though she were sleeping, then wiping the floor of blood.

When Sy finally finished searching the main floor, he shifted the mountain rock over the hall's entry, hopefully sealing them in and whatever evil creature out. They would have to open the seal eventually to leave, but they hoped this would buy them some time in safety.

Only then did Coren lead him back to Damren's room, where she placed two chairs beside the bed and lit the room with as many candles as she could find. She sat by his side through the long hours of the night vigil, and she lent her voice to the funeral song she had learned in so many hard ways over the years.

In the early dawn hours, when a sliver of light was beginning to arc into his bedroom from the single skylight, Coren followed him to his bed and curled behind him. Her arm circled his chest, the connection keeping them grounded, not in reality but in the comforting presence of each other.

After several minutes Sy rolled to face her, and she leaned into his shoulder, then let him turn her face up to his.

He sought solace in her lips, his fingers shaking as they traced her neck, collarbone, then down her sides above her thin tunic, coming to rest heavily on her hipbone. Their lips met again and again, but more gently each time, and with less passion.

Coren wiped each tear from his cheek as it appeared.

She wasn't sure how she was supposed to feel. She mourned the loss of Damren, but her ache came from seeing him in such pain. His touch was warm, but it didn't stir her heart or the core of her body, where love and lovers were supposed to dwell.

The light above them strengthened and Sy blinked away what turned out to be his last tear.

"I'm sorry, Corentine. I just can't do this." He pushed away from her on the narrow bed, covering his eyes with his arm. "I can't do this with you."

And then Coren understood. Her heart was closed. She'd walled it away to avoid hurt, like Sy shifting the mountain rock to keep out Shadow. His words *should* have hurt her, but all she felt was relief that she didn't have to unseal that wall quite yet.

She didn't think she could live through it if the wall crumbled and exposed her heart to the wrong person.

"I once thought I might fall in love with you," Sy murmured, his voice muffled beneath the fabric of his sleeve. "But even as little as I know of love, I can tell we're not meant to have it. Whatever we do here, in a bed like this, is just an extension of the hunts." He pushed up on his elbow, looking at her again.

"I feel it here," he touched his temple, "but not here," and his heart. Laying one hand gently over hers, he watched her for a reaction. She nodded, hoping he would continue to explain, so she wouldn't have to.

"All this time, I thought I was resisting my father's wishes, but everything I've tried to force with you only extends what he wants."

"He wants a magical heir," Coren said, and Sy nodded, his eyes dark and closed.

"A magical heir isn't the answer to Weshen's problems." He sat up farther. "Coren, I'm tired of waiting. I don't want to sit and grow old hoping for the next generation to be the one."

"It has to be us," she clarified, and finally a weak smile broke onto his face. She sat up and crossed her legs beneath her. "Sy, I know nothing of romantic love either, but I do know friendship, and that's what I feel here." She touched her own heart.

"I'll follow you, but I'll also lead you, and together we can *become* the magical Weshen heir he wishes for - the creation won't be a helpless baby, but the magic inside each of us. We will rise like the sun and burn away Zorander Graeme's hold on Riata."

Sy laughed then, the sound triumphant and strong. Grief lingered in his eyes, but Coren knew he was ready.

"Shall we go to EvenFall today?" she asked. "We have Wesh to rescue."

His face settled into a hard, handsome line that she was proud of. "Pack for cold and climbing."

26

Climbing down the mountain was easier than climbing up, and Sy was grateful for it. He felt drained, exhausted from the night's vigil and full of a terrible regret for what had happened.

He would never tell her, but he suspected Damren's death was Corentine's fault. He guessed Shadow had entered when she opened the rock door of Damren's home in anger.

Sy didn't want to live his life with blame, but he knew there was a part of him that might never forgive Coren for her rash disbelief in the dangers of Umbren. He only hoped now she might take him more seriously when he warned her about danger in Sulit and Riata.

They spoke little on the journey down the slick rock, stopping only once for a hurried meal.

"Do you feel any of the shadows around us?" Corentine asked, warming her hands above the small fire.

"It's Shadow, singular, and no, I don't," Sy answered, knowing his voice was harsh but his fatigue made him unable to temper it.

"Sy, I'm really sorry. I know how much Damren meant to you. How much her knowledge could have meant to everyone."

He turned away, closing himself to her words. He couldn't stop to think about it, and right now he didn't care a bit about the lost magical knowledge. Damren had been more parent to him than his father, and losing her was a wound that felt like it would never heal. "Let's keep going. I want to be inside the mountain passage before night."

Corentine nodded and repacked their remaining food without another word. They made good progress, but still night descended before they reached the Weshen City wall. Sy hated to admit it, but he knew they needed rest. Although desperation to rescue the Wesh was beginning to needle his every thought, he knew pushing forward until he collapsed would help nothing.

"We need to sleep for a few hours," he said, not waiting for a response. He lead them to a tiny cave he knew of, just beyond the grove of lemondrine trees where the *Alimente* still waited, untouched. The cave was too small to hide Shadow, and after cramming their bags and bodies into the cramped space, they both worked quickly to shift rock across the opening, walling themselves in.

"This feels like a tomb," Corentine whispered, lighting a single candle.

"Well, for a shifter it's not," Sy said, draining the last bit of a water skin and closing his eyes to rest. He slept hard for several hours before the dreams began: Damren, alone and walled forever in a real rock tomb. Sitting up too quickly in the darkness, Sy smacked his forehead on the rock ceiling. Cursing, he fumbled for a candle. The light showed nothing threatening, though. Corentine slept peacefully, and their shifting had held, keeping them safe inside the rock.

Still, time was running short. He pulled bread from a bag and began to eat. Soon Corentine stirred too, and rubbing her eyes, she tried awkwardly to stretch her legs. Silently, she took the offered food.

"Ready?" He zipped the bag closed a few minutes later. She nodded, and he shifted away enough rock for a tiny peephole. The world outside was still dark, but all seemed quiet and still. He widened the opening and shoved a bag through.

"The passage isn't far, and it's only a few hours' journey under the mountains."

"So it's an underground passage?" she asked, and he heard the nervousness in her voice as they stepped out of the cave.

"Yes," he answered, shouldering his bags and setting a quick pace. "But it's not so tight as the one from the city. And Shadow could never follow us there. It can only go where there's both light and dark. Plus, the passage was enchanted by the Magi as part of the barrier. Only full-blooded Weshen can pass through unharmed."

"Full-blooded?" she repeated, following him closely across the moonlit sand toward the city wall. "But how will we get the Wesh back through the passage once we rescue them?"

"As long as they have some Weshen blood in their lines, they may pass through. They just won't be unharmed," he said. "I traveled through once with a guard whose family had lived in Riata, and mixed their blood with a Riatan family. He grew weak and sick inside the mountain, but he made it through. The effects aren't permanent."

Her eyes were wide, and he shrugged. "I doubt the Wesh will mind the sickness if it gains them their freedom."

"So how has the Restless King not breached the mountains, then?" she asked. "Surely he's tried with Wesh soldiers."

They were nearing the entrance to the passage, and the wall loomed in the distance. Sy hushed her with his finger. "There are always guards watching the passage here. They check everyone who comes out. We've killed many of Zorander Graeme's attempts."

"You mean you killed our own people!" she whispered back, fury in her eyes.

Sy regarded her grimly. "We killed traitors." He shushed her again, and they crept closer. Just as he'd said, there were two guards standing watch at the mouth of the passage.

He motioned to her to wait, and he slunk between the trees, using their early-morning shadows as cover. Once he was close enough to see the iron gate that barred the entrance, he began to shift the metal bars, careful to remove only what they would need to slip through. He turned to beckon to Corentine, only to find her mere feet behind him.

Smiling for the first time since Damren's death, Sy pointed to the two guards, then up to the rock face. Corentine nodded in understanding, and as he removed the last bar, she shifted part of the mountain face into fist-sized rocks that tumbled down the cliff just beyond the entrance. The guards snapped to attention, leaving their posts to investigate.

Sy and Corentine sprinted to the passage opening and shoved their bags through. They had just made it into the darkened entrance when the guards returned, arguing about what they'd heard and seen. Sy quickly fused the iron bars in their original position, and silently, they backed into the Weshen passage.

Coren was struggling to keep up with Sy's pace through the mountain tunnel, but it was as though her limbs were filled with sand. She fell farther and farther behind, finally stumbling to her knees with barely enough strength to call out to him.

She heard Sy's steps rushing back to her, but when she tried to look up at him, the candle he held grew in her vision until it was all she could see, and she screwed her eyes shut against the brightness.

"Corentine?"

His voice sounded so far away, like he was calling her name from the very beaches of Weshen Isle. She smiled softly, thinking of running the plains there, free and carefree. Her stomach churned then, and the image behind her eyes grew sinister. She imagined herself running the plains, but running from Shadow, and nearly being caught. In her imagination, she jumped from the cliff, but Shadow clung to her, wrapping around her body as she fell, splashing into the sea and sinking and sinking and sinking and-

"Corentine!"

Her body was shaking, or someone was shaking her body.

"Open your eyes and look at me!"

She tried to obey, but even her eyelids were too heavy to move. She struggled and finally peeled open one eye.

"Hmm?" she breathed.

"Are you going to be sick?" Sy asked. Syashin, she remembered. He would help her. He always did. He liked her. He didn't like kissing her, though. Her brain began to spin again, and she closed her eyes against the nausea, but that made it worse, like she was spinning away into nothingness.

Her stomach churned from the imagined movement, and she rolled to her knees, heaving, gulping at the cool cave air.

"Coren, we're only halfway through. Can you stand?" Sy held out a hand and she took it, stumbling to her feet. She swayed, and the sick bubbled in her belly, but she nodded hesitantly. Sy pulled her hand out to rest on the rough passage wall.

"I'll carry the bags. You go in front, and I'll be right here in case you fall again."

Their progress slowed to nearly nothing, as Coren repeatedly had to pause to rest and dry heave every dozen steps.

"I need to stop," she said finally. There wasn't a scrap of energy left in her body.

"No, we need to move," Sy answered, prodding at her back. "We have to get you out of here." But her legs buckled, and she sat right down on a bag, pulling it from his shoulder. She blinked up at him, the near-darkness and the shadows in the cave passage making her dizzy and fearful again.

"Don't you know what's happening?" he asked. Her mind was like mud. "You're obviously reacting to the passage. This is just like what happened to that guard. You have the strongest magic in decades, and you're not even a full-blooded Weshen," he said, ending on a sort of strained laugh.

"Wesh," she managed, unintentionally cutting the word to its appropriate label.

"Don't call yourself that," Sy said, anger drawing his mouth into a tight line. "After we finish with the Restless King, no-one will ever have to call themselves that. Now get up. You'll only feel like this - or worse - as long as you're in the passage."

Coren groaned inwardly and struggled to pull herself up. One foot at a time, she instructed herself, fixing her eyes on the semi-circle of light thrown out by the candle.

It felt like hours passed, but eventually the candle was not the only light in front of her.

"There's the exit," Sy said, breathing hard. She could feel him behind her, nearly pushing her along with a hand on her back, the bags bumping between them.

She tripped over her own feet trying to hurry toward the light, and as she stumbled into the bright morning sun, Coren dropped to her hands and knees in the grass, breathing a prayer of thanks to the Mirror Magi for the impossibility of yet another safe journey.

"We made it," she grinned, rolling over onto her back. The dizziness was already subsiding somewhat.

"Welcome to Riata," Sy said, letting the bags slide from his shoulders and dropping to sit next to her.

Coren closed her eyes against the sun for a moment, noticing how the sickness in her belly and the heaviness in her limbs was dissipating. She breathed deeply of the fresh air. It was warmer already.

But then a chill slunk over her, and she pushed herself up, staring at the mountain above them. The morning sun was still weak, and the clouds hung low, filling the cliffs with undulating shadows that strummed at her nerves. She turned her gaze back to Sy. He looked exhausted.

"How am I not a full Weshen?" she asked, wondering what other family secrets her blood might hold.

"Many Weshen had children with Riatan noble families. Your grandmother lived in Riata, didn't she?"

Coren nodded and reached into her bag for a skin of water, not certain that was a sufficient answer. "We have to rescue those slaves, Sy."

"We will," he said, the certainty in his voice reassuring as she closed her eyes to drink.

"How far to EvenFall?" she asked, putting the skin away and standing shakily to look at the flower-pocked meadow spread before them, and the dark woods beyond. But the answer never came, because an icy wind blasted down from the mountain, knocking her off balance and sucking the air from her lungs.

Her face smashed into the grass, and her eyes screwed shut against the freezing air.

"Coren!" Sy screamed, but it was too late.

Darkness was covering her, the sensation just like her vision from the passage. Shadows slunk over her skin, blackening it, crawling down her throat and behind her eyes. She tried to scream, but her voice strangled in her throat, and she felt herself falling and falling. Coren rolled, trying to curl in on herself, to protect herself, but her muscles spasmed and stretched, flattening her face-first on the ground.

Another scream filled the air, and Sy shouted, but all Coren could do was struggle to resist.

Her blood swirled and bubbled in her veins, her mind filling with a war between light and dark, and all that was winning was Shadow.

Sy was desperate to understand what was happening.

A tall shape had leaped from the cliff, darkness trailing its insubstantial form as it landed on Coren, somehow both covering her and dissolving into her. Her pores oozed the blackness, but as Sy scratched her skin, his fingers grasped nothing. Somehow, an oily smoke was attacking her.

Was this Shadow? It seemed so different from what he'd beaten at Damren's. He fought to help her, but she only twisted away from him, screaming as though his touch were worse than whatever grasped her mind.

This couldn't be happening. His brain swirled with panic. They'd come so far. Why wouldn't the Magi protect them now? Coren was going to die here, at the base of the NeverCross Mountains, barely two steps into Riata.

And then a different sort of scream registered, coming from far above them, and Sy's heart dropped.

It was over.

A flap of giant, gray-shaded wings knocked him to the ground and away from Coren's writhing form. He rolled head over heels several feet, then managed to scramble up and pull his dagger, but he was too late.

An enormous Vespa crouched directly on Coren's back, wings spread wide as its golden, deadly claws sunk deep into her skin. It screamed and she screamed as it raked those poisonous talons across the whole of her back, leaving bright streaks of blood beneath the shredded fabric of her shirt.

Sy lunged at the MagiCreature, slicing at its wings, but it only batted him away like he weighed nothing. He hit the ground hard, the dagger bouncing away into the grass.

The Vespa flapped its wings and rose a few feet, kicking out at her and rolling her body. She moaned as the creature lifted in the air, hovering just out of Sy's reach. He cursed and yelled at the MagiCreature, trying desperately to fixate on its sources and dissipate it like Coren had once done.

But his magic was not strong enough, had never been strong enough, and the great bird only dodged and swooped in the air.

Shouting in frustration, Sy dove for his bag. If he could find his bow sword and assemble it and take good aim…yet even as he rushed through the motions, he knew there was no time.

The darkness was beginning to flake from Coren's skin like scales from a fish, and she moaned, clawing at her mottled and bloodied flesh. The Vespa ducked and dove at her again, another claw swiping across her stomach, bringing more blood and screams. Sy tugged desperately at the weapon, which was caught on something inside the overstuffed bags.

The Vespa screamed once more, and Coren yelled wordlessly back at it, her voice hoarse with pain and outrage and anguish. She cradled her arms over her bleeding stomach, but as she twisted, Sy saw the braid of her whip loose around her middle.

"Coren! Whip!" he shouted at her, finally breaking the bow sword free and rushing to click its parts together. She fumbled with the handle, gritting her teeth as the whip rubbed against her raw skin. But when the Vespa dived once more, she struck out at it, severing a single golden claw that fell to the ground near her hand with a thud.

Sy finally loosed an arrow, but the Vespa jerked away at the last second, screaming in what sounded like rage. It circled away, higher and higher, until Sy couldn't see it anymore. He didn't think it was coming back, but he didn't even care. He scrambled to Coren, gathering her into his arms as she shook with pain and knowing.

His back was exposed to the sky as he held her close, but he cared nothing for the threat of the creature. He rocked her like a child, smoothing her hair and brushing away the strange dark ash that was still flaking from her skin. Blood soaked her shirt, and any remaining shreds of hope disintegrated as he saw the Vespa's blue-gold poison shimmering in each wound.

"I'm going to die," she whispered. "After all this, I'm going to die."

Shadow hurt. It felt pain, a new sensation.

Or rather, a sensation it hadn't felt in many, many years.

The Vespa - yes, Shadow knew those - it had turned on its creator and chosen the girl instead. It had denied its dark-earth, bloody origins and taken to the clean, smooth glass of the sea and sky instead.

But Shadow wasn't as worried about the Vespa as it was worried about its own broken skin. No, not broken. Shattered.

Its own shattered skin.

Shadow was not supposed to be in pieces. That meant there was too much light. Shadow was supposed to join the light and dark.

Shadow knew it was not all bad, but neither was it all good. One piece slunk across the blades of grass, latching onto another piece, and then a third piece joined, the magnetic pull growing stronger with each addition.

Soon there were enough pieces in one place for Shadow to see the boy again, and the girl.

Oh, the girl.

Shadow wanted the girl. Her blood. Her blood, her blood, her blood.

It would make such powerful, powerful magic.

But the boy stood then, cradling the girl in his arms. He kicked at the brown-like-dirt bags, shoving them away into the too-dark passage where Shadow couldn't go, and then the boy took the girl.

He took her, and Shadow wanted her.

Another splinter of darkness moved silently through the grass to join the others, but progress was slow, and soon the boy and girl were gone.

Sy stumbled into the outer banks of EvenFall, his eyes searching desperately for a reputable hotel. There were many places to stay, but very few who wouldn't call the Riatan guards, or where he would be comfortable leaving Coren while he left to get a doctor for her wounds.

Sy refused to admit that no Riatan doctor could help her now.

He rounded a corner and finally saw a familiar sign: the NightGuard.

The man at the counter inside wasn't familiar, though, and he gave Sy a highly suspicious glare on seeing Coren in his arms, bloodied and now unconscious.

"Please, sir," Sy begged. "We were attacked by an animal. I need a bed and a maid with warm water. I have plenty of money."

"Pay now," the man responded sourly.

Somehow, Sy resisted cursing him up and down. Keeping one arm firmly under Coren's limp body, he braced her back against the wall to dig in his pocket, finally pulling out a sack of Riatan coins and tossing them on the counter.

"Now, a bed please!"

The man nodded but continued to count the money out carefully before turning to ring a brass bell on the wall behind his desk. A girl appeared shortly, her eyes growing round at the sight.

Sy groaned when the girl led him down a long, darkened hallway and up a ridiculously steep staircase, finally unlocking the door to a narrow attic room crowded with a single sagging bed. Sy tried to lay Coren gently on the bed, but his strength was gone, and she moaned as she hit the blanket, her eyes fluttering.

"You need water?" the girl asked, her voice barely a squeak.

"Hot water, and towels, and food, if you can. My bags aren't here yet, and I have nothing to clean her wounds with. But I have money," Sy repeated, as though coins could solve such a problem. He wrapped the rough blanket around Coren as gently as possible, then collapsed in the room's single chair, breathing heavily.

Coren moaned again, and the girl jumped. "I can send for the doctor," she whispered.

"Please!" Sy said, smiling gratefully at her and digging again in his pocket for the coins. Now he could tend to Coren until the doctor arrived with medicine for the pain. And perhaps then he could find one of his contacts and retrieve their bags from the passage.

His brain pulsed with a list of things to do, even as his heart twisted in half, knowing all of this was false industry.

The girl came back quickly with a bowl of water and a few threadbare towels, then again with a plate of bread, cold sliced meat, and a hunk of white cheese. Sy poured some of the water into Coren's mouth, and she gulped and coughed, silent tears leaking from her closed eyes.

He lifted the remains of her shirt, peeling the fabric as gently as possible from the dried blood and dabbing the dampened towel to her shredded skin. Where the iridescent, blue-gold Vespa blood had swirled with her bright red was now a shimmering purple.

Sy blinked back tears as he worked.

There was no way to save her, he knew. Even a Weshen healer had no power against a Vespa's poison, but he couldn't just let her suffer. He couldn't just do nothing. He regretted any anger he'd shown her over the last days.

"Sy," she whispered, her eyes fluttering open.

He bent near to her. "It's okay. I have a doctor coming."

She shook her head weakly. "No. Leave me to die and rescue those Wesh. Promise me you'll rescue them. There's nothing left for me now." Her voice ended in barely a breath, and her eye drifted closed again.

Her breathing slowed so much that Sy panicked, pressing his cheek to her lips. He felt warm air, but he feared she had nearly run out of time and energy.

"Sir?" the girl called from beyond the door. "Sir, you have a visitor."

"Send him in!" Sy yelled, turning to greet the doctor.

But it was no doctor who opened the door to Sy's room.

"Resh!" Sy choked. "What? How?"

"And why, I suppose? No matter - it looks like you've nearly managed to kill the witch yourself. I admit I hadn't thought of Vespa poison to do the job."

Sy rose and shoved his brother against the door as it closed behind him. "She is no witch. She's just a girl who's lost everything," he gasped, losing his strength on the last word. Slumping into the chair, Sy held his head between his hands.

"Brother, I saw it all. I've been in EvenFall for days, watching the passage for you. Why was she so weak coming out of the tunnel?"

"Wesh," Sy mumbled, too spent for these questions.

"And I saw Shadow jump from the cliffs and coat her body. Did you know about this dark magic? Does she control its power as well?" Resh took a step toward Coren's limp form.

"Did it look like she had control of that power?" Sy spat back. "Shadow is Umbren. We have nothing to do with that. Her magic - *our* magic - is pure Weshen."

Another knock sounded at the door, and the girl called, "Another visitor, sir!"

"Come in," Sy managed, staggering to his feet to greet the doctor.

But again, it was not the doctor who pushed open the door.

Instead, a slight girl stood before them, her hair a mass of dark waves, her face shadowed by a deep hood.

"Shanta," Resh said, extending his hand. She pushed back her hood enough for Sy to see her eyes and her glare for his brother.

She brushed past his hand and strode to the bed, bending over Coren. "Vespa?" she asked, poking at the slice on Coren's stomach.

Sy nodded. "On her back, too."

"By the Magi," the girl cursed and shook her head. "I have herbs that will ease her pain. And I have some that will put her to sleep until she dies. But she *will* die."

Sy blinked at her, unable to respond. She ignored him and began rummaging in her pack, pulling out a jar of thick yellow cream and spreading it on the wound, then rolling Coren's unresisting form over to add the cream to her back.

All Sy could do was stare numbly at the skin that was once so smooth and beautiful, now sliced to ribbons of red mixed with the shimmering blue poison.

"Shanta is a Wesh healer. I thought her presence would be more helpful than some ignorant Riatan doctor," Resh offered. "I met her last year on a mission in here in EvenFall."

"He means to say he was caught by my crew," Shanta said, a hint of derision in her voice. "Caught trying to cheat us with a false talisman."

"What can I say?" Resh grinned. "I make my money the dishonest way."

"Shut up, both of you!" Sy exploded finally. "Corentine is dying, and I promised her I would complete the rescue, and I can't leave her!" He broke down, slamming both fists into the wall and hanging his head between them. His muscles shook from the fatigue of the day, of the week, of the month.

"She has lost everything," he whispered. "And I very nearly have. And all of it - all of it - is the fault of the Restless King."

Shanta glanced at him. "What rescue?"

He shook his head.

"What rescue?" she repeated.

"The Wesh," Resh guessed, and Sy found the strength to nod.

"They were to be sold today, I think," he said, knowing in all reality the auction had likely already happened. They had taken too long with Damren, too long in the passage, too long with Shadow and the Vespa.

"The auction was held early on special request," Shanta said, breaking into his thoughts. "Two days ago."

Sy felt himself slump even farther down in the chair, defeat resting heavily on his shoulders.

"But I could still find out who purchased them. Rumor has it that the king bought many of them," Shanta said, a dark look crossing her face.

"The Restless King?" Sy asked stupidly, fear and hopelessness growing in a tangled mess in his gut. He'd never be able to rescue them now. His father had been right. The mission would be suicide.

Shanta nodded. "He still collects any Wesh or Weshen he finds, to test their power. But like I said, if you're willing to pay, I can find out more."

"You want payment for helping your own people?" Sy asked, his dislike for Shanta growing.

"No-one works for free in EvenFall," she shrugged.

"I won't pay you to do something I could do for free!" Sy exclaimed.

"Then pay me for a map of the route they'll take to StarsHelm," she suggested. "Oh, and for the herbs."

"I'll wait for the doctor," Sy said, turning away. He had no intention of paying this girl for anything.

"He isn't coming," Resh said. "I intercepted your message and saved you from a load of trouble. Didn't you even pause to think of what her blood might be worth?"

Sy felt his own blood drain from his face. He hadn't. But obviously Weshen blood was still valuable, and a dying girl would certainly be too tempting for the average medicine man. Sy hated to admit it, but Resh had been helpful.

Sighing, he began to dig in his pack for coins to pay Shanta.

Coren stirred just then, rolling to her back as her arms and legs went rigid. She whimpered and thrashed her head, but her eyes remained tightly closed.

"*Vespa*," she whispered hoarsely, and the cut on her stomach seemed to glow.

Sy bent over her, using the towel to wipe the sweat from her brow. Something clutched in her hand began to glow, and he grasped her wrist, spotting the single severed talon burning her palm.

He pried it from her fingers, careful not to touch the needle-sharp end, but he gasped at its heat.

Shanta sucked in a breath and stepped closer, but then the talon flared even hotter in Sy's hand, and he dropped it. It wormed across Coren's stomach like a thing alive, and Coren clamped her hands over the claw, sealing it between her fingers and her skin. She twisted and writhed on the bed, a low moan turning quickly to a growl.

Sy shouted at Shanta, who shoved at Resh, but none of them could manage to grasp her writhing body or pull her hands away.

And then her eyes flew open, a scream like nothing Sy had ever heard bursting from her lips. Her hands flew out straight as though someone had tied them back, and Sy gasped as he saw how the claw had pierced the skin above her belly button, curving itself into a shining, glowing golden circle.

"A true talisman," Shanta breathed and began to step backward toward the door, edging away from Coren with a look of mixed horror and awe in her silver-blue eyes.

27

The whole world was burning, and Corentine Ashaden was the sun.

She knew it now.

This was how she was going to die. Not in the darkness or the shadows. But seared by the light of the noon sun on the summer water, her body skipping helplessly across the ripples like a flat stone, the salt scrubbing mercilessly at her wounds.

And her back bore the brunt of it.

The sun was burning away her skin, her muscle. Her blood boiled in her very veins, as they too were opened to its rays. Her body was disintegrating, and she had no idea how she could possibly fuse her own sources together again.

This was how she was going to die.

Her spine curved as she curled into herself, shifting smaller and younger, the bed and the blanket swallowing her whole.

Perhaps this was also disintegration, and she would shrink and shrink until there was nothing left of her but sources - orderly piles of bone dust and flakes of skin and droplets of her cursed, poisoned Weshen blood.

But just as she'd grown small, her limbs rebounded and began to stretch back to their normal length, then longer. Her throat was raw from screaming, and still she screamed as the bones remade themselves inside of her, thinner and longer.

And different.

Her skin tried to stretch to accommodate these new bones, but there simply wasn't enough of it, and the bones burst through the source that was her skin, showering her back and the tattered blanket in ruby droplets.

"Jyesh, I've failed," she whispered to the darkness hovering in her mind, "Even your power can't save me."

Now face down and spent on the bed, she could still feel her arms pulling and stretching wider and wider, and *backward* - the wrong direction for arms. They swooped behind her and up and up, and down, and a single iridescent Vespa feather floated down from the skies to cause a new ripple in the sea and remind her again that she was dying because of this cruelest of MagiCreatures.

"Corentine!"

The voice sounded familiar, and as it shouted her name again, Coren realized it had been calling her for some time now. With tremendous effort, she raised her head. The feather tangled in her matted hair, and she paused to watch its beautiful shades of gray flicker in the sun streaming in the window. Where had it come from?

She was so sore. Every bit of her ached as though it had been pummeled from the inside out for hours.

"Coren?" the voice tried again, closer now.

She pulled an arm from beneath her and pushed up. That wasn't right…her arms had been twisted and tied behind her. She could feel them behind her. Yet here they were, before her eyes. She sat back on her heels and nearly fell backward over the edge of the bed as the unnatural weight of her back pulled her off balance.

Strong arms caught her and righted her in the bed. "Coren, look at me!" the voice pleaded. She turned and blinked until the form took focus. A blanket was pulled up her front, and she realized her skin was naked beneath it.

"Sy," she whispered, as he held the blanket gently to her shoulders. She watched, puzzled, as tears slipped down his face. "Mourn me when I'm dead," she said, her voice stronger now.

"You're not dying," another voice said. A girl. Coren swiveled her head and tilted her face to examine the girl before her. She looked like an arach, all shadows and gleaming silver eyes crouched in the corner, her arms splayed as though she were ready to scale the wall and disappear if needed.

"I was poisoned by a Vespa," Coren said. "Of course I'm dying." She no longer felt sad about it, either. It was a fitting end to her pointless life. Maren would care for the twins. They would be better, even.

"You're not dying," the girl insisted, the aggravation clearer in her voice. "You're *shifting*."

"Look at your Magi-cursed hands!" Still another voice. Coren peered into the shadows of the other corner, and her eyelids lowered in recognition.

"Second Son," she said. Her head swiveled back to Sy, who still clutched the blanket around her nakedness. She pushed the edge away, revealing her hands.

Dizziness washed over her, and she slumped against Sy as she twirled her hand in the sun-dappled room. Each finger now ended in golden, curved claws, glittering like glorious death.

"And you have wings," Sy whispered, his finger pulling her chin up and around, so she could glimpse what waited over her bare shoulder. Giant wings crowded the room behind her, crushed beneath the rafters of the room. Feathers shone softly in the mix of shadows and sunlight that was created by their downy drape against the room's grimy attic windows.

"I am both light and dark," Coren whispered, pulling a clawed hand away from her back, where the feathers of those wings did indeed seem to meld with her skin, connected to her bones beneath. "I am a shadow."

"You are *not* Shadow," the other girl cried, a panicked look on her face. "You're a Weshen shifter!"

Coren suddenly felt a surge of strength, and she leaned away from Sy, careful not to snag him with her golden talons.

"I'm a monster," she breathed, staggering to her feet. She stood before them, swaying, clutching the blanket to her chest. The fabric seemed to catch on something at her waist, and she lifted it, revealing the Vespa's golden claw, now looped and curved through the skin of her stomach. The wings trembled, their tips brushing the cobwebs from opposite corners of the room.

"I'm a *monster*," she repeated, her voice growing to an inhuman shriek on the last word. Her brain itself felt shifted, and where she once yearned to run the plains of Weshen Isle, now her wings ached to test the breeze. Clumsily knotting the edges of the blanket around her breasts and tangling the braid of her whip in her awkward talons, she scrambled across the bed and to the window, throwing it open, clawing her way out in a mess of arms and feathers and too many wings.

Someone, maybe left behind in the room, or maybe in the streets far below, screamed as Corentine burst into the summer sky above EvenFall.

Resh whirled on his brother. "Where is she going?" He had no idea what that girl had just turned into, but he recognized that they could use her power.

Sy barked out a laugh, shoving his hair from his too-wide eyes. "How should I know?"

The door slammed just then, and Shanta was gone. Resh muttered a curse. Wasn't that just like her?

"We need to find the witch before she hurts someone," he said, bending to tug Sy's bow sword from the bag in the corner.

"She is not a witch, and you will not harm her!" Sy cried, moving to wrest the weapon from Resh, but he was too slow. Resh was out the door and down the stairs before Sy could catch him. Out in the street, all he had to do was follow the screams.

Sy's footsteps pounded after him, but Resh's training was as good as his brother's, and *he* was not emotionally compromised. Was it Sulit magic? Umbren? Resh had never studied Weshen history like Sy, but surely he would have remembered Vespa-girls.

The city streets quickly turned to the selvage of dirt paths and fallen barns, and then the open field stretching into the forest and mountains beyond. Wings flapped high above Resh, and a cackle of laughter floated down from the air. He knelt on one knee and steadied his aim on the bow sword, the sun glinting down at him as the girl-turned-witch-turned-monster swirled above.

"Reshra, no!" Syashin yelled, crashing into Resh just as the arrow left its notch, soaring up into the air.

There was a beat of silence, and then again, the laughter. The sky seemed empty above him. A trick of the Vespa that any hunter knew - from a certain height, their bodies and wings blended with the pale sky. A single opalescent feather drifted down to land at Resh's feet, and when he stooped to gather it in his fingers, he saw one bright drop of blood resting on its spine.

He began to smile, but a whoosh of air nearly knocked him off his feet, and the punch of feather and bone against his shoulder finished the job. The bow sword tumbled to the ground, and Resh with it, a searing pain in his neck and shoulder and all the way down his arm.

His head thumped against the ground, and when his eyes opened, the sun was blotted out by the girl standing above him. Crouching, she pushed a knee into his chest, her wings draped around them like the curtains of a private tent. The blanket wrapping her chest fell open at the waist, and he could glimpse the gold talon piercing her skin, as well as the coil of her whip around her slim stomach.

"I should kill you for trying to kill me," she murmured, leaning close to his face and demanding his attention with her bronze-fire eyes. "But I won't, because I care for your brother, and he cares for you." She lay a hand on his chest, five golden claws stroking the skin around his heart. "I may be a monster on the outside, but you, Second Son. You are a monster on the inside."

She watched him for a long second, and Resh marveled at her control. And, certain parts of him admitted, her fierce, beautiful power. He knew she could kill him with a single swipe, and yet she didn't. Even after he had tried to kill her, she resisted.

He'd never known a witch who resisted using whatever power was available.

Corentine stood suddenly, folding her wings against her back.

"Sy," she whispered, suddenly looking very, very afraid. "Will I stay like this forever?"

Sy only shook his head and stepped toward her, running a finger reverently down the feathers of one wing. She shivered in the summer sun, and something stirred inside of Resh, awakening a dangerous, jealous interest. Sy was taller and stronger and a better hunter, and held all the rights of First Son, but girls had always been the exception.

Girls fell easily for Resh, but never for Sy.

Yet here was one girl who preferred the First Son, and Resh wanted to know why.

Resh staggered to his feet, clutching his arm. "You truly think this is Weshen magic?" he asked Sy, grimacing against the pain. He was certain his shoulder was dislocated, and possibly the bone of his arm had broken.

"Of course it is," Sy said. "I have a book in my bag at the hotel. I'm sorry you never sought any of these secrets. But they were always there for you to find. And now you have them all. What will you do with them?"

Resh ignored the gruff question that poked at how he'd betrayed Sy once. He hadn't decided what he might do with this new knowledge. He hated the idea that Sy had been keeping so many secrets. Not only from him, but from all the Weshen people, who didn't have Sy's access to travel and books.

"What can she do?" he asked instead.

"*She* can do a lot of things," Corentine bit out, her amber and gold eyes sparking. She drew the blanket from her bare stomach, running a shining claw across the braid of the whip circling her sun-brown skin. "And not all involve magic."

Resh nearly grinned, catching himself just in time.

Sy stepped forward, moving between them. "Both of us can SourceShift, disintegration and fusion. That's what you saw on the beach. SelfShifting, now within and without."

Resh nodded, although he knew what none of those words truly meant.

"Resh, Corentine is the strongest shifter Weshen has seen since before the Separation. None of what you've seen her do is Sulit magic, no matter what her family did before."

The brothers locked eyes in a challenge, and for once Resh backed down. He and Sy were different, but they were brothers: Weshen alone in the kingdom of Riata. Whatever this girl could do, he hoped she could be convinced to do it for their people.

"Can we go back to the hotel to figure this out?" he asked, rolling his neck to loosen the knot of pain. "I think I'll go ahead and call for that doctor after all, since Shanta ran the second she saw this mess."

"I would say I'm sorry," Corentine said, "but I'm not a bit." She turned away from them and stripped off the blanket, throwing it higher around her shoulders and pulling it tight. The wings weren't visible, but her back looked deformed and hunched. It would probably pass in the streets of EvenFall, though.

Sy glared at Resh, then gathered his bow sword from the grass, and the three of them slowly walked the road to EvenFall for the second time in a single day. Silence accompanied them, as though even the small birds of the air were afraid to squawk at Corentine's form.

Resh trailed slightly behind Sy and Corentine, his eyes fastened on the restless, shifting mass beneath her blanket. He was even more uncertain what to think of this girl now.

First, she had been nothing more than another island girl, safe and protected and faceless to someone like Resh. Then as Sy had fixated on catching her, she had grown into an aggravation, a problem Ashemon had asked him to solve so Sy might have an heir. And not that many days ago, he had labeled her a witch before the entire Weshen community.

Although he still didn't understand her magic, he'd never seen a Sulit witch take the shape of a MagiCreature. And Shadow, which he knew was from Umbren, had been torn apart by the Vespa at the base of the mountain, releasing its hold on her before the shift had happened.

But what kind of Weshen magic would join a MagiCreature with a human, when all they'd done for generations was try to kill each other? There was too much he didn't understand.

Resh decided that for now, he would trust Sy's claim that Corentine wasn't a witch.

By the Magi, she was terrifying, and if she were loyal, that terror could be turned on their enemies.

Resh was also forced to admit that the skin on his chest still thrilled where her claws had skimmed his heart. He'd known so many, many girls, but this Weshen woman was different.

The Sulit witch leaned back from the glass-smooth surface of the scrying pond and stared at the hard-faced Weshen woman. The two young Weshen watched her back with matching eyes of pale sky, appearing much older than they should have.

"Does she live?" the woman asked, her eyes pinched in concern.

"She more than lives," the witch assured her customers. She pushed aside the braids of her black-blue hair and clutched her fingers in the folds of her dress. Her excitement must not show, or the woman might grow suspicious. "She and the boy have defeated Shadow for now, and she found the strength of the Vespa. Her body accepted its poison, and her magic shifted her very bones into the wings of death."

"ShapeShifting," the woman murmured, her eyes shining with tears.

The witch shrugged. Her people had their own names for what the Weshen had once been able to do. The important part was that their shifter power was indeed returning. The girl would be sought after by many, and the witch was nearly bursting with excitement.

"You have given me something valuable to use against my sisters," she said. "And for that, I will tell you my true name."

"Thank you for your help," the Weshen woman answered, bowing low to the ground.

"I am StarSeer."

"And I am Maren," the old woman responded, raising her head. "These are-"

"I know these children. They have been spoken of in prophecies, nearly as often as their elder bloods. Do not spend the currency of their names too easily, Maren. My sisters have many things in mind for the future of your people."

"Won't your sisters know us by sight?" the boy asked then, and the witch smiled at him. He was far too young now, but perhaps one day, his heart might be hers.

"My sisters know many things, but there are always spots of blindness. Do not open the eyes of your enemy before you are ready to gouge them out."

The girl shuddered at this, and StarSeer studied her. She was as delicate and beautiful as the pink leaves floating around them, but surely there was the strength of the black bark within. That strength shone easily through the boy's matching features, and StarSeer wondered for a moment if they would both live long enough.

She might be able to look into her pond, of course. Her family's ability to cast their eyes across the MagiSea could sometimes be stretched. Her grandmother had begun teaching her to cast her eyes across the seas of time before the Sisters of the Heart had found them.

"We travel to Rurok now," Maren said, rising to her feet and gathering her things. The young ones rose with her, flanking her like miniature guardians.

"You should know this, then," StarSeer said, and the woman paused. "There is one who waits in the black city. He sits on a throne of mockery in a tower of Rurok."

"A man? On the throne before witches? That must indeed be a mockery."

StarSeer nodded. "He has given up much to sit there, but some will give more to see him fall."

28

"**W**hat am I supposed to do with all of this?" Coren demanded, gesturing to herself with golden-clawed fingers, once they were again enclosed safely in the attic room.

Sy didn't answer because he truly had no idea. Not that he knew much about this sort of shifting, but he kept expecting her form to shift back to normal, just as it did when she SelfShifted to a younger form. Her magical energy should have depleted, forcing her back. After the day they'd had, they were both nearing exhaustion.

The Weshen magic was finally awake, and neither of them had any idea what to do next.

Sliding her wings from beneath the blanket, she rummaged in her bag and shrugged an unbuttoned tunic on backward, so it covered her chest but left her wings free and her back exposed.

Resh, of course, had immediately sent for the doctor,

then sprawled on the single bed, nursing his injuries while leafing through the book Sy had salvaged from Damren's room.

"These are incredible," he murmured. "Not only a Vespa, but every MagiCreature we know of could join with a shifter. The Restless King would sell his soul for an army of these shifters."

"He likely did once," Coren muttered, still pacing. "Does it say anything about how to shift out of these stupid wings?"

Resh smacked the book shut with one hand. "Now why on earth would you want them gone?" He stood and stepped toward her, stalling her pacing as she edged away from him in the narrow space.

"It's going to be a bit hard to *blend in* like this," she bit out. Sy smiled, making sure to keep his back turned to them. Of all the possibilities Coren's new form had opened, the one he liked best was that she no longer had to fear anyone, including his brother. Her abilities with a whip were certainly frightening, but these wings...these wings would reduce any attacker to a babbling mess.

"Now, Corentine," Resh practically purred. Sy bit at his lip to keep from laughing. She was going to break another of his bones if he treated her like one of his summer girls. "These wings - these beautiful wings - they will scare the whips right out of the hands of those slavers."

"The Wesh!" she said, suddenly understanding. "Sy, he's right! We can rescue the Wesh anywhere now!"

Sy did turn then, considering the two of them. Resh was still holding his left arm tight to his chest, but with his right hand, he had reached up to touch a feather. And even more impressive, Coren was allowing it.

"We could," Sy said, and Resh dropped his hand, blinking. "But we've missed the auction. We have no idea what happened to the Wesh. The ones the king bought are gone, and the others are probably scattered across the Riatan countryside by now."

Coren's face fell. He almost wished he hadn't said anything, but it was the truth. She needed it.

"It was me, wasn't it," she said, twisting toward the window. "I caused us to miss the auction."

"I think these wings are worth it," Resh said, stepping closer to her again, his eyes following the dance of feathers across the walls.

"Nothing is worth someone else's life!" she snapped at him. "If I were a true Vespa, I'd be flying straight for StarsHelm right now. Vespas deal in revenge. They carry the stench of death and iron," she murmured, and Sy shivered even in the muggy heat of the attic room. He knew that smell, and she'd named it perfectly.

"Maybe I should forget these men and their petty battles for power, and fly to Sulit and rescue my family," she continued, her voice taking on a menacing lilt as she turned to face them. "You wanted so badly for me to be a witch, Second Son. Perhaps I'll go be one."

The gold in her eyes shone as brightly as her claws in the shadows of the room, as though they were pulling the light from the dark. Sy glanced at Resh nervously. The corners of the room seemed darker in an instant, and Sy scanned the room, looking for the slink of Shadow among the shadows.

Could it have survived the Vespa attack, too? Would it find them again?

"Corentine." Resh's voice was quiet in the stale air. "You aren't a Vespa. You aren't Shadow. All my life I've prayed half a prayer, and now I've been shown the rest." He held up the book of magic. "You're a Weshen warrior, and you were made like this to protect your people."

She turned wild eyes on him, the feathers of her wings seeming to glow as they swished behind her. "Revenge on the king is a sort of protection, is it not? And who is deserving of protection more than my innocent twin brother and sister? My own twin was ripped from me when he was eight! What a warrior he could have become!" Her voice had risen to a sort of shriek now, and Sy stepped forward cautiously.

She turned toward the window again, her eyes seeking something in the sky. "You two can rescue the Wesh. You don't need me. I can fly to Sulit. I can *fly*," she repeated. Sy was growing more anxious at the wild twisting of her words. Her face flickered with indecision and regret.

"I know nothing of your family," Resh began, reaching a hand toward her and letting it fall. "But I know Sulit witches. They take, and take, and take." He had advanced with each step until he was toe to toe with her.

"Sounds like what I know of you, Second Son," Coren replied, her voice glittering with warning.

"With these wings and claws, you've just become the most valuable weapon the Weshen people have against the king," Resh said, not backing away. Sy kept watching, uncertain how he could help, or even who he might side with. He understood Coren's desires. He knew she was right about the Wesh, too. He and Resh could handle it.

But he also knew he didn't want her out of his sight, and including her in the rescue greatly increased their chances of getting everyone out without injuries.

"Is that what you both want of me?" Coren asked, turning to Sy again. He blinked at her, not understanding. "Do you want me to be a weapon in the hands of men?"

Sy startled, shaking his head.

"Good. Because your father," she pointed to both of them, "my *General*, did not want such a weapon when he was asked to reconsider. If these wings and claws are used against the Restless King, I am the only one who will wield them. Get your own," she added, and before either of them could react, she scrambled out the window and shot into the air.

"Nice," Sy said, glaring at Resh. "Now I have to go find her again."

"Let her go," Resh replied, shaking his head and massaging his temples with his good hand. Sy realized his younger brother suddenly looked quite tired. "She needs to figure this out. I may have said the wrong thing, but you're doing the wrong thing. Stop trying to protect her, because she doesn't need it."

Sy opened his mouth to retort, but then he realized Resh was right. On both accounts. "You can stay here in case she returns. Rest your arm. I'll go find Shanta," he said.

Resh's return smile was grateful and almost shy, the look reminding Sy of when they were just boys, still new to Weshen City and learning to be brothers and sons.

Those lessons had been hard, but they had driven Sy and Resh close for many years until the hunts had begun to separate them.

When Coren had been a girl on Weshen Isle, dreaming of freedom and the ability to travel, never once had she imagined it would come to her like this.

She stretched her wings in the sun, still in awe of their width and strength. She marveled at how they allowed her to swoop through the treetops of the nearby forest and wondered at how natural she felt - as though she'd been in this form her whole life and only just discovered how to use it. She swung toward the NeverCross Mountains, shooting up its icy vertical face and then plummeting down again, testing her balance on the wind.

Had it been only this morning when Sy had dragged her, helpless, from the passage? Only this morning when she thought she was dying of the Vespa's poison? How could this form feel as strong and natural to her as the body she'd been born into?

Even stranger, she'd eaten and drunk nothing all day, had no lemondrine tonic, and yet her strength felt immeasurable.

She felt more than human, more than Weshen, more than creature. She felt magical, as though nothing could touch her as long as she stayed aloft in the white-blue sky.

Certainly there were no shadows here in the clouds, and no men either.

What did she owe anyone, after all this? Sy and Resh would rescue the slaves. Sy could teach the others to find and use their magic. She could fly away now, all the way to Sulit, and be with Kosh and Penna. They could make a new life, in a new country.

Weshen City had not protected them, so what obligation did she have to protect the city?

None.

These thoughts and more like them flitted through her mind as she flew. Higher and higher, until she shot through a misty cloud. The fog and minute droplets blinded her for a second, but then she was even above the clouds. In every direction, there was white. The feathers of her wings glistened with moisture.

Up here, Coren didn't need to reach to feel the sources around her; they pushed against her senses, demanding her attention. She closed her eyes, drawing the water sources around her together in a palm-sized sphere that she brought to her lips.

It was cold and clear as crystal, and she drank deeply, enjoying the freeze that slipped down her gullet and rested in her belly.

How long would it take her to fly to Sulit? Could she cross the MagiSea without resting?

Coren slowed her wings and leaned back, sinking backward beneath the clouds again, falling faster and faster until she righted herself just in time to perch on the top branches of an ancient tree. She wished for another message from Maren, but there was nothing up here except her. No-one to make this decision easier or harder.

Perhaps the very form of the Vespa was a distraction, clouding her ability to decide.

Dropping to the ground between the trees, where the foliage was too dense for flight, Coren began to walk instead, cutting a blind path through the woods. Her wings brushed the tree trunks, and her feathers acted as a thousand sensitive fingertips, letting her feel the living sources inside each tree.

Soon she came across a narrow stream, and she began to follow it idly, her thoughts still pulsing with indecision. The sound of the water soothed her somewhat, though she would have preferred the crashing of the ocean waves and the cries of the Weshen Isle dawngulls.

For a second, she almost imagined she did hear the snap of ocean against cliff, and the cries of the birds wheeling in the clouds. Rounding a bend in the stream, Coren stopped dead.

The water before her was no longer empty and still, but occupied with a horror she could barely understand.

Two stakes were plunged deep into the mud of each opposing bank, and between them slumped a young boy, each arm stretched wide and tied to a stake. He was naked from the waist up and seemed barely older than Kosh. Her heart stuttered between pangs of grief and surges of rage at whatever was happening to this child. Even as she watched, the water rushed faster and higher past his thighs, wetting the fabric in gulping splashes.

It rose inches with every second.

"The water will continue to rise, Nikesh, and you will drown, unless you stop this stubbornness and shift the sources away, or grow that pitiful form a little taller," a male voice called from the opposite bank, followed by a gruff laugh. The sound of a whip snapping through the air reached Coren a second before the boy cried out mournfully - the ocean and the dawngull she had heard.

"No-one is coming to help you," the voice added cruelly as the boy hung his head, almost seeming to strain toward the water.

Coren ducked behind a tree, still searching the area for the boy's tormentor but saw no-one.

"Shift, boy!" the voice yelled, and this time Coren followed the voice to the branches of a tree across the stream. She could barely make out the shape of a man in the low branches, where a whip did indeed dangle from an unseen hand.

The boy's head jerked up, and Coren saw gashes across his pale chest, blood-encrusted trails of a whip. His blue eyes were murky and unfocused as he pulled his arms against the stakes again, grimacing as the leather ties dug into his skin. Then his head lolled back down, as though staring directly into the water, which was now nearly to his ribcage. He was giving up.

There was no more time. Coren raced the short distance to the bank, where her wings could spread wide, and she flapped hard, rising above the boy, then settling down in the water. It was as high as her waist now, and her wings were sodden and heavy. She began to tug at the leather bindings, but they were solid.

"What is this!" the man cried, dropping from the tree. Wide-eyed, he stared at Coren, pulling a familiar string of prayer beads from beneath his shirt. His lips moved in silent supplication. She heard the words *Mirror Magi* cross his lips, and her horror at the situation doubled.

"You are Weshen?" she asked, nearly forgetting why she was in the water. Her talons scrabbled clumsily with the thick leather that bound the boy's wrists to the poles, but as soon as she sliced one, it fused together again.

"Stop shifting the sources!" she yelled in frustration, but she wasn't even certain who she was yelling at. The water was now to the boy's armpits, and his eyes had fluttered closed, his body limp and lifeless. With a roar, Coren focused on the poles and managed to shift the wood into pieces. The boy's body slumped against her, heavier than expected, and she stumbled backward, the imbalance of her wings dangerously close to pulling them both under.

Staggering to the bank under the boy's weight, Coren saw the man still standing there, watching her with the sort of awe reserved for the Mirror Magi themselves.

"You would do this to your own people? To a child?" she cried, heaving the boy onto the slick bank. Still the water rose, sucking at her legs and her water-soaked wings, even threatening to overflow the riverbed. Her words seemed to break through the man's trance, and his face set in a grim look.

"I do this to set his power free. He is a slave to the king. We are all slaves to the king, even if we have never been sent to the palace! We must access our true power if we are to break free. Power like yours!" There was a manic look in his eye, and Coren felt the pull of shifting around her. The water rose in columns, blocking her access to the boy and the bank and her own safety.

Flapping her wings against the surge of water, she managed to rise a few inches, but the man only laughed, forcing the water down onto her in rivers flowing up and down, swirling around her in a cage of murky river-water bars.

"But you…you could be more than a slave!" he cried. "You are magnificent!"

The water crashed down on her head, pushing her under. Coren fought her lungs' natural motion and forced herself to locate the muddy bottom, using the strength of her legs and arms to propel herself up and up. She burst from the water, wings spreading to their full length, and shifted enough air around herself that the feathers were sucked dry in seconds.

She knew her strength wouldn't last long, but it had to be enough. Barreling down on the man, she knocked him to the ground and crawled into his chest, her talons grasping at his neck. The columns of water crashed back into the riverbed. His breath pushed from his lungs, and his mouth gaped open like a fish deprived of water.

"I would have loved to learn from you," she said, her voice low with regret for what she was about to do. Her talons tightened on the man's neck, and he shook his head, frantic as he also realized his fate. Coren closed her heart against his panic and sliced deep into the flesh of his throat, opening the vein of life.

The water immediately receded, bubbling down to its natural banks as the red of the man's blood gurgled into the grass, a river of blood flowing to mix with the murky water beside him. His limbs grew still, and his eyes dimmed, and finally Coren pushed to her feet, her wings drooping with exhaustion.

She turned to the boy, who had curled in on himself, shaking, watching her with a mixture of amazement and terror.

"I won't hurt you," she said, softening her voice. She tucked her wings back and hid her bloodied hands. Now that the threat was gone, her adrenaline ebbed as well, and a deep exhaustion pulled at her muscles.

The boy lifted a finger and pointed to the tree where the man had been hiding. A pack rested at the base of the trunk, and Coren hurried to grab it. Inside were two skins of what smelled like lemondrine tonic and a cloth-wrapped hunk of bread with cheese inside.

She offered everything to the boy, and he took one skin, then pushed the rest at her. They both drank deeply, and Coren relaxed into the sensation of renewal. Her wings stretched and shuddered in the dappled light of the forest, shaking away the droplets of river water and blood.

"Nikesh?" she asked, remembering the man's taunts. The boy nodded, his blue eyes fluttering open and closed. "Are you injured?" she asked, kneeling next to him. The gashes on his chest weren't bleeding any longer, but there were also older wounds, some green with infection. His wrists were still bound to the stumps of wood, and she busied herself shifting it all away. Beneath the bands, his skin was raw and blistered.

"You're safe now," she whispered, and a ghost of a smile crossed his face before his head fell limp against the grass again. Coren cursed, darting to the dead man and tugging his shirt free. She wrapped the boy as gently as possible and gathered him in her arms. He was small, but she still staggered a bit under his weight.

Gritting her teeth, Coren spread her wings and pushed off the forest floor, breaking through the canopy in a burst of broken twigs and stripped leaves.

It had begun to rain, making her wings soggy and unwieldy, but she turned her body toward EvenFall. The flight back would be hard, but she owed it to this boy to get him to true safety.

If it had been Kosh himself, she could not be more determined to save this young life from Riata's horrors.

Wind rattling the window drew Sy's attention from the map he was copying. After receiving his message, Shanta had delivered a map of the surrounding area. Resh had convinced her to stay, and now she lounged near the fire, waiting to help them with the Wesh rescue.

As Sy stared into the stormy darkness beyond the panes, a flash of lightning illuminated a winged figure outside the building.

"Corentine!" he cried, dropping his pen. Shanta snatched it up before the ink could blot out the map, but Sy was already at the window, pushing it open.

"Take him," Coren gasped, shoving a sagging, wrapped bundle at Sy.

Sy wrapped his arms around the form and Coren climbed onto the sill. Her wings, dripping from the rain, remained half in and half out of the room, and Sy noticed her clothing was barely hanging on her shoulders, red with blood and soaked with rain.

"What happened?" he asked, forcing himself to stay calm as he placed the form gently on the bed. He unwrapped one end of the ratty blanket and winced at the pale, starved face that lay motionless beneath the fabric.

"He's alive, but barely. Slavers. He's a Wesh," Coren said, her words coming with difficulty.

"Are you injured?" Sy asked, moving toward her. But she only held up a hand, shaking her head.

"I'm fine. Take care of the boy."

The door banged open then, and Resh entered, balancing a wide tray of food, wine, and a grin that slid off his face when he saw Coren crouched in the narrow window. His moans about a broken arm had been quickly put to rest by Shanta, who forced some herbs down his throat and pronounced him healed.

Resh cursed mildly at the scene and set the tray down on the table, smudging the map. Shanta cursed fluently back at him, but Resh ignored her, glancing from the still body on the bed and back to Coren, hunched on the windowsill.

Sy had a flash of fear that perhaps she might stay in this half-Vespa form forever, and that she would hate him for it.

He blinked as Resh squeezed around him to reach the other side of the bed, offering Coren a towel. She dried her face and arms, eyes sliding between the brothers.

"I found the child in the woods, close to drowning in a stream."

"There are lots of estates where slavers hide between here and StarsHelm. Mostly abandoned," Shanta said, her eyes on the map.

"This child was being whipped and tortured to try and force his magic. He's probably not even old enough to display it, if he has any." Disgust and horror wrapped her words as she turned her face back to the storm outside.

"I'll be back in the morning to hear your new plan for rescuing the Wesh, and I'll tell you then what I'm willing to do. Treat his wounds, or he won't live until morning," Coren added, and then she pushed off the windowsill into the night sky. A few seconds later, though, Sy heard a thump on the roof above them, then footsteps.

Sy felt his rage growing. How could Coren even think of running from her people now? How could there even be a decision left to make? If this scrap of a boy on the bed hadn't convinced her to help the Wesh, he didn't know what would.

But Magi be damned if he was going after her now.

He pushed aside the boy's dark curls and pressed his palm to the child's forehead, cursing at the fever he found there. Looking up, he caught Shanta's eye. She nodded and stood, pulling several vials and wrapped pouches from her bag. They both bent over the child, Sy peeling the blanket back so Shanta could work.

"I should go up there to talk with her," Resh said, uncertainty in his voice. He bent and pulled a cloak from a bag and held it up in question, but Sy just waved him away, more intent on saving the tiny life before him than on Coren and her continued indecision.

As the door closed behind Resh, the boy's eyes fluttered open, making contact with Sy's anxious gaze.

"Are you here to save me?" the boy whispered, staring up at Sy.

Sy flushed and moved back. The boy was delirious: his forehead hot with fever, but his chest like ice.

"I'll build up the fire," he said to Shanta as she bent to rip open the ragged cloth. She rubbed her palms briskly over the boy's clammy skin, skirting around his open wounds. He began to shake as his body warmed enough to circulate its own blood.

Sy hurried to finish the fire and dug a fur-lined cloak from his bag, spreading it over the boy's legs.

"What a beautiful boy," Shanta murmured, spreading her thick yellow cream over the wounds on his chest. Sy glanced down, relieved to see color returning to the boy's s cheeks. His bluish tint cleared to a smooth olive hue.

"Are you Weshen?" Shanta asked the boy as his eyes fluttered open.

"Once," he whispered, closing his eyes again and turning his face away. "Once upon a time."

Shanta glanced to Sy. "He'll be fine, I think, no matter what Corentine said. Give him plenty to eat and drink when he wakes, but do it slowly and start with broth. If he's been starved, his stomach might reject the food."

"Thank you," he said. "I'm growing more in debt to you each hour we stay here," he added ruefully.

Shanta grinned, pressing a poultice to the boy's temple. "Something's still bothering me, though. I don't know where she found him, but even among the local estates, it's rare to see such wounds on a Wesh slave. Their blood is too valuable for the king's men to spill recklessly. As soon as I'm done here, I need to go check the news with my crew," she said, glancing to the ceiling, where Coren's footsteps could still be heard pacing the roof tiles.

29

Coren didn't know where to go.

Despite struggling with wanting to leave, she wasn't quite ready to do such a drastic thing, but she certainly didn't want to be in that room. It was too crowded for these cursed wings, and she couldn't bear to watch the little boy die.

All she could think of was Kosh, and how he could be undergoing the same sort of torture this very minute.

And she would never know. She had abandoned her family to the mercy of the Hungry River and the Sulit witches. How was she any better than that slaver she had just murdered, really? She had killed another of her own people. Yes, the man had been cruel, but it could be argued so had she.

The rain slowed again, allowing the moon to poke through the swift-moving clouds. Still, she was soaked and chilled to her very bones from the trauma of the day.

Her feathers shook as she curled her arms around herself, trying to think through the mess of wants and needs in her mind - desire and fear swirled with obligation and responsibility.

She wrapped what was left of her tattered shirt more tightly around her, shuddering at the bloodstains that covered the front. And then she stiffened.

Something was there, watching her. She felt it, like the slitted eyes of a catten tracking her every movement.

"Do not come closer." Her voice was so quiet it was nearly lost in the night, but the shadows stopped moving. "I feel you moving, gathering strength. But know that I'm stronger, and I will beat you again and again, until the threat of Shadow is no more."

She heard what could have been the low rumble of thunder, or what could have been the laughter of a beast of Umbren. Either way, she immediately stretched her wings in a wide threat, feeling the cool breeze ruffle the damp feathers.

Crouching low on the roof tiles for balance, she scraped her talons against the tiles, scanning the roof for signs of Shadow. As she turned toward the far end of the roof, she glimpsed a slim form watching her.

Cloaked in black, it was much more human than Shadow should be. She stood, her eyes struggling in the darkness and mist. The form took a single step toward her, though, and she flapped her wings just enough to rise her feet from the roof tiles. She could be off and in the sky in seconds, but if this were Shadow, she needed to protect the people in the room below.

"Who are you talking to?" a familiar voice asked, and the figure stepped closer. A cloud stripped itself from the moon, and a shaft of silver light broke over the roof.

"Reshra," Coren murmured, landing back on the tiles gently. He grinned and stepped forward again.

"Is there someone else here?" he asked, glancing around at the gathered shadows.

Coren closed her eyes and sifted through the sources around her. She felt the clay of the roof tiles, the warm and cold of the night air, the droplets of rain. But she no longer felt Shadow. Opening her eyes and turning a full, slow circle, neither did she see a gathering of darkness that might point to the Umbren presence.

"It's just the two of us," she answered finally, turning back to Reshra. "How did you get up here?"

"There's a balcony off the dining room with stairs leading up here."

"Shouldn't you be resting?" she asked, keeping her eyes on the city below, where the streets were dark except for a few windows.

"Shanta popped my shoulder back in place and gave me strong medicine. I feel very nice, actually," he answered. Coren turned back to him, curious at the friendly tone in his voice. He was even closer now, close enough to reach out and touch, or to grab her arms as he had once on Weshen Isle before claiming her with a kiss for Sy.

Coren nearly grinned at how poorly that had played out. She scanned her eyes down Resh's body, conscious that she could do anything she wanted now. Never again would she need to fear a boy like Reshra.

She allowed herself to notice how handsome he truly was. The opposite of Sy, with his sly smile and thick-lashed eyes that could harden or turn curious in a blink.

Right now, they were curious. He didn't hide, and she could tell he was puzzling out her motives. She noticed he held a thick cloak, and she ached to snatch it from him. He already wore a black coat, slicked with wax against the rain, the collar turned up against the wind drifting from the NeverCross Mountains. His shirt opened deep at the throat, and she could see jewelry sparkling there, diamonds and onyx in the dark.

"So," he began, gesturing toward her. "Two arms, two legs. Four wings. Eight ways to help our people. Will you do it?"

"The Magi number," she whispered, realizing he was exactly right. He turned to gaze out at the city, and the necklace shining on his chest glinted in the moonlight - prayer beads. "I never thought of you as prayerful," she said, immediately regretting the slight tease of her words.

"I am in debt to the Mirror Magi for everything I have. How could I not be prayerful?" he asked with a sincerity that surprised her.

A beat of silence swelled between them, and Coren shivered. The rain had begun again, and she watched as the soft mist dampened his hair. She longed for the cloak in his hands, but she was too proud to ask for it, and he had yet to offer it to her.

"The child is about the same age as your brother, isn't he?" Reshra asked, turning back to pin her in his gaze, and Coren closed her eyes against the pain his question brought.

"He's just a child. They're all just children," she whispered.

"So help them," Reshra hissed, and her eyes flew open. "Look, Corentine. I'm sorry for what I've done. I know I'm to blame for your banishment, and I've questioned that morning with each new morning that has dawned since. But I was only acting on what I knew then. I know more now, so my actions will be different."

She eyed him, not ready for what he was about to say, but knowing he would say it anyway. He wouldn't hold back like Sy might.

"You know more now. How can your actions be the same? Your siblings are no more important than that boy. Your family is no more special to the Magi than any other Weshen family. But *you* are. You can save them all, Corentine."

She bit at her lips, resisting the harsh words that bubbled inside her. Kosh and Penna *were* more important, if only to her. But hadn't the child on the bed been important to someone once? Maybe there was a sister or brother or mother desperately seeking the boy right now.

"No-one can save them all." This part was easier to address.

"*You* can," he insisted. "Your power. It's incredible." He reached out to grasp a wing, drawing his fingers down the slick, rain-darkened feathers. Coren felt the touch vibrate in every part of her body, and to her embarrassment, she had to bite back a moan. Closing her eyes against the awakened desire and what it would mean to a boy like Reshra Havenash, she backed away a few steps.

"You can change the world we live in," Reshra continued. "You can kill the king with the power you have."

"Or he could just shoot me out of the sky."

Reshra stepped forward again, and Coren stepped back. But this time, her wings brushed the stone chimney behind her, and she would have to fly if she wanted to move farther away. And she wasn't certain she wanted to. Not just yet.

Reshra closed the distance between them, reaching around her and finally slipping the cloak up behind her wings, a newly-cut slit in the fabric allowing the cloak to part around them and still fasten close about her neck. She sighed into the dry warmth of the silver-black fur, hugging it close to her soaked body.

Then Reshra's hand slipped beneath her chin and tilted her face up. His eyes were heavy-lidded, as though he'd had too little sleep or too much drink. They dropped to study her lips, and Coren suddenly wished she *had* taken the opportunity to fly away.

Her magic shuddered, clamoring to help her escape, but she fought to control it, staying still beneath his touch.

She was stronger than the girl who used to run from the boys. That had been a sort of strength, certainly, but now her power was so much more. She would no longer be intimidated by Reshra. What harm was a touch or a kiss from a vain Second Son to a warrior woman like her?

He was only a man, and she had killed a man for less. She straightened and looked him directly in the eye, knowing she could do the same to him if needed.

Reshra stopped, dropping his hand.

He angled his face back to better see her in the faint moonlight. "You've changed more than your form in Riata, haven't you," he said, his voice smooth as the evening shadows. "What wicked have you done, Weshen woman?" His congratulatory grin and the wonder that accompanied it was contagious, and Coren felt her own lips stretch into a smug smile. She knew she shouldn't be proud that such a change had happened.

It should sicken her that the deed of murder was so visibly written on her face.

But it didn't. It proved she did not have to be a victim, and that none around her need suffer. "That child had a cruel master, and that master is now dead," she answered, holding his eyes. No, she wasn't proud that she'd slain another man, especially a Weshen shifter, but she also knew she would make the same choice again and again.

Reshra watched her several more moments, as though deciding whether to believe her.

"So it's true. You. And not Syashin. You did kill that guard in the armory." His voice held interest, but not surprise.

"I am no helpless island girl," she said, leaning close enough to hear the catch in his throat as she twisted a single talon in his prayer beads, the other golden claws scratching lightly at his bare skin. She didn't try to wound him, only warn.

But then he laughed, the sound blending with the quickening rain around them, and his fingers closed over hers. Her talons turned inward toward her palm, tangling in the beads as he pressed his entire body against hers, pinning her completely to the stone chimney.

He dropped his head and crushed his lips over hers, sucking greedily at her mouth, one hand clutching her waist beneath the cloak that was suddenly too hot, and the other hand moving to clasp the back of her head, holding her lips just where he wanted them.

She thought he breathed her name in stuttering syllables as he broke the kiss abruptly, and her eyes fluttered at the odd sensation.

Somewhere deep in her core, her body realized that this was an entirely different sort of kiss than the one she'd shared with Sy, and she clamped down on the growing need. *Traitorous wings*, she thought, as his fingers dredged them again. She closed her eyes to keep them from rolling back in her head.

Reshra stepped back then, glancing up at the night sky, where the clouds had begun to part, allowing moonlight to stream down on them. Grinning, he reached for her hand, unfolding the golden claws. His prayer beads had snapped and were wound around each talon, and a tiny dot of her blood rested in the center of her palm, her skin pricked open by her own needled talons.

He stroked her palm, blending the red with the rain, then slipped the beads into his pocket.

"I'm not all bad, Corentine. There are parts of me that can be very, *very* good," he said, and a shiver slunk across her shoulders.

Then he leaned close once more, his eyes glittering black in the shadows as he looked down at her lips, then up again. "You kissed me back," he whispered, then swiveled and was gone in a swish of black cloak, his tall leather boots quiet against the roof tiles. She heard the noise of a raucous crowd as the balcony door opened to the dining area, then silence as it closed again.

Coren blinked after him, uncertain whether she could honestly argue his parting comment.

Surely she had done no such thing. Had she?

Then again, she certainly hadn't tried very hard to stop him, Vespa talons or otherwise. She looked down at the smeared red on her palm and pulled the cloak tighter around her.

Only then did she recognize it as being the same cloak she'd taken from Reshra's room so many days ago. She scowled; that meant he'd been in her bag.

Shaking her wings dry as much as possible, she dropped off the roof and ducked into the attic window. Instead of finding Sy and Shanta tending a sick child huddled on the bed, she found a boy nearly as tall as Sy, holding a rusted dagger before him as Sy crouched protectively over Shanta.

"Stop where you are," the boy said, holding a hand up to Coren at the window, but keeping his blue eyes fixed on Shanta and Sy.

"Coren, he SelfShifted," Sy informed her. He kept still, though he was still reeling from the boy's ability to hold his shifted form for so long, then still have enough strength to bring part of the wall down onto Shanta, knocking her unconscious. "This is the child you brought."

"Stop!" the boy cried again, slicing his dagger through the air. Sy knew he could easily overpower him physically, but he was uncertain what further magic the boy might be hiding.

"Nikesh? Isn't that your name?" Coren asked from her crouch at the window. Her voice was low and soothing. Sy noticed that the cloak Resh had taken draped around her shoulders. She folded her wings back and tucked her talons beneath the cloak. "I promise we aren't going to hurt you."

Nikesh snorted a cynical laugh. "I have been told that many times, and each time it was a lie." But Sy noticed that the rusted dagger he'd pulled from a sheath on his thigh a few minutes ago had begun to lower a bit. The shirt he'd been wrapped in lay in tatters on the bed, and his pants, too loose only moments ago, were now fitted perfectly to his slim waist.

"Is this your regular form?" Coren asked, stretching one leg down to the floor.

Nikesh glanced back at her and nodded. "I'm nineteen."

"We're of similar age," she said, lowering the other foot gently. "I'm just going to shut the window," she added, reaching behind her to the flapping shutter.

Sy watched Nikesh carefully, risking the boy's anger to lower one hand to check Shanta's breathing.

"I'm sorry I hurt her," Nikesh said, his voice softer now. He looked again at Coren. "Thank you for saving me. But I'm afraid it will mean your death."

"What is that supposed to mean?" Sy asked, the growl in his voice barely contained.

Nikesh snapped his sky-blue eyes to Sy. "She killed my master. Someone will come looking for him. They have Sulit magic, too. They can do tracking spells. Binding spells. That's what they did to me."

"Would you like something to eat?" Coren offered, pointing to the tray still on the table. "Did you know your master was Weshen?"

Sy sucked in a breath. She had killed a Weshen? Another?

He saw the moment when Nikesh decided to trust them. He finally lowered the dagger, laying it on the table. His eyes fixed on the food. "Of course I knew. His training methods, like trying to drown me in river water, were obviously Weshen shifting." He shoved a piece of cheese in his mouth, his eyes drifting closed as he chewed. "But the Sulit magic was in the leather ties, binding me in child form," he mumbled around a bite of bread.

Sy stood slowly, testing the boy's new calm. Nikesh watched him closely but continued eating. The two boys were nearly the same size, though Sy's build was thick with muscle, and Nikesh looked as though he'd been long without a full meal.

Shanta began to stir then, and Sy held up a hand to warn Nikesh. "She won't hurt you, either."

Shanta sat up, holding her head and brushing wood dust from her eyes, from the wall planks Nikesh had shifted down on her. She blinked up at the others.

"Are you feeling okay?" Sy asked, bending back down to her. "Stay calm," he whispered.

She glared, turning her attention to Nikesh, who was already on a second piece of bread. "Why did you do that? We aren't the enemy! We're all Weshen!"

He stopped chewing and looked at all three of them in turn, darkness sliding over his face. He swallowed and put his food back on the table, sinking into the chair. "When your own people turn against you, it's hard to tell. For me, everyone is an enemy."

"I know what you mean," Coren said, stepping toward the table. "Sy and I were banished from our homes for using Weshen magic. By his own father. My siblings fled to Sulit to escape, and I may never see them again. But we have a plan," she added.

Sy nodded, helping Shanta to the bed and coming to stand next to Coren. "We know of a group of Wesh who were recently sold as slaves, and we plan to track them and rescue them. Then we'll go on to StarsHelm to attack the king."

Nikesh's eyes grew wide, and his face broke into a grin. A laugh bubbled up, filling the room, and Sy glanced at Coren, uncomfortable.

Nikesh snapped his lips shut, ending the laughter. "You will all be dead by summer's end."

Coren moved to stand over Nikesh then, her wings spreading as wide as they could in the cramped room. She bent down, her face close to his, her talons resting on the table on either side of him. "Have you ever seen a Weshen who had this form of SelfShifting?"

"No." Nikesh stared up at her without fear. "My master and I are the strongest Wesh we know of. And he was only stronger than me because of the witches."

Coren straightened and folded her wings, pacing the length of the room with measured steps. "Do you know any of the Sulit magic?"

"None," he answered.

"Will you let me leave now, or are you going to freak out again?" Shanta asked, sitting up on the bed. "I have to check in with my crew soon, or they'll start scouting the streets for me."

"I'm sorry," Nikesh said again, gesturing at the door.

"I'll send you my bill through Resh," Shanta grinned wickedly at Sy, gathering her bag and slamming out the door. He sighed, sagging against the wall.

"Where is Resh?" Sy asked, looking to Coren. He raised an eyebrow when she startled at the question, her cheeks flushing. She turned toward the fire, her wings brushing the walls as she gathered them to her back.

"He brought me this cloak and went back down to the dining area."

"We decided to set out at first light," Sy said. "Traveling at night might be safer, but we don't have a good idea where we're going. And we're all exhausted. I'm going downstairs to reserve another room, so we can all have somewhere to sleep a few hours. Unless you've decided on a different plan?" He stepped next to the fire, turning her shoulders to face him. He fixed her in his gaze, challenging her. Nikesh blinked between them, watching carefully.

"No. I'm coming with you. When I thought he was a Weshen child," she gestured to Nikesh, "all I could think of was Kosh. I don't want any other children being hurt, or any other families being torn apart. Maren will take care of my family. I need to help you. I'm sorry," she added, reaching her arms around his waist and sagging into him.

"I'm sorry," she repeated, her whisper dissolving into his shirt, tugging at his heart. He ran a hand through her hair and held her close.

"If you're going to get naked, I should probably go," Nikesh said, breaking the silence of the room. He stood, grabbing more of the bread and cheese.

Sy and Coren pushed apart a little too quickly. "We're not like that," Sy said, glancing at Nikesh. The other boy's eyes sparked, and a sly grin turned up the corners of his lips.

"I'll come with you to get the keys, then. I could use a stretch," Nikesh answered. Sy shrugged. He glanced back at Coren, but she had already turned back to the fire, watching the flames do their own shifting with the sources of the wood there.

Resh sat alone at a dark corner table in the dining area, letting the noise of the other patrons drown out all but the most important of his thoughts.

Coren had kissed him back: she was letting him in. Of that he was certain. But why? And why had he pushed himself on her again?

He'd been so wrong about her. So wrong, yet so right. "Little Weshen witch," he whispered to himself, taking a deep draught of the wine before him. But the words had grown from a curse to something more familiar,

412

somehow almost endearing. Resh had been trained all his life to disbelieve and hate the magic.

But he was no fool, either. Things were changing in the world, and he intended to ride the crest of the wave that was about to sweep across Riata.

Sy's plan was short-sighted as always.

He and Corentine could kill Zorander Graeme with their magic, Resh was certain of it. But when the Restless King was no more, who could step up to put the pieces of an empire back together? Sy wouldn't want such a responsibility. He barely wanted to lead his own people.

Without the Restless King, Riata would dissolve into civil war, as all the nations the king had forced to unite tried to separate themselves again.

Resh smiled to himself, absently rubbing a finger over his lips. He could lead them, though.

True, he knew nothing of kings and court games. But he knew people, and he could guess their reactions often before they knew themselves.

He stared into the crowd, seeing nothing except the image in his mind of a beautiful girl, wings curled around them both, lips turned up in a beckoning smile.

Coren's magic made her a beautiful, deadly weapon. She was uncertain of her power - mistrustful of her instincts to rule those around her.

Her life had done nothing but teach her submission, yet still she did not cower. All he needed to do was push her a little farther, and she would come into her destiny.

Finding and rescuing this child was a boon to all Sy and Resh had discussed. If the boy reminded her of her brother, even better. Now Resh could lure the magic in her to notice the atrocities all around her. Everywhere, there were people taking advantage of innocent Weshen children.

He had seen the darkness swirling in her eyes when she claimed her kill, and he intended to use that darkness to smother the evil in StarsHelm.

Using dark to overpower dark sounded counterintuitive, but he had felt the song of her blood rising when they kissed.

He knew the blood magic of Umbren chased her. If they could find and merge the light of Weshen, the dark of Sulit, and the Shadow of Umbren, they would be unstoppable.

Sy was the strength, Resh was the sly, and Coren was the shifter.

Together, the three of them could rule Riata.

30

Coren took advantage of the empty room to strip her wet clothes and gather clean, dry ones. Wrapping again in her cloak, she hurried down a flight of stairs and found the hotel bathrooms, locking herself in the single bathing room.

The water wasn't very warm, but it was a relief to rid herself of the crusted blood and dirt. Feathers were difficult to wash, and she finally gave up, drying them as best she could. She wished for her own body again, or for the ability to shift in and out of these Vespa wings, the way she could with her younger form.

She even tried SelfShifting, but that only resulted in a young Corentine with wings that were far too heavy to lift.

Sighing, she shifted back and dressed as best she could in the cramped space, her sleeping gown thin against the night air. She threw the cloak over her wings and hurried back to the room, uncomfortable in the knowledge that so many strangers waited around her, down the stairs and behind so many closed doors.

Locking the door behind her, she decided she did not like city life.

"I can help you cut that gown so it fits your wings properly," a voice sounded from the darkness.

Her grasp on the cloak faltered, and it slipped to the floor as a single candle flamed to life. "Reshra? What are you doing? Get out!" she cried, her words running together. She clutched at the untied neck of the gown.

He didn't move, his eyes roaming over her form in the thin dress. "Don't worry. I'll be sleeping in another room with Sy and Nikesh. You'll be alone with your thoughts soon enough."

She glowered, uncertain which was worse - alone with her thoughts, or alone with Reshra.

"You would look stunning in my clothes, though," he murmured, standing and holding up one of the dresses she had stolen from his closet in Weshen City so many days ago.

"I wish I had been the one to present you with this dress. It would have given me much…pleasure." He stepped closer, a smile spreading across his face.

"I took what was mine by right," she retorted, finding her pride and using it to prop herself up taller. "You claimed me, so I chose a dress."

"And this?" he asked, holding the stiletto out toward her.

"Why have you been going through my things?" she asked, refusing to take it.

"Because you went through mine. It seemed fair." He dropped the dress onto her open bag and stretched out on the bed, toying with the stiletto.

"What do you want, Reshra?" she asked. Now that she was clean and dressed for bed, her body strained for the warmth of the blanket and the relief of a pillow.

He fixed her with his dark eyes but said nothing. She shivered beneath his gaze, the question hanging between them like a flag of war, or possibly surrender. A log in the fireplace broke, sending a brief spurt of light in the air, and Coren watched each spark die, glad for the distraction.

"Would you laugh if I said I wanted magic?" Reshra asked, his voice barely a whisper. When she turned back to him, his face was open in a way she had never seen. "I want what you and Sy have. I want that power." He sat and leaned forward, and she sensed a rare simplicity in the openness of his eyes. "I don't want to be left behind, Corentine."

Her feet carried her the few steps to the bed without her permission, and she hovered at its edge. His words had pulled her in too easily, as though he already possessed some strange magic. He reached out hand, palming her stomach over the nightgown and stroking the golden circle at her waist with his thumb. Her wings floated out lazily, responding to the touch.

Somehow Coren sensed the severed claw in her skin was the source of her power.

Could it be removed? Was that the secret?

"A true talisman," Reshra whispered, sliding his hand around her waist to her lower back and tugging her closer. Coren's mind felt blank with fatigue as she allowed him to pull her onto the mattress, her legs slipping beneath the blanket. Even alone in a room, there was no more reason to fear him. She lay on her side, facing Reshra with sleep-heavy eyes. He pulled the blanket up around her.

"You're exhausted. I'll go now, so Sy doesn't come rushing up here." He smiled, slipping off the bed. She felt him pause, and his hand brushed the length of her wing, sending her eyes rolling back in her head again. She pressed her lips closed, pretending sleep.

Did he know how much that single touch affected her?

His fingers left her feathers, and she heard the door open. "Sleep well, my Weshen witch," Reshra murmured, and then the door closed softly behind him.

His words no longer sounded like a curse, Coren thought as she drifted to sleep.

When Sy knocked on Coren's door the next morning, it swung open. The three boys filed in, finding her standing dressed and ready at the window, staring into the bright morning sun.

Nikesh set a tray of breakfast on the table and sat, keeping close to the food. Sy smiled at him. Nik had eaten his weight in food the previous night, then fallen asleep curled next to the fire. Sometime in the night, Resh had joined his brother in the bed, but he looked less awake this morning.

"Out late?" Sy asked Resh, smearing butter on a chunk of bread. It would be just like his brother to chase a girl the night before a mission. Resh's eyes flicked to Coren's back. He shrugged and chose an apple from the plate.

"What can we expect today?" Coren asked, turning. She wore the boys' clothing they had stolen from Weshen City - a burgundy shirt tucked into tight breeches, and a leather vest with new slits cut for her wings. Her hair was braided away from her face, and her whip wound around her arm, its handle resting on the inside of her wrist.

She strode around the bed, her borrowed boots echoing on the wooden floor. The outer feathers of her tucked wings brushed the walls. She paused before Resh, and when he didn't move out of her way, she leaned across his chest to spear a piece of roasted meat. Resh choked on his bite of apple, hiding it with a cough.

Nik's blue eyes widened, and he arched his brow at Sy, asking a question about something Sy was only beginning to notice. Resh was watching Coren stand by the fire, seemingly mesmerized by her form in the fitted clothes. Sy frowned. Why would Resh suddenly gain an interest in Coren?

He cleared his throat. He had no time for this today. "We have a map with abandoned estate homes marked, where slavers often hide the Wesh." He glanced at Nik, whose face was storm-dark with fury. He rubbed at the scars on his wrists, and Sy swallowed. "But we aren't sure where the slaves were taken. They might even have been sold to someone outside of EvenFall."

"If only we could find out who bought them," Coren muttered.

"We can," a voice said from the door.

All three of them startled as Shanta closed the door silently behind herself.

"While you were all sleeping, I broke into the auction house." She pulled a folded paper from inside her leather vest. "The bill of sale," she added, handing the paper to Resh.

"Shanta, I could kiss you for this," Resh said, scanning it.

She smirked. "I prefer Riatan gold, thanks."

"I have that, too," Resh nodded, glancing up. Then he grinned wickedly. "Though that wasn't always your preference, was it?"

Shanta glared at him, her hand drifting toward the knife strapped to her belt, and Sy bit back a laugh. Coren swiveled and stalked toward them.

"If you're done trying to bed another unwilling girl, can you please share the paper?" she said, holding out her clawed hand. Resh placed the paper in it, holding her eyes a beat too long. Sy felt discomfort flush into the room, and he sighed.

Why did his brother have to turn every interaction back to his bedroom?

"My crew and I can hunt down single slaves pretty easily, but I suggest you going after the main purchaser," Shanta said, turning to Sy. "A single person bought ten of the thirteen Wesh."

"Who?" Sy asked.

Shanta flicked her eyes at Resh, whose face had grown hard in realization. "The Prodigal Knight," she answered.

"Who's that?" Coren asked, looking up from the paper.

"Zorander Graeme's general, in charge of the Alchemists. And of all Weshen prisoners," Resh spat. "He belongs to the Restless King, and now so do those Wesh."

Coren cursed and punched her hand against the wall. Her wings shuddered and pulsed with pale colors, and her claws scraped at the wood. "They'll be tortured, won't they," she whispered. "Because of me."

"Because of *Graeme*," Shanta said harshly. "Don't place blame where it doesn't belong. If you want to help those Wesh, stop feeling sorry for yourself, and take back what's ours."

Coren turned to Shanta, and the two girls locked eyes, each measuring the other. "You're Wesh?" Coren asked. Shanta nodded, glaring. "Why haven't you tried to get through the mountains?"

"Because hiding is pointless! The Restless King never stops hunting our people. He will find a way to cross those stupid NeverCross Mountains, and all you people hiding on that island won't be safe - you'll be *trapped*."

Sy's heart dropped, realizing just how right Shanta was. "The barrier will fall soon," he muttered. Three pairs of eyes turned on him, and he began to rub at his temples. "Now that the magic is returning, the barrier will fall, right?"

Resh cursed. "Let's figure out this rescue, and then we can take them back to Weshen City to heal. We'll get the General to let you two back in the city, and we'll get the army ready again."

"I'm not going back there," Coren said. "But I'm up for the rest of your plan."

Sy grinned down at his breakfast.

Coren soared above the trees, watching for glimpses of movement. She had already doubled back to check on Sy, Resh, and Nik several times before she saw the party of Wesh slaves. They were tied together with loose ropes, and she counted maybe a dozen prisoners and at least two guards following a dirt path through the forest. The trees were thick here, though, and somehow she doubted all those slaves were being held by just two men.

Her boys were still several minutes behind the traveling party and would need to cross a wide part of the stream first.

Just as she swooped down to land near the water and scout a good crossing point, she noticed movement among the trees, too close to be either the slaves or her friends. She scanned the foliage, her nerves thrumming as she noticed how thick the shadows were in this part of the forest. Even the water of the stream was dark, with the sun barely reaching through the dense canopy.

Then voices reached her, and she quickly ducked behind a trunk, her breathing already calming. Shadow, at least, did not speak.

"There are at least ten, according to the auction records," one voice said, not so much loud as near.

Coren shrunk in on herself, praying her wings would not catch any of the few dappled sunspots.

"I wish we knew who had ambushed Oren. That still unsettles me," another answered. "Losing Nik was a disaster."

Hearing the gruff voice speak Nik's name nearly drove Coren from her hiding spot. These men had tortured Nik, and who knows how many others. She should attack. She could beat them. A small whisper echoed in her mind, encouraging her to cut them down with her talons. Coren shook her head, trying to free it from the images playing there.

A figure passed closer now, and then a second. Both men were carrying bow swords, shining daggers strapped to their waists. She saw the glint of Weshen prayer beads at one's throat as well, and the whisper in her mind grew louder.

These were Weshen, preying on their own kind. Their blood should spill.

A branch snapped beneath her foot, and she ducked to the ground, cursing under her breath. She hadn't even realized she'd taken a step. She gritted her teeth against the overwhelming need to go after the men - even in her Vespa form, she may not be a match for two grown men with powerful weapons.

Only the sort of discipline she had gathered from her summers in the hunts allowed her to stay still in the brush, watching them until they disappeared. Then she raced through the trees to find Sy and the others.

"Do you think they could be after the slaves to free them or capture them?" Sy asked Nik when Coren had described the men.

"Capture," Nik answered, his face dark and drawn with a violent sort of hatred. Coren found satisfaction thinking that now, Nik could repay what was taken from his youth.

"Either way, we need to reach the slaves before they do," Resh said. "Let's move."

Sy heard the man running through the trees for him before he saw the movement, and he ducked low. When the man burst onto the dirt path, he nearly sailed over Sy, who had his longknife ready.

He slashed at the man's outstretched arms, knocking the crudely-made bow sword away. The man shrieked in rage and whipped a dagger from a sheath on his thigh, charging Sy again. He was large but less trained, and Sy danced around him, almost teasing. Just as the man was about to lunge again, he cried out, and his eyes grew wide.

The gleaming tip of a bow sword push through his chest from behind. The man began to gurgle, blood leaking from between his lips, and he fell like a stone to the ground. Standing just behind him was Nik, a satisfied grin stretching his lips wide.

"This one was especially cruel to me. I know you didn't need help," he said, holding Sy's gaze a beat longer than expected. Sy wondered what Nik was trying to tell him, but another Weshen traitor bore down on them, yelling all-too-familiar curses.

The second slaver was much more skilled, and Sy leaped at him. Nik had been slow to recover his shifting strength, and Sy wondered if Nik might be permanently affected by the Sulit spells.

The man got past his guard and sliced Sy's forearm. The bright spark of pain reminded him to focus on the fight before him, not figuring out the boy behind him. Sy latched onto the sound of weapons clashing in the brisk morning air.

The man fell to his knees in the grass, clutching his bloodied side and holding up his hands in surrender. "Please don't kill me!" he begged. Sy hesitated, and Nik shrugged.

"I'll watch him," he said cheerfully, moving to stand above the man, sword point pressing into his chest. "Coren and Resh went on. I think the other slaves are right ahead."

"Let him live," Sy said. "I want some questions answered."

Nik just grinned, winking. The gesture shot through Sy's chest in an odd way, and he turned quickly, scanning the trees for Resh and Corentine. He wasn't worried about either of them, but he had the odd sensation that Nik wanted to tell him a secret, and it might be something he wasn't ready to hear.

He saw a flash of wings, and he dashed through the trees, finding Coren swiping her claws across the neck of a third Wesh slaver. She screamed at the man as he yanked at one of her wings on his way down, but before Sy had the chance to intervene, she kicked the man violently in the gut. He sprawled on the ground, his eyes turning dull and lifeless even as he hit the forest floor.

"Came out of nowhere," she muttered to herself, jerking her wing back into place with a grimace.

"That's three slavers," Sy said.

She whirled on him, claws raised and a startled fire in her liquid amber eyes. Sy's grip on his weapon faltered. Coren looked every bit like a demon from the Sulit forest, or something from deep in the Umbren shadows. But as she focused on Sy, the look softened, and he began to breathe again.

"Where's Resh?" she asked, scanning the trees.

Sy shrugged, but the thrum of an arrow and a shout reached them from beyond a thick copse of trees. They both broke into a run, Coren shoving her wings behind her as they tangled in the foliage.

"Resh!" she cried out as they entered a wide clearing, but he didn't turn, his attention focused on fighting the tall, brawny guard before him. The man was decorated with too much brass to be a mere guard.

"Prodigal Knight!" Sy warned. The man's head whipped around at the name, but when he saw them, his mouth and his weapon both dropped.

"Sorenta?" he said, the name floating in the air as he stared at Coren, his face ghostly pale in the shadows of the forest.

Coren knocked Resh aside and was on the man in a second, her wings stretching wide and blocking the brothers' view of either of them. Resh kept his bow sword up and ready, glancing back at Sy, who shrugged in uncertainty.

Coren trembled, holding the man's jacket tight in her talons, searching his face from a mere few inches. It was older, certainly, but the familiarity was there. The amber eyes matched her own. But it just couldn't be true.

Not after all these years. Not here.

"Corentine…" he said, whispering now. "It's me. Kashar. Your father." His voice sounded uncertain of the words it was pronouncing, but his eyes had filled with tears.

Tears that she wanted nothing more than to smack away. She loosed her hold on his palace uniform and backed up several feet, relishing the awe spilling over his face as he took in her full Vespa form.

"Traitor," she spat at him, and his face hardened. She glanced back at Sy and Resh, who were still alternating between scanning the woods around them and the scene before them, ready to fight and protect her. She shook her head at them.

"If anyone fights this man, it will be me," she snarled.

Sy raised his brows in question.

Turning back to Kashar, she said, "Call your men here. I want no surprises."

"This is my father, Kashar the *Deserter*," she said to Resh and Sy. The shock on their faces would have made her laugh if not for the rage bubbling in her veins. "This is Kashar…who left me with a suicidal mother and twin babies to care for, and apparently came to work for the *one man* who his people hate most in all the world."

"Corentine, I'm so sorry," he began, but she snapped her wings at him, their momentum pushing him backward. He stumbled to one knee.

"You do *not* get to apologize for those years," she said, infuriated even more by the obvious hurt in her voice. "Now call your men," she repeated. "Bring all the Wesh. Or I will slice you open where you stand."

He searched her face for something, and apparently didn't find it. Casting his eyes down, he put his fingers between his lips and whistled, long and clear.

Coren hated the relief that began to filter through her.

No, she didn't want to kill her father. But she also couldn't bear to gain a new weakness, just when she'd become so strong.

Kashar could bring her to her knees if he remembered how to speak just the right words.

Two men appeared momentarily, both trailing several Wesh behind them, still in their rope bindings. They hadn't been far, and Coren realized that if they hadn't come upon the three Weshen slavers first, much more blood would have spilled.

"Where are the traitors?" she asked Sy.

"Two dead, and Nik is watching a third," Sy said quickly.

"Bring him here," Coren said. Her control threatened to snap at any second, sending her into the sort of spiral that had already killed a guard in Weshen City, and several more since.

She felt Resh step next to her, but she ignored him. Kashar was all that mattered.

They must take the slaves, so he could no longer do harm. "We're taking all of these Wesh with us. They will not go to the palace, but home to Weshen City," she said, glaring at Kashar.

The huddled Wesh muttered to each other, disbelief and fear on their faces. The guards yanked on their ropes, calling threats. Kashar's expression hardened, and he shook his head.

"That is impossible. My life is forfeit if I do not bring them."

"You are a traitor. Your life is already forfeit."

He shook his head, and she bit down on a yell of rage.

"I am your *daughter*," she said instead, taking a menacing step toward him. "These are your people. Or they were, once. Before you traded them for the luxuries of a tyrant."

"There's so much you don't understand," he replied, and her vision tunneled to his eyes, everything else turning to darkness. How dare he? "Corentine, these Wesh are safer in StarsHelm with me than anywhere else. The passage through the mountains would kill some of them. As I'm sure you also found out," he added.

Coren startled, her thoughts stumbling from black thoughts of murder.

"You knew I was Wesh?"

He nodded. "Sorenta was Wesh. Helping her escape Riata through the passage was the worst thing I'd ever had to endure. We were so young, and we knew nothing of Weshen City, except that it waited on the other side of the mountains. It was supposed to be safe. I loved her, and she was dying before my very eyes. There was nothing I could do."

"And yet all those years later you abandoned her and your children and your people," Coren said, her voice slicing like steel through the plea on his face.

"I'll explain everything, but we cannot stay here. I promise you, things will be much worse for all of us if I return to StarsHelm without these Wesh."

Sy returned with Nik, half-dragging the wounded slaver between them. She spared a second to check on Resh, who was strutting up and down across the line of guards and Wesh, soaking in her words.

"What do you want?" Sy asked Kashar.

"He does not get terms!" Coren cried, but Resh stepped forward and drew a hand along her trembling wings, leaning to whisper a warning of calm. She made a noise nearly like a growl, but then she nodded to Kashar. "What is it that you want?"

Kashar hesitated, then nodded. "I will compromise. These are good men. My guards, loyal to me even above their pledge to Zorander Graeme. For years, we've helped collect the Wesh and bring them to the palace, but you must believe me. I swear on the Mirror Magi themselves that I help the Wesh in every way I can. You've seen what happens to them on their own," he said, gesturing to Nik, who stiffened and stepped closer to Sy.

"The king mandates his Alchemists to learn from the Wesh, and while it's true they are prisoners, if I'm in charge, I can ensure they're treated better than many of the king's friends. I'm learning from them, Corentine. We're collecting the magic again, and recording its ways for the time when the magic returns to Weshen."

"In case you hadn't noticed, the magic is here," Resh said, stepping slightly between Coren and her father. "That means you no longer need to carry on this sham.

Simply free these Wesh and return home. I will see to it that my father pardons you."

"A First Son?" Kashar asked, raising a brow. Resh flushed.

"I am First Son," Sy responded, stepping next to Resh. "And my father is not one to discuss magic lightly." He glared at Resh. "But we can ensure their safety in other ways."

Coren bit back a snort, and Sy gritted his teeth. "Let us take the children, then," he said, gesturing to the few small bodies in the lineup of Wesh. "Tell the king they didn't make the journey, or they didn't have magic. I'm sure you can figure out a believable story. Take the healthy adults, and leave us the children and the wounded," he requested.

Kashar was silent, seeming to consider the offer.

"Or, we can simply kill you now," Nik said, raising his stolen bow sword. Sy held up his hand, and Nik sighed, disappointment slouching his shoulders.

"Fine," Kashar bit out. "But only because of my daughter."

Coren felt her rage reach a tipping point. She was about to lift her father from the grass when Sy jumped and shoved her back, sending her stumbling into Resh's arms.

"Watch out!" Sy yelled, waving his arms at everyone in the clearing. The guards yanked at the Wesh, pulling them together automatically against the unseen threat. Nik and Resh and even Kashar whirled in circles, trying to locate the new danger.

"Shadow! It wants the magic!" Sy cried, and several of the Wesh screamed.

Coren brushed Resh away and prowled the trees, soon finding the type of darkening mass and flickering movement she would never again take for granted.

She let out a wordless scream of rage just as Shadow slunk from behind a tree, its form the most substantial she'd seen it yet. Low rumbles of something between a creature's growl and the threat of thunder echoed through the forest, and more of the Wesh screamed, huddling closer to each other.

Kashar and his guards circled the group, weapons brandished as Shadow dissolved again between the trees, reappearing several feet closer each time.

"What is it?" one of the guards yelled, just as the darkness slithered over him, and his scream was cut short with the severing of his head. Blood gushed into the grass, and Coren heard someone retching among the screams and whimpers.

Leaping into the air, she flapped her wings and located Shadow. She dove, ignoring the crunch of feather against tree branch as she bore down on the darkness, but Shadow was too fast. Colliding with a Wesh woman at the edge of the circle, it sliced her deep enough that the red of her insides became a gruesome tangle on the forest floor.

Shadow flickered and grew more defined, as Coren's stomach churned at the mess of a human before her. But in the split second she had looked to the dying woman, Shadow darted to her and sliced at her with its trailing talons, opening her leather vest and tunic from her waist nearly to her neck.

Old instincts took over, and her whip slid down her arm to flick at the air like the tongue of a snakka.

The remaining Wesh and even the guards were panicking behind her, crushing each other in their haste to flee. But she focused on the darkness before her, and the odd stretch of light within it, almost as though the creature were trying to smile at her.

A low rumble shook the ground at her feet, and she sliced the whip through its middle. It dissolved like smoke, and she flapped her wings at it, spreading it farther. The rumble turned to something more like laughter as the bits of darkness slipped away.

Its kills had been making it stronger.

"Blood magic," she whispered, glancing behind her. Sy and Nik were struggling to corral the hysterical Wesh, and Kashar was tending to a wounded guard.

She spotted Shadow gathering itself together at the edge of the clearing. She began to run, but Resh was also striding toward the monster, bow sword drawn and murder on his beautiful face.

"Reshra, no!" she cried, but it was too late. He was too close.

Shadow leaped at him with a guttural roar that seemed to shake leaves from the trees, the edges of darkness twining around Resh's arms and legs, tumbling him to the ground.

Coren half-flew, half-ran and crashed into the black mass settled above Resh's chest. Swiping her talons through the amorphous form, she shrieked and beat her wings, loosing all her rage on the creature as they rolled together into the grass. Its form was solid and smoke, darkness and light, all at once.

Finally, it burst and shattered into pieces that fell like shards of glass and scraps of sodden fabric into the grass around them. Heaving, she picked up a piece and felt nothing in it, no living source.

She crawled and knelt in the blood-soaked grass next to Resh, her wings enclosing them in a different sort of shadow, draped like a shroud.

"Resh?" she whispered, unashamed at the desperation in her voice. She wasn't sure why yet, but she needed him to be alive. His eyes fluttered open, and his face was drawn in pain. She carefully sliced away the tattered shirt to reveal deep gashes across his stomach and up his side, the skin flayed back to expose several white ribs.

"Thank you," he said, reaching a bloodied hand to cup her cheek. She smiled into his fingers, about to tease him, but something grabbed her from behind.

White pain ripped through her abdomen, and she curled around herself, moaning.

Agony reverberated through every limb in her body, and the world flashed dark and light, dark and light.

Someone screamed her name, but she was lost again on the MagiSea, just a pebble skipping over the salty water, stumbling over the ripples but no longer making them.

31

Despite his own injuries, Resh had barely left Coren's side in three days.

Three days he had watched her wrestle with her mind, muttering incoherently about ripples and shadows and the cruelty of family. He'd never cared enough for anyone to spend this much time with them, but when Sy had questioned him, Resh used the last of his resolve to avoid punching his brother.

Whatever hold this girl had over him, it hadn't been exclusive to her beautiful, sensual Vespa wings.

Resh was certain of that because now, the wings were gone.

Sy told him later that Shadow had ripped the claw from Coren's stomach, sending her into this dreamlike state. Her wings had begun to shrivel and shrink into her back immediately.

Resh remembered none of this. Neither did he

remember Sy's story of shifting apart the forest floor with Nik's help, then overturning the dirt, trapping Shadow deep in the earth.

All Resh remembered after being attacked were Coren's eyes, locked onto his, fear and pain and desperation swirling there and tugging him under like a drowning man with a weight on his chest. So he stayed by her side, watching for the slightest change.

He wasn't certain why, but he needed her to live.

"Any change?" Sy asked, opening the door to the attic room of the NightGuard.

Resh shook his head, standing to stretch and wincing as the bandages pulled at the edges of his wounds. "Is Shanta here? I need to change these bandages and take a piss," he said. Sy nodded, and Resh shoved past his brother before he could ask another question.

Coming out of the bathroom, he sought Shanta in the boys' room. She'd been visiting two and three times a day, checking on Coren and bandaging Resh's ribs and stomach.

"How are the Wesh?" he asked, peeling the cloth from his skin.

"You're healing nicely," she answered instead. Her ice-blue eyes blinked up at him. "So far Kashar hasn't bothered us. He let me take the kids and the few wounded ones. He didn't even have a guard follow me."

"How can you be certain?"

She glared, taping the clean cloth to his skin with more force than was necessary. "Because I know my city, Resh. I know everything that goes on in my quarter."

Nik entered the room just then, bearing yet another full tray of food. "I sure hope you have some money.

We're starting to run quite the tab here," he said, grinning. Resh only narrowed his eyes. Something about Nik bothered him, but other than the boy's incessant cheerfulness, he had yet to figure it out. Sy seemed intent on keeping him around, though, so Resh tolerated the feeling.

He would figure it out eventually.

"Any luck finding the source of the magic?" Resh asked, trying to keep his voice neutral. Shanta and her crew had been interviewing people and scouring the city for reasons why some of the Wesh had magic while others did not. So far they'd found nothing new - most of the patterns traced back to powerful families, when the lineage could be discovered.

"I'm sure you'll get your powers soon." She knew what he really wanted.

Resh scoffed. "I'm fine with my bow sword, thanks. Leave the wings to that one." He gestured above them to the attic.

"I'd be happy to torture the magic from you," Nik added. "I've seen lots of techniques."

Resh grimaced. "None of that. But if you can play nice, I think you'd do well to come to Weshen City when we take the Wesh there. You can help smooth things over with the General."

Nik scowled. "I'd rather not help that man." He sat down before the food and began to eat, closing his expression from Resh and Shanta.

"Well, I'm off," Shanta said abruptly. "Send a message if bird-girl wakes up."

Resh shrugged. Grabbing a plate of food, he followed her out the door, turning up the stairs when she turned down. He clomped up to the attic, passing Sy on the way down.

"Nik has the food," he said. Then he stopped mid-step, and Sy glanced up at him from the bottom of the staircase. "You're coming home, aren't you? You and Coren?"

Sy opened his mouth, then closed it again. He shook his head. "I don't know. I don't think she'll want to go anywhere near Weshen City or the island for a long time. And I promised her the king."

"She can't do much to the king without her wings," Resh muttered.

"She made that decision long before the wings were even a thought on the horizon," Sy said, opening the door to the boys' room. "I doubt she'll back down now."

Resh sighed and continued to the attic, where Coren lay motionless on the bed, just as he'd left her. He knew Sy was right. He tried to settle in a comfortable position in the chair, but his ribs ached, and the bandages seemed too tight.

Nothing was working out the way he'd hoped.

"Any change?" Nik asked as Sy came into the room. He shook his head, weary of the question and its same answer.

Nik handed him a plate filled with Sy's favorites from the downstairs tavern. He smiled and sat at the table.

Over the last three days, their eyes had met over mugs of tea and sandwiches, in the early morning hours, and just before the last candle flame flickered out. Sy had grown used to looking for Nik's easy smile and raised, questioning brows, although he still wasn't certain what Nik wanted to ask him.

"Your brother offered me a teaching position in Weshen City," Nik said, his eyes twinkling.

Sy snorted. "He's only trying to get out of it himself. But you'd do well at it," he added. "You know as much as any of us. Maybe more."

Nik nodded. "You plan to go to StarsHelm?" he asked after a few moments.

Sy gazed out the window. "I promised Coren the king. Graeme's time is done."

"There are rumors that he has Sulit magic. That he's far younger than his years should make him. It would be too dangerous to attack him without a trained army of shifters."

Sy didn't respond, instead standing to stretch. He'd been sitting far too much these last few days. Besides, these rumors meant nothing. He'd heard them all and more, and there was no way to confirm them.

He should have asked Kashar, but the man had disappeared immediately after delivering the wounded Wesh to Shanta. Sy assumed he had returned to StarsHelm with the remaining slaves.

He dreaded that conversation when Coren woke. And she *would* wake. He still clung to that belief. They all did.

"She has a hold on you yet, doesn't she?" Nik asked, his voice almost too soft to hear. "Corentine. Do you love her?"

Sy glanced at Nik. This was the question. But now that it had been asked, Sy realized he feared answering it even more. What would his answer mean to Nik? His storm-dark eyes caught Nik's crystal-sky eyes, and they held.

A challenge, an evaluation, a measuring.

A wanting waited there for him, and Nik didn't look away when Sy noticed it.

Sy shook his head. No, he didn't love Coren. Not that way.

Nik pushed his plate away and stood, facing Sy, his eyes hopeful and wide with a new question.

Suddenly a coward, Sy turned away, ruffling his hair from his brow. What was he doing?

Nik made an odd noise. "Where did you get that scar?"

Sy startled, and his hair feathered over his eyes. Nik stepped into the light and pushed his black curls from his temple, revealing a grid of eight circular scars, tiny but distinct.

"You have that, too. On your temple," he said.

Sy pushed his hair away and felt for the circles he knew were there. He'd had them as long as he could remember. "I didn't think it was a scar," he admitted.

Nik shook his head. "It's from a test. Someone tested you for magic."

Sy felt the blood drain from his face, and he leaned against the edge of the bed. Had Ashemon tested him?

"It's not always accurate, though. If you don't have a true talisman, the magic sometimes doesn't show. The slavers who kept me did it to all the new Wesh. They'd do it every few months, sometimes, just to be sure," Nik explained.

He stepped forward again and lifted Sy's hair to study the marks. Sy barely breathed, his mind whirling with too many unanswered questions.

Nik's hand slid from Sy's temple, tracing a gentle line down his cheek, and Sy burst away. He paced to the window and stared, seeing nothing.

He should be wondering about Ashemon's intentions, but all he could focus on was the feel of Nik's calloused fingers.

And suddenly Sy's cheeks were hot and his chest was hotter and everything clicked as the machine of desire rumbled to life in his body. Everything slid into place and he finally understood. He hadn't disliked the hunts because of the indignity of chasing girls. Well, yes to the indignity.

But he had disliked the hunts because hunting the girls was wrong in an entirely different way.

Nik stepped close behind him, interrupting Sy's churning thoughts.

Sy turned and focused on how full Nik's lips were, how soft they looked, despite everything he'd suffered. His eyes flickered down the lean muscle of Nik's chest under its thin shirt and stuttered over the narrow waist tapering into low-slung pants.

Sy blinked up just as Nik pulled his lips apart in a soft smile, and Sy's breath thickened in his throat.

"General...First Son," he muttered to himself, shaking his head. He couldn't...wasn't supposed to...

"I know what you are," Nik whispered. "And I know how he treated you." He took another step, and Sy's back touched the window's warm glass. They were close enough to touch now, but they didn't. Sy felt dizzy from the heat swirling around them.

"You're not a General's son anymore. He doesn't deserve you," Nik continued, erasing all the distance. His slippered feet rested at the tips of Sy's boots, his chest rising and falling only inches from Sy's chest. "And by the Magi, I don't either, but I want you," he finished, and Sy stopped breathing altogether.

They were nearly the same height, and all he needed to do was lean forward, cross the tiniest channel of air from between their lips. Sy closed his eyes to keep Nik from seeing the fear he knew was creeping in, turning him to stone.

He tried to move, to show Nik what he wanted - what he now felt like he'd always wanted - but his muscles were locked down from fear.

"Sy," Nik said, and the word was barely a breath on Sy's face, pushing away the fear, and then Nik slanted his lips over Sy's, pressing him to the window. His hands slid up Sy's arms, squeezing the corded muscle there, then into his hair, pulling the strands as he kissed harder than Sy thought he could bear.

Still, he hesitated to touch Nik. He didn't know what to do or where to begin, and his chest was near to exploding with indecision when Nik broke away, fear now transferred to his hooded eyes.

"I-I'm sorry," Nik whispered, backing away a single step. Uncertainty twisted that incredible mouth into a frown, and Sy realized this might be his only chance to tell himself the truth.

He forced his feet to advance, prowling like the animal he felt he'd turned into. His lips were rough and used, and it was glorious. Sy had waited his entire life to feel like this, and now that the door had been opened, he wasn't backing down.

Nik must have caught the look in Sy's eye because his lips broke into a sly grin.

"I guess I'm not sorry," he said, tilting his head, a challenge lifting his brows.

"Definitely not," Sy answered, his voice barely above a growl. But he made it only far enough to grasp Nik's narrow waist before the door flew open, revealing a very angry Kashar.

"I've waited long enough. We need to talk about Corentine," he said, his eyes flicking between the two boys. Sy had jumped away from Nik like an electric charge separated them, and he flushed now, wondering what this man thought he'd seen, or who he might tell if provoked.

And then, seeing the hope mixed with disappointment on Nik's face, he wondered if he even cared what others would think.

In the attic room, Coren opened her eyes, blinking into the afternoon sun streaming in the window.

Turning her head, she saw only Resh there, his head tilted back, eyes closed in sleep. Her limbs felt filled with sand, and she pushed herself up to sitting with difficulty.

Stretching each muscle slowly, she watched Resh's chest rise and fall gently. His lashes cast thick shadows on his flushed cheeks, and his lips were slightly upturned with a content she'd rarely seen on him.

He had filled her dreams. They all had. She had flown the length of Riata, to Sulit and Umbren and back again, bringing the head of King Zorander Graeme to place on the spikes of Weshen City. She had danced with Sy and embraced Resh, and he had kissed her, long and without reason to hurry.

She was still rifling through the odd images and studying the scruff of unshaven beard on his jaw when his eyes opened, locking on hers.

"I knew you'd wake again, little witch," he said, his mouth pulling up on one side in a sly grin.

Coren glared, the moment of remembrance from her dreams gone. "You still believe my wings are not Weshen?" But as soon as she said the words, she became conscious of the weight that no longer pressed at her spine. She reached her hands around her back and felt nothing.

"My wings!" Her eyes flew to Resh's, and she noticed a hesitation there. "What happened? Resh, how did I shift back?" Her strength…her beautiful power. Gone.

"Shadow stole the claw from your stomach. Kashar believes that was the key."

"The talisman," she whispered, and he nodded. She pulled up the edge of her tunic, noticing it was clean and wondering who had changed her. Her stomach was bandaged, and when she peeled away the edges of the cloth, she could see the hole in her flesh. It was healing, as were several fierce red slashes across her middle.

"Shadow did that," Resh said, and she glanced up to see his face full of fury, all trace of content gone.

Coren swung her legs over the edge of the bed, standing and swaying a bit. Resh caught her gently, his hands careful around her injuries.

"Where is everyone?" she asked, steadying herself enough to push away his touch. She was beginning to remember other things, like the moment they had shared in between Shadow attacking him, then her.

"Sy and Nik are downstairs eating. Are you hungry?" Resh's voice was soft in her ear.

She shook her head, taking a step back from his grasp. Her balance was imperfect, though. As her body overcompensated for the lack of weight on her back, she stumbled again.

Resh was there a second time, his arms strong and ready. For a moment, she allowed herself to sag into his strength, to be gathered against his chest like a scraped-kneed child. A wave of grief shuddered through her as she mourned the loss of power.

Resh pulled her close, his arm firm around her waist. Her cheek rested on his collarbone. And for the space of a few breaths, she soaked in the comfort of his warm, smooth skin.

When she pushed away again, he didn't resist, and when she leaned a hand against the nearby chair, he didn't suggest that she lie back down.

For all of that, she was grateful.

She couldn't learn to care for or depend on anyone now. Not yet. She needed to regain her strength.

Wings or not, she had a king to kill.

"Come back to Weshen City with me," he whispered, and her eyes flashed to his. They were close enough that she could read the hesitance in the set of his jaw, and something that looked for a mere second like pleading.

"I'm sorry, Resh, but I'll never go back there," she said.

"Then I'll come with you and Sy to StarsHelm."

She shook her head. "Someone has to go back and tell Ashemon all that has happened. He needs to be readied."

The excuse seemed valid enough as she said it, but really she wasn't ready to travel those miles with Resh so near. She could focus with Sy nearby, but she was beginning to suspect this would not be so with Resh.

He nodded with guarded eyes and glanced away. She raised a brow. He had accepted her rejection too easily. Perhaps he was as conflicted as she. All the better for them to go in separate directions.

"I should eat," she said, taking the few steps around the chair and sinking into it. Dizziness pulsed behind her eyes, and she wondered if she should drink some of the lemondrine tonic as well.

"I'll go fix a plate and bring it back to you. Sy will want to know you're awake." And with that, Resh slipped out of the room, leaving Coren alone in the attic. She glanced around, noticing that someone had shifted together the broken panes of glass and the scratches in the wall. There was no more evidence of her Vespa form.

Not in the room, and not on her body, except her healing wounds.

Remembering her triumphant dreams again, Coren wondered how she could possibly be strong enough to become a killer of kings.

Now that she had known true power, without it she felt insubstantial and silly, like Penna playing at war with her wooden sword.

Still, it changed nothing. She hadn't been born a savior of her people, but she could become one.

32

When Resh entered the boys' room, he was irritated to see Kashar pacing the room. Sy sat on the bed, a half-eaten plate of food next to him, his knees drawn to his chest. Nik sat at the table, still eating, but his back was to the others.

The tension between them all was like the air before a summer storm breaks the horizon. And by storms, Resh thought, he really meant accusations.

"She's awake," he said, grinning to himself as the tension ratcheted several notches. A dark look passed between Kashar and Sy, and Resh straightened. "What is it?"

"This one," Sy said, gesturing rudely at Kashar, "wants to take her back to the palace with him. He claims he can get her in undercover and that she'll be safe there."

Resh examined his brother. There must be more to the plan. "Isn't that exactly what you wanted?"

Kashar turned and nodded at Resh, but Resh wasn't about to side with this traitor.

"He doesn't want Sy to go," Nik said from the table. "He wants me instead."

Sy stood, his energy barely contained in the small room. "I don't care what he wants. You're still not leaving with either of them," he said to Kashar, as though he'd said it a few times already.

"Why would you want Nik?" Resh asked.

"Because he's stronger than any Wesh I've met. We could learn a lot from him," Kashar answered.

"I will not teach you methods to torture the magic from someone's veins!" Nik burst out, nearly overturning the table as he stood and strode out the door, slamming it behind him.

Sy took a few steps toward the door, as if to follow, then glanced back to Resh, a puzzling guilt on his face.

"Why don't you just let Coren decide what she wants to do?" Resh asked. "She's awake," he repeated. Sy nodded and squared his shoulders.

"Come upstairs, then. We'll figure this out now. Then you leave," Sy said to Kashar. The older man's jaw twitched, but he nodded silently, and the three men headed up the stairs.

When Resh reached for the door, however, he found it locked. He rattled the handle, and Coren's voice called, "Wait! I'm changing!"

In the locked room, Nik grinned. "Now you have to actually change."

"Not with you in here," Coren whispered. "And keep your voice down."

"Relax. I'd much rather see Sy's naked chest than yours," Nik replied, and Coren snapped her eyes to his, her jaw slack.

He raised his eyebrows, challenging her to find fault.

"Sy?" she managed. He grinned, his dark eyes sparking.

Coren was about to ask another question when the door rattled again. She hurried to slip off her tunic and pull on another one, just as clean as the first. It *had* been a silly excuse.

"You can't let him take us to StarsHelm," Nik repeated, advancing on her as she pulled her hair forward and began to braid it. "None of the Wesh who go there ever come back. And you may be his daughter, but to the king, you're just another powerful Wesh."

"I don't trust him at all," she agreed. "But he could be my way into the palace. You could go back to Weshen City with Resh."

Nik glared. "I don't want *that* brother."

Despite his petulance, Coren grinned. The grin faded as she imagined Sy's reaction to Nik's interest. "He won't be with you, though," she said. Nik raised a brow. "He's too loyal to the General still, and Ashemon wants heirs."

"Have you been with him?" Nik asked, his eyes turned toward the cold fireplace.

"Coren!" Sy called from beyond the door, and their eyes met.

"I'll never be with him," Coren whispered. "Or any boy. I need all of my magic."

Nik tilted his head as though puzzling out her answer, then a smile edged back onto his face. "Good. Because he kissed me back."

And before Coren could recover from that revelation, he strode to the door and threw it open, amusement splashing across his face as he took in the startled looks on Sy's and Resh's faces.

"Why are you in here?" Resh asked, his voice harsh as he pushed past his brother and Nik, peering around them to see Coren.

She crossed her arms over her chest, her eyes narrowing as Kashar followed the boys into the room. There was suddenly too little space and too much disagreement.

"Nik came up here to tell me the plan you were all discussing. He's the only one who thought I might like some input." She was pleased with the flashes of guilt on the brothers' faces. Kashar simply leaned against the closed door, mimicking her crossed arms and blocking the way out.

"Coren," Sy started.

"I'm going to the palace," she interrupted. "I don't care if Kashar is with me or not, but a guide would be useful. When I rescued Nik, I decided I should help where I could, however I could. My power wasn't given to me to save my family only. Maren will keep the twins safe." She paused to glare at Kashar. "But I'm not going to be one of your experiments. I'm going to help all the Weshen and all of Riata. The Restless King has lived his last cursed year in this world."

Resh's black eyes connected with hers across the room, and she felt a spark like lightning pass between them.

She knew he liked her power, and she liked that he did.

Flushing, she turned away. Sy was watching her carefully. He flicked his gaze at Resh, then back to her, and Coren swallowed hard.

Then she almost laughed. Neither of them had any business kissing anyone back, and yet there they were.

But they couldn't let themselves get distracted.

"I'm going to StarsHelm," she repeated, making several decisions at once, and basing them solely on the looks both brothers had given her. "And I want Sy to come with me. Resh and Nik should go back to Weshen to inform the General that the world has changed."

Across the room, Kashar smiled at her, and though she still didn't trust him, she nodded.

Her father had been a traitor to the king once, and to the Weshen once. His loyalty could never be trusted, but for her, it might be like fruit ripe for picking.

Once upon a time, Kashar had been a good father to her, and she planned to make him remember that. He would help them, and he would meet Penna and Kosh, or she would make him pay in ways only a daughter might dream of.

"I promise to keep her safe," Sy said to Resh in a low voice as the brothers packed their bags, alone in the room below the attic. He had to believe he was capable of such a task. Together they had already done so much. The magic was awake, and even without her wings, Coren was more powerful than he'd hoped.

"I realized she'd gotten under your skin, but I still never dreamed you'd let her tell us all what to do," Resh muttered, shoving weapons on top of his clothes.

"Resh, I care about her."

Resh stopped packing, a cold challenge in his stare. "You think you love her?"

"Not like that," Sy said, flushing as the memory of Nik's kiss overwhelmed him. "Like a…like a sister."

Resh watched him a moment longer then nodded. "Even Weshen don't bed their sisters," he said, contradicting the familiar EvenFall slur.

"You and Father can join us when he has the men ready," Sy added, ignoring the implied warning. He'd never had that intent with Coren, anyway.

"Oh, I plan to join you. But not with Father. Once I get Nik and the other Wesh through that passage and make sure Father knows what he's supposed to do with them, I'm gone. I won't sit back and train troops while my brother fights all the battles."

"Just make sure our Father General doesn't abuse Nik. That he doesn't reject the magic again." Sy hoped he'd kept the emotion he felt for Nik out of his voice, but Resh noticed.

"What is this Wesh to you?" Resh asked, straightening and pinning Sy with a stare.

Sy faltered, then gathered his courage. "Something worth coming home for," he said, his voice strong in the silence.

Resh's eyes widened, and he searched Sy's face as though wondering what piece of the puzzle he'd missed. But he nodded.

"Well, Coren may be my reason to leave home," Resh returned, and it was Sy's turn to wonder. He remembered something Damren had told him once about love and magic.

"Love is something Weshen denied themselves for generations, but it's as strong as the magic. If we can learn both again, nothing can stop us," he said.

"Well, I used to think both were a children's bedtime tale, and now I've seen one. Why not the other, too?" Resh smiled, zipping his bag shut.

"You've come a long way in your beliefs, brother," Sy observed, wondering if Resh were serious.

"Maybe the little witch enchanted me, too," Resh offered, just as the door opened.

"The little witch is leaving," Coren said, but she was smiling. "Take care of the Wesh," she said, staring at Resh. He nodded. She glanced at Sy, then stepped toward Resh. "And take care of yourself," she whispered, embracing Resh quickly.

Sy had just enough time to catch Resh wink at him before Coren pulled back and bolted out the door.

"Go settle your bill and say your goodbyes to Nik. I'll be outside," Resh said as he followed her out. As Sy watched them go, Nik appeared in the door.

He hovered on the threshold of the room, suddenly hesitant.

"Come here," Sy said, his voice gruff. Nik slipped inside, and Sy took the few steps toward him quickly, backing him against the closed door. "My brother will watch out for you, but I need you to do the same for him. Resh is impatient."

"So am I," Nik said, his gaze even with Sy's. He slipped a hand onto Sy's waist, and Sy's breathing stuttered. "But I could learn patience for you."

Sy watched the blue sky of Nik's eyes for a spare second, then he leaned in to cover Nik's mouth with his. He tried to be gentle, to say goodbye without asking for more, but the wanting was too much. Nik pulled him closer until Sy wasn't certain where he ended and Nik began, and in that tangle was a freedom he'd never expected.

The clomp of boots on the stairs just outside the door broke them apart.

"Are you sure I can't come with you?" Nik asked, his mouth quirking up at the corner.

Sy grinned, feeling invincible and vulnerable all at once. "My city needs a man like you."

"You need a man like me," Nik said, the smile slinking farther across his face.

"And I'll come back to just that." Sy picked up his bag from the bed, glancing around the empty room. He knew Kashar waited downstairs with Coren and Resh. "Please," he said to Nik, and his heart nearly stopped as he waited for Nik's answer.

"I'll wait for you," Nik said, then leaned in once more with the gentle kiss Sy had meant to begin with.

Sy breathed in his scent, taking strength from the freedom Nik was offering.

Freedom to make a promise and freedom to trust in its power.

Freedom to love and to be loved, and freedom to invite the magic in his blood to take back what his people had been waiting for.

Nik broke away and opened the door, and they walked down the stairs and into the sunshine where the others were waiting.

Kashar reached to shake Resh's hand, then Nik's. "You know I've made good on my promise to deliver the children and wounded to Shanta. You'll find them ready to travel in a few days. I'll make good on these new promises as well."

Resh nodded, glancing at Nik. "Long live the king," he said, smirking, and they turned to leave.

Sy finally acknowledged the dark underside of freedom as he watched them walk away, disappearing into the EvenFall crowds.

He had gained much from this portion of their journey, but what clutched at his heart now was the freedom to lose everything.

"We can do this," Coren whispered, stepping closer to him. "They'll be fine, and so will we." Sy felt her lean against him briefly, and he offered her his strength while also taking some of hers.

Kashar cleared his throat. "Are you certain about this? I have no love for the king either, but this is no small task you've set for yourself. I don't want to take you to the palace against your will."

Sy recognized the words, and he looked to Coren, who nodded.

"Nothing is small when it is against your will," she said.

Kashar tilted his head, measuring. "I used to tell you that when you were a child."

"And I've told it to myself ever since," she replied. "But the death of Zorander Graeme is no longer just a hope of the Weshen people. It will be our legacy. My family's greatest redemption. One day, children will not hear bedtime stories of the king's monstrous crimes, but stories of the Weshen who rid the world of a monster."

Sy felt his chest swell with the same anticipation and interest he'd felt all those days ago when he'd watched her jump off the cliffs of Weshen Isle, diving into the great unknown below.

He hadn't followed her then, but he would today, and every day forward.

They had gained friends and let go of love in the hopes it would wait. They had buried a teacher, and now they traveled with a traitor in hope that he might turn again.

The magic was awake in Riata, and the struggle between dark and light had begun.

ACKNOWLEDGEMENTS

TO BE HONEST, by the time a book gets to this page, most people have stopped reading. If you're still here, then I want to thank YOU!

I love to write, and you love to read, so let's be friends! Seriously.

There are a ton of people who helped whip this story into the warrior it is today, though. My ever-supportive parents and my beautiful family and friends win the favorite fans of all time award. They give me motivation, time, babysitting, and even a little cash to follow this dream of storytelling, and all of those things are priceless. Well, except for the cash., but that's a secret.

If you're looking for a great developmental editor, I wholly suggest Mary Rosenblum of New Writers Interface. Unless she's reading my next story, and then you can't have her! Gold, I tell you.

Likewise goes immeasurable gratitude to my favorite beta reader slash legal advisor, Cecily. She has a few other titles, but those are also a secret.

Can I say Deranged Doctor Design covers are amazing? You saw it. You bought it. Amazing, right? I'm looking forward to sharing many more of their covers with you. If you have the ebook version of this story, please check out the hardback and paperback for more gorgeous design work from DDD and Eight Little Pages. This story has such a rockstar wardrobe.

I'm forever grateful for the marketing advice from friends and fellow warrior-women Margo Bond Collins and Rebecca Hamilton, for their work in pushing authors to succeed.

I can't possibly name all the fantastic people I've met and worked with on social media, and my wonderful Stargazer Reading Group. Special shoutouts to Melle for a fantastic buddy read (down with passive voice!), and to the AAYAA and For Love or Money groups. Y'all are amazing, and worth everything a girl has in this life.

Should I say something cheesy now? Yeah. I totally should.

Keep your sights in the stars, and stay out of the shadows. You've been welcomed and warned.

Hilary used to be such a practical girl. Then she let the stories out, and claimed the titles of stargazer, daydreamer, and believer in all things magical.

Fairy tales, myths from all cultures, and the wonderful "what if" are the foundation of her stories. Villains, heroes, and sidekicks clamor for equal attention. Happily-ever-afters, too (of course), but be warned that the road will twist and turn and seem to dead-end before the magic of a sweet romance leads back into the sunlight.

When she's not writing, Hilary teaches Creative Writing, Literature, and College Writing, drinks too much coffee, and reads as much as her eyes can handle. She plays superheroes and dress up games and reads books in bed with her independent, willful children, and plays at homesteading and world traveling with her soulmate of a husband. She tends to ignore laundry and dirty dishes.